The Fairy Godmother's Tale

Also by Robert B. Marks

The *Re:Apotheosis* series:

Re:Apotheosis
Re:Apotheosis – Aftermath
Re:Apotheosis – Metamorphosis
Re:Apotheosis – Genesis

The *Road of Legends* series:

The Traveller on the Road of Legends
Magus Draconum
War of Succession

The Eternity Quartet, with Ed Greenwood

Seizing the Torch
Of Wizards and Watchers
The Conjurer's Treason
Hunting the Future
The Confession of C. August Gaston
Foolish Ideas Involving a Volcano

The Fairy Godmother's Tale

Robert B. Marks

Published by Legacy Books Press
RPO Princess, Box 21031
445 Princess Street
Kingston, Ontario, K7L 5P5
Canada

www.legacybookspress.com

This edition first published in 2025 by Legacy Books Press
1

ISBN: 978-1-927537-93-0

Cover art by Dabdab
(https://dabdab.carrd.co//)

This book is typeset in a Times New Roman 11-point font.

Library and Archives Canada Cataloguing in Publication

Title: The fairy godmother's tale / Robert B. Marks.
Names: Marks, Robert B., 1976- author.
Description: Includes bibliographical references.
Identifiers: Canadiana (print) 20240540379 | Canadiana (ebook)
    20250100983 | ISBN 9781927537930 (softcover) | ISBN
    9781927537947 (EPUB)
Subjects: LCGFT: Fantasy fiction. | LCGFT: Historical fiction. |
    LCGFT: Novels.
Classification: LCC PS8626.A75417 F35 2025 | DDC C813/.6—dc23

To my wife and children,
and all lovers of fairy tales.

Once upon a time...

...in a forgotten island kingdom on the Baltic Sea in the Year of Our Lord Sixteen Hundred and Fifty-Eight...

Part I
Once Upon a Revolution

Chapter I – Birth of a Fairy Godmother

As Elisa stared out at the distant mainland, the warm sea air brushing against her and gulls swooping down to the water, her best friend Charlotte said, "There's no point. They'll never let you go."

Elisa sighed. "Because it's so dangerous."

Charlotte looked at her and grinned. "You know what's on the other side of that water – heretics. *Protestants*. Followers of *Martin Luther*. People whose souls are damned and won't even lift a finger to save them. And among them are even *Jews*!"

Elisa looked at Charlotte and scowled. Charlotte's free-flowing brown hair was a stark contrast to her own blonde ponytail, her face round and eyes mischievous. Her red headband, which marked her as unmarried, was embroidered with flowers – something Elisa had never bothered to do with her own. *If only I could be as happy as she is here*, Elisa thought.

Elisa glanced around, her gaze falling upon an old man sitting on a wharf, casting a fishing line out into the water. She had noticed him a while ago when she and Charlotte had first arrived. The bucket beside him was empty. She turned back to Charlotte.

"There are merchants who are allowed to go," Elisa pointed out. "It's safe enough for them. We'd starve if it wasn't for them."

"They're specially trained," Charlotte said. "And there's only a handful of them."

"I could marry one of them."

"They're all married."

"Then I could become one of them."

"The guild would never let you join."

"I could ask St. Christopher for help."

"It would still be a longshot."

Elisa sighed again. "How do we *know* it's dangerous on the mainland?"

"You've heard all the stories that I have," Charlotte stated. "Come on...let's go to the bathhouse."

Elisa shook her head. "I don't really feel like a bath."

Charlotte grinned again. "Then go for the view. I'll bet Peter will be there – he's always worth looking at."

Elisa chuckled. "Okay, but I want to visit my brothers first."

"Have you got the flowers?"

"I'll pick them up along the way."

"Then I'll meet you at the bathhouse," Charlotte said. As Charlotte made her way away from the shoreline, Elisa looked back at her best friend, whose deepest wish was that Peter would ask for her hand in marriage.

Elisa blinked. *How do I know that?*

Elisa made her way through the headstones in the

graveyard, the church looming at the top of a hill. Finally, she made her way to her brothers.

She took a deep breath as she looked at each headstone. She remembered each one of them. Little Joseph, who had been so cheerful, had died before he had ever learned to walk. Franz, so curious about everything, had died of a pox when he was five. Adam had been quiet, watching everything as though it was the most fascinating thing in the world, and died just after he had begun to walk. Anton had been sickly since the beginning, a tiny infant dying in Elisa's arms as her mother had attended to making supper.

She laid a flower at each grave. "I wish you could still be here," she muttered. She glanced around. The children's section of the cemetery stretched almost as far as her eye could see. Several of the graves were fresh, tiny mounds of earth far smaller than they ever should be. She wiped tears from her eyes. Then her stomach growled. *I wish, just for once, we had enough to eat*, she thought.

Her mind cast back to Charlotte at the shoreline. Elisa knew her deepest wish, but how? Had Charlotte told her about it some time ago? Had she figured it out from the way Charlotte looked at him in the bathhouse?

It had to be something like that. She'd known Charlotte since she was a little girl. Charlotte had probably figured out her deepest wish as well.

"They are in a better place," a voice said behind her. She turned to see Father Xaver approaching, a kindly look in his eyes, his short hair mostly grey. "No just god would keep such innocent souls in Purgatory. Not with so many good Christians like yourself praying for them. They are all in Heaven right now, looking down on us."

Elisa gave him a sad smile. "I still wish they could be here."

"The way the world is, it might be a mercy that they

aren't," Father Xaver said. "At least they aren't hungry like the rest of us."

Elisa took a deep breath. "The mainland...is it really that bad?"

Father Xaver shrugged. "Today, I have no idea. But back when I made my way here twenty years ago, the things I saw...this island is a haven, my child. Nobody is hanging people from trees here, or burning down their village because they won't accept a heretical faith."

"I still want to see what's out there," Elisa said. "I can pray for the souls of my brothers on the mainland too."

"Maybe you'll get to," Father Xaver suggested.

"What, by joining the Church?"

The priest shook his head. "The king is going to make an announcement at the festival on the weekend. The rumour I heard was that he's planning to re-establish ties to the mainland, now that it's been ten years since the Peace of Westphalia."

Elisa's eyes widened. "That would mean..."

Father Xaver smiled. "That people would be able to go, yes."

Elisa closed her eyes and sighed happily. In that moment, she wanted to hug Father Xaver, whose dearest wish was to know if his mother was still alive.

Her eyes opened in shock. Father Xaver had never mentioned his family to her, or in any of his sermons. How could she know that?

"Is something wrong, my child?" Father Xaver asked.

Elisa took a deep breath. "I was just thinking about my family," Elisa said. "How much we've lost. And I was wondering about you...is your family...?"

"Alive?" Father Xaver replied. "My father died just before I entered the priesthood. My mother was still alive and saw me off when I left to come here. As to what happened...well, we get very little news here. So, I just don't know."

"I'm sorry to hear that," Elisa said.

Father Xaver shrugged. "My mother is a good, pious woman. If she is gone, she'll be in Heaven by now."

"I need to go," Elisa stated. "Charlotte is expecting me at the bathhouse."

Father Xaver gave her a quick blessing. "Enjoy yourself, my child."

As she walked away, Elisa mind churned. She knew Father Xaver's wish. There could be no question now. But how? How far did it go? And was this a miracle from God, or a temptation from the Devil?

The bathhouse was not large, but it was well decorated. Stepping into the changing area, Elisa slipped out of her dress and removed everything except for her headband. Then she walked into the main area, where a musician played on a lute. Large baths lined the wall, with two people to each bath. Across the middle of each bath was a table covered by a white cloth, most of which had steins of beer.

"There was a time when they served food here too," an older man with white hair said to the younger woman bathing across from him. "But that was a long while ago."

"What a thing that must have been," the woman replied. "Enough food to eat while you bathe. I'd love to have seen that."

"Elisa!" she heard Charlotte call from the far end. Charlotte was standing and waving. "I saved you a spot!"

Elisa stepped over to Charlotte's bathtub and slid into the warm water. Charlotte sat back down across from her and pointed to a second stein on the table. "I saved you a beer too. It's good today."

Elisa took a drink and nodded. It was indeed good.

"So, how was your trip to see your brothers?" Charlotte asked.

15

"It was good," Elisa replied. "Father Xaver was there. I asked him about his family."

Charlotte leaned forward, a gleam in her eyes. "Oh?"

"Apparently his father died when he entered the priesthood, and his mother may still be alive."

Charlotte sighed. "And here I was hoping for some scandalous story. This island can be so *boring*!"

"Sorry to disappoint you," Elisa said.

"Anyway, I'm going to visit my sisters and brothers there tomorrow. How are the prices for flowers?"

"Pretty good," Elisa said. "I paid less than a *thaler* for mine. I think they were around twenty *groschen*."

"Well, it's better than last week," Charlotte said. "Still, they're getting pretty expensive. I can remember when it was less than half a *thaler*."

"You seriously think *that's* what the king is going to announce?" a raised voice called. Elisa and Charlotte turned to see two men arguing a couple of baths down.

"It makes sense!" the second man said. "It's been ten years since the Peace of Westphalia. Surely it's safe to make contact with the German lands again."

"Just because the French and the Swedes aren't fighting here anymore, it doesn't mean that fighting stopped," the first man declared. "I've been to the German lands – you haven't. You have no idea what it's like."

"You've been to the German lands?" Elisa blurted, then realized she was standing in the bath. A merchant! She had actually encountered a merchant!

"You splashed water in my beer," Charlotte groused.

"I was there last autumn," the first man said.

"What's it like?" Elisa demanded.

She felt Charlotte tugging at her elbow. "Will you sit down already? You're dripping in your own beer now!"

"There's not a lot of people left," the merchant replied. "At least, not to the east. A lot of empty villages, or what used to be villages. And those who are there are pretty hungry – we have to go quite far to find food. A lot of times, we're having to buy from heretics."

"Are there a lot of those?" Elisa asked as Charlotte finally pulled her back into the tub.

"Most of the north of the German lands are Lutheran," the merchant said. "You have to go pretty far south to find any Catholics."

Elisa frowned. "And you said there was still fighting?"

"It's not as bad, but yes, there is," the merchant said. "The Prussians, the Swedes..."

"I told you," Charlotte declared. "It's not safe there."

"But you're able to travel," Elisa pressed. "You come back safe, with your family."

"We hire mercenaries to help us," the merchant said. "And everybody is sworn to secrecy. If anybody remembers this island exists...it would be bad."

"When the king announces that we're going to rejoin the *Reich*, they'll remember we exist," the man in the bath across from the merchant stated. "We may even finally have enough to eat!"

"I keep telling you, he's not going to do that!" the merchant declared. Elisa was about to look away and turn back to Charlotte when his wish became clear in her mind: he wanted to have more children to replace the ones he'd lost.

Elisa took a deep breath and started looking around the room at the other bathers. As she did, all of their wishes flooded into her mind. The older man wished that his wife was still alive. The woman across from him wished that her sickly daughter would recover. The merchant wished that he could have more children. The man sharing his bathtub wished that he could have a bigger house.

"Are you okay?" Charlotte asked.

Elisa looked back at her. "I'm fine. I'm just...did Peter show up?"

Charlotte shook her head. "Not yet. If he doesn't, I'll see him tomorrow anyway when I stop by the smithy."

"When his apprenticeship is done, he'll make a good husband," Elisa said.

"He's also very nice to look at," Charlotte added, grinning. "Especially when he swings that hammer."

Elisa chuckled.

"Is that a blush I see?" Charlotte laughed. She leaned forward. "You know, Peter and I will need to find out if I'm fertile before getting married, and there's only way to be sure—"

"Enough!" Elisa laughed.

"You know, some day, if you stop spending all your time staring at the mainland, you might find somebody you want to start a family with too," Charlotte said.

"I'm only fifteen," Elisa stated. "I've got lots of time."

"I'm fifteen too," Charlotte said. "Some things are worth doing sooner rather than later. Speaking of which, there he is!" She stood up and waved.

At the door to the changing area, Peter waved back. Elisa looked at him, his wish to become a great blacksmith becoming clear.

An attendant poured some hot water into the bath. Elisa settled in as Peter came over and started chatting with Charlotte. As she leaned back in the bath, enjoying the fresh hot water, her mind began to wander. She could look at people and know their true heart's wishes, that much was now certain. But what else could she do?

Could she grant them?

Chapter II – The King's Festival

Elisa had always enjoyed watching her father work in the bookbindery downstairs. Her father worked in silence as he sewed pages together into a bundle, each stitch given care and attention. A copy of the Bible sat in a finishing press against the wall.

Her father had once told her that back when he had apprenticed, before he bought out the bindery, there had been five people working in it. She liked to imagine that – a bustling workshop making no end of books. But now it was just him. Not enough people needed books, and almost everybody had to work fishing to the north or growing what few crops the island could support in the fields around town.

As she watched her father, his wish became clear in her head – he wanted a happy future for his daughter. But was it God telling her this, or the Devil?

Elisa took a deep breath. "Father?"

Her father looked up. "Yes, Elisa?"

"I was thinking," Elisa began, picking her words with care. "You've taught me so much. I know how to read and write, and I can do sums."

Her father nodded. "You're very good at all of them. When things are better and there's more business, you'll be a great help to me in the workshop."

Elisa swallowed. "But, I'm also fifteen. And I thought, perhaps, that I might be able to apprentice to a merchant."

Elisa's father sighed and put down the bundle of pages he had been working on. "You know that can't happen," he said. "The guild would never allow it, no matter how talented you are."

"But maybe I could prove myself to them," Elisa pressed. "I could be the first woman to apprentice into the guild."

"They'd never go for that, and you know it."

"But the guilds allow widows to inherit their husband's businesses all the time!" Elisa protested. "Why can't a woman just be an apprentice to begin with."

"Because that's not the way it's done."

Elisa forced back tears. "Maybe you could marry me to an apprentice merchant! Then I could join them when they–"

"Elisa!" her father barked.

Elisa swallowed and tried not to cry.

"I know what this is about," her father said. "And it's all terribly unfair. But you don't understand how dangerous it is out there." He rubbed his temple. "You were probably too young to remember this, but for most of my life you could see the pillars of smoke from villages being burned on the mainland. We haven't seen one in years, but..."

"A merchant at the bathhouse said that most of the fighting was done," Elisa said. "If I was careful, I would be safe."

"Most of it, but not all," her father declared. "I've heard this too. Just because a bunch of powerful kingdoms declare a peace doesn't mean that fighting will ever stop." He sighed. "Look, I've got to get some supplies from the guild merchants after tomorrow's festival anyway. I'll bring you with me, and you can ask if there's any way they'd let you in. But, be ready for disappointment."

Elisa smiled. "Thank you father!"

"Now, I've got to get back to this," her father declared. "And then I've got that 'special project' to work on."

"I wish you'd tell me what that is," Elisa said.

"All in good time," her father said. "Now hurry upstairs and help your mother with dinner. She's going to need help with the mustard sauce."

"I wish we could afford meat," Elisa muttered.

Her father chuckled. "Perhaps one day we will. But for now, it's whatever the fishermen can catch."

The festival began with a Mass in the church, Father Xaver blessing the congregation and King Martin, and then delivering a sermon on the need for temperance in all things. As he spoke, Elisa glanced at her mother, her wish becoming clear in Elisa's mind – she wished that they could never worry about having enough money again.

Elisa blinked. Something was different this time. It was as though there was a thread attached to the wish, and all she had to do to grant it was give it a tug.

She looked around the congregation, each person's wish flowing into her mind. Each one with a little thread that she could pull. And if she could grant wishes, then...then...

...then if they caught her doing it, they might burn her at the stake for witchcraft.

The Mass concluded, and the congregation filed

outside. The road was filled with flowers and banners leading to the town square. In the centre of the square was a raised platform, a procession from the palace approaching. In the distance, the royal castle stood on a hill, ancient and craggy.

King Martin and Queen Elisabeth, white haired but still robust, ascended the platform, flanked by musketeers. Their son, Prince Amadeus, took his place beside them. Elisa's mother tapped her shoulder, pointed at the queen, and whispered, "I named you after her."

"I know, mother," Elisa whispered back, staring at the royal family. Their wishes became clear in her mind – the king wished for prosperity for his people, the queen for a good match for her son, and the prince wished for excitement. Elisa smiled. The prince *did* look quite bored.

King Martin raised his hands. The murmuring crowd fell into silence.

"It has been forty years since the great war began on the mainland," the King began. "Forty years since the ruling council and my father decided that the best way to protect ourselves from the violence was to separate from the *Reich* and become forgotten. Few will ever know how much was sacrificed in those days – how much was paid in bribes to remove our island from maps, to swear the leaders and merchants of any towns or villages on the coast to secrecy about our existence, to erase us from the rolls in the College of Princes, and how many suffered and died to keep our secret while our merchants make connections whose silence could be trusted. But St. Michael the Archangel granted us his blessings and prayers, and we succeeded in our efforts.

"But we have also suffered," the King stated. "Our fishermen have made heroic efforts, but they have never been able to bring in enough to feed us all. We have all spent years tightening our belts, and losing children who should not be lost. And our family has suffered alongside you, waiting for the moment when our kingdom could end our self-imposed exile and rejoin the *Reich*."

The king raised his hand with a flourish. "That time has come! It has now been ten years since the Peace of Westphalia, and the merchant guild reports that most of the fighting on the mainland has died down. We may finally be able to resume trade and let ourselves be known without fear of armies of heretics coming across the sea to raze our fair kingdom!"

The crowd cheered. Elisa realized she was grinning.

"But we must still tread with the greatest of care," King Martin warned. "We do not know what dangers may still lurk on the mainland. Before we reveal ourselves to the *Reich*, we must know for certain that it will be safe to do so. We must know that we will be welcomed back to the College of Princes and the Reichstag. And for the next year, determining this is what we shall be doing. The Merchant's Guild will begin by sending emissaries to Regensburg. Should their reports be as promising as we hope, we will send a formal representative to request reinstatement in the College of Princes. Our days of hunger will be over!"

The crowd roared with approval.

"Now let the festival begin!" the King declared. As musicians began to play, he stepped down from the platform.

Elisa turned to her mother and father, a wide grin on her face. "We really are going to rejoin the *Reich*! I'll get to see the mainland!"

Her father smiled, but held up his hand. "If the Guild emissaries say it's safe, we'll rejoin the *Reich*. But, it's going to take time. Remember what his Majesty said – we paid bribes to have our kingdom erased from the rolls so that we could hide. Adding them back on won't be easy."

"Your father isn't saying that it won't happen," Elisa's mother added. "Just that it won't happen this year."

Elisa took a deep breath. "I don't want to wait. When we go to the Merchant's Guild, I'm going to ask if I can apprentice."

People's wishes began popping into her head as they crossed her line of sight, each one with a thread that could be pulled to grant them. They were coming so much more easily now – she barely had to glance at them any more.

The Devil wouldn't grant somebody the power to help others, would he? she thought. *No. He wouldn't. This had to come from God. Surely it came from God.*

"Just be ready for disappointment," her mother warned.

Elisa nodded. "I will, mother. I'm going to go find Charlotte and Peter."

"You take care," her father said. "And don't stay up too late!"

Elisa wound her way through the crowd, wishes popping into her head, crowding out her thoughts. It would be so easy to start granting them. All she'd have to do is pull on each thread with her mind. But would they thank her for using magic to help them, especially without asking for permission first? Could she even ask for permission without being denounced as a witch? And what if she just granted the wishes and didn't take credit for it – would that be the right thing to do?

She spotted Father Xaver enjoying a stein of beer by the seamstress' shop and talking to a couple of parishioners. She took a deep breath and stepped over to him.

"Father," she asked, "might I have a word with you?"

Father Xaver gave her a kind smile. "Of course." He turned to the two parishioners. "Please enjoy the rest of the festival."

As the parishioners left, leaving Elisa and Father Xaver alone, he said, "Now what is it, my child?"

Elisa steeled herself. "I think I might be able to do something to help a lot of people. But, I'm not sure if I should."

Father Xaver raised an eyebrow. "Oh? What is this thing you think you can do?"

"I can't really say," Elisa replied. "At least, not now."

"Is it something that will endanger your immortal soul?"

"I don't think so."

"I see. Will it require you to commit a sin?"

"I'm pretty sure it won't."

Father Xaver paused. "Okay. What is your concern?"

"What I could do...I think it could help people a lot. But I could never ask for permission to help them first, or tell anybody that I had done it."

"So you're wondering if it's okay to help somebody without their knowledge?"

Elisa nodded.

"I think most charity should be anonymous," Father Xaver began. "Charity is like a penance – it should be done for the good of your soul and your community, not for worldly glory or recognition. Can it really be called charity if the most important part is being recognized for it?"

Elisa smiled. "I guess not."

Father Xaver raised his hand. "But, one must always be careful. It is very easy to assume that you know what a person needs, only to discover after trying to help them that you were wrong, and things are now worse. People often know best what they need in this worldly life. So, if you can truly help them, you must take pains to learn what they need from them first. Does that clarify things?"

Elisa nodded. "I think it does, yes."

"I'm glad," Father Xaver said. "Now, you should go find your friends, and I should take care of some chores in the church. Festivals like these are for young people like you, not old men like me."

Elisa smiled. "Thank you so much, Father."

Father Xaver smiled back. "Go find your friends."

As Elisa made her way back into the crowd, looking for Charlotte and Peter, her mind kept coming back to her precious new gift. *I know what people most wish for*, she thought. *I don't need to talk to them first. I can just help them. God has given me the miracle of being able to help them!*

Chapter III – A Simple Wish

Elisa and her father left for the trading house early in the morning the day after the festival, her father carrying a couple of books in a bag around his shoulder. Their path took them down the winding streets, the half timber buildings looming over them, dirty white plaster and windows between the exposed dark wooden support beams. A pleasant smell wafted through the air.

Elisa looked at her father and grinned. They were approaching Mrs. Becker's bakery. Mrs. Becker gave them a wave from the door, her deepest wish that her husband was still alive shining through.

Her father chuckled and handed her a few *Pfenniges*. "Go on, then," he said. "Get yourself a bun."

"Hello, Elisa," Mrs. Becker said. "Hello, Thomas. How are you this fine day?"

"Not too bad," Elisa's father replied. "And how are you, Johanna?"

Mrs. Becker took a couple of *Pfenniges* from Elisa and handed her a warm bun. Elisa bit into it, savouring its flavour.

"A bit hard to get wheat and grain right now," Mrs. Becker said. "The merchants haven't been able to bring in as much as I had hoped. I expect to be out of stock by midday. And how is Helena?"

"My wife is helping out at the church, as usual," Elisa father said. "Not enough work to bring her into the family business at the moment."

Elisa swallowed the last of the bun, and asked, "But won't all that change once we rejoin the *Reich*?"

"We hope so," Mrs. Becker mused. "But it will still be a lean and difficult year while we wait for it to happen."

"We should go," Elisa's father declared. "I don't want to keep the trade master waiting."

Elisa waved goodbye to Mrs. Becker as they made their way down the street towards the centre of town. The trading house rose before them, larger and more decorated than any of the buildings around it.

"Well," Elisa's father declared as they came to the door. "Let's see what they have to say."

The guild master was at the desk when they entered, sorting through some papers. It only took a moment for his wish to clarify in her mind, a longing to make enough money to leave the trade behind and spend the rest of his life in leisure. He looked up and gave Elisa and her father a welcoming smile. "Thomas! So good to see you again. And this must be this daughter you keep telling me about."

Elisa curtsied. "It's a pleasure to make your acquaintance, sir."

"No need for that formality," the guild master said. "What can I do for you, Thomas?"

Her father pulled the books out of the bag. "I've got these for you, Henry," he said. "They're hymnals. I was thinking that you might be able to sell them on the mainland. I've made sure that there's nothing in them that can expose our island."

Henry frowned and flipped through one. "Bibles would be easier to sell," he said. "Most of our dealings right now are with heretics. They don't use our hymnals, no matter how good the quality may be. Are you sure you can't print us some bibles?"

Elisa's father shook his head. "That's what we were doing when I bought out the shop, but there just wasn't any demand on the mainland for them."

"I don't understand," Henry said. "How can there not be a demand for bibles in Christendom?"

Elisa's father stroked his beard. "Right, you only took over as guild master around eight years ago. The village parishes we were selling them to were razed, and further inland the churches were able to buy them for cheaper than we could sell them. You first need a church and a congregation before you can sell a bible."

Henry sighed and put the books behind the desk. "Well, I guess you don't know until you try. Perhaps, God willing, we'll find somebody on the mainland who needs hymnals."

"Thank you, Henry," Elisa's father said.

"Is there anything else?"

Elisa's father handed Henry a piece of paper. "This is for my special project."

Henry took a look at the page, and then glanced at her father. "And you have the money for this?"

Elisa's father placed three groschen on the desk.

Henry took a deep breath. "You understand the risk I'm taking for you here, Thomas? If you hadn't saved me from that fire, I wouldn't do any of this for you."

"I understand," Elisa's father said.

"Fine, then," Henry declared. "You can pick it up tomorrow at the warehouse. Anything else?"

Elisa's father gave her shoulder a supportive squeeze. "Elisa here has something to ask you."

"And what can I do for you, young Elisa?" Henry asked.

Elisa steeled herself. "I'm fifteen years old, and I can read, write, and do sums. I was wondering if I could become an apprentice to the guild."

Henry's eyes narrowed.

"I really can read and write, and my sums are very good," Elisa added. "And if I become a merchant, I can go to the mainland and–"

Henry held up his hand. "I'm sorry, but the answer is no."

"But widows inherit their husband's business all the time," Elisa declared.

"I know," Henry stated. "And one day, if I die, my wife will inherit my business. But the answer is still no."

Elisa fought back tears. "Why not?"

"Because I'd be setting you up to fail," Henry replied.

"I wouldn't fail," Elisa mumbled.

"Yes, you would," Henry said. "Look, I believe you about being able to read and write, and I'm sure you're wonderful with your sums. But you have to be very good at reading people to be a good merchant, and that's why I can tell that you don't really want this in the first place – you just want a way to get to the mainland. You're not excited by the thought of making a good deal, or negotiating to increase your profits. And those are needed for success."

Henry leaned forward. "But even if you did truly want the life of the merchant, and it is a hard one, you need to be taken seriously by your customers. A widow who learned her husband's trade at his side will be respected, and treated well. A single woman will be seen as weak, or an upstart, or even worse, a loose woman trying to ensnare a man under the guise of being a merchant and then leaving the trade the moment you're married. Nobody would respect you well enough to give you a good price on your goods.

"And then there's your immortal soul. Most of our trade right now is in principalities filled with heretics. There are no churches of the true faith where you can confess your sins. Dying unshriven in the heretic lands is a risk we all take when we go to the mainland to trade."

Elisa's shoulders slumped. "I hadn't thought of that."

"Look," Henry said. "Once we have returned to the *Reich* and our trade is fully restored, if you still want to try being a merchant I'd be willing to consider giving you a chance. But, by then I don't think you will – you'll be able to just go to the mainland without spending years learning the merchant trade. Until that time, however, this island depends on our success in trading amber for its basic survival – we do not have the luxury of sending somebody out into the world who might fail."

Elisa sighed. "I guess so."

Henry turned back to her father. "Thomas, before you leave, I'm not going to give up on this. It would be very helpful if you took on a family name. Most people have one."

Elisa's father scowled. "There's nothing wrong with 'Thomas the bookbinder'. I'm the only bookbinder on the entire island."

"And if you take an apprentice who is also named Thomas?"

"Then you'll have 'elder Thomas' and 'younger Thomas'."

"Most choose their trade as their family name, just to make it easy to remember. You could just call yourself Thomas Buchbinder or Buchmacher."

"And what about Elisa?" her father objected. "If she

doesn't become a bookbinder, should she really have a family name that tells the world that she is one? That would be ridiculous."

"You're being difficult," Henry declared. "It would tell the world that her father is a bookbinder, and make her name different from all of the other Elisabeths on the island."

"Everybody would know which Elisabeth Elisa is."

Henry rolled his eyes. "You could use something else, you know. You hair colour, what you look like, anything you want. So long as you don't suggest you're royalty by choosing 'Konig', you'll be fine."

"I'll consider it," Elisa's father said, shaking his head. "Come along, Elisa, we're done here for now."

She followed her father out of the building into the street, the familiar smell of sea air with a tinge of human waste wafting into her nostrils. "It's ridiculous," her father muttered. "If somebody doesn't know you by your given name, how will adding another name to remember help?"

I'd like a family name, Elisa thought, but held her tongue.

"And it's not like there's another Thomas the bookbinder here anyway!"

Elisa took a deep breath. "Father, can I join you back at home later? I'd just like to take a walk and get some of the sea air."

"Okay," her father said. "Just remember that your mother will need help with the household, so don't take too long."

Elisa smiled. "I won't, father."

As she turned to walk away, her father said, "Elisa – never allow somebody to define you the way Henry is trying to define me."

Elisa turned back and nodded. "I won't, father."

Her father gave her a kind smile, and then headed off.

Elisa made her way to the waterfront, her mind churning. She could look at people and know what their wishes were, but could she really grant them? The only way to be certain would be to try. But what if she was caught doing it? Would Father Xaver really understand, or would she be burned as a witch?

She sat down on the side of a path overlooking the wharfs. If she was going to grant a wish, it had to be a simple one. One that would look like somebody had gotten lucky, instead of magic.

Her gaze fell upon the end of a wharf, to the old man she had seen fishing a few days ago, his bucket empty. His wish crystalized in her mind – just once more, to land a great big fish. The thread attached to his wish beckoned, just waiting to be pulled.

She mouthed a silent prayer. Then she reached out with her mind and pulled on the thread.

Reality shifted.

Elisa blinked. That was...odd. She looked around. The sky, the earth, the buildings, the people walking along the path behind her, they all seemed the same. But she could feel that something had changed, something deep in the fabric of the world.

Movement from the wharf caught her eye. The old man began to pull at his fishing rod, the rod bending under the strain. He stood and pulled, putting the weight of his body behind it.

Elisa's eyes widened. She grinned. It had worked! It had actually worked!

The old man gave a massive heave, the fishing line taut, the rod bending to its limits. A giant pike erupted from the water and fell onto the wharf in front of him, twitching. Elisa began to laugh in delight. It had to be at least seven feet long!

The old man looked at her, a gleeful grin on his face.

"Did you see that?" he called to her. "I caught it! I caught it all by myself! Just like I could when I was younger!"

"I saw it!" Elisa called back. "It looks amazing!"

"God has smiled upon me!" the old man shouted.

"He certainly did," she said under her breath. *With a little help from me.*

Elisa yawned. Then she blinked and looked at the sky. It was not even close to midday. *Why do I feel this tired already?* she wondered.

Then she shrugged and headed home, smiling as she thought of the old man and his giant fish, possibilities upon possibilities passing through her mind.

Chapter IV – An Island Full of Wishes

Elisa was amazed that she slept at all that night. The possibilities were endless. She could grant anybody's wish whenever she wanted. She could walk through the marketplace, granting wish after wish after wish.

The realization hit her. Her eyes widened as a grin spread across her face.

She could grant *everybody's* wish.

"Are you okay?" her mother asked as they cleaned up after lunch. Her father had gone back downstairs to the shop to work on a new bible for the church at the other end of the island.

"I'm fine," Elisa replied, grinning.

"You met a boy, didn't you?" her mother asked.

Elisa shook her head. "I didn't."

"It's okay to tell me!" her mother declared. "Do you think I didn't feel this way after meeting your father?"

"It's not a boy!" Elisa laughed.

"Then what is it?"

Elisa grinned. "It's about a fish. A really, really big fish!"

Her mother frowned. "A fish. Elisa, if you're fooling around with a boy, be careful. Make sure he'll marry you before giving him your maidenhood."

Elisa laughed even harder. "Mother, it's not a boy, and my maidenhood is quite safe. The old man at the wharf – I watched him catch an enormous fish yesterday. It made him so happy, and watching him be that happy...it made me happy too."

Her mother's eyes narrowed. "This is all about an old man catching a fish?"

"I promise, it is."

Her mother shrugged. "If watching people fishing gives you this much joy, who am I say otherwise. If you meet a boy you like who's a fisherman, just make sure he's a successful one. Love is important in a marriage, but so is your husband being able to support you and your children."

Elisa dried and put away the last of the lunch dishes. "I understand. May I go for a walk?"

Her mother smiled. "Go ahead. But be back by the time I'm home from the market. We have a dinner to make."

"I will!" Elisa said as she headed down the stairs. She waved at her father, working away at sewing pages together, as she passed through the shop. He glanced up and smiled at her, then went back to his sewing.

As she stepped out into the street, her mind raced. Could she grant more than one wish at a time? How many could she grant at once?

Elisa took a deep breath and closed her eyes. She reached out with her mind. Wishes upon wishes filled it, each with a thread to pull. Her mind gathered all of the threads into a bundle. Yes, she could pull them all at once.

She opened her eyes and grinned. A couple of passersby glanced at her with detached interest. She didn't have to grant wishes one at a time. If she cast her net wide enough, she could grant every single wish on the island in a heartbeat! What an amazing miracle that God had granted to her!

She stopped in her tracks. But what if she was wrong? What if it wasn't God? What if this came from the Devil instead?

Elisa swallowed. Surely this couldn't be the Devil's work. What could be bad about granting somebody's deepest and dearest wish? But...how could she be certain? The Devil was powerful, and could use deceit to make his work look like a miracle, couldn't he?

She took a deep breath and steeled herself. There was only one thing to do – she needed to ask Father Xaver. If she was very, very careful, she could hide that she had granted a wish, and perhaps determine if it was the Devil's magic or God's miracle.

She made her way to the church. It was the only stone building in the neighbourhood, the grounds and cemetery surrounded by half-timbered houses. She pulled open the door and stepped inside.

The space was bright, lit by the sunlight through the stained glass windows. An ornate vaulted ceiling towered above her. She made her way to the votive candles and lit one for her brothers.

"I want to wish you back," she muttered. "But that would take you out of Heaven, and I could never be so selfish. When you look down on me, know that I miss you, all of you. And so do mother and father."

She sighed and sat in a pew, praying for guidance. "If this is not a gift from you, O Lord, give me a sign," she muttered. And if this is your gift, give me the wisdom to use it well."

Elisa looked up from her prayer. The church was the

same as it was before, save that Father Xaver had come from the sacristy and was changing the cloth over the altar.

"Father, may I have some guidance?" Elisa asked.

Father Xaver looked over to her. "Of course, my child." He walked over and sat beside her in the pew. "What is troubling you?"

She took a deep breath. "How can I know if something is a miracle from God or a trick of the Devil?"

Father Xaver leaned back and chuckled. "That's never an easy one. The Devil is very good at his tricks. He can take many forms to tempt one's soul into corruption and mortal sin. And he can use his powers of trickery to create the illusion of the miraculous."

"So how do you tell the difference?"

"The Devil cannot create, not truly," Father Xaver stated. "Nor can he heal. He can deceive, he can harm and injure, and he can take away that injury to make it look like he has healed and performed the miraculous. Only a miracle can contain true creation."

"Like granting a wish?" Elisa asked. "Something that makes one's life better?"

"That depends on the wish," Father Xaver replied. "I think the Devil could certainly grant a wish that causes harm to the soul, or at least make it look as though he has granted it. But, remember, it is creation that is the key. The Devil cannot create. Only God can do that."

"I think I understand," Elisa said.

Father Xaver smiled. "I'm glad I could help. Do you need anything else?"

Elisa shook her head. "I think I'm good for now. I'll see you on Sunday, Father."

"I'll look forward to hearing your voice during the hymns then," Father Xaver declared, rising and returning to the altar.

Elisa watched him replace the candles in the

candlesticks for a short while, and then rose and headed back outside. As she wandered towards her favourite spot on the waterfront, she mulled over the wish she had granted.

Had she created a fish for the old man to catch, or caused one to come to him? If she had created it, then it must be creation. But if she had only caused a fish to swim to him and be caught, there was no creation there.

She approached the wharf where the old man had been fishing. It was empty.

Of course it is, she thought with a smile. *He caught his fish.*

A new thought crossed her mind. *How fast can a fish swim?* Surely a fish that large would not be in shallow water. It would have had to swim there. And the fish had appeared very quickly. Could there have been enough time to swim? No, it couldn't have. And were there even fish that big in the water? She had never seen one.

Elisa smiled. The fish must have been created. That was the only explanation. It was creation, and therefore it must have come from God.

"I thought I'd find you here!" a familiar voice said. Elisa turned to see Charlotte approaching her, waving. "How goes the day?"

"Wonderful!" Elisa replied. "You?"

"I spent time watching Peter work, so it was good," Charlotte said. "Did you ever speak to the merchant's guild?"

Elisa nodded. "They turned me down."

"I told you that would happen," Charlotte stated. "Also, I'm sorry you didn't get in."

"It doesn't matter," Elisa declared. "We're rejoining the *Reich* anyway, right? So, I'll get to go to the mainland in a year or two no matter what."

"That's assuming they'll let us rejoin," Charlotte

pointed out. "It's not certain that we'll be welcomed back. And what about all the heretics? Can you imagine going to the mainland and getting killed where there are no priests of the true faith to give you last rites?"

Elisa grinned. "It will be fine. They'll welcome us back with open arms."

"How can you be sure?"

"I have *faith*."

Charlotte stared at her. "Have you had too many beers?"

Elisa laughed. "Just one at lunch."

"You sure about that? Maybe I should smell your breath."

Elisa took her friend by the shoulders. "I can't explain right now. One day, I hope I'll be able to tell you everything. But I know that we're going to be welcomed back into the *Reich*, and everything is going to be good for all of us. We'll all have enough food, and we'll be safe, even from the followers of Martin Luther."

"You're worrying me, Elisa," Charlotte said. "I'll give you today, but you're going to tell me everything tomorrow."

"Okay."

"Promise on the blood of our Saviour."

Elisa crossed herself. "I promise on the blood of our saviour, I'll explain it all to you tomorrow."

"Good," Charlotte said, stepping away. "I've got some things to do. I'll see you back here tomorrow."

Elisa smiled. "I'll see you tomorrow."

As Charlotte walked away, Elisa took a deep breath and closed her eyes. She opened up her mind, reaching out to all of the wishes around her. They began to flow in.

I wish that Peter would propose to me. I wish that I had a bigger house. I wish that I could have another child. I wish I could live in the world as I see fit.

She gathered the threads of all of the wishes together, casting her mind even wider. The multitudes of wishes became a legion.

I wish my husband would return to me I wish my son would stop wasting his life I wish I had a proper dowry for my daughter I wish my father would stop beating me I wish people would just do what they're told to I wish that the guild would be mine I wish to be the greatest poet in the world I wish my wife could make a better beer I wish my husband could give me children I wish that people would see that I'm right.

She gathered the new threads together, the bundle linking to hundreds upon hundreds of wishes. Still she cast her net further, across the entire island, the wishes so numerous that she could no longer distinguish between one and another.

I wish – I wish –

She strained to gather the last threads together, thousands of wishes ready to be granted, thousands of people whose dreams would come true, all with a single pull of her mind.

She opened her eyes, and pulled on the threads.

Reality shifted with the force of an earthquake.

Darkness took her.

Chapter V – The Head of a King

Elisa opened her eyes, then winced. She turned her head away from the light streaming through the window, and stared at the wall. As she blinked, her eyes adjusted.

She sat up, looking around. She was on her bed in her room, in her nightgown. The bare plaster walls were illuminated by the morning sun. She swallowed again, then winced once more. She had never felt so parched in her life.

She tried to remember how she got here. *I had been on the wharf*, she thought. *I was on the wharf, I talked to Charlotte, and then I did something...and then I was here. What did I do?*

A memory resurfaced. She had told Charlotte that everything would be fine. Why had she done that? There was something else, something she could not put her finger on...

She shook her head and rose from the bed. She sat back down, her head swimming. Her stomach growled. Elisa took a deep breath. *I'm going to get out of bed and ask my parents what happened.*

She took another deep breath and stood. Her head swam, but not as badly. She made her way out of the bedroom and into the main room of their apartment above the book bindery. Her parents, both pale and haggard, stared at her.

"You're awake!" Her mother cried, wrapping her arms around Elisa. Tears streamed down her cheeks. "Thank the saviour you're awake!"

"Mother, I'm okay, I..." Elisa began, but then stopped. She closed her eyes and enjoyed the embrace.

"We were so worried about you!" her father said. "You were asleep for so long, and–"

Elisa looked at her father, as he wiped away tears of his own. "I'm fine – just really hungry and thirsty, that's all."

Her mother stepped back and gave her a fragile smile. "I'll get you something to eat. We still have some smoked meat."

Elisa blinked. "Sorry, did you just say 'smoked meat'?"

"Yes," Elisa's mother declared. "Although, with you asleep, we...we..."

"We haven't felt much like eating," her father stated.

Elisa stared at the food her mother placed on the table in front of her. The plate was brand new, the nicest plate she had ever seen. On it was a slice of smoked pork. Her mouth watered.

"We have plenty," her father said. "Eat however much you want."

As Elisa said her grace, her mind wandered. How could this happen? We had barely been able to keep food on the table at all! And they keep talking as though...

Elisa looked at her parents. "How long was I asleep?"

Her parents glanced at each other. "Two weeks," her father replied. "We were afraid you'd never wake up. They found you unconscious on the wharf. But, this is a time of miracles, after all."

Elisa blinked, a memory trying to resurface. "Miracles?"

"Miracles all around us," her father said. "All of the granaries and stored filled with food, and they never run out! Some childrens' toys have come to life! Some houses were suddenly two storeys taller! And some of the dead, they...they..."

"They came back," her mother said. "Mrs. Becker's husband showed up at the door, as though he had never been taken by the Lord into Heaven! And he's not the only one. And there are empty plots in the children's section of the graveyard, and nobody can remember there being any graves there!"

"Show her your coinpurse," her father said.

Her mother held out her coinpurse. "It never runs out of money. It doesn't matter how expensive something is, all I have to do is reach into it, and the money is there!"

Elisa's eyes widened as it all came back to her. Miracles...but they weren't miracles – they were *wishes*. Wishes that she had granted.

It had worked!

"But that's all wonderful, isn't it?" Elisa asked, a smile crossing her face as she bit into the smoked pork, relishing the taste. "If all these miracles have happened, then surely everybody is..." The smile fell off her face. Her parents were staring at her with a look of terror akin to a hunted beast.

"There are things you need to know before you go out there," her mother stated.

"Let her finish eating first," her father begged. "She only just woke up!"

"She *needs* to know," her mother stressed. "If she goes out there and says the wrong thing–"

"What's going on?" Elisa asked.

Her father shook his head. "Look, she doesn't have to go out today. Today, of all days, she can just stay home. We can tell them that she's still asleep, they'll believe us!"

"Everybody is expected to be there, and she needs to know! And what if our neighbours hear something and turn us in?"

"What is happening out there?" Elisa demanded.

"They're executing the king today!" her mother cried, burying her head in her hands. "The king, the queen, and the prince, they're all losing their heads today."

Elisa swallowed, a feeling of nausea rising. "You can't be serious. What do you mean they're executing the king? Who is executing the king?"

"The ruling council of the Republic," her father replied. "The miracles were wonderful, and the king declared that this would make the *Reich* even more likely to welcome us back. But, there were some people who thought that now that we had everything we needed, we didn't need the *Reich* anymore, and it would be safer to remain isolated. King Martin disagreed."

"They overthrew him a week and a half ago," her mother added. "Most of the royalists are in hiding..." Her voice fell to a whisper. "Well, those of us who weren't already hanged."

"You can't tell anybody that we're royalists," Elisa's father hissed. "There are guards everywhere now, and a single one overhears you...we'll be hanged in the town square."

"And you can't say anything in support of the king either," her mother added. "You don't know who will overhear you, or if they'll take it to a guard."

Elisa began to feel faint. "This can't be. How can this

be?"

Her father sighed. "It doesn't matter. It just is. So long as we keep quiet and don't criticize the Republic, perhaps they won't find and execute us."

Elisa buried her face in her hands, her appetite gone. "I don't understand. I just don't understand." *Did I do this? But...I granted everybody's wishes! I made them happy, didn't I?*

Her mother turned to her father. "We have to take her with us to the execution. If they find out that she woke up and we didn't take her..."

Her father clenched his fist in frustration. "Fine! We'll take her. But..."

Her mother embraced him. "We do what we must to survive. That's all that matters now. We just need to make it to–"

Her father shook his head. "Best not mention that."

Elisa's mother glanced at her. "You should finish eating."

"I think I need to pray," Elisa said, rising from the table. "And go to confession. I think I have sins I need to confess, and–"

"You can't," her mother said.

Elisa took a ragged breath. "What?"

Her mother sat down at the table across from where Elisa had been sitting. "Father Xaver wouldn't support the Republic, so they hanged him. They said that the Church must serve the Republic in all things. His church has been shuttered, and the other priest at the church across town, he..."

"He's with them," her father said. "Any royalist who goes to confession there is likely to be arrested and executed."

Elisa's eyes widened. "Priests aren't supposed to do that!"

"It's a time of miracles," Elisa's mother said, bitterness in her voice. "Lots of things that aren't supposed to happen are happening."

"We need to leave soon," Elisa's father said. "It won't look good if we're late."

"You'd better wash yourself and brush your hair," Elisa's mother said. "I'll prepare you a wet sponge."

Elisa nodded, her hand shaking as she made her way back to her bedroom. *What have I done?*

Elisa swallowed as she entered the square, glancing at the guards watching her and her parents as they joined the crowd. The platform had been turned into a gallows, but that wasn't what drew her eye. In front of the gallows was a block and basket, an executioner in a black hood standing holding a large axe.

"Elisa!" a familiar voice called. "You're awake, thank the Lord!"

Elisa turned to see Charlotte rushing to embrace her. "I'm sorry I scared you," she said. "I had no idea that I would–"

"Just so long as you're awake and safe," Charlotte declared. That's all that matters now."

"She visited you every day," Elisa's mother said. "Well, almost every day."

A memory flashed through her mind. Charlotte's wish...had it...?

"Peter," Elisa asked. "Did Peter–"

Charlotte broke into tears. "They hanged him. We'd been engaged for less than week, and they hanged him!"

"Don't say any more," Elisa's mother warned in a quiet voice. "Remember who could...just, be strong, Charlotte."

Charlotte wiped the tears from her eyes. "I know. It's what Peter would have said."

"I'm so sorry," Elisa said. "That thing I told you about, I'll explain it all to you, and–"

Charlotte gave Elisa a sad smile. "That's a wonderful offer, but it doesn't really matter anymore, does it?"

Elisa read Charlotte's wish and suppressed a gasp. All she wanted to do now was join Peter in Heaven.

"People of our glorious Republic!" a voice called from the podium. Elisa turned to see a man she didn't recognize, dressed in fine clothes. Behind him, guards were escorting the royal family, the king and prince both looking beaten and bloody. A priest she didn't recognize walked beside them. The crowd, already quiet, went silent.

"We live in an age of miracles!" the man in fine clothes declared. "For the first time in a generation, we have enough to eat! Our storehouses are never empty! We can now live on our own, without help from the *Reich*! We need never fear hunger again!"

Elisa heard a scattered applause from the crowd.

"Our safety came from our isolation!" the man continued. "Our hunger made us weak, and our king played on that weakness. He gave us a false promise of safety and prosperity for rejoining the *Reich*, but there is no such safety in that action! There is no prosperity to be found! God has given us miracles that will enable us to never need help again! We will never cease to be surrounded by heretics and Jews! Had this traitor of a king restored our place to the College of Princes, he would have sold us to the followers of Martin Luther!"

Elisa looked at the king. His head was slumped, his eyes downcast and dejected.

"But, this council stopped him!" the man said. "We saved this island from the clutches of Protestants and Jews, no longer a kingdom, but a republic, like Rome was long ago! And one day, we may even be an empire!"

The applause became a ragged cheer.

Elisa swallowed, nausea rising.

The well dressed man turned to point at the king and his family. "King Martin, Queen Elisabeth, and Prince Amadeus, this Republic finds you guilty of high treason and sentences you to death! May God have mercy on all of your souls!"

As Elisa watched, the guards pushed the king to the block as the priest followed at his side, performing last rites. They forced him to his knees, putting his neck on the block. The executioner raised his axe to strike. The axe fell. Then it fell again. At the third strike, the king's screams became a strangled whimper. After the fourth, the executioner pulled the king's head out of the basket, displaying it to the crowd.

The crowd cheered. Her mother and father joined them.

"Cheer," her mother whispered. "You need to cheer."

The guards picked up and tossed the king's body to the side, and then dragged the queen to the block as she sobbed.

Elisa shook her head. "I'm sorry, I can't–" She bolted from the crowd, making to the corner of the street before the contents of her stomach spilled out onto the flagstones. She fell to her hands and knees, gagging as the taste of bile filled her mouth, and then heaved again.

Behind her, the queen's screams ended and the crowd cheered.

Elisa felt a hand on her shoulder. She looked to see Charlotte holding her. "Don't worry," Charlotte said. "You'll be okay."

Elisa felt somebody's gaze on her. She looked up to see a guard staring at her, his wish clear in her mind – to punish every single traitor.

"Please excuse my friend," Charlotte said. "She's never seen anything like this before, and she's been sick. We'll rejoin the crowd."

Elisa took a ragged breath, swallowing, trying not to retch once more. "Long live the Republic," she rasped.

"Come on, get up," Charlotte whispered, helping Elisa to her feet. Behind her, the prince began screaming. "Just look at the ground, Elisa. Just keep your eyes on the ground."

The crowd cheered as she rejoined her mother and father. A moment later, Charlotte said, "You can look up now."

Elisa raised her gaze to the platform. The bodies of the royal family were being tossed onto a cart. The well dressed man returned to address the crowd.

"This is the true dawn of our great republic! We have now cast off the shackles of a corrupt monarch, and we look forward to a future of safety and prosperity! But, our struggle is not yet complete! We must face the dangers ahead with unity, and any who threaten this unity will be committing treason. But we *will* face the coming days despite the machinations of royalists and traitors! And every one of us will have a part to play in creating the future of this great republic!"

He stared at the crowd, his wish for never-ending dominance sending a shiver down Elisa's spine. "Every single one of us."

Chapter VI – Reign of Terror

Elisa hugged her legs in a fetal position as her mother knocked on her bedroom door. "Elisa? You have to come out."

I did this, Elisa thought, King Martin's screams and whimpers of agony ending with his head falling into a basket flashing through her mind. *This is all my fault.*

"I tried something new with the beer," her mother said. "I added some...well, it's very good. You should try it."

Maybe I should just go to the other side of town and confess my sins. They might burn me as a witch, but don't I deserve that now? She frowned. *And if I go there, they might find out that my parents are royalists, and then I'd get them killed too.*

She buried her head in her hands and wept.

I got Peter killed. I got the royal family killed.

She heard her father's voice at the door. "Elisa, sweetheart, I need your help."

Elisa looked up. The sun had risen far enough into the sky that her room was cloaked in shadows. She wiped the tears from her eyes, swallowed, and said, "With what?"

"In the shop. There are some pages that need sewing into bundles, and they have to be done soon."

"Shouldn't you be getting an apprentice for that?"

"Getting an apprentice to help out wouldn't be spending time with my daughter," her father said through the door.

Elisa choked back a sob, then took a deep breath. "I'll be right down."

"Take a moment to have something to eat, first," her father said. "This is hungrier work than you'd expect."

She composed herself and opened the door, walking into the main room. Her mother opened her mouth to speak, but then closed it again. Elisa glanced at her, and then glanced away.

"I'm sorry mother, for all of this," she said.

Her mother shook her head. "It's not your fault."

"Yes, it is," Elisa stated. "But, I'm not...I'm not ready to tell you about it yet. I'm sorry."

"Anybody would have been sick seeing that execution."

"I'm not talking about the execution."

"Whatever it is, when you're ready to talk about it, I'll be there."

Elisa gave her a fragile smile and spread some butter on a piece of bread. She finished off the bread as she made her way downstairs. The shop was filled with thin volumes, with stacks of page bundles waiting to be sewn on a table.

Elisa blinked. "That's a lot of books."

"The Ruling Council of the Republic needs somebody to print and bind their decrees," her father said. "And I'm the only bookbinder on the island."

52

She picked up one of the books and read the title. She suppressed a shudder. *The Willful and Terrible Crimes of King Martin Against the Republic.*

"It's best if you try not to think about it," her father said. "Just think about the work, and put everything else out of your mind. Here – let me show you what to do."

Elisa sat down as her father ran her through the fine points of sewing a bundle of book pages together. Then she picked up the needle and started sewing the bundles together.

She was halfway through the pile when the workshop door opened. Elisa glanced up, her eyes widening in fear. The well dressed man from the execution walked into the shop, flanked by four guards, all carrying muskets.

Her father rose to greet him. "You honour us with your presence, First Consul. We will have the contract finished by the end of the week, as promised. You can examine the completed books on that table, if you wish."

The First Consul gave her father a cold smile. "That's not necessary. I have a more urgent matter that needs to be completed first. Hand him the decrees."

One of the guards handed her father a stack of papers. Her father flipped through them.

"We will need three hundred copies to start," the First Consul said.

"That should only take us two to three weeks," her father muttered, then looked up in shock. "You're decommissioning the fishing fleet?"

"We live in a time of miracles," the First Consul declared. "Our food stores are always full. We have no more need for fishermen. We are *dismantling* the fishing fleet. The decree was made today, and the destruction of the boats has already begun in the harbour. We must move quickly on this – after all, we don't want royalists escaping to the mainland and begging heretic princes for help."

Her father's face was expressionless. "I see the reason in that."

"And how is your dear wife, good bookbinder?" the First Consul asked.

"She is well," Elisa's father replied.

"I would give her my greetings," the First Consul stated. "Do bring her downstairs."

"Elisa, please go and fetch your mother," her father said.

The First Consul stared at her as she rose from the table. "Elisa...short for Elisabeth?"

Elisa swallowed. "Yes, sir."

"I was told that you were quite distraught when the royal family received their justice."

Elisa forced down a rising panic. "It was all the blood, sir. I had never seen so much."

The First Consul laughed. "Well, it's a good thing you don't work with animals! There's a lot of blood in the pigs that died so that you could have that tawed leather for your book covers. And it all comes out when they're slaughtered."

Elisa nodded, praying she had nodded fast enough. "I guess so, sir."

The First Consul fixed his cold smile upon her. "Go fetch your mother. Don't be long. I do hate being kept waiting." He turned back to her father. "The rest will be announced and implemented once the books are ready. No need to change everything all at once."

As Elisa reached the top of the stairs, the First Consul called out, "Now that you're awake, perhaps you should attend some of the executions in the square, Elisabeth. It might toughen you up for the days to come."

Elisa swallowed. "I'll consider it, sir."

Her mother was chopping vegetables when Elisa came into the kitchen. Her mother glanced at her, and then put down her knife.

"Elisa, what's happened?"

Elisa took a deep breath. "The First Consul is here. He wants to speak to you."

Elisa's mother stiffened. "Did he say about what?"

"Just that he wanted to give you his greetings."

Her mother closed her eyes and composed herself. Then she opened them and said, "Whatever happens, let your father and I do the talking."

"Yes, mother."

Elisa followed her mother down the stairs. The First Consul greeted them with his cold smile. "Ah yes, the lovely Helena. How are you this fine day, Helena?"

Elisa's mother curtseyed. "I'm good, First Consul. Thank you for asking."

"Very good to hear," the First Consul declared. "It is a good day for the Republic as well. The Royalist threat will soon be eliminated." He turned to her father. "Oh yes, how can I forget! Payment, for the work done thus far, and an advance on this new more urgent job."

The First Consul handed her father a purse of coins. Elisa's father opened it up, his eyes widening.

"First Consul," her father said, "I fear there may have been a mistake. This is a pittance. It doesn't even cover the costs of the materials to print the pages."

"There is no mistake," the First Consul stated. "This is what the Republic can afford. We face many challenges, and the Republic needs all of the resources it can get. All citizens of the Republic must contribute as best they can. Too many do not understand this obligation of charity towards their home. Take Henry Wagner, for instance."

Her father stiffened. "Henry Wagner?"

"Yes," the First Consul said. "The former master of the Merchant's Guild. On the day of miracles, he came into a fortune and resigned his position. But he did not wish to share any of it with the Republic. After being arrested he denied being a royalist, but what can be more royalist than depriving the Republic of the funds it needs to survive? He's being hanged today, and all of his money has been confiscated. I do feel for his poor widow and children. They will be relying on the charity of the Church from now on.

"I must admit surprise, however, at your concern. I was under the impression that you can come into quite a lot of money as well, based on how you have been spending it. In fact, you seem to never lack for money. I've even heard stories of a coinpurse that is never empty of coins."

Elisa suppressed the urge to scream.

"The money that we received appeared in a pile in our home, First Consul," her father said. "We spent the last of it yesterday. We simply kept filling up my wife's coinpurse whenever it was empty. She does most of the shopping, you see."

"Nevertheless, I would very much like to see this wonderful coinpurse," the First Consul stated. "Where is it?"

Elisa's mother and father shared a guarded look. "It's on the mantle of our fireplace," her mother said. "I can go and fetch it if you would–"

The First Consul shook his head. "I would not dream of inconveniencing you by making you go up and down the stairs over and over again! One of my guards will fetch it for us." He glanced at one of his guards, who headed up the stairs. Elisa steadied herself against the table.

The First Consul glanced at her. "You seem to be faint, Elisabeth. Perhaps you're not eating enough."

Elisa swallowed. "I'm fine, First Consul."

The guard returned down the stairs, her mother's magic purse in his hands. He handed it to the First Consul, who opened it up and looked inside.

Elisa closed her eyes, trying to control her breathing.

"I guess you haven't filled it yet today," the First Consul said. He turned to the guard. "Did you find any piles of money upstairs?"

"No, First Consul," the guard replied.

The First Consul looked the purse over. "The stitching is good, but I've seen better." He tossed it to Elisa's mother. "I wish you all a good and productive day. I look forward to seeing the books when they're done in a couple of weeks. Long live the Republic."

"Long live the Republic," Elisa's mother and father said.

"Long live the Republic," Elisa repeated.

The First Consul and his entourage swept out of the workshop and back into the street. Elisa collapsed onto her chair, shaking.

Elisa's mother stared at her father, tears running down her cheeks. "Henry..."

Elisa's father embraced her, shedding tears of his own. "I know. I know."

"What do we do now?" her mother asked.

"We do what we're told," her father said, handing her the purse of money from the First Consul. "And this is what we have to spend until some more work comes in. I'll see if I can get the materials we'll need on credit. Elisa, get back to your work."

"Yes father," Elisa said, willing her hands to steady enough to start sewing pages again.

Elisa stared at the ceiling, that terrifying meeting with the First Consul repeating in her head over and over. He had held all of their lives in the palm of his hand, and he had known it. Just the thought of seeing him again chilled her blood.

How did somebody like him exist on this island in the

first place? And what would he have become if she hadn't granted his wish? How many people would still be alive?

I did this, she thought for the thousandth time. *This is all my fault.*

"You think she's asleep?" she heard her father's voice say quietly.

"I hope so," her mother replied, her voice barely a whisper.

Elisa's eyes widened.

"They know about us," her father said.

"Can we be sure of that?"

"They're having us followed."

"But they haven't arrested us yet."

"They still need books bound. But once this job is done..."

"Maybe we can delay."

"They're watching us, remember?"

"Perhaps you won't be able to get the credit for the materials – maybe they'll need to make you do something for them first, and that–"

"It's work for the Republic. If somebody did deny me the credit, they'd be hanged as a royalist."

Elisa swallowed, a cold sweat running down her back.

"Maybe they'll spare Elisa," her father added.

"Who have they spared, Thomas?" her mother demanded. "Sending her to the Church for scraps after leaving her an orphan isn't mercy."

"I know. But, I can pray."

"They got Henry. Do you think he told them about–"

"Henry would never do that. And it's well hidden, I made sure of that."

"Then we need to use it."

"We can't do that without cover of darkness. The moon won't even be *full* for another week. And, even if they're weren't watching us, if they saw two or three people walking alone in the dead of night, they'll know something was happening."

"So we're stuck," her mother stated, a note of disgust entering her voice.

"All we can do is lay low, do the work, act like everything's normal, and hope we get an opportunity."

"Let's get to bed, Thomas. I just want this day to be done."

As her parents footsteps moved away, Elisa wondered what they could be doing that would put them in such danger, and began to weep.

Elisa's life became the work and spending time with her parents. She stopped enjoying going out to the wharf. The streets had gone from a place where she could overhear pleasant conversations to silence, people walking with their eyes downcast, trying to avoid attracting attention. Wherever she looked, there were guards. And then there were the hangings in the public square.

Every day there was a new hanging of a "royalist." Sometimes it was as many as five. Sometimes she knew one or two of them, but most of the time she didn't. She tried not to look and just get through the square as quickly as possible, walking with her mother to get what little food they could afford off the payment the Republic had given them.

In the meantime, her father printed bundle after bundle of pages for the Republic, giving them to her to bind. But, for the most part, they worked in silence, knowing that every book they finished brought them one step closer to arrest and the gallows.

It was a week after the First Consul's visit that Charlotte came into the shop and stood before her.

"We need a break," she said. "Both of us."

Elisa looked up at her. "If I don't work, they'll–"

"If your *father* doesn't work, they'll know," Charlotte stated. "They don't care about unmarried girls like us. So, let's go to the bathhouse. Besides, I have news."

"We don't have any money," Elisa said. "They gave us a pittance, and they're watching everything we spend–"

"I've got some money," Charlotte declared. "I'll pay for it. We need to get a proper meal into you anyway."

"But–"

Charlotte frowned. "We're probably going to be moving to the farmland outside of town. They hanged some farmers who tried to horde some food, or, at least, that's what they said. And my parents are considered loyal enough that we might be able to acquire one of the plots." She sighed. "It will get us away from all the guards, at least."

Elisa's father nodded to her. "You go with Charlotte. I can spend more time working with you tomorrow."

Elisa rose and gave her father a kiss.

As they stepped out into the street, a guard at the corner stared at them. She tried to avoid his gaze.

"Are you okay, Elisa?" Charlotte asked. "I haven't seen you since...well, that day."

"I'm surviving," Elisa replied, glancing at the guard they passed as they crossed another street. "The work for the Republic keeps us busy."

"Maybe I could join you," Charlotte said. "I wish I was busier. Gets me thinking about something other than...well, you know."

They crossed through the town square. An elderly man and a woman hung suspended from the gallows. Elisa tried not to look at them. Finally, they came to the bathhosue.

The door was shut, a notice hammered onto it.

"You can read," Charlotte said. "What does it say?"

Elisa took a closer look. The notice had been printed,

but not as expertly as her father would have done. "'By order of the Consuls of the Republic, this bathhouse is closed to ensure the prevention of immoral, disgraceful and lewd behaviour'."

Charlotte stared at the notice in shock. "...the prevention of immoral, disgraceful and lewd behaviour..." Her face curled into a snarl of outrage. "What in the fucking hell is immoral about people *bathing*?"

Elisa gasped. "Charlotte, please, don't attract atten–"

"I don't care anymore!" Charlotte screamed. "First they murdered my fiancé, then they killed the king, and now they're taking away my bath!"

Elisa glanced around the street. Two guards were starting to make their way towards them.

"What good is having enough food when everything else that makes life worth living is taken away?" Charlotte raged.

Elisa waved her hands at the guards. "Please, she doesn't mean it, she's just having a bad day–"

"Fuck the Republic!" Charlotte shouted. "The First Consul deserves to eat shit in Hell!"

The guards broke into a run towards them.

"Please, she's not in her right mind!" Elisa cried, trying to step in front of Charlotte. The guard pushed her aside, sending her falling back against the cobbled road. She looked up to see the guards taking a firm hold of Charlotte by the arms.

"Peter wasn't a royalist!" Charlotte screamed as they dragged her away. "He was just against *you*!"

Elisa knew that she should get up and move. She knew that she should turn her face into a mask so that the guards wouldn't see any weakness or discontent. But she couldn't – all she could do was curl up into a fetal position and cry.

"And it was a *printed* notice?" Elisa's father asked, taking a bound book out of a press and placing it in a stack. "Not handwritten?"

Elisa nodded.

"That is troubling," her father said. "It means that they have already established their own printing shop. I suppose we shouldn't be surprised by that."

"And what about Charlotte?" Elisa asked.

"I'm sorry," her father stated. "If she was arrested today, she'll be hanged tomorrow. They work very fast."

"Is there anything I can do to–"

Her father shook her head. "Saving her would require a miracle. And as far as miracles go, I think our island has used up its allotment."

Elisa took a ragged breath. She could do miracles. She had done them before. She could do it again. The wishes she saw in her mind still had a thread she could pull on to grant.

That night, she lay in her bed, concentrating. *I wish Charlotte was safe at home.* She took a deep breath, looking for a thread to pull to make her wish come true.

Nothing.

She wished even harder, searching for even the tiniest thread that could make her wish come true.

Nothing.

Her wish became a silent prayer.

Our father, who art in Heaven, please forgive me my sins. Please don't punish Charlotte for what I have done. If somebody must be hanged, please, let me it be me.

She was still praying when the sun rose.

Maybe if I go there I can wish her off the scaffold, Elisa thought. She dressed herself and made her way to the town square, where the crowd was already gathering. An empty noose hung from the gallows, a short stepladder underneath it. Behind it, they were already leading

62

Charlotte, her hands bound behind her, to the noose. Beside her was the priest, giving her last rites.

I wish she was safe, Elisa thought. *Please, Christ in Heaven, let Charlotte be saved from this!*

She searched her mind for a thread to pull, to make the wish a reality. Still, there was nothing.

The executioner helped her up the ladder, and then put the noose around her neck.

Please, I wish she was safe! Please, God, let her just disappear from the gallows and re-appear beside me! Please!

"For crimes against the Republic, the royalist Charlotte Koch is sentenced to death," the executioner announced. "May God have mercy on her soul."

"I'm coming, Peter!" Charlotte cried, her voice ragged.

Please, get her off of there! Please!

The executioner pulled the ladder out from under Charlotte, her body dropping. The noose pulled tight. Charlotte's legs began to twitch.

Please, I wish she wouldn't die! Please, don't let her die!

Charlotte twitched, like some obscene dance at the end of the rope. Her face went purple.

Please!

The twitching began to slow, Charlotte's body finally becoming still. The executioner and priest stepped off the platform. The crowd began to disperse.

Elisa walked to the street, steadying herself against a building, resisting the bile rising in her throat. Silent tears flowed down her cheeks.

A couple of lowered voices caught her attention.

"Enough is enough," the first said.

"Agreed," the second said. "We begin at dusk."

Chapter VII – Escape

Elisa staggered into her father's workshop, collapsing into her chair. From the corner of her eye, she saw her father glance at her, open his mouth to speak, and then close it again.

I wish I had never granted all of those wishes, she thought. *Please, I'd give anything to have never granted those wishes!* She cast around in her mind, looking for a thread with which to grant the wish, but there was nothing.

I can't grant my own wishes, Elisa realized. She rested her elbow on the workbench, buried her head in her hands, closed her eyes, and sobbed.

Elisa felt somebody's hand on her shoulder. She opened her eyes. By the shadows on the street, it was already late afternoon. Her father stood by the window, looking out onto the street.

"You need to eat this," her mother said, putting a plate of food in front of her.

Elisa blinked. "Did I fall asleep?"

"Yes, you did," her mother said. "And you need to eat this. Quickly."

"There's four now," Elisa's father reported.

"What's going on?" Elisa asked.

The expression on her mother's face broke Elisa's heart. "Please eat, sweetheart."

"Mother, father, what's happening?"

"You're leaving the island today," her mother said. "And you need your strength. So, eat."

Elisa's eyes widened. "We're escaping?" She began to wolf down the food in front of her. Her mother and father exchanged a look.

Elisa's father knelt down beside her and said, "There's a boat. I'd been preparing it for weeks when all the miracles happened. I was going to take us to the mainland...I figured that maybe there we'd find a place with a guild that would accept me, a place that had enough food. I...I..."

"That was your special project," Elisa breathed.

Her father nodded. "Henry was helping me with all of the provisions. And, he wouldn't have talked about this to anybody, so the boat is probably still there. I made sure to hide it so that the tide wouldn't expose it. It's got oars, spare clothing, blankets...all that's missing is food."

"As soon as you're done eating, you're going to leave and head to the wharf," her mother said. "You'll get the boat out, and make your way to shore."

"It's under Pier Four," her father said. "Right under the dock where it meets the land. All you have to do is unmoor the rope to the left when you're facing the water, and then use the rope on the right to pull the boat out. With the fishing fleet destroyed, they shouldn't be watching the docks much anymore."

Elisa's mother handed her the magic coinpurse. "You

should take this. When you have to buy something, just reach inside and however much money you will need will be there."

Elisa's heart skipped a beat. "And you're going to follow, right?"

Elisa's mother and father glanced at each other.

"I'm sorry, sweetheart," her father said. "They're coming to arrest us today. The guards are already gathering. But, they're not interested in you, at least not yet. They may even be hoping that you'll leave, so that you won't get in the way."

Elisa shook her head. "No, no! Please, Mama, Papa, don't do this! Come with me...or leave right after me! Maybe if you left one at a time—"

"I'm sorry, Elisa," her father said. "It's too late for that. Helena and I would just get arrested as soon as we left. But, you can get away, and that's all that matters to us."

"I can't...please...don't make me..."

Elisa's mother took her by the shoulders. "You need to go to the mainland," she declared. "You need to live a good life, one full of happiness and children. And then, when you're done, your father and I will be waiting for you in Heaven."

Elisa began to cry. "Please...please..."

Her father embraced her, and then wiped away her tears. "You need to be strong. When you leave, you need to act as though you're just going off on an errand. Do *not* run. You need to act as though everything is normal. Can you do that?"

Elisa swallowed, and then nodded.

Her mother embraced her and kissed her on the cheek. "We love you, Elisa. Do you remember where the boat is?"

Elisa nodded.

"We're not going to go easy," her father said. "We'll keep them busy as long as we can."

"She needs to leave," her mother told her father.

"Goodbye, Elisa," her father said. "Go now."

Elisa closed her eyes and took a deep breath. Then, she opened the door and stepped out onto the street. The sun hang low in the sky. Six guards stared at her from the street corner, their muskets unshouldered.

She walked in the other direction, resisting the urge to run with each step.

Don't look back. Everything is normal. Don't look back. Everything is normal. Don't look back.

She rounded the street corner and kept walking. When she got to the next corner, she took a ragged breath and looked back behind her.

Nobody was there.

Elisa took another deep breath, and made her way toward the wharf. Bored guards barely glanced at her as she passed.

A strange popping sound erupted behind her. Her breath caught in her throat.

Is that what gunfire sounds like? Are my parents—?

She forced herself to keep walking. Finally, the docks came into view. She made her way down to the pier, checking for ropes.

Nothing.

Her heart skipped a beat. Had they found the boat? She forced down a rising panic as she looked around. The sign for the pier read, "Pier 5."

I'm in the right place, Elisa thought. *They must have found the – wait, no, the boat is on Pier 4! I'm in the* wrong *place!*

She glanced over at Pier 4. The mooring poles closest to the shore had ropes tied around them, leading under the dock.

Elisa forced herself to walk to the pier, and glanced around. She pulled the rope on the left side off the pole, startling as it splashed into the water. She glanced around again. Nobody in sight. She pulled on the rope attached to the right mooring pole. A rowboat slid out from under the pier, two pairs of oars, and a full sack inside, full of changes of clothing and a couple of other necessities, by the looks of it.

Elisa pulled the mooring rope off the pole. Then she climbed into the boat, bracing herself as it rocked under her. The sun hang even lower in the sky, forcing her to shade her eyes as she looked at the distant mainland. She picked up one of the pairs of oars, staring at it for a moment.

"It's rowing," she muttered. "How hard can it be?"

She put the first pair of oars in the water and began to row, staring down at the water to keep the sun out of her eyes. The boat slid away from the docks, its movement sluggish.

Concentrate on the rowing. Don't think about what's happening to Mama and Papa.

"Stop!" a voice called. She looked back to see a guard on the dock, levelling a musket at her. He was so close that he couldn't possibly miss. Two more guards approached behind him.

"Row back here now, or die," the guard said.

Elisa closed her eyes, forcing back tears. No, not when she was this close to getting away! Not when her parents were sacrificing themselves for her!

She looked at the guard, his wish flooding into her mind. He wanted to be rich, to have enough gold to bury himself in it. The thread to his wish hung there, waiting to be pulled.

She pulled on the thread. Reality shifted. Gold coins began to fall from the sky around him.

The guard stared at the coins, and then spun to aim his gun at the approaching guards. "They're *mine!*" he shouted, firing the musket. The nearest guard fell, clutching at his neck as blood flowed. The guard behind him didn't even stare at his fallen comrade, but leveled his own gun and fired back. The guard under the coins clutched at his side with his left hand, drawing his sword with his right.

An explosion sounded behind them.

Elisa blinked, and then turned around and started rowing. Behind her, the guard screamed, "They're mine! They're all mine!" and then was silent.

"They've blown up the food stores!" a new voice shouted behind her. "To arms! The royalists are attacking!"

Elisa stared at the water and rowed. The popping of gunfire sounded behind her, but still she rowed. Then, her arms gave out, the oars sliding into the water, the shore still distant.

Elisa looked back. The island seemed so far away. Pillars of smoke rose from several locations, the fighting now little more than a faint rumble. An explosion rocked the castle on the hill.

All of this is my fault. If I hadn't granted those wishes...

The boat drifted with the current towards the shore, the sun so low it almost kissed the horizon. She stared at the other pair of oars, the muscles in her arms in agony.

She began to pray for the forgiveness of her sins, the souls of her parents, and the souls on the island. As she did, the boat came closer to the shore.

My parents are probably in Purgatory right now, she thought. *Mama, Papa, I'm so sorry for everything I've done.*

The shore came within sight, a sandy beach waiting

for her. The current began to pull the boat parallel to the beach.

Elisa took a deep breath. *Just a little further.* She pulled out the second pair of oars, her arms screaming in agony. She gritted her teeth and began to row. Pain shot up and down her arms.

The boat slid up onto the beach. Elisa let go of the oars, her hands and arms shaking. She took a ragged breath. Then it hit her.

I'm on the mainland.

She stood and looked around. Beyond the beach was a tree line and a thick forest. Hills rose in the distance. At the tree line was a thin but noticeable foot path.

Elisa climbed out of the boat, grabbing the bag and slinging it over her shoulder. Then she looked back across the water.

A thick pillar of smoke rose into the air. The entire island was burning.

I need to find help, Elisa thought. *The survivors, they—*

The realization landed on her shoulders like a ton of boulders. She had heard a guard say that the royalists had destroyed the food stores. The merchant had told her that there was almost nobody left on the coast. And even if there was somebody, they'd be protestant heretics, and not likely to care about an island full of Roman Catholics.

There was no help coming.

The thought came unbidden to Elisa's mind. *I'm the only survivor.*

Elisa took a deep breath, entered the forest along the foot path, and left the boat and the beach behind.

Part II
Once Upon a Fairy Tale

Chapter I – The Wandering Jew

Elisa woke up in a clearing, her back sore from sleeping on the hard ground. She stretched her arms, and then rose to a kneeling position and began to pray.

First she prayed for the souls of her parents, and that their time in Purgatory would be shortened. Then she prayed for Charlotte's soul. Then she prayed for Father Xaver. Finally, she prayed for herself.

Her stomach growled as she pushed the blanket and rolled up clothes she had used as a pillow back into the bag. Part of her wondered if the fire on the island had burnt out yet. She pushed that to the back of her mind. Better to focus on the present.

She needed food. The path through the forest was overgrown, but it still existed, so at least some people must still be using it. If she kept following it, surely she'd come to a village of some sort.

Elisa shouldered the bag and started down the path, heading deeper into the forest. Birds chirped high in the canopy. She swallowed, her throat parched.

After what felt like hours, she came across a creek. She leaned down and drank her fill, the water sweet to her lips. Her stomach rumbled again.

"Just a bit further," she muttered. "Just a bit further and there will be something to eat."

The path opened up into a village.

A smile crossed Elisa's face, but then faded. It had been a village once, but it had been abandoned long ago. Most of the frames of the buildings still stood, but few were intact. At least half of the roofs had collapsed.

Elisa walked through the empty village streets. Once she reached the village square, the buildings stopped. The ground became rough and lumpy. Her foot knocked up against something hard. She knelt down and poked at the earth, uncovering the charred remains of a piece of wood.

A memory from a conversation with a merchant in the bathhouse came into her mind. *"There's not a lot of people left. At least, not to the east. A lot of empty villages, or what used to be villages."*

"But I rowed to the west," Elisa muttered. "So what will I find?"

She knelt down and prayed for the souls of the people who had once lived in the village. Then she stood and stared up at the sky. The sun hung low. Her stomach growled.

I deserve this, she thought. *It's because of me that my home was destroyed.*

"Who the Hell are you and what are you doing here?" a voice with a strange accent demanded.

Elisa turned to see a man staring at her. He was dark haired, with a long, bushy beard. His clothes were shades of black and bluish grey, and he wore a wide hat on his head. His wish came into her mind – nothing more than to be left alone.

"I'm looking for food, and a place to stay," Elisa said. "I'm sorry, but I'm very hungry."

"You won't find much here," the man stated. "This place was destroyed fifteen years ago. Nobody lives here now."

Elisa swallowed. "Do you have any food? Please, I have money, I can pay however much you want."

"If you have so much money, why are you here?"

Elisa stared at the man. His eyes were cold and calculating. "It's a long story."

"It always is."

"Please, if you could share some food, I would–"

The man rolled his eyes. "Enough whining. I'll share some food with you. But, you'll have to pay for it."

"However much money you want, it's yours," Elisa promised.

"I don't want your money, *gentile*," the man said. "I've had enough of gentiles talking about my kind ripping them off. You'll pay with your labour. Gather firewood."

Elisa chewed on the smoked meat, savouring every bite. She looked over at the strange man, tending the fire he had made in the town square with a stick.

She took a deep breath. "I'm sorry for asking, but are you...are you...are you a Jew?"

The man sighed and shook his head. "Fucking gentiles. Yes, I am a Jew. Or, I guess, I'm not so much *a* Jew as *the* Jew."

"I'm sorry," Elisa said. "I don't understand. What do you mean by '*the* Jew'."

"Work it out, you idiot girl," the Jew said. "You've heard of me – everybody has. Cursed by your saviour to walk the earth until his return...now do you remember?"

Elisa's eyes widened. "You're the Wandering Jew."

"There you go," the Jew declared. "The more interesting question is what you are."

Elisa stiffened. "I'm just a daughter of a bookbinder."

"Don't lie to me, girl," the Jew snarled. "You're not smart enough to do that. You're like me. *Special*. I could feel it as soon as I saw you. I walk the world and never grow old or die. What do you do?"

Elisa took a deep breath. "I grant wishes."

"Wishes."

Elisa nodded.

"And what are you doing out here?" the Jew asked.

"I come from this island named..." Elisa sighed. "I guess the name doesn't matter now. We'd left the *Reich* before I was born, and kept ourselves safe my making sure nobody knew we were out there. I granted everybody's wishes, all at once. It went wrong, and..." She stared at the fire. "I think I'm the only survivor."

The Jew began to laugh.

Elisa glared at him. "It's not funny."

"Oh yes it is!" the Jew chortled. "And here I thought I'd heard every single reason that gentiles would kill one another."

"Stop laughing!"

"Make me!" the jew laughed. "Everybody who wished for wonderful nice things, you granted their wishes, but everybody who wanted power and domination over their follow man, you granted their wishes too! Just how old are you?"

"I'm fifteen," Elisa muttered.

"Fifteen!" the Jew said. "Well, that explains it. Most people are fucking stupid when they're fifteen. But you...I think you've managed something truly exceptional!"

"Stop laughing!" Elisa shouted. "Thousands of people are dead because of me! It's not funny!"

"They can join everybody else here then, can't they!" the Jew declared. "You think you gentiles killing each other is something new? The Catholics and the Lutherans, they fought and raped and murdered each other across this land for thirty years! Then they got together and declared that the 'Peace of Westphalia' would set everything to rights. But then a few years later the Swedes and the Poles and the Prussians were all fighting over the land again anyway. Gentiles killing each other is the rule, not the exception. I guess that's what happens when your saviour is a carpenter with pretensions. So long as they're not killing my kind, what do I care what the reason may be? One of these days, you might just realize how lucky you and your island had been."

"Well, it's not lucky now," Elisa stated. "And it's my fault. And I...I...I just don't know what to do."

"Yes you do," the Jew said. "You may be an idiot of a girl, but you're smart enough."

"You just met me," Elisa declared. "What would you know?"

"You're *here*," the Jew stated. "And you're tearing yourself up for what you did. I think that if you were a wicked person, you'd have just walked away without a care. If you were a weak person, you'd have killed yourself. Since you aren't either of those, I think you know what to do."

Elisa took a deep breath. "Penance."

The Jew shrugged. "Whatever you gentiles call atonement."

"How do I atone for the destruction of an entire kingdom?"

"You can grant wishes, can't you?" the Jew said. "So grant wishes."

"The last time I granted wishes, I destroyed my home and everybody I love."

"Be careful this time."

They fell into silence. Elisa watched the flickering of the fire. Then the Jew spoke.

"If you head down the path to the northwest," he said, pointing, "you'll come to a village. It will take about three days, if you walk quickly. I just came from there – they're friendly enough."

"Are they Catholic or Lutheran?"

The Jew shrugged. "You gentiles are all the same to me."

"And you, will you–"

"I'll be long gone by then," the Jew said.

"Will I see you again?"

"Not if I can help it."

Elisa sighed. "Can I at least know your name?"

"No."

Elisa stared at the fire. "My name is–"

"I don't care or want to know."

"I guess you wouldn't."

The Jew lay down on a bedroll and closed his eyes. "Go to sleep, girl. You've got a long road ahead of you."

Elisa awoke in the village square, birds chirping. The fire had gone out long ago. She glanced across where it had burned. The Jew was gone, along with his bedroll. Where they had sat was a small package.

She got up, wincing as her muscles complained after a second night sleeping on the ground, and picked up the package. Inside was some more smoked meat.

"Thank you, Jew," she muttered, taking a bite. As she swallowed, she added, "I wish I'd known your name."

After she had finished her breakfast, she knelt and began her prayers, this time adding the Wandering Jew to the souls she prayed for. Then she prayed for wisdom as she began her penance.

She stared at the roll of clothes she had used as her pillow. Half of them had belonged to her father. She glanced up at the sky, wishing that he would be out of Purgatory already, but knowing it couldn't be true. But, perhaps, if God was kind and willing, he could hear her there.

"Papa," she began. "Mama...I'm sorry for everything. I should have told you that I could grant wishes. I should have asked you for advice on how to use this gift. I should have thought more before I acted. And everything that happened, it was because of me.

"I'm sorry, because I'm not going to live a happy life with lots of love and children like you wanted me to, at least not yet. I need to atone for what I did first, and it's going to take a very long time. My penance may not be finished by the time I come to join you. But it's what I need to do."

She sighed. "I'm going to take a family name, Papa. I know you didn't see the point in one, but I always wanted one. I kind of hoped that it might be one that would remind me of you. But, I don't deserve that. Not anymore, anyway. I'm going to name myself Elisabeth Beichtkind – 'Elisabeth the Penitent'. That way, anybody who meets me will know what I am, and what I must do."

Elisa wiped a tear from her eye. "Please don't hate me for what I did, Mama and Papa. Please forgive me for what I was too afraid to tell you. And please, when you get to Heaven and are able to look down on me, please know that I will do whatever I need to in order to atone for my sins."

Elisa stuffed the bundle of clothes and blanket back into her bag. Then she threw it over her shoulder, took a deep breath, and began her penance.

Chapter II – In a Land of Heretics

The first thing Elisa saw as she approached the village, weak and light-headed from hunger, was a man arguing with frogs.

Elisa blinked, staring in disbelief. He was a peasant in ragged clothes, his hair going to grey, gesticulating with wild abandon.

"It's seven *Thalers*, I'm telling you!" he cried. "Not eight!"

The frogs croaked at him.

"I'm the one who sold the cow, you idiot frogs, and I'm the one who knows how much I sold it for! It's seven *Thalers*! Seven!"

The frogs croaked at him again.

"What, you think that you can just see through my coinpurse?" the man demanded. "It's seven, and that's all there is to it!"

Elisa looked closer, the peasant's wish becoming clear in her mind. He wanted, more than anything in the world, for the frogs to admit he was right.

The frogs croaked. The peasant opened up the coinpurse and brandished a handful of *Thalers*. "It's seven, see!" He counted them out. "One, two, three, four, five, six, seven, and no more! Just seven, not eight!"

The frogs croaked.

The peasant snarled and tossed the coins into the pond. "If you don't believe me, then count them yourselves! But I want every single one of them back once you're done!"

The frogs croaked.

"Well, come on, give them back!" the peasant demanded.

The merchant at the bathhouse said that you had to go pretty far to get away from the heretics, Elisa thought. *So, these have to be heretic lands. But...this man is insane! Are all heretics like this?*

The frogs croaked.

"Typical!" the peasant roared. "You're going to take all the time in the world to count them, aren't you? Well, you've wasted enough of my day! I'm not going to stand around and wait for you to count them one at a time – I'm leaving! But when I get back, every single *Thaler* had better be there waiting for me!"

The peasant gave the frogs his middle finger, stomped his feet and turned his back on them. Then he noticed Elisa staring, her mouth agape.

"When somebody is wrong, never give them the satisfaction of thinking they might be right," he declared, and then stormed off, shouting insults back at the frogs.

Elisa realized her mouth was open and closed it. She took a deep breath, and then walked into the village.

A cacophony of sounds and smells greeted her. Livestock bleated, honked, oinked, and crowed. People milled around, talking to each other. She stared as a boy drove a flock of geese across the village square.

A creaking caught her attention. Elisa looked down the river to see a large water wheel turning. "What's that for?" she muttered.

"It's a sawmill," a voice replied. "It cuts wood. You've never seen one before?"

Elisa turned to see a young woman regarding her. Her hair was brown, her eyes a bright blue, but her dress was grey and dirty, stained with soot.

"We didn't have one where I was from," Elisa said.

"You look lost," the young woman said.

Elisa nodded. "I guess I am."

"You hungry?"

Elisa's stomach growled. "I haven't eaten a proper meal in days. I've got money, though."

"Good," the young woman said. "Let's get some food and beer. There's a tavern just over there. You can pay for it."

Elisa blinked. "You have enough food?"

The young girl smiled. "This year, we do. We've finally got enough people to work all of the fields again. Come along – let's eat."

The tavern was small but clean, the ceramic floor recently swept. They took a seat by an open window, a serving girl taking their order. Then, after the girl brought the beer steins to the table, the young woman smiled and took a long, deep drink.

"Oh, that's good," she said. "My stepmother can't brew a decent beer to save her life. Not that it stops her from trying, unfortunately. So, what's your name?"

"I'm Elisabeth," Elisa replied. "But, everybody calls me Elisa."

The young woman smiled. "Good to meet you, Elisa. I'm Eleonore, but everybody calls me Ella."

Elisa took a drink from her stein. Ella was right – it was a good beer. She watched Ella finish off her beer and call for another. Ella's wish crystalized in her mind: escape.

Elisa blinked. Escape from *what*?

"So, what's your story?" Ella asked.

Elisa gave her a fragile smile. "I'm from this island a few days from here, but...there was a revolution. They killed the king, and my best friend, and my parents, and...the last time I saw it, the entire island was burning. That was just a few days ago."

Ella frowned. "I'm sorry to hear that. I'll pray for all of their souls."

Elisa stared at the table. "No you aren't, and you won't. We're all – we *were* all Catholics."

She felt Ella's hand on hers. "You're wrong. I *am* sorry, and I *will* pray for them. I don't care if they haven't seen the light of Protestantism. Nobody should have to go through that."

Elisa looked up at her, a tear rolling down her cheek. "Really?"

Ella gave her a kind smile. "Really."

"Thank you."

The server arrived with their food. Elisa's eyes widened as she saw the size of the pork cutlet in front of her, covered in a mustard sauce.

Ella chuckled, taking a bite out of her own cutlet. "You really haven't eaten a proper meal in days, have you?"

Elisa began eating, scarcely stopping to savour so much as a single bite. After she had polished off the cutlet, she looked up at Ella, who watched her with an amused grin. "So, what about you?" Elisa asked.

"My father owns a large farm," Ella replied. "Around a hundred acres. Most of the food here probably comes from our land, in fact. Not that I get to see it very often."

"Why's that?"

Elisa raised her stein to take another drink and then stopped. Ella was staring out the window, her face pale, her hand clenching the table.

Elisa leaned forward. "Ella, what's wrong?"

"You have a little friend!" an arrogant voice declared. Elisa looked out the window to see a pair of young women, one tall and one short, but both beautiful and well-dressed, staring at Ella with a malignant smile.

Ella averted her gaze to the table. "Errands are my own time," she mumbled. "I'm not late getting back yet. I'm allowed to be here."

"What do we care what the kitchen wench gets up to?" the short one laughed. "But have you told your friend who you really are?"

"Ella the kitchen wench," the tall one laughed with a singsong voice. "Ella the fireplace cleaner, always covered in ashes and cinders...I know! We should call you 'Cinder-Ella'!"

"When I get home I'll do all my work, I promise!" Ella whimpered.

"You're eating such a good meal here," the short one mused. "Must be on somebody else's coin. Can't have you getting uppity and thinking that you're allowed to eat like this, though. Let's put her peas and lentils in the ashes tonight. Remind her of her place."

"That sounds like a wonderful idea!" the tall one cried. "Don't be late, 'Cinder-Ella' – lots of work to do at home!"

The two women walked away, laughing. Ella began to shake. Elisa put her hand on Ella's, only to have Ella jerk it away.

"I'm sorry," Ella cried. "I'm sorry, I didn't mean – you didn't deserve–"

"Ella, it's okay," Elisa said. "Who were those people?"

"My stepsisters," Ella said. "My father remarried a couple of years ago, and my stepmother brought them with us."

"And he lets them treat you like this? How can he do that?"

"I don't know," Ella sighed. "No, actually, I do. It's because of my mother."

Elisa leaned forward. "I don't understand."

Ella took a deep breath, a tear rolling down her cheek. "My father took me with him on a trip to talk to the Merchant's Guild in Stralsund about a dozen years ago. You should have seen him back then. He was so loving...people kept teasing him for doting on me so much. But when we came back...the French had come, and they'd slaughtered half the village and razed our crops. We found my mother and my brother hanging from a tree, along with all the rest."

Elisa placed her hand on Ella's. "I'm so sorry."

Ella nodded. "Thank you. Everybody lost somebody in the war, we're no different. My father never forgave himself for not being there to protect them, even though if we had been there the French probably would have killed us too. But, when I grew older, I became the spitting image of my mother, or, at least, that's what people tell me. And my father...he can't even look at me anymore."

"Is there any way you can get out of there?" Elisa asked.

"Where would I go?" Ella replied. "I've got no money, and if I haven't been properly disinherited, I may as well have been. Most of the villages around here were destroyed, and we've only been able to feed everybody here for a year."

"What about marriage?" Elisa asked. "Surely if somebody married you, they wouldn't be able to touch you."

Ella sighed. "I've thought of that. It's no good. My stepmother insists that since her daughters are older, they need to get married first. And, well, there's a reason they aren't married yet."

Elisa glanced out the window. Ella's stepsisters were nowhere to be seen. "They seemed beautiful enough."

"They are indeed beautiful and fair of face," Ella declared. "And they have had plenty of suitors – but all of those courtships ended shortly after they opened their mouths and started talking. They are very...unrestrained...in their cruelty. Nobody in the village will touch them." She chuckled, a sparkle returning to her eyes at last. "Hell, nobody in the principality will touch them."

"There's got to be something," Elisa muttered.

"Well, there is, but...it's a dream, nothing more."

"Tell me," Elisa said.

"Prince Johann is holding a three day festival at his palace over this weekend to find a bride for his son," Ella said. "All of the families of the landowners have been invited. If I could catch his eye, and the prince's son wanted to marry me, my stepmother could never refuse the match."

Elisa smiled. "Well, that's something! So, if you could just get to the festival and charm a prince, you're out."

Ella frowned. "Elisa, look at me. My hair is a mess, my face is never cleaner than this, and I have no nice clothes, or any way to get them. Anything I had that could be worthy of the gaze of a prince my stepmother and stepsisters either took for themselves or destroyed a long time ago. And even if I did manage to clean myself up, I've got no way to get there."

"Suppose I can make all of that happen," Elisa said.

Ella gave her a skeptical stare. "The half-starved Catholic heretic girl is going to help me get engaged to a prince?"

"Please don't call me that. I'm not a heretic."

"Elisa, I'm not the one whose church does whatever they want instead of sticking to the word of the Bible."

Elisa sighed. "We can agree to disagree on that, okay? But, please, let me help you. I think I can make your wish come true."

"And why should I do that? My home is a hell, but it's one I know how to navigate, and most days I don't get beaten. Why should I take the risk?"

Elisa took a deep breath. "Because I'm a penitent. The person who destroyed my island...it was *me*. I made this terrible mistake, and destroyed everything I care about. I need to find some way to make this right, and if I can help you get away from those horrible women, then maybe it's a first step to saving my soul."

Ella chuckled. "You know, some people just go to confession. Don't you Catholics just do that along with some 'hail Mary's?"

"I'm not one of those people."

Ella shrugged. "Well, what do I have to lose? If nothing else, while you're around you can buy me some decent food. Go ahead and try."

"Do you know a place I can stay? I can sleep on the ground again, if I have to, but it would be nice to have a roof over my head."

"There's an inn just down the street," Ella said. "I don't know why Jakob and Anna kept it open during all of the lean years, but they did. You can stay there."

Elisa sighed. "Thank you."

"Well, I can't wait to see this," Ella said, grinning and leaning forward. "You've got three days until the festival begins. Let's see what you can do, half-starved Catholic girl."

Chapter III – Preparations for a Festival

Elisa sat at the table as Anna took her empty plate, saying "At least you're a good eater. We'll put some meat on those bones yet!"

The grey-haired innkeeper's wife bustled off to the kitchen, leaving Elisa with her thoughts. Ella's wish was there, the thread waiting to be pulled. But what would happen if she pulled it? Would Ella just find herself somewhere else, with no money or way of finding her way back? Would her parents and stepsisters die? They probably deserved that to some degree, but killing somebody just because they had hurt a person Ella wanted to help wasn't the Christian thing to do, and causing them to die unshriven would do nothing to save their souls. Or would there be something else, something Elisa couldn't foresee?

Elisa sighed. She really needed to figure out how granting wishes worked.

"What's on your mind?" Jakob asked. Elisa turned to find the innkeeper, his hair and beard also going to grey, at the door to the dining room, staring at her.

"I'm trying to help somebody," Elisa replied. "I promised her I would. But, I'm just not sure how."

"Who are you trying to help?"

"Her name's Eleonore."

"Ah, Ella," Jakob said, sitting down across from her. "Now that's a tale of woe."

"She told me that her mother was murdered by the French in the war."

Jakob nodded. "That's true enough. They killed half the village. Georg and Ella were lucky they weren't there – the French burnt down their house, too."

"Sorry, Georg?"

"Ella's father."

"I see."

"He spent the next ten years keeping her alive," Jakob said. "Ran the entire household by himself, although once Ella was old enough, she helped too. Most people would have tried to remarry, but he didn't...not that there were many eligible women left around here anyway."

"Ella said that once she grew old enough, she reminded him of her mother."

"That she did," Jakob declared. "It was like looking at a ghost."

"So, why did he remarry?"

"Why does anybody?" Jakob mused. "Loneliness, needing help running the household. It would probably be a few years before Ella could marry anybody – after all, it's hard for anybody to put together enough land or money to provide for a family these days – but once she did, Georg would have been left alone. And then that harridan got her claws into him."

"Ella's stepmother?"

Jakob nodded. "Some people, they're very good at hiding their true nature. That woman Georg married, she seemed decent enough at first. But, then she'd laugh at some cruelty, or find some excuse to berate somebody who was helping her...let's just say, she didn't hide it for long. I think we even saw her smirking during church. And her daughters, they just never even tried. If they didn't have Georg's money and land...well, even with that, they're going to die as spinsters – I'm certain of it."

"I saw them mistreat her," Elisa said. "They did it right in front of me at the tavern. They called her 'Cinder-Ella'."

Jakob sighed. "I know. The entire village knows. I thought that maybe we could make enough money to offer her a job her, get her under our roof. But, even with the war now over, there's too few people travelling. We mostly support ourselves by brewing and selling beer, and my wife mends clothes."

Elisa smiled despite herself. "Your beer is pretty good."

Jakob nodded. "Thank you. It's the same for everybody. We'd all help her if we could, but there's nobody who can take in an extra mouth to feed. And even if we could...well, Georg owns the largest farm in miles. If we tried to interfere, the harridan could starve us."

"Why doesn't Georg do anything about it?"

"The harridan took control of his household as soon as she got there," Jakob replied. "In his own way, Georg may be as much of a prisoner there as Ella."

Elisa sighed. "If I can figure out how to help Ella, I will."

"I hope you do," Jakob said. "If anybody needs it, it's Ella."

Elisa woke with the dawn, the sunlight light streaming into her room. Her sheets were soaked with sweat – perhaps she had been having nightmares? Either way, it didn't matter now. She could walk into the main room, and tell her father about this dream she'd been having, where she'd had to escape the island and had met the Wandering Jew and...

She blinked. This wasn't her room. The bed was comfortable, but it wasn't quite as soft as the one at home. And she'd never had a chest for her belongings like the one in the corner.

Elisa curled into a fetal position and began to cry. It wasn't a dream – it was reality. Everybody and everything she had loved was gone, and it was her fault.

She took a ragged breath, and wiped the tears from her eyes. She couldn't change what had happened, but she could help Ella. She just needed to figure out how...and if possible, to do it without granting her wish. If Elisa was going to use her ability to know and grant wishes to carry out her penance, she was not going to let anybody get hurt by accident ever again.

She spent breakfast lost in thought. *Put yourself in Ella's shoes – what would she need?* She's need a dress, to begin with. And enough time to clean herself up and take care of her hair. And then she'd need transportation to the palace...and then she'd need to be back home before her stepmother and stepsisters, so that she could hide the dress and make herself look dirty again.

Elisa nodded to herself as Anna cleared the table. She had her mother's magic coinpurse. Almost everything Ella would need could be bought. She'd just need to find it. *Time to explore the village.*

She made her way out of the inn, a large structure catching her eye as she glanced around. It was a half-timbered shed of some sort, with three large wooden doors on one side. Elisa grinned as she realized what it had to be – a carriage house. She'd seen one on the island once. Then the grin faded. It had probably been unused for years.

"Do you like our carriage house?" a voice said behind her. Elisa turned to see Anna carrying a basket of clothes. "We keep it in good shape, not that there's much call for it these days. Nobody really travelling at the moment."

Elisa nodded. "I'd love to."

"Have you ever been inside one?" Anna asked.

Elisa shook her head.

Anna put down the basket and opened one of the gates. "Well, I'm afraid you'll probably find it a bit disappointing. It's just a big building that keeps the rain and snow off of carriages."

Elisa's eyes widened as she saw what was inside. "You have a carriage?"

"It's not really ours," Anna declared. "Well, I guess it is now. The owner was killed when the French attacked our village, and we never found out who his family was or where they might be. It's probably not in very good shape anymore – we were planning to sell it once somebody wealthy came along, but the war put a stop to that too. We've kept it in here, but we don't know much about taking care of carriages. It almost certainly needs a lot of work before anybody can take it anywhere."

Elisa smiled. "Is there anybody in the village who can fix it up?"

"Oh yes," Anna replied. "We have a good wheelwright. Mostly he handles the wagons used for the harvest and the sawmill. But, we'd need to be able to pay him for it, first."

I could pay for it, Elisa thought.

"Jakob told me that you're planning to help Ella," Anna said. "I really hope you can – I hate seeing my niece treated like that."

Elisa blinked. "Your niece?"

Anna nodded. "Ella's mother was my sister. I still have a couple of her things. I didn't dare give them to her, well, because..."

"Because you were afraid of what her stepmother and stepsisters would do if they found them."

"Yes." Anna picked up the basket. "I should get to this laundry – they won't walk themselves to the river for cleaning, after all!"

"I'll see you this evening," Anna said.

As Anna walked away, Elisa grinned. She had a carriage! Now what she needed was somebody to drive it and a dress...

Elisa found Ella making her way through the village square. Ella gave her a mischievous grin. "Hello, half starved Catholic girl! Are you going to buy me a lunch again?"

Ella nodded. "It's the least I can do."

"Good," Ella declared. "But there's something I need to do first."

"Oh?"

"I need to check in with the butcher to see if the cow we had slaughtered is ready, and then I need to visit my mother and brothers." Ella smiled. "Want to come?"

Elisa nodded. "I'd love to."

The butcher was close enough that it only took a couple of minutes to get there. Once Ella had finished her business, they followed the river out of town into Ella's family farm.

"So, how goes the plan?" Ella asked with a smile.

"I've found a carriage," Elisa replied. "And I'm pretty sure I can get somebody to fix and drive it."

"Any wagon driver can do that," Ella stated. "No shortage of them around here."

"So, what I need next is a dress."

Ella stopped. "Elisa, are you certain about this? If they catch me..."

"They won't," Elisa declared. "I'm already taking that into account."

"But where are you going to get a dress that will fit me?" Ella demanded. "That takes time, and you'll need me there for fittings."

Elisa shrugged. "You look about the same size as me. If it fits me, it will probably fit you."

Ella shook her head. "You really are still a kid, aren't you?"

"I'm fifteen!" Elisa protested.

"And I'm *twenty*," Ella stated. "Trust me, you're a kid. Don't assume everything will just go to plan. Something *always* goes wrong."

"I'm being careful," Elisa said.

Ella looked at her and smiled. "Okay then. Come along, we're almost there."

They walked a bit farther. The first Elisa saw of the graves was a large hazel tree. In front of it were three headstones. A white bird perched on one of the lower branches, watching them.

"They're not on consecrated ground?" Elisa asked.

"When Heinrich died as a baby, father and mother decided that they wanted him close," Ella said. "It was comforting, really. But then the French came, and, well, you know the rest." She pointed at the tree. "I planted that on mother's grave, so that I'd always be able to find her. Even now, it feels like she's looking down on me from Heaven."

Or waiting to get there, Elisa thought, but held her tongue. Ella had enough problems – no point in reminding her that her mother was probably still in Purgatory, assuming that she hadn't been sent straight to Hell.

94

Besides, even if she was in Purgatory, she'd be able to look down on and pray for Ella.

Ella knelt down by her mother's grave and started to pray. As she did, Elisa frowned.

She needs to know, Elisa thought. *It's not right to hide it from her.*

Ella finished praying and rose to her feet. "Okay, let's go to lunch."

"Before we do," Elisa said, "I have something I need to tell you."

"What is it?"

"Please don't think I'm a witch. I'm not."

Ella blinked. "I didn't think you were."

Elisa took a deep breath. "But, I can grant wishes."

Ella shrugged. "Okay."

Elisa realized that she had been holding her breath. "You're not afraid of me?"

"Why would I be?" Ella asked. "You're working hard to make my wish happen. Nothing wrong with hard work. It's good for your soul, after all."

Elisa sighed. "You don't understand. I can grant wishes...as in making them just happen."

Ella crossed her arms. "You're right. I don't understand."

"Back on the island, there was this old man who wished he could catch a giant fish. It was like his wish was there, flowing out of him, and all I had to do was pull on it to make it happen. And, as soon as I did, he caught this massive fish, the biggest I had ever seen."

"Elisa, that's just coincidence," Ella said. "The fish was probably just there, and that's the moment it chose to bite."

"But, there's more," Elisa declared. "My mother's wish was to always be able to pay her way, and when I granted it, it made it so that her coinpurse always had the money she would need in it. And when I was escaping from the island, there was this guard who was about to shoot me, and his wish was to be so rich that he could be covered in gold, and when I granted his wish, coins just fell from the sky around him."

Ella stared at her. "So when you say that you can grant wishes, you mean that you can actually perform miracles."

"I don't think they're really miracles," Elisa said. "I'm not a saint. But, they're not from the Devil either, I'm sure of that."

"Wait...when you said that what happened to your island was your fault..."

Elisa stared at the ground. "I wanted to make everybody's lives better and I thought it was a good idea to grant everybody's wishes at once. It...it wasn't." A tear rolled down her cheek.

She felt Ella embrace her. "Oh, Elisa, you poor thing."

Elisa looked up. "You don't think I'm a witch?"

"I don't think there's such a thing as a penitent witch," Ella said. "Even among the Catholic heretics."

Elisa's body shook as she sobbed in Ella's arms. "I killed them all, Ella! My parents, my best friend and her fiancé, they all died because of me! And I tried to wish that I had never made my mistake, but I couldn't! I can't grant my own wishes! I can't fix any of it!"

"Listen to me, Elisa," Ella said. "It is going to be okay. You'll help lots of people, and you'll atone."

"Thank you," Elisa muttered, taking a ragged breath.

"You okay now?" Ella asked.

Elisa nodded. Ella let go and took a step back.

"So, you can grant wishes, right?" Ella asked.

Elisa nodded.

"So, why not just use your power to grant mine? Why go through all of this?"

Elisa sat on the ground. Ella sat beside her.

"I don't really understand how it all works yet," Elisa said. "I don't know how to control it. I don't know if granting your wish would make you disappear to some strange unknown land, or kill your family, or what it could do. Your wish...it's too vague."

"I thought my wish was to go to the festival."

Elisa shook her head. "It's to escape."

Ella sighed. "Well, you're not wrong."

"Look, I have enough money...why don't you come to the inn with me? Get away from those terrible people."

Ella recoiled, abject fear in her eyes. "I can't do that! What will they do to me if I come back? What happens if you can't get me to the festival, and then you leave and I've got nowhere to go? I don't want to become some poor beggar selling my clothes for scraps of food!"

"That wouldn't happen," Elisa pressed.

"You can't know that!" Ella declared. "And what happens if they come looking for me? What would they do when they found me? Who's going to protect me against them?"

"If I have to, I can bring you with me when I leave," Elisa said. "You don't have to stay here."

Ella held up her hand. "Elisa, we'll stick to your plan. And if it fails, and you can't get me to the festival, that's fine too. I won't mind, really. I'll be fine once you leave. Now, let's go get some food."

Ella gave Elisa a hug and a promise to meet again the next day before she went home, leaving Elisa alone in the village square. Elisa took a deep breath. She was going to get Ella out of there even if she had to drag her out kicking and screaming.

She had the carriage. Now she needed a dress made. She glanced around. Back on the island, there would have been a colourful sign marking the seamstress' shop. But here...

A memory flashed through Elisa's mind. Anna was mending clothing to help make ends meet. Perhaps she would know who could make a dress.

Elisa made her way back to the inn. Anna and Jakob were in the kitchen, chopping vegetables and dropping them into a soup. Elisa knocked on the door.

Anna looked up and gave her a smile. "Elisa! How goes your afternoon?"

"Good so far, but still a lot to do," Elisa replied. "Might you know where I can have somebody make me a dress?"

Anna shrugged. "I could make you one. Workaday clothes are pretty easy."

"It's not for that," Elisa said. "It would have to be something fancier."

Anna frowned. "That's harder. We had a proper seamstress, but she died during the war. Right now, everybody is pretty much making their own clothes. I just fix them for those who don't have time to do it themselves."

"Is this part of your plan to help Ella?" Jakob asked.

Elisa nodded.

Jakob blinked. "You're going to take her to the festival, aren't you?"

Elisa grinned. "If we can get her in front of the Prince's son..."

Jakob laughed. "Her stepmother wouldn't be able to do a thing to stop her! The prince could take her into his household, and she'd be safe at the palace. That's brilliant, Elisa!"

Anna smiled and poked her husband. "Forget taking her into his household – the prince's son could marry her! She's still the daughter of one of the wealthiest landowners in the principality!"

"So, I need the carriage to take her to the festival, and a dress," Elisa said. "I've got money – I can pay to get the carriage fixed, and hire a driver. That just leaves something for her to wear."

"If it's to help Ella, you might not need to pay a cent for any of those things," Jakob declared. "And we'll definitely do whatever we can."

Anna looked thoughtful for a moment. "I'll be right back," she said, and left the room.

"Everything will need to be ready in two days," Elisa said.

"That's not a problem," Jakob stated.

Anna came back through the door. "Let me handle the dress."

Elisa grinned. "Then I guess I'd better get Ella here for lunch tomorrow."

Elisa grinned as Ella sat at the table in the inn, her eyes wide. Jakob and Anna sat across from her.

"You...you actually made all this happen?" Ella said.

"Everything is ready," Elisa declared.

"The carriage?" Ella asked.

"It's being fixed right now," Jakob stated. "It will be done by sundown."

Ella blinked. "And horses?"

Jakob smiled. "Gotthelf Wagner is bringing his very best. As soon as we told him what we're doing, he insisted, in fact."

"One of our friends who works for your father will be keeping an eye on your house," Anna said. "Gotthelf has arranged for a horse to be waiting for him. As soon as the carriage carrying your stepmother and stepsisters leaves, he'll ride to fetch us, and we'll come with the carriage to get you. I'll get you cleaned up and ready, and then we'll take you to the palace."

"And if on the third day the Prince hasn't taken you into his service, or the prince's son hasn't selected you as his bride, you're going to come stay with us," Jakob added. "Whatever we need to do to protect you and keep all of us fed, we'll figure it out. We won't let you go back to being abused by that harridan and her daughters."

"Uncle Jakob, Aunt Anna...I don't know what to say," Ella stammered.

Anna leaned over and placed her hand on Ella's. "Ever since that harridan and her beastly daughters came into your life, we have been praying for some way to help you. The entire village has. And God sent us Elisa. Bless you, Elisa, bless you!"

Elisa blushed. "It's the least I could do."

Ella leaned forward. "I'll still need something to wear. I can't go to a festival to meet a prince's son wearing this!"

Anna pulled a dress out from under the table. It was a fine yellow, almost gold, embroidered with silk. "Your mother wore this when your father was courting her. She had planned to wear it as her wedding dress, but your father paid for something better. When she got married and moved out, this was one of the things she left behind. I've kept it, just in case you would ever need it."

Ella stared at the dress, a tear rolling down her cheek. "This belonged to my mother?"

"It may need a few adjustments," Anna said. "So, you're going to put that on right now, and I'm going to do them as quick as I can. But, I have a suspicion that you're close enough to your mother's size when she was your age that it won't be necessary. Now, what are you waiting for? Get changed!"

Elisa watched the fitting, then closed her eyes and took a deep breath. It was going to work – she'd be able to grant Ella's wish without using any of her powers.

"Just as I thought," Anna declared. "It fits you perfectly."

"Aunt Anna," Ella said. "Can I...can I take this with me? I don't have anything of my mother's left. I'd just like to have this near me tomorrow. Please."

Anna and Jakob traded a concerned glance. "That's not a good idea, Ella," Anna said. "If the harridan or your stepsisters find it..."

"They won't," Ella promised. "I know just where to hide it."

Anna nodded. "Okay. Your mother would have wanted you to have it anyway. Anyway, change out of it and I'll put it in a bag that won't look too conspicuous."

Elisa grinned. Tomorrow, Ella would go to the festival!

Chapter IV – When a Prince is Not a Prince

Elisa checked the carriage one more time. She could still smell the fresh coat of dark blue paint. The horse looked at her and snorted. The mid-afternoon sun shone bright in the sky.

"Will you please relax?" Anna said. "You're making *me* nervous now."

"They should have left by now," Elisa declared. "Maybe we should just get started."

"If we show up before they have left, it will ruin *everything*," Jakob warned. "They're going. We need to be patient."

"Suppose something happened to our 'scout'?" Elisa protested. "What if he fell off his horse, and is lying hurt at the side of the road?"

"Gustav's parents raised horses," Jakob stated. "He was in the cavalry during the war. He's an expert rider."

Elisa sighed. "We've got everything we need to clean Ella up, right?"

Anna chuckled. "Yes, for the fifth time, we've got everything."

Elisa's heart skipped a beat. Was that a rider on horseback she just heard?

Jakob looked down the cobbled road. "That's Gustav."

The rider brought his horse to a halt in front of them. "They've left, Jakob," he said.

"Thank you so much," Jakob said. "We'll see you tomorrow. Anna, Elisa, let's do this."

The carriage ride was short, but Elisa spent the time wishing it was shorter. They pulled up to the front of the farmhouse, Elisa jumping out as soon as the carriage had stopped. She threw open the door and dashed into the house.

"Ella," she declared, "it's time to...to..."

Ella was curled up on the floor sobbing, surrounded by ashes. Behind her, Elisa heard Jakob and Anna follow her in.

"My God," Elisa breathed. "Ella, what happened?"

"They found the dress," Ella cried. "I don't know how, but they knew where I had hidden it. They took it out and cut it up in front of me, and then threw it into the fireplace! Then they scattered the ashes and told me to clean them up before they get home!"

"Oh, Ella," Anna said, pulling her up and embracing her. "I'm so sorry."

"I finally had something of my mother's," Ella sobbed. "And they destroyed it!"

"That's it, then," Jakob said. "We don't have another dress, and there's no way we can get one in time. The plan won't work. Let's get Ella out of here and back to the inn."

"But, if I don't clean this up, they'll beat me!" Ella cried.

"Ella, you're never coming back here," Anna declared. "Let them clean up their own mess."

Elisa closed her eyes and resisted the urge to scream and punch the wall.

"It's all my fault," Ella said. "If I hadn't brought the dress home-"

"It's not your fault," Anna snarled. "You didn't destroy that dress. Those terrible women did, and I'll give them a piece of my mind if it's the last thing I do!"

Ella waved her hands. "No, no! I can't let you do this! What are you going to do if you take me in? My stepmother will decide you can't buy food anymore, my stepsisters will beat me when I'm out and alone in the town!"

"Then we'll sell the inn and move somewhere else," Jakob said. "We'll do whatever it takes."

"But, wait!" Ella protested. "The plan can still work! Elisa can make it work! She can grant wishes – she can perform miracles!"

Jakob and Anna exchanged a concerned look.

Ella stared at them, desperation in her eyes. "No, it's true! Elisa, tell them what you told me!"

Elisa swallowed. "But they're not miracles. They're *wishes*. Miracles come from God and the saints, and I'm not any of them. I'm just...me."

Jakob and Anna turned to stare at Elisa. "Wait, you can grant wishes?"

Elisa nodded. "It's true. And it's not witchcraft, I promise! But, I also don't know it works, and I don't know what will happen if I try here. Almost every time I've done this, it's gone wrong! You could just disappear and re-appear somewhere far away!"

Ella sighed. "Try. Please, just try. I can't let Uncle Jakob and Aunt Anna get punished because of me. I just can't. I'd rather be a beggar in some foreign land."

Elisa opened her mouth to object, but then closed it again. "Okay. But, please forgive me if...if..."

Ella stood, wiping the tears from her eyes. "I forgive you. Now, do it."

Elisa took a deep breath, reached out with her mind, grasped the thread attached to Ella's wish, and pulled. Reality shifted.

A dress floated down from the ceiling, landing in Ella's arms. Two silver slippers followed.

Jakob and Anna made the sign of the cross. "You really can perform miracles," Jakob said.

"It's not a miracle," Elisa stated. "I don't really know what it is. All I know is that it's not from the Devil."

"That's silver thread!" Anna breathed, touching the dress in Ella's hands. "Actual silver! And, the rest – I've never seen anything so like gold! Ella...this dress might be worth more than our inn!"

Ella breathed a sigh of relief. "So, I'm going to the festival."

Anna took the dress from Ella. "Well, you can't go looking like this. Let's get you cleaned up and dressed. Jakob, Elisa, can you please sweep up all of these ashes?"

Elisa grabbed the broom and Jakob a dust pan. Together, they swept up the ashes until there were none left on the floor. As they did, Ella and Anna came out.

Elisa's eyes widened as she saw her. Ella was so radiant and beautiful that she almost looked like a different person.

"Alright," Anna declared. "We need to get this maiden to the festival!"

As they made their way to the carriage, Jakob said, "Remember, Ella, don't let them announce you by name. And make sure you are one of the first to leave, so that we can get you home in time. We'll be waiting for you with the carriage just down the path to the palace."

Ella hugged each one of them. "I will. Thank you so much, Uncle Jakob, Aunt Anna, Elisa."

They got into the carriage. With a crack of the whip, the carriage began making its way to the palace.

Elisa leaned against the carriage wheel, looking out into the darkness. The moon and stars shone bright overheard.

Jakob moved to rest beside her. "So, miracles," he said.

Elisa shook her head. "I told you, they're not miracles."

"Has it occurred to you that maybe they are?" Jakob asked. "That maybe, even if you hadn't...procured...that dress, just being able to save Ella from those terrible women is a miracle?"

"You would have done something," Elisa said. "You're her family."

Jakob shook his head. "Not in time. It never occurred to us to use the festival to rescue her. And the harridan and her daughters, well, there's a better chance of a blizzard in Hell than there is of them charming the prince or his son. This is the only opportunity the harridan has left of securing a good marriage for her daughters. Who do you think they'll take that out on at the end of the festival once they've failed? They could beat Ella to death. You probably saved her life."

"But, I'm not more pious than any other Christian!" Elisa protested. "I don't pray any more than anybody else, and I probably pray the rosary less often than–" She winced.

"Ah," Jakob said. "You're a Catholic heretic."

"I'm sorry," Elisa mumbled.

Jakob shrugged. "We won't hold that against you."

Elisa blinked. "Why not?"

"Too many people have died over how you confess your sins," Jakob replied. "The Peace of Westphalia was the right thing to do. Perhaps it doesn't matter in the end, and all that matters is that you're Christian. Perhaps one day that's how people will think. Regardless, only God's mercy determines who is saved and who is damned, nothing else. What happens to your soul is between you and God, not us."

Elisa sighed in relief. "Thank you for not hating me."

Jakob chuckled. "You're too kind a person to hate."

Elisa stared off into the darkness towards the front door. "I wonder how it's going in there."

"So long as she doesn't come out running for her life, it should be fine," Jakob said.

She heard Ella's voice approach behind the carriage, panting. "Aunt Anna! Uncle Jakob! Elisa! We have to go!"

Elisa blinked and stepped away from the carriage, looking behind it. Ella was running towards them as though her life depended on it, gasping. A feather fell off her dress as she ran.

"What happened?" Anna demanded. "Why didn't you use the front door?"

"I'll explain once we're off," Ella panted. "Just go!"

They climbed into the carriage, the driver whipping the horse into action. As they sped down the road, Ella collapsed back into her seat, a grin on her face.

"Your stepmother – did she recognize you?" Jakob asked.

Ella shook her head. "They thought I was some foreign noble lady! It was wonderful!"

"And the prince's son," Anna said. "Did you offend him in some way?"

Ella shook her head, laughing. "I was the only one he danced with! I don't think I've ever met a man so kind and wonderful in my life!"

Elisa glanced at Jakob and Anna. "Well, that's great, then! Did he ask you to marry him?"

Ella's smile faded. "No. And I don't know if he will. There are a lot of beautiful and charming ladies there."

"Okay, so maybe he proposes to you tomorrow," Anna said. "But that's a great start!"

"I don't get it, though," Elisa said. "Why were you running?"

"He didn't want me to leave!" Ella laughed. "I had to escape by running through the pigeon house and locking the door behind me. I think they were knocking down the door with an axe when I went out the window."

The carriage turned onto the road leading to Ella's home. "Right then," Anna said as it stopped by the door. "Let's get you dirtied up before they get back, and try to think unhappy thoughts when they arrive."

Ella grinned. "Tonight, I may have to work at that."

Ella lunched with Jakob, Anna, and Elisa at the inn. Elisa found herself missing the food at the tavern, but it would be too risky – if Ella's stepsisters found her acting too happy, they'd know something was up.

"You should have seen it," Ella gushed. "The ballroom is enormous, and it's got lots of people in it. They have these musicians playing the dance, and their music is wonderful. And they have this wonderful food."

"It sounds delightful," Elisa said.

"I wish you could come tonight," Ella declared. "It's so wonderful, and there are so many gentlemen – maybe you could find a gentleman for yourself, too!"

Elisa held up her hand. "It's not my place. Remember, this is my penance. I'm not supposed to be attending fancy festivals and wearing fine clothes."

"Well, at least let us wash that dress you wore from last night," Anna said. "You got ashes all over it when you cleaned up the room."

"I can wash it myself," Elisa said. "And I have this one, anyway. I can wear it for a while."

"Please," Anna begged. "Let us do this for you. You've helped us so much."

Elisa sighed. "Okay."

"Thank you," Anna said. "I'll pick up the dress from your room after lunch."

"And you can sit with us at church tomorrow," Jakob offered.

Elisa shook her head. "I'm sorry. I can't pray or take communion in a...in a church that isn't Catholic. It wouldn't be right."

"Well," Ella declared. "I have to get back before I'm missed. I'll see you later this afternoon."

After Ella left, the afternoon passed quickly. Elisa insisted on helping Anna clean her dress, and then she helped out with the rest of the laundry. Ella's dress from the festival proved to be a minor nightmare – every time they thought they had removed all of the feathers stuck in it, Elisa or Anna found another. Then they ate an early supper. Gustav arrived shortly after it was finished.

"They've left," Gustav declared.

Elisa, Jakob, and Anna hopped into the carriage and made their way to the farmhouse. Elisa was the first through the door, finding Ella standing before her and grinning.

"You're happy," Elisa said as Jakob and Anna came through the door, bearing Ella's dress and shoes.

"And you're my size," Ella declared.

Elisa blinked. "I don't understand."

Ella pointed at a beautiful gold and silver dress on a table, accompanied by a pair of silver shoes. "That fell from the ceiling right after they left."

Anna moved over to the table, running her finger along the fabric. "This is even nicer than the last one!"

Ella stared at Elisa, her grin widening. "We have two dresses now. And pairs of shoes. And we're the same size."

Elisa shook her head. "Now wait a moment. I can't come with you!"

"You can and you will," Ella declared.

"But I'm a penitent! I'm not supposed to be *enjoying* this!"

Ella shrugged. "Well, then come and be miserable. Turn down anybody who asks to dance with you. But you *are* coming."

Elisa shook her head again. "No, I can't do this. I'm sorry."

Ella folded her arms. "Well, if you don't go, I don't go."

Elisa's eyes widened. "What?"

Ella smirked. "You heard me."

Elisa heard Anna laugh behind her. "Elisa, let me give you one very important piece of advice – know when you've lost. Come on, both of you – we need to get you both ready for the festival, and we haven't a moment to lose."

Elisa swallowed as she gave her name to the herald at the door to the ballroom, trying to feel comfortable in the fine clothes...and with the lie that was about to be announced.

"Elisabeth Beichtkind and her sister, Eleonore," the herald announced.

Elisa looked around the ballroom with awe. A balcony overlooked it, some gentlemen and ladies standing upon it and chatting quietly. A handsome young man in expensive looking clothes approached them and offered his hand to Ella.

"You have returned, my lady," he said.

"How could I not?" Ella replied with a smile. "This is Elisa. I wouldn't be here without her. Elisa, this is Prince Karl, the son of Prince Johann."

Elisa curtseyed.

Prince Karl bowed. "You have my eternal gratitude, Lady Elisa."

Elisa blushed. "I'm not a lady. My father was a bookbinder."

"And how can our people be noble without books?" Prince Karl declared. "So, I will continue to call you 'lady'. That said..." He gave Ella an adoring gaze. "...this is my partner. Shall we dance?"

"I'll see you around dinner, Elisa," Ella said, taking Karl's hand. He swept her off onto the dance floor, the musicians playing. Elisa allowed herself a slight smile, took a deep breath, and then headed to the balcony. At least there she couldn't embarrass Ella.

Once she got up the stairs, Elisa leaned on the railing and looked down at the floor. Ella and Prince Karl danced as though they had known each other their entire lives, surrounded by other dancers. It took Elisa a moment to spot Ella's stepsisters – they stood to the side, gossiping. Nobody paid them any mind. Beside them was an older woman, and a tall man with grey hair.

That must be Ella's father and stepmother, Elisa thought.

"You're allowed to enjoy yourself, you know," an unfamiliar voice said.

Elisa looked up to find a well dressed man with piercing grey eyes, black hair and a close cropped moustache-less beard regarding her. "I'm just here for my friend," she said.

The gentleman grinned. "And here I thought she was your sister."

"She insisted that we be announced that way," Elisa

111

stated. "It's not what I would have preferred, but I'm here for her, so I guess I just have to accept it."

"If you say so, 'Elisabeth the Penitent'," the gentleman said. "Not the family name I would have chosen for myself, but I imagine you had your reasons. Mind you, everybody here chose their family names, or had their fathers choose them. That's one of the benefits of being a peasant, particularly a wealthy one."

"My sin was very grave," Elisa said.

"I have no doubt you will atone for it," the gentleman stated. He cocked his head as he looked at her. "What is it?"

Elisa grimaced. "I don't understand this."

The gentleman shrugged. "It's a festival. There will be dancing and feasting. At the end the prince's son will have a wife. What else is there to understand?"

"But why do it this way?" Elisa asked. "Why invite peasants to find a bride for a prince? Why not invite nobility?"

The gentleman chuckled. "Permit me to answer your question with a riddle. When is a prince not a prince?"

Elisa blinked. "I don't know."

"When he's in the German lands," the gentleman declared. "In any other place – France, or Spain, or England – Prince Johann would be a duke, or a count, not that the *Reich* lacks either of those. But this is the German lands, the *Reich*, the Holy Roman Empire, and here the nobles have pretensions. These men are not royalty, and this principality is not a kingdom. It's not wealthy, it doesn't have an army, and there's nothing to recommend it to a noble bride. No prince would send their daughter here, and if the prince's family is left without an heir, when the last prince dies the entire principality returns to the *Reich*."

Elisa blinked. "So he doesn't have a choice."

The gentleman nodded. "Take a look around. A close look. This is an old palace – it's been around for a hundred years. Some of the finish is starting to wear off of the furnishings, and it hasn't been repaired or replaced. The musicians aren't from a city, or deep inside the Empire – they're provincial, playing old tunes. This is all Prince Johann could afford, and he is ailing. If he can marry his son off to a wealthy landowner, then he can save his legacy. And if not...well, perhaps before he goes bankrupt his son can sell his land and title and not die in disgrace."

"It's a last chance," Elisa breathed.

"There's a lot of that going around. Happily, Prince Karl does seem rather taken with your friend."

"I hope he marries her," Elisa said.

"They would be very happy together. At what about you?"

"What about me?"

"Surely there might one day be some gentleman you fancy."

Elisa shook her head. "I'm a penitent atoning for a grave sin. Maybe when I'm done, I might think about that, but until then..."

"Your penance might take a very long time," the gentleman observed.

"It would be what I deserve."

"Well, for the sake of the dashing young men of the world, I hope one day you feel differently."

"There you are!" a singsong voice called. Elisa looked up to see a beautiful woman with raven hair approaching. "Chatting up a younger woman?"

The gentleman turned to her and bowed. "You know I can never ignore the ladies."

Elisa allowed herself a smile. "Your wife?"

The gentleman chuckled. "No. I've never been married, and never will be. But, I do enjoy the company of the fairer sex."

"Well, *this* member of the fairer sex wants a dance," the woman with raven hair declared. She shot Elisa a mischievous glance. "Be careful of this one, whoever you are. There's no man more charming in the world."

"Who am I to refuse such an offer?" the gentleman laughed, and offered his arm to the raven haired woman. The two made their way off the balcony and onto the dance floor. Elisa watched them for a moment, and then turned her gaze back to Ella and Prince Karl.

Marry her, Elisa thought. *Please, for the love of all that is holy, marry her.*

The dancing came to an end, and the festivities moved to the dining hall. Ella took a seat beside Prince Karl at the high table, positively glowing as she talked with him. Elisa found herself seated beside two chatty matrons, but no matter how often they tried to pull her into their conversation, her eyes kept being drawn back to the end of the table.

Ella's father, stepmother, and stepsisters sat at the very end, away from everybody else.

"You haven't done a very good job, have you Georg?" Ella's stepmother said. "We need to get an audience with Prince Karl, and give my daughters a chance to show off their charms and...assets. You don't want them to become spinsters, do you?"

"Of course I don't," Ella's father said, his eyes downcast.

"If we can't get an audience, it will be your fault. We have to do something before that foreign hussy steals him away from us."

"I'll do what I can," Ella's father said. Elisa looked down at her food with a pang of regret. He looked like he needed saving as much as Ella did.

Worry about Ella first, Elisa thought. *Then see what we can do for her father.*

The dinner finished up as the sun began to set. The festivities moved back into the ballroom, servants lighting chandeliers and candelabras. Elisa leaned against the wall, watching Prince Karl and Ella dance. She whispered a quiet prayer that God would shine down upon this match.

Ella broke away from Prince Karl, the young prince looking back at her with adoration as she made her way to Elisa.

"That's looking good," Elisa said. "Did he propose?"

"I need a distraction," Ella stated.

Elisa blinked. "What?"

"A distraction," Ella declared. "Distract everybody so that they're looking somewhere else while I get away."

"I don't know how–"

"Think of something!" Ella hissed. She glanced back. "He's starting to come this way! Do it quickly!"

Elisa drew up to her full height and pointed out the window. "Everybody look!" she shouted. "It's...something interesting!"

As they looked, Ella bolted for the door. Elisa glanced around the room to see the gentleman watching her, failing to suppress his laughter. Then she curtseyed, forced herself to walk to the ballroom door, and ran down the hall.

She got outside and sprinted to the carriage where Jakob and Anna were waiting. "Has Ella made it yet?"

Anna shook her head. "She's not with you?"

"She had me create a distraction while she escaped," Elisa said. "She was gone by the time I got to the front door."

Jakob cursed. "We need to find her." He handed out oil lamps. "Split up. Start searching the grounds. Count your paces. Once you reach two hundred, make your way back here."

Elisa walked away from the carriage, trying to

115

approximate the direction she had come from the previous night. She had counted a hundred and twenty three steps when she was nearly bowled over by Prince Karl and two guards.

"Lady Elisa!" the prince said, bowing. "Have you seen your sister?"

"I'm afraid not," Elisa replied.

"You're looking for her as well?"

Elisa swallowed and nodded.

"If you find her, bring her back to the palace!" Prince Karl commanded, then turned to the guards. "Men, search this way!" The prince and the guards ran off into the darkness.

Elisa took a deep breath, and then resumed walking and counting paces, using a large pear tree as a landmark. She had reached the tree and was almost up to two hundred when she heard Ella's voice.

"Psst!"

Elisa looked around. There was nobody there.

"Up! Look *up*!"

Elisa looked up, then blinked. Ella was standing on a tree branch, at least ten feet off the ground.

"What are you doing up there?" Elisa whispered.

"I'm hiding!" Ella hissed. "What does it look like I'm doing? Will you help me down from here? I'm stuck!"

Elisa put the oil lamp on the ground, and reached up, giving Ella a place to put her foot as she climbed down. Then she picked up the lamp, and she and Ella dashed back to the carriage.

"Oh good, you found her!" Anna said, emerging from the darkness.

"Ella's been found?" Jakob said, coming out of darkness behind her.

"We need to go, quickly!" Ella declared.

They got into the carriage. With a crack of the driver's

whip, it was on its way down the road, away from the palace.

"What happened?" Elisa asked. "Everything looked like it was going so well!"

"He wouldn't let me leave again," Ella replied. "That's why I wanted the distraction. About that... 'Look, something interesting!' – *that's* the best you could do?"

"I wasn't expecting to have to do anything at all!" Elisa protested.

Anna leaned forward. "Did he ask you to marry him?"

Ella's voice was almost a whisper. "Yes."

Jakob and Anna looked at each other and grinned. "That's great news!" Jakob said. "It worked! The plan actually worked!"

"I told him I'd think about it," Ella muttered.

Anna blinked. "Sorry, you did *what*?"

"I told him that I'd give him an answer tomorrow."

Elisa stared at Ella in disbelief. "But why? This is what we working towards! We got it – all you have to do is say 'yes', and you'll never be treated like a kitchen maid in your own house again!"

"How do you know that?" Ella snapped. "How can you possibly know that? How do you know that once I'm in the palace, I won't be treated worse? How do you know that the prince's family will accept me, or that any of the other noble families will? I'm not one of them! I'm the daughter of a farmer! I'm a peasant whose family owns land! I've got *nothing* of my own! He could promise to marry me, and then put me on the street, and nobody could do anything about it!"

"You don't know that," Anna said.

"And neither do you!"

"Ella, we can't protect or provide for you like the prince can," Jakob pointed out. "If you marry him, your stepmother and stepsisters will never be able to touch you again. But if you don't..."

Ella wiped tears from her eyes. "I need to think about it.

Just...give me a day to think about it. I'll see you tomorrow afternoon."

"What about lunch tomorrow?" Elisa asked.

Ella took a deep breath. "I need to spend it thinking. I'll see you at the house tomorrow afternoon."

Elisa, Jakob, and Anna sat around the table at the inn, lunch going cold on the plates in front of them as they wracked their brains.

"In a worst case, we can sell the dresses," Anna said. "They'd be worth a fortune. With that money, we could just take Ella and settle in a town, or open a new inn somewhere that wasn't as badly hit by the war."

"She's better off with the prince," Jakob declared. "We all know it. His family has a good reputation, and Prince Karl is known for being kind and gentle...at least when people can see him."

Elisa sighed. "Maybe we just shouldn't give her a choice."

"We're not her father," Jakob said. "We can't force her to marry anybody. And even if we could...I don't think I could face her after doing something like that. Not after what she's been through."

"She'll do the right thing," Anna said. "Nothing that harridan and her daughters have done could ever take that away from her. She wouldn't be Ella if they could."

"We have to play this out, and trust Ella," Jakob said. "That's all we can do."

"But what if she's too scared?" Elisa asked. "You weren't at the festival, you didn't see what she and Prince Karl were like together. They were so happy! When they talked, or danced...they were meant to be together, I know it."

"There's only so much we can do," Jakob said. "Look,

let's not lose sight of our goal. Getting Ella married to the prince would be great, but anything that gets her out of that house is a victory. If she doesn't marry the prince, but she stays here with us, *we've still won*."

Elisa opened her mouth to protest, but then closed it again. There was no point. Whatever was going to happen would happen. She made the sign of the cross and whispered a silent prayer. Then she looked up to find Jakob and Anna doing the same.

"Right," Anna said. "Let's get ready for tonight." She looked at Elisa. "And today, we'll have enough time to make you look absolutely beautiful before we leave."

As the carriage drove to Ella's house, Elisa wondered if she would ever get comfortable wearing a dress this fancy.

"You look beautiful," Jakob assured her.

Elisa gave him a faint smile. "It's not that. This isn't how a penitent is supposed to behave."

"A penitent is supposed to do whatever is necessary, right?" Anna asked. "We need you inside looking after Ella, and you need to look like this to be there."

"It's not modest," Elisa muttered.

"It's appropriate," Anna stated. "That's what matters today."

Elisa looked out the window, trying to take her mind off it. They passed the odd fellow she had seen arguing with the frogs when she first came to the village. "Who is he?" she wondered.

Jakob glanced out of the window. "That's Hans. He's...unique."

"I saw him talking to a bunch of frogs," Elisa said. "It was an argument. He lost."

"Sounds tame for Hans," Jakob mused. "He once had a cow slaughtered, and then gave the meat to hungry dogs to deliver to the butcher. He was furious when he found out it had never arrived."

Elisa couldn't help chuckling. "Why would he do that?"

Jakob shrugged. "It made sense to him, I guess. He wasn't always this way. Before he joined the militia during the war, he was kind, generous, and sensible. Then, when he came back, he was...broken. None of us know what he saw or what happened to him out there – he doesn't talk about it to anybody. His wife takes care of him – she's a saint."

Elisa stared out the window. The carriage turned onto the road leading to the farmhouse. "My island was able to stay out of the war."

"They were very lucky," Jakob said.

Until I granted all those wishes, Elisa thought. She took a deep breath. "If it goes wrong, and something happens to me, please promise you'll leave me and get Ella to safety."

Jakob looked at her with concern. "Are you sure that's what you want?"

Elisa nodded. "I'll be fine."

The carriage rolled to a stop. Elisa stepped out to find Ella at the door, waiting for her with a grin on her face.

For a moment, Elisa's heart soared. "You've made a decision?" she asked.

Ella shook her head. "Another dress fell from the ceiling...this time with gold slippers!"

Jakob and Anna shared a look. "Those dresses are worth a fortune," Jakob said. "And now there's three of them!"

"I really need to figure out how granting wishes works," Elisa muttered.

"You look wonderful, Elisa!" Ella declared.

Elisa sighed. "Thank you, but this all seems a bit too

fancy for me."

Ella shrugged. "Well, you only have one more day of it. Let's get ready to go to the festival!"

Getting Ella ready took little time, and soon they were pulling up to the front door of the palace. Ella and Elisa stepped out of the carriage, attendants bowing to them. Elisa blinked. There seemed to be more of them than on either of the other two days.

"They're really going all-out for the last day, aren't they?" Ella asked with a happy smile.

"That they are," Elisa said as they stepped through the door. "Ella...how do you really feel about Prince Karl?"

Ella stopped, a look of heartbreak crossing her face. "Please, just enjoy the festival with me, okay? Let me finish sorting this out on my own."

Elisa sighed and nodded.

They made their way into the ballroom, where they were again announced as being sisters. Prince Karl stepped up to them, bowing and offering his hand to Ella.

"You are more beautiful than ever, lady Eleonore," he declared. "I am so happy you returned."

A look of bliss crossed Ella's face as she took his hand. "How could I stay away, my prince?"

Prince Karl bowed his head to Elisa, and then swept Ella onto the dance floor. Elisa frowned and headed up to the balcony, where she leaned against the railing, watching Prince Karl and Ella dance as though they were the only ones on the floor.

"Something is troubling you, 'Elisabeth the Penitent'," the gentleman's voice said behind her. He joined her, leaning on the railing.

"Elisa," Elisa muttered. "Everybody calls me Elisa."

He gave her a wry smile. "Okay, 'Elisa the Penitent'. What's wrong?"

Elisa sighed. "I don't want to trouble you with my

problems."

"Consider me here to be troubled. Please, I'm a good listener. I even, every now and then, give good advice."

Elisa took a deep breath. "I'm trying to help my friend, down there on the dance floor. And, I'm trying to figure out if I should do something."

"What thing?"

"Stop her from running away," Elisa replied. "Hold her down, tie her up if I have to. Anything to keep her from going back to that terrible house."

"Ah."

"She's so...happy down there! They love each other, you can see it. But, she's so afraid of what might happen, that..." Elisa shook her head. "I just want her to lead a good and happy life, but she keeps running away from it."

The gentleman cocked his head. "Well, they are in love, that's for certain. A life with him would be good, happy, and safe. And, if you wanted to keep her from running, I would be willing to help. But, if you did, there would always be a part of her that would feel as though the choice had been made for her, just like in that 'terrible house'. There would always be a part of her that is unhappy because of that. And, I don't think she would ever forgive you...and I think you know that."

Elisa sighed. "So what do I do?

The gentleman shrugged. "It has been my experience that most people will get to where you want them to go with just the right nudge in the right direction. Your friend Eleonore may need additional help, and you should be ready to provide it. But, start with the nudge, and see what happens."

Elisa took a deep breath. "I will. Thank you."

"Now, let me take your mind off of this terrible subject with a bit of wonder," the gentleman said. "Tonight will be clear, and the stars will come out. Each of those stars is a sun, like ours, and many of them have planets like ours rotating around them, just like ours."

Elisa frowned. "I thought the sun revolved around the earth, and the stars were just heavenly spheres."

The gentleman chuckled. "Galileo and Copernicus are out of favour at the moment, but that doesn't mean they're entirely wrong. No, I assure you, they're just like our sun. And they're so far away that their light takes many, many years to reach us. Sometimes, it takes hundreds and even thousands of years." He grinned, a twinkle in his eyes. "And that means that you can never see the stars as they truly are in the moment – only as they once were. Just to look into the night sky is to look centuries into the past. Now, how's that for wondrous?"

Elisa allowed herself a smile. "It's pretty amazing." She looked around. "So, where's your friend?"

The gentleman shrugged. "She's around. No doubt trying to charm the pants off some poor fellow with money who has no idea what he's getting into."

The herald called the guests to the dinner table. The gentleman bowed. "I will see you later, 'Elisa the Penitent'."

Elisa nodded her head, and then made her way to the table. For a moment as she sat down, she thought Ella's father was staring at her, but when she turned to look he was talking to his wife, his stepdaughters hanging on his every word.

"I am in negotiations with Prince Johann," he said. "They are going well."

"The prestige of our family depends on marrying one of my daughters to the prince," Ella's stepmother stated. "You know what failure means. That foreign hussy he spends all of his time with cannot be allowed to undermine us!"

"I know," Ella's father said. "She won't. I'm meeting with Prince Johann tonight after dinner. I should be able to seal the deal then."

"Just get my daughters in front of Prince Karl. They will do the rest."

A server put a plate of food in front of her. It smelled and tasted delicious, but she barely picked at it. She looked to the high table, where Ella sat beside the prince, chatting away with a smile on her face. *If Ella runs...*, she thought.

A tall gentleman with light grey hair wearing regal clothes rose from the high table. "Thank you all for coming to our festival," he began. "I am your host, Prince Johann. I apologize for not appearing these last two nights, but even a principality as small as this one always has something to keep you busy.

"We are a rich principality – not rich in wealth, or resources, but in the quality of our people. My family has ruled here for five centuries, and it has been our privilege to be your lords and protectors. And soon, it will be our privilege to bring one of you into our family as an equal."

The assembled crowd clapped.

"So, enjoy this last day and night of the festival!" Prince Johann declared. "And know that you are our strength – we have only flourished over the centuries because of you."

Prince Johann sat down. The crowd fell into the buzz of conversation, many wondering who the foreign beauty was sitting at Prince Karl's side. Elisa, however, was lost in thought. *What do I do if she runs? What* can *I do if she runs?*

Her plate was taken away, the assembled festival-goers rising and returning to the ballroom. Elisa took a deep breath and followed them. *Please don't run*, Ella, she thought. *Please, just don't run.*

The shadows grew long and then disappeared as servants lit the chandeliers and candelabras. Ella said something to the prince and hurried over to Elisa.

"I've made up my mind," Ella said quietly. "I'm going

to go live with Uncle Jakob and Aunt Anna."

Elisa's eyes widened. "But the prince–"

"He's wonderful," Ella said. "But I can't do it, I'm sorry. Please give me a distraction so I can get away."

Elisa shook her head. "This is the wrong thing to do!"

"But it's what I have to do," Ella hissed.

"Please, just tell me if you love him!" Elisa demanded. "Do you love him? Do you want to marry him?"

"Of course I love him!" Ella whispered. "He's kind, and generous, and handsome, and wonderful! I never believed in love at first sight until I met him! To spend the rest of my life as his wife would be a dream come true!" Tears ran down her cheeks. "But, I can't Elisa! I just can't...and I wish that I could. Please, I'm going to have Uncle Jakob and Aunt Anna take me back to the house, and then I'll join you all at the inn tomorrow."

Elisa shook her head again. "No! That won't be safe!"

Ella took a deep breath. "If I am missing when they get home, they'll know exactly what I did, who helped me, and they'll come to find me. Trust me, this is safer – I'll go out for my daily errands, I'll come to the inn to have lunch with you, and then I'll stay." She took Elisa's hands in hers. "Please, give me a distraction."

Elisa wiped tears from her eyes. "Okay. But I wish you'd change your mind and stay here."

"I wish I could do that too."

Elisa took a deep breath, stepped into the ballroom, pointed at the window, and called out, "Look everybody, there's something exciting!"

The crowd turned and looked. The gentleman watched her with a sad smile and mouthed "I'm sorry."

Elisa walked out of the room, her eyes downcast. *Remember what Jakob said – so long as we get her out of the house, we win.* Then she stopped dead in the hall. Two guards with muskets at the ready blocked her path. She heard footfalls behind her, and looked back. Two more guards moved into position, blocking any retreat, followed by Prince Johann.

Prince Johann stared at her and said, "I think you had best come with us."

Chapter V – To Rescue a Princess

Elisa resisted curling into a fetal position as she sat on the chair. The room they had taken her to was on the third floor, and two guards stood by the door, muskets ready. Prince Johann loomed over her.

"You were announced as Elisabeth Beichtkind," Prince Johann stated. "Is that your real name?"

Elisa swallowed. "Yes, Your Royal Highness."

"Where are you from?"

"I'm from an island kingdom a few days from here," Elisa said. "You wouldn't have heard of it...and besides, it's gone now."

The door opened and Prince Karl stepped into the room, followed by Ella's father.

"Oh good, Georg, you're here," Prince Johann said. "As you can see, we caught her."

Elisa's heart skipped a beat as she stared at Ella's father. "Why are you here?" she breathed.

"This is Georg Bauer," Prince Johann stated. "He's here to negotiate a dowry."

It was all Elisa could do to suppress her tears. "Please, no!" she cried. "Prince Karl – I mean, his Royal Highness Karl – he loves Ella – I mean, Eleonore! Just ask him!"

Prince Johann sighed. "It's not–"

"Please, let him marry Ella!" Elisa begged. "I'll do anything! Please, you need to let them be happy together, and–"

"Shut up, you idiot girl!" Prince Johann roared. Elisa recoiled as though she had been struck. "Let us speak."

"The dowry is for *Eleonore*," Georg said.

Elisa blinked. "What?"

"We started negotiations as soon as his Royal Highness Karl told me he had proposed to her," Prince Johann stated.

Elisa swallowed. "How can this be? Nobody knows who she is. We were so careful about that."

Georg sighed. "She is the exact image of her mother when I married her. Do you really think I didn't recognize my own daughter as soon as I saw her?"

"We've known who she was all along," Prince Johann said. "And her circumstances."

Georg kneeled beside her. "I owe you such a debt of gratitude, I will never be able to repay it! I came here to try to get Ella either married to Prince Karl or brought into Prince Johann's household as a servant. But, once I got here and talked to his Royal Highness, I found out that they don't have the money to hire another servant...and he would never marry his son to a woman he had not even seen. And then, as I feared all hope was lost, Eleonore appeared at the festival, as radiant as her mother had been while I was courting her! And you made this happen, didn't you?"

Elisa opened her mouth to speak, then closed it again and nodded.

Georg kissed her hands. "Thank you, dear girl! May God bless you for ever and ever! I have not been the parent I should have been to Ella these last couple of years – by the time I discovered the true nature of my wife, it was too late and she had taken complete control of the household, including overseeing our children. And, whenever I looked at Ella...all I could see was her poor mother hanging from that tree, when it should have been me instead. But, thanks to you, I can finally set things right."

"I had help," Elisa said. "I couldn't have done any of this without Jakob and Anna." She glanced at Prince Johann. "They're Ella's aunt and uncle."

"When this is done, I'm going to everything I can to thank them," Georg stated.

"Why is she running?" Prince Johann asked. "Surely she knows that we can give her an apartment here and protect her."

Elisa looked at the three men and took a deep breath. "She's terrified. She afraid that she'll be mistreated here like she is at home, or that she won't be accepted, or abandoned because she's just a peasant. Even though what she wants to do is marry his Royal Highness...she's too scared."

Georg's shoulders slumped. "I had hoped her spirit had not been this badly broken. God forgive me."

"Don't worry," Prince Karl said. "She's not going anywhere tonight."

Prince Johann, Georg, and Elisa stared at him. "What do you mean?" Prince Johann asked.

"As soon as she arrived, I had the servants spread pitch on the stairs outside," Prince Karl replied.

Prince Johann blinked. "Why in God's name would you do that?"

"So that she would get stuck when she walked through the pitch, of course," Prince Karl said. "Now, we just need

129

to send somebody to collect her, and we can convince her to follow her heart and stay."

"But, Your Royal Highness, Ella doesn't leave through the main doors," Georg pointed out.

Prince Karl grinned. "I know. I had the servants spread pitch on *all* of the stairs outside."

Prince Johann's eyes widened. "There are over a hundred guests at this festival."

A puzzled look crossed Prince Karl's face. "What's the problem? Once we've collected the good lady Eleonore, we have the servants douse it with buckets of water."

Prince Johann rubbed his temples. "My son, pitch doesn't work that way." He turned to one of the guards. "Get the servants, have them see if Eleonore Bauer is stuck on the stairs. If she is, bring her here. If she isn't, have them get some rugs – any rugs – and cover the stairs with them. And make it fast – we don't want to have a hundred angry guests trapped in the palace."

The guard bowed. "Yes, Your Royal Highness," he said, and left.

"Pitch on the stairs," Prince Johann muttered, shaking his head. Elisa's thought of Ella stuck in a pear tree the previous night, and picking pigeon feathers out of her dress from the night before. *They're a match for each other, that's for certain...*

The guard returned. "Eleonore Bauer is not on the premises," he reported. "Neither is her coach. We did find a single gold slipper at the top of the stairs, however."

"That's hers," Prince Karl said. "She was quite proud of them while we were dancing. Please give it to me."

"We don't have it yet, Your Royal Highness," the guard said. "The stewards are still trying to free it from the pitch on the stairs."

"So she made it off the grounds," Georg said. He

turned to Elisa. "You said that Jakob and Anna were helping her. Please tell me she went back to the inn with them."

Elisa stared at the floor. "She went back home to the house. She was afraid that if she was missing when her stepmother and stepsisters came home, they'd know it was her."

Georg cursed. "That's the worst thing that could have happened!"

"But, her stepmother kept talking about her as a foreigner," Elisa protested. "And if you didn't tell her that it was Ella, then surely–"

Georg cut her off with a wave of his hand. "My wife may be wicked, vindictive, and manipulative, but she is not an idiot. If she didn't figure out that it was Ella as soon as she was announced by name, then she figured it out shortly after."

"So we need to rescue her," Prince Karl said.

"It's the only way," Georg stated. "I can tell my wife that negotiations have been successful, and that her daughters will receive a private audience with Prince Karl to try to woo him. But, that won't forestall violence against Ella for long. We need to get her out tomorrow morning, and no later."

"Fine," Prince Karl said. "I'll take some guards first thing in the morning, and get her out."

Georg shook his head. "It's no good. She saw how much his Royal Highness and Ella cared for each other, and she knows it was Ella. She'll have the staff watching for any carriages or guards, and the minute she gets word of them, she'll know why they're come."

Elisa glanced at the two princes and Ella's father, reading their wishes in her mind. None were helpful. She grimaced.

Prince Johann scowled. "Then we need a subterfuge.

Something that will allow us to get into the house without that terrible woman realizing it's a rescue attempt. And all we've got is a gold slipper...once it's out of the pitch."

Elisa blinked. Perhaps one of the wishes was helpful after all. "If I may ask, how are his Royal Highness' Karl's eyes? I mean, how well does he see?" she asked.

"They could be better," Prince Karl replied. "Why?"

Elisa suppressed a smile, thinking of the prince's wish – *I wish I could see things in the distance.*

Georg blinked. "Oh! That could work."

Prince Karl glanced at them. "I don't understand."

"What if we tell my wife that your eyesight is very poor, and you didn't get a good look at the woman you were dancing with," Georg said. "And the only thing you have to know that it's her is the gold slipper she left behind."

"We're very careful," Elisa said. "Jakob and Anna make sure that they take the clothes Ella is wearing back to the inn with them, so they can't be discovered. Ella's stepmother won't have the dress or the other slipper."

Prince Johann grinned. "That would work! None of them got close to you, and they won't have any way of knowing that your eyesight is mostly fine. So, we say that Prince Karl is on a search for the woman he was dancing with, and he's going to the homes of every single woman who attended to make every eligible lady in the house try on the slipper, with no exceptions even for serving girls, starting with the Bauer farm."

Georg nodded. "Alright. We do this first thing in the morning, before my wife can figure out some plan to substitute one of her daughters for Ella."

"I want to be there," Elisa said. "I helped her get here, and...she's my friend. I need to see this through."

Prince Johann nodded. "Be waiting for us on the road to the property. I'll have the guard call you a carriage to take you back to your inn."

"Bring Jakob and Anna in on this as well," Georg added. "My wife lies very easily – we may need them to vouch that Ella was there."

Elisa nodded. "Can you protect them too?"

Georg gave her a knowing smile. "That's already in hand."

As Prince Johann instructed the guard to fetch her a carriage, Elisa allowed herself a smile and a thought of the gentleman's advice. *How was that for a little nudge?*

Elisa took a deep breath as she stood with Jakob and Anna at the corner of the road leading to Ella's farmhouse, waiting for the prince's carriage. She rubbed her eyes – rather than risk waking up too late, they had all just not gone to sleep.

"That's quite a plan Georg came up with," Jakob mused. "I hope it works."

"It feels over-complicated," Anna said.

"That may be, but we've got nothing better," Jakob stated.

Elisa swallowed. "I've got a favour to ask."

Anna looked at her. "What is it?"

"Whatever happens, when you tell people about all of this, don't tell anybody I was here or what I did," Elisa said. "Just make something up if you have to, but don't mention me."

Jakob blinked. "Why not? None of this could have happened without you."

"This is my penance," Elisa replied. "I shouldn't be receiving credit or praise for good deeds." She sighed. "Besides, I don't want anybody trying to find me so that they can burn me as a witch."

Anna nodded. "Okay. We'll tell people that Ella was helped by her mother's spirit up in Heaven."

"And the dresses were brought by birds," Jakob added.

Anna blinked and stared at him. "Why birds?"

Jakob shrugged. "I like birds."

The creaking of wheels and clopping of horseshoes sounded from around the corner. Two carriages pulled to a stop in front of them, Prince Johann opening the door and stepping out.

Jakob bowed, and Anna and Elisa curtseyed.

"I'm familiar with Elisabeth here," Prince Johann said. "You must be Jakob and Anna."

Jakob bowed again. "It is a pleasure, Your Royal Highness."

"We are returning with Ella in our care today," Prince Johann stated. "But, I must ask you to continue to the house on foot. That will allow you to appear as though you are curious bystanders who saw the carriages drive by."

"We'll do that, Your Royal Highness," Jakob said.

"Godspeed to you," Prince Johann said, climbing back into the carriage. With a crack of the whip, the carriage hurtled down the street.

Elisa looked at Jakob and Anna. "Well, let's go," Jakob said.

By the time they reached the farmhouse, the carriages were already unloaded. Georg beckoned to them from the door, letting them into the house. Both princes and four guards were crowded into the main room, along with Ella's stepmother.

"I was so sorry to hear of your son's affliction, Your Royal Highness," Ella's stepmother was saying. "I cannot imagine what it would be like to have troubles seeing the world. Shall I bring my daughter who shared so many dances with out so that you can take her home?"

"I must be sure it is her," Prince Karl said. "You cannot imagine how many unscrupulous souls might try to take advantage of my...problem...by passing off their daughter as somebody she is not. And we have so many houses to visit today."

"You do not, Your Royal Highness, for the maiden you danced with is indeed one of my daughters," Ella's stepmother said. "Give me the slipper, and I will produce her for you."

"Where's Ella?" Elisa whispered to Georg once Ella's stepmother had left the room.

"I don't know," Georg whispered back. "I haven't seen her since I got back last night. Don't worry – neither of my stepdaughters have feet that will fit in that slipper."

The door opened, and Ella's stepmother re-entered the room, followed by Ella's taller stepsister. "This is my daughter, Hilda," she said. "As you can see, she fits the slipper to perfection."

Elisa's eyes widened in shock. *That can't be!* Then she looked down at the golden slipper. Blood seeped through the stitching at the toe.

"The slipper," Elisa breathed, pointing.

"What treachery is this, madam?" Prince Johann demanded.

Ella's stepmother looked at her daughter in shock. "Hilda, how could you?"

Hilda shook her head. "But mother, you–"

"Silence!" Ella's stepmother screamed, striking Hilda so hard that she fell to the ground. "How dare you try to deceive a prince of the *Reich*!"

"Get the slipper back," Prince Johann instructed. Elisa swallowed hard as one of the guards pulled the slipper off, Hila's big toe little more than a bloody stump.

"I must have been mistaken about which daughter of mine you had been dancing with," Ella's stepmother declared. "Please forgive my mistake, and my daughter. I fear that while I tell people that my eyesight is perfect, I do so to save face. It must be my daughter Maria you were

135

dancing with. Hand me the slipper, and I will fetch her and prove that it is Maria's hand you desire."

"Do not deceive me further," Prince Johann warned. He nodded to the guard holding the slipper, who handed it to Ella's stepmother.

Jakob, Anna, and Elisa exchanged worried glances as Ella's stepmother left the room. "Let this play out," Georg whispered. "Trust in God's mercy."

Ella's stepmother returned, followed by her shorter stepsister. The girl looked pale, giving Prince Karl a fragile smile.

"My daughter, Maria," Ella's stepmother announced. "The woman you danced with these last three days. As you can see, the slipper fits perfectly."

Elisa forced down a wave of nausea as she looked at the slipper. The heel was covered in blood.

"My God, what have you done," Georg breathed.

"Mother, please, I–" Maria began, and then doubled over and retched. Ella's stepmother kicked her in the side, sending her sprawling in her own bile. "Have I taught my daughters nothing!" she screamed. "Trying to deceive a prince of the *Reich*! You both deserve to rot in Hell!"

She turned to Prince Karl and curtseyed. "Please accept my deepest apologies for my treacherous and deceitful daughters. They will both be severely punished for their actions. I fear that we have wasted your time, and you will need to visit other houses today."

One of the guards recovered the slipper. Elisa looked away from the bloody mess that was left of the poor girl's heel.

"And are there any other daughters in this house?" Prince Johann asked.

"None at all," Ella's stepmother replied.

"There is my daughter, Eleonore," Georg declared. "She should come out."

"There's no point," Ella's stepmother said. "She was not at the festival."

"Nevertheless, I would see if the slipper fits her," Prince Karl stated. "Please bring her out."

"You have already wasted so much time here," Ella's stepmother began. "Why waste it further on such an unworthy creature. She could not possibly have been at the festival for she was here, cleaning the house. She is also a clumsy thing, she can't dance to save her life, and sad to say the only thing she is good for is domestic labour. She cannot have been the woman you danced with."

"Where's Ella?" Georg demanded.

"She's locked in her room, being punished," Ella's stepmother replied. "She was quite disrespectful to me last night after we got home, and it is my right to keep discipline in my own household."

"Where's her room?" Elisa asked.

"Up the stairs, first door on the right," Georg replied. Before he had finished speaking Elisa was pounding her way up the stairs, Karl close behind her. She came to the door and shouted, "Ella, it's me! We're here to get you!"

"Step aside," Prince Karl said. Elisa stepped back. Prince Karl kicked the door under the doorknob, breaking it open. Elisa gasped at what she saw.

Ella was in a crumpled heap on the floor beside a bed of dirty straw, sobbing, her face bloody and bruised. She looked up at Elisa, one of her eyes swollen shut, and said, "She knew...somehow she knew...how did she know?"

Elisa knelt down beside her. "It's okay," she said. "It's over now. Prince Karl is here too – we're here to rescue you."

"Karl?" Ella said, looking up. "You're really here?"

"I am my love, I am," Prince Karl said, embracing her. Ella sobbed in his arms.

"I'm sorry! I'm so sorry! I shouldn't have run! I was just so scared!"

"I know," Prince Karl said. "Elisa explained everything."

"I'm just a peasant," Ella cried.

"I don't care," Prince Karl declared. "You're a princess to me. If you won't live in the palace, I'll come join you on a farm. Now let's get you up."

Prince Karl helped Ella up and out of the room. They made their way down the stairs, Ella leaning on Karl and Elisa behind them, where Ella's stepmother watched them with a sneer.

"The slipper fits," Prince Karl said. "This is my bride."

"You didn't even try it on her, not that it's in much shape to try on anything now," Ella's stepmother declared. "You have no idea of who she is, do you? She doesn't like princes, or fancy balls, she likes cleaning! Do you know what we call her? We call her 'Cinder-Ella'. It wasn't our choice – she insisted on it. She loved cleaning the cinders and the ashes out of the fireplace that much."

"She's the one I danced with," Prince Karl stated.

"Well, then, let's hear her say it for herself," Ella's stepmother declared. "Go on, 'Cinder-Ella', tell us about how you were at the ball!"

Ella stared at her stepmother, and then at the prince, and shook her head, her eyes wild with fear.

"She was there," Elisa declared. "I provided the clothes she wore. On the second and third days of the festival, she was announced as my sister."

"And my wife and I drove her there and back," Jakob added. "She used our carriage to get there."

"A pack of lies, and 'Cinder-Ella' still hasn't confirmed that she was there with her own words," Ella's stepmother said. "And by your own admission, Your Royal Highness, you couldn't see her well enough to know. If she was there, let her say it! But she won't, because she wasn't." She turned to Elisa. "But you were. I remember you. Have any more 'interesting' and 'exciting' things to show us before I beat you to a pulp?"

Ella's stepmother raised her hand to strike, Elisa flinching and raising her arm to protect herself. And then a voice brought the entire room to a frozen tableau.

"*Leave her alone!*"

Elisa blinked. Ella had risen to her full height, her good eye glaring. "I was at the festival," she stated, her voice strong. "I asked Elisa to allow me to be announced as her sister to protect myself. I danced with Prince Karl on all three days, and I fell in love with him. I ran away on each night because I was too scared to stay, but I'm not going to let myself be scared any more. I accept Prince Karl's proposal of marriage, and I will be his loving wife to the day I die."

"And I consent to the marriage," Georg declared.

"But I do not," Ella's stepmother said. "We had an agreement when we got married, and that was that my daughters would be married first. Did you forget that?"

Prince Johann glared at her. "You mutilated your own daughters and then beat them in front of us. You are not part of this decision."

Ella's stepmother shrugged. "Fine. Have it your own way. But as for you, Jakob and Anna the innkeepers, I hope you enjoyed eating. I do not forget those who wronged me, and there will be consequences for this."

"You'll do no such thing," Georg stated.

"This household is *mine*," Ella's stepmother said. "And, thanks to your weakness, so is the family business. I'm the one the merchants deal with now, I'm the one who sets the prices, and I'm the one who decides who can buy food from our farm."

"You may think that," Georg said. "But you forgot about Ella's dowry – the one I negotiated with his Royal Highness."

Ella's stepmother scowled. "What about her dowry? What dowry can a lowlife cleaning maid warrant, anyway?"

Georg smiled. "The house, the farm, all related businesses, and the fortune."

Ella's stepmother stared at him in shock. "What?"

"I will help his Royal Highness' staff take over the farm and the businesses, and then I will retire with a reasonable pension. You and your daughters will be sent to a little house far away from here with a couple of attendants and receive a much smaller pension. And you will never again darken my door or show your face to me or my daughter."

"Fine!" Ella's stepmother barked. "If you want to get rid of me so badly, divorce me!"

"And let you get your claws into somebody else and mistreat their children?" Georg said. "No. You're going to stay married and separated from me, and be happy with what you get."

"Come on, my love," Prince Karl said to Ella. "Let's get out of this dreadful place."

Ella nodded and leaned into him. He helped her out the door and towards the carriage, followed by Prince Johann and the guards. Elisa, Jakob and Anna walked behind them.

Just before the carriage step, Ella turned to face her stepmother and stepsisters, who had gathered just outside of the door. "My name is *Eleonore*," she said.

Prince Johann stepped over to where Elisa, Jakob, and Anna were standing. "Please ride with us back to the village. It's the least we can do to repay your for all of your help, and we will do more to repay you in future."

Jakob and Anna nodded. "Thank you, Your Royal Highness," Jakob said.

Reality shifted.

Elisa startled. Ella, Jakob, and Anna stared at her. "What is it?" Anna asked.

Then the screaming began.

Elisa looked back to the house, her eyes widening in horror. Pigeons were descending on Ella's stepmother and stepsisters, clawing and pecking at their eyes.

They fell to their knees, Maria screaming, "Get them away, get them away!" as a bird plucked out her bloodied eyeball and flew away with it.

Ella staggered over to Elisa and grabbed her shoulder. "Are you doing this?"

Elisa shook her head. "No! I would never, I–"

The three women writhed in pain as the pigeons flew away, their faces a ruined mess, their eyes gone.

Ella looked at Elisa with her good eye. "But if you didn't do this, then..."

"Then there's somebody else like me here right now," Elisa said, glancing around. Some workers stood in the fields, watching them. For a moment, she thought she saw somebody slip behind a tree, but it was so fast that she couldn't be sure.

And whoever it is, I need to find them.

Chapter VI – A Parting Gift

Elisa watched in horror as Charlotte twitched on the gallows, wishing and praying to no avail. Then she opened her eyes.

She took a deep breath, reality asserting itself as sunlight streamed in through the window. Her bed was comfortable, the most comfortable bed she had ever slept in. Ornate patterns covered the walls. Even the ceiling was divided into decorated panels.

I'm in the palace, Elisa remembered. *I'm here for Ella.*

Elisa had been preparing to leave the inn when a messenger had been sent from Prince Karl and Ella, begging her to come to the palace and stay with them until Ella was better. After a single thought of the wreckage that Ella's face had been reduced to, Elisa had agreed, gathered her few belongings, and gotten into the carriage.

A week had passed. Ella's face was still swollen, but not as badly as before. She could see through both eyes again. A physician Prince Johann had summoned had declared that there was unlikely to be permanent disfigurement.

Elisa rose from the bed, used the chamber pot, and then dressed herself. After the first morning at the palace, Elisa had wandered the halls with her full chamber pot, asking where she was to dispose of its contents, and refusing all offers to take it off her hands. Ella had given her a stern talking to, insisting that Elisa had to let the household servants do their jobs and take care of her. Elisa had reluctantly agreed. She still wore her own clothes, instead of the more luxurious dresses that had been provided in her room – Ella couldn't take *that* away from her.

She knelt on the floor and prayed, begging for forgiveness for her sins, and for God to speed Ella's healing. Then she prayed for the souls of all the people she had met, including Ella's stepmother and stepsisters. Then she prayed for the souls of all the people on the island, asking God to shorten their time in Purgatory.

Elisa stood up and sighed. It felt like weeks since she had been able to hear a Mass or confess her sins. But she was in the Lutheran lands – there were no churches for a Catholic to attend.

She made her way out into the hallway, and down to the kitchen. Ella had tried to get her to take her breakfasts in the dining hall, but that had never felt right. Besides, she was a penitent – enjoying fancy meals with the nobility was not what a penance was about.

Elisa was sitting at a table, finishing off some bread covered in butter when Ella opened the door and walked into the room. The kitchen staff bowed and said, "Your gracious lady."

Ella sighed and sat down across from Elisa. "I will never get used to that."

Elisa swallowed. "Once you're married, they'll be calling you 'Your Royal Highness'."

Ella chuckled, and then winced in pain, pressing her hand to her bruised face. "Don't remind me. Sometimes I think I should have taken Karl up on his offer to join me on a farm. But...this is better, and I think I can use this marriage to help people. That's the least I can do for *you*. Maybe it will help you along in your penance."

Elisa drank down some water. "How are you doing?"

Ella sighed. "I still keep having this nightmare that I'm waking up in that dirty straw bed back at the farmhouse, and that I deserve to be beaten for wanting something better. But, then I wake up, and I'm here, and I know Karl is in the apartment beside me, and it feels better. What about you?"

Elisa stared at the table. "I keep dreaming that I'm back at the island, watching my best friend Charlotte die because I gran–...because of me."

Ella took a deep breath. "Well, we're both safe now."

"You know I can't stay."

Ella nodded. "I know. But I wish you would. There are other ways to do a penance, even if you're not in Catholic lands. Anyway, we do need you to stay a bit longer. Having you here is a great comfort to both of us. And, you're joining us for lunch today in the dining hall."

Elisa raised her hands. "You know I'm not comfortable doing that. I'd rather eat in the kitchen, with the servants."

"You're joining us in the dining hall because we have things to discuss with Prince Johann and Prince Karl, including plans for my wedding. And, we have something to give you, but it won't be arriving for another couple of days."

Elisa scowled. "Ella, I'm a *penitent*. I can't be accepting gifts like this."

Ella smiled. "This one you can accept – I guarantee it."

Elisa sat beside Ella at the high table in the dining hall, looking at everybody else in fine clothes and pushing down her instinct to bolt. With the room containing only herself, Ella and Prince Karl, Prince Johann and his wife, Princess Katharina, and Ella's father Georg sitting at a single table, the hall felt deserted.

"Your wife and stepdaughters are settled," Prince Johann was saying to Georg as a servant brought out plates of sausages. "Your wife has been informed that there will be severe consequences if any of the servants are mistreated, or if there is any further mistreatment of her daughters."

Georg nodded as a plate was placed in front of him. "Thank you, Your Royal Highness."

"We're about to become family. Please call me Johann."

"We're going to hold our wedding in two weeks, once most of the bruises have faded," Ella told Elisa, stabbing one of her sausages with a two-pronged fork and slicing it into pieces. "We would really like you to be there."

Elisa shook her head. "I'm sorry, I can't. I've probably spent too much time here already."

"Jakob and Anna will be attending," Georg said. "They send you their best wishes, by the way."

"Please thank them," Elisa said. "And, please tell them that they are in my thoughts and prayers."

"And you are in all of ours," Prince Karl stated.

"I've been told a remarkable story, Elisabeth," Princess Katharina began. "And I would hear the truth from you. How did you know about my son's eyesight?"

Elisa stiffened.

"We know you're not a witch," Prince Johann stated. "We once had an encounter with a witch. Believe me, nobody could mistake you for one."

Ella blinked. "You met a real witch? What happened?"

Prince Johann took a deep breath. "She had been the secret leader of a group of brigands, but what they were doing went far beyond mere brigandage. They would get one of their number engaged to some peasant girl by posing as a wealthy suitor. Then, they'd take her back to their house deep in the forest, murder her, and eat her. If it wasn't for some miller's girl getting suspicious after her engagement and going to investigate, we never would have found out about it."

Elisa realized that her jaw was open, and closed it. Beside her, Ella asked, "How did she survive?"

"They had an old woman they had captured and forced to be their servant," Prince Johann explained. "The girl arrived when only the old woman was there, and she hid her – I think it was behind a giant hog's head. Then, the old woman put a sleeping draught into their wine, and they both escaped. Somehow, the miller's girl managed to recover the finger and ring on it from their most recent victim, and brought it to the attention of our guards. Apparently, she had watched them murder, butcher, and salt the poor girl. We didn't know about the witch until we stormed the place. Only half of us made it out alive, and what we found in that cellar..."

"It was the last time I allowed Johann to go out on an expedition with his guards," Princess Katharina stated. "We kept the existence of the witch a secret and burnt down the house...best not to panic the our subjects and cause a witch hunt. But, back to the matter at hand. Elisabeth, how did you know about my son's eyesight?"

Elisa swallowed. "It's true. When I look at somebody, especially if I concentrate, I can know and grant their deepest wish. When we were talking about rescuing Ella – I mean, Eleonore – I hoped that somebody had a wish that would be useful. Your son's was to be able to see things from far away. That's what gave me the idea."

Princess Katharina leaned forward. "Then you could grant his wish and fix his eyesight?"

Elisa's breath caught in her throat. "Your Royal Highness, I...I..."

Prince Johann placed a hand upon his wife's. "Don't pressure the poor girl, Kathy. She's already done so much for us."

"It's okay," Elisa said, and turned to face Princess Katharina. "Your Royal Highness, I don't understand how this...gift...works. I granted Eleonore's wish to escape, and fancy dresses and slippers fell from her ceiling...and she was still almost beaten to death before we rescued her. I granted my mother's wish to always have enough money to feed us, and her coinpurse was enchanted to always contain enough coinage to buy whatever is needed. I granted my best friend's desire to have the boy she loved propose to her, and he was hanged right after they became engaged. If I grant your son's wish, he will be able to see things that are far away, but I don't know what else will happen."

She felt Ella's hand on hers, giving it a squeeze. "It was *my* choice to run," Ella stated. "I put *myself* back in danger, even when I knew I shouldn't. Nothing you could have said would have stopped me."

"But, we almost didn't make it in time," Elisa said.

Ella squeezed her hand again. "You *did* make it in time."

"Elisa," Georg began, "have you considered that Eleonore's rescue could have *only* happened because you granted her wish and got her to the festival? Once the prince proposed to her, nothing could have stopped us from carrying out a rescue, even if we had to just leave that night and storm my house to get her back. Your idea ensured that we didn't have to take her by force, or risk an altercation that might have caused panic inside the village. It wasn't the granting of Eleonore's wish that put her in danger – it's the thing that *saved* her."

"Your gift bestows blessings, not curses," Prince Johann added. "It wouldn't fix our son's eyesight just to damage him in some other way."

Ella placed her hand on Elisa's shoulder. "Wouldn't you like to be able to grant a wish with no complications, just to see that it works? There's no danger here, no need for a rescue to take place. Just a simple wish among people who already owe you everything."

"I would be happy to let you try this on me," Prince Karl stated. "And if it doesn't work, or something goes wrong, no harm will come to you. You are forgiven for anything that happens."

"As the ruler of this land, I declare that to be so," Prince Johann added.

Elisa took a deep breath. Beside her, Ella said, "Elisa, I think deep down inside, you need to know."

Elisa sighed and nodded. "You're right, I'll do it." She reached out with her mind to the thread attached to Prince Karl's wish, and pulled on it. Reality shifted.

"So what happens now?" Prince Karl asked. "Do you have to wave your arms, and speak an incantation, or..."

Elisa took a nervous breath. "You look out the window and see if it worked."

Karl blinked and stared at her. Then, without a word, he rose from his chair and stood by the window.

"I can see those trees!" he breathed. "And the wildflowers around them! And the hills! They're so beautiful."

Ella gave Elisa's shoulder a squeeze. "I told you it

would be okay. Now, if you could fix my face, we could get married even sooner..."

Elisa gave her a sad smile. "I can't. Your wish has already been granted, and you know that your face will heal. All I'm getting from you is happiness."

"Maybe my father's wish, or Prince Johann or Princess Katharina's wishes – you could practice on them!"

Prince Johann smiled at Ella. "Our wishes were granted as soon as you came into our son's life."

Georg wiped a tear from his eye. "Mine was granted as soon as Eleonore was freed."

"What about the servants?" Ella gushed. "Maybe you could practice on them!"

Prince Johann chuckled. "Eleonore, let the poor girl be. Elisabeth took a big step today. Let her do this at her own pace."

A servant came into the hall with a message. He whispered it into Prince Johann's ear.

Prince Johann smiled and turned to Elisa. "It seems, Elisabeth, that our gift for you has made excellent time, and will be arriving tomorrow morning. Please, stay with us until then. I promise you, it will be a benefit to your penitence, not a hindrance."

Elisa sighed and bowed her head. "I will, Your Royal Highness. But, Eleonore is healing well enough that I should be leaving."

"Then we will ensure that you have a proper send-off tomorrow," Prince Karl declared.

Elisa stood in the ballroom, staring out the window, wondering what this "gift" was that was supposed to be arriving today. Her bag with the clothes that her parents had packed and left for her escape was packed and leaning against a wall.

She had spent part of the morning talking to the servants, taking in each one of their wishes. Most of them were small, and didn't require a wish granter. A couple weren't – ailing parents or siblings at death's door that they wanted healed, and Elisa granted them without a word. It was the least she could do before she left, and it was better for her penance that they didn't know who made their wish come true.

The door opened, a small procession entering containing Prince Johann, Princess Katharina, Ella, Prince Karl, and a priest. Elisa curtseyed as they approached.

"Elisabeth," Prince Johann began, "this is Father Gabriel from the Roman Catholic Archdiocese of Posen. He is here so that you may hear Mass and, if you wish, receive the sacrament of Confession."

The priest stepped forward. He looked to be in his mid-forties, with a clean shaven face and kind blue eyes. "It is a pleasure to meet you, Elisabeth. They have told me a great deal about you."

Elisa blinked back tears. "You...you brought me a priest? I can confess my sins?"

"Of course we did," Ella said, stepping forward and taking her hand into hers. "You care so much for your soul, we could not ever deny you this. And you're going to be spending so much time in Protestant lands...we wanted you to give you the best start to your penance that we could."

"We had to agree to allow him to proselytize to us once you've left," Princess Katharina added. "That's how much what you've done means to us."

"I promise I will go gentle on them," Father Gabriel said with a smile. "Shall we begin? I just need a table."

"You can use the high table in the dining hall," Prince Johann said. "It's just through there."

"Come Elisabeth," Father Gabriel said. "Let us see to your soul."

Elisa followed Father Gabriel into the dining hall, and watched as he laid down a cloth and the accouterments of the Mass, then made the sign of the cross and said a blessing to sanctify the space. Then Father Gabriel asked, "Would you like to confess your sins?"

Elisa nodded and knelt. "Forgive me father, for I have sinned. It has been...at least three weeks since my last confession."

"And what are your sins?" Father Gabriel asked.

"Pride," Elisa replied. "So much pride, and so many people were killed because of it." She began to pour out her heart, telling Father Gabriel about the first wish she had granted, the revolution, the death of King Martin and his family, and Charlotte, and finally how her parents had sacrificed themselves to save her. Then, tears streaming down her face, she told him about her penance.

When she was done, Father Gabriel shook his head. "That...was not what I was expecting to hear. So many souls to pray for...and poor Father Xaver."

Elisa blinked and wiped the tears from her eyes. "You knew him?"

"We were at the seminary together. He was a good friend, and a good man."

Elisa stared at the floor. "I'm sorry I got him killed."

"You're not the one who killed him. But, you certainly made some grave errors in judgement."

"I've been so afraid that people would think I'm a witch," Elisa muttered.

"A witch would not care so much for her soul or the souls of others," Father Gabriel stated. "Nor would she use her talents to help people the way you have."

"So, this comes from God?"

"I think so," Father Gabriel said. "Why would the Devil give anybody such a talent?"

"I guess he wouldn't," Elisa said.

"As far as your penance goes, what you have chosen is appropriate. It may even be what you were given this gift to do. That said, I can provide you an alternative if you wish – one that would allow you to stay with these people who care for you so deeply."

Elisa thought for a moment, and then said, "I don't."

"Well, then," Father Gabriel stated. "Are you sorry for all of your sins and any sins you have forgotten to mention?"

"I am, Father."

Father Gabriel made the sign of the cross. "God the Father of mercies, through the death and resurrection of his Son has reconciled the world to himself and sent the Holy Spirit among us for the forgiveness of sins. Through the ministry of the Church may God give you pardon and peace, and I absolve you from your sins in the name of the Father, and of the Son, and of the Holy Spirit. Amen."

Elisa crossed herself, tears flowing again. "Thank you, Father."

"Do not fall back into the sin of pride," Father Gabriel warned. "Know when you have done enough, and it is time to stop being a penitent and lead a good life."

"I'll do my best."

Father Gabriel smiled. "That is all I can ask. Now rise."

Elisa climbed to her feet. Father Gabriel began to recite the liturgy. Elisa's tears flowed freely as Father Gabriel blessed the host and she stood to receive Communion.

"You have dear friends here," Father Gabriel said once they were done. "They sent a rider on horseback to the Archdiocese with instructions to do and promise whatever was necessary short of conversion back to the True Faith to bring me here. You are well loved, Elisabeth."

Elisa nodded. "I know."

Father Gabriel smiled again. "I might make good Catholics of them yet. But first, say your farewells and take however long you need. I have been allowed all the time in the world here by the Archbishop."

Elisa made her way back to the ballroom, where Ella and the others were waiting.

"Are you sure we can't get you to stay until the wedding?" Ella asked.

"I'm a penitent," Elisa replied. "And I need to earn my absolution. I can't do that by staying here."

"You come back and visit," Ella said. "Promise me that. Swear it."

Elisa smiled. "I will. Besides, I need to find that other wish granter. I need to know why she blinded your stepmother and stepsisters. As soon as I know who they are, I will return with the news so we can figure out what to do."

"So you *can* smile," Prince Karl said. "I hope you won't wait that long to come back. And come straight to the palace when you return – so long as we are alive, you will have a home here if you wish it."

Prince Johann stepped forward. "Are you certain you have everything you need?"

Elisa nodded. "Thank you, Your Royal Highness, for your consideration. I have everything I need."

"Will you at least let us give you a horse and a carriage to take you to the edge of our land?" Princess Katharina asked.

Elisa shook her head. "Wouldn't be right for a penance."

"Then Godspeed to you," Prince Johann said. "You will be in our prayers, always."

Elisa curtseyed. "And you will all be in mine, always."

"Well, then," Ella said with a grin. "So long as one of ours is the True Faith, we should all be good, then."

Elisa chuckled. "I guess so."

Ella stepped forward and embraced Elisa. "Goodbye, my friend. Come back soon, and be safe. And get going before we all start begging you to stay."

"Goodbye, Ella," Elisa said, and then smiled. "Or, I guess, Princess Eleonore."

She took a deep breath and began walking away. With every step, she wanted to turn and return to their company. It was only once she was off the palace grounds and standing on a fork in the road that she allowed herself to look back.

"Goodbye Ella," she said again. "I'll miss you."

She looked at the fork in the road. One path led back to the village with Jakob and Anna's inn. The other led out into the Protestant lands. For a moment, she longed to go back to the village and spend time with Jakob and Anna again.

I'm a penitent, she reminded herself. *I'm not here to enjoy time with friends.*

Elisa took a deep breath, and then headed down the road away from the village, out into the Protestant lands.

Chapter VII – A Princess in a Tower

Elisa watched the little girl walk down the path into the forest. She wore a red hood and cloak, and her deepest wish was that her grandmother would be safe from hungry wolves. Elisa reached out with her mind, pulled on the thread attached to her wish, and reality shifted.

Now, if a wolf did show up, there would be hunter too. The wolf would not know that the hunter was on its tail. Nothing would appear magical or miraculous to the little girl or her grandmother.

The little girl continued on down the path, lost in her own thoughts. Elisa allowed herself a slight smile. The red-hooded girl would never know that Elisa had been here. Then she moved on.

She had lost count of the number of wishes long ago. It didn't take her long to figure out that if she concentrated, she could shape how a wish was granted. It also didn't take her long to realize that the best way to grant wishes was from a distance.

It wasn't a terrible life, this penance. She moved from village to village, spending a bit of time in each and granting as many wishes as possible before moving on to the next one. Sometimes she would find a pretext to talk to somebody before granting their wish, to ensure that she understood all of the circumstances around it before deciding if she should pull the thread attached to it. But most wishes weren't like that. Most people's dearest desire was that their children would survive the winter, or that they would have enough to eat, or that they would find a good wife or husband that would make them happy.

Some wished that a boy or girl that they loved would love them back. She left them alone – after all, they could figure it out between themselves.

Then there were the people who wished that their recently departed were in Heaven. She never touched those – those wishes were the sole purview of God and his church.

When the village she was staying in was bringing in the harvest, she'd remain long enough to help. Whenever the weather grew cold and the snow began to fall, she would buy plain winter clothes and serviceable boots. Once the winter passed, she would donate them to the nearest church. Every now and then she had to replace her dress, undergarments, and shoes. Always she kept with her the change of clothes her father had packed for the three of them in preparation for escaping the island. Sometimes when she got to the room of whatever inn she was staying in, she allowed herself to take them out of the bag, lay them on the bed, and enjoy fond memories of her parents. Then she would pray for their souls to have a quick exit from Purgatory, and pray for the souls of all the other people she had helped.

Her hunt for the other wish granter continued, but without success. Everywhere she went, she asked if anybody had seen miraculous or magical things. The answer was almost always a "no," and in the few cases where something had been seen, it had been so many years ago that whoever had caused it had almost certainly moved on.

She sighed as she walked, coming to a large river. She walked down the road to where a ferry waited, the ferryman waving at her. She waved back.

"I'm a bit lost," Elisa said as she approached. "Which river is this?"

"This is the Rhine," the ferryman said. "Would you like to cross?"

Elisa nodded, reached into her magic coinpurse, and paid the toll. She stepped onto the ferry, and as the ferryman pulled them away from the shore, her mind went back to that fateful day at Ella's farmhouse.

Who had that shadow been? Had that been the other wish granter? Or had the wish granter been one of the hired help working the fields? But if it was the hired help, why would they make the birds attack when the royal family had been there? But that just brought her back to the shadow behind the tree...and Elisa hadn't gotten a close enough look to even tell if it was a man or a woman.

She cursed herself under her breath for not having chased after them.

"We're here," the ferryman said, snapping Elisa back to the present. She thanked the ferryman and made her way up the hill. It was what she saw once she reached the top that made her stop in her tracks.

The road was packed with people and families, all heading towards the ferry. Many walked alongside wagons filled with their belongings. Most looked hungry and exhausted.

Elisa reached out with her mind. All of their wishes were about safety and escape. She took a deep breath.

There's too many! If I grant all their wishes, it could kill me.

"Turn back, good maiden," one of the first men in the column warned, followed close behind by his wife and three children. "You don't want to go down that way."

"What's happening?" Elisa asked, but the column was pressing onwards, the man and his family already past her. She stepped up to a woman who appeared to be travelling alone. "Excuse me, can you tell me what's happening?"

"The French," the woman spat as she moved on. "It's the fucking French."

"But what are they doing?" Elisa said. The woman just shook her head and walked on.

Did another war start? Elisa thought. *Could another war have begun so soon?*

Elisa gritted her teeth. If these were refugees from a war, then there were people who needed help. She had to go. But, first, she needed to do something about this column.

She started walking down the column, checking each wish as she did. Somebody had to be thinking of more than just their own family. If she could find just one person whose wish was for all of them to get to safety...

In fact, if she could find a priest in the column, that would be ideal.

The first priest she found wasn't. His wish was simply for the members of his congregation. Elisa shook her head. She needed somebody whose wish would cover the entire column.

The second priest wasn't any better. His wish only covered their souls. But after a couple of hours she encountered a third priest, whose wish was for all of the refugees in the column. Elisa pulled on the string, crafting it so that the column would find safety once they crossed the Rhine, and that they would not come under attack before they had crossed.

Reality shifted, and she moved on. It took until almost sundown to find the end of the refugee column.

158

She spent a night in an almost empty village. "It's lucky you got here tonight," the innkeeper told her as she paid for her room and a meal. "We're leaving tomorrow."

"How bad is it?" Elisa asked.

The innkeeper didn't answer, but the look on his face told Elisa everything she needed to know. She granted his wish to get himself and his family to safety, and reality shifted once again.

That morning, she brought what few supplies she could, and made her way down the road. It was the middle of the day when she came to the first village that had been razed to the ground.

All that was left was charred remains, both of the buildings and the people. Elisa pushed down a wave of nausea, looking for survivors but finding none. Even the crops in the fields had been burned to ashes.

She walked down the road, finding another empty, burned village. That night, she slept under a tree, thankful that it was summer and not one of the colder months. She woke with the dawn, her back stiff and sore.

I've gotten too used to sleeping in inns, Elisa thought. *It would do me some good to spend a few nights outdoors.*

She ate a small breakfast from her dwindling supplies, and made her way further down the road. It was around midday when she came to the tower.

It was short and squat, made from dark grey basalt, without so much as a single window. An iron door hung open. The inside was pitch black.

Elisa was about to move on when she heard a faint scratching sound from inside. She blinked, and stepped into the tower, finding herself in a small ante-chamber with a large wall at the back and no doors save the one she had come in through. With what little sunlight shone in, she could make out a tiny hole at the bottom of the wall facing her, just large enough to pass something through...something like food.

A chill went down her spine at the implications. Then she heard the scratching again, coming from behind the wall.

"Is somebody in there?" Elisa called.

"Yes!" a woman's hoarse voice replied. "We're still alive in here! Please, help us get out! This mortar around the bricks – I don't know if we can scratch it away!"

"Keep trying – I'll do what I can!" Elisa declared, kneeling down to look through the hole. It was too dark to see anything, but a wish formed in her mind – a wish to escape. Elisa pulled on the thread attached to it, shaping the wish so that the mortar would give way.

Reality shifted.

A brick fell down onto the stone floor, and then another. Elisa reached into the hole and pulled out another brick. She heard the impact of a foot on the other side of the wall, the mortar between the bricks flaking off.

"Keep kicking!" Elisa shouted. "It's working!"

Another kick sounded behind the wall, the bricks shaking. One more kick, and a slab of brickwork crashed to the ground, leaving a jagged hole. Elisa strained to see into the darkness.

A woman climbed out of the hole, shielding her eyes from the light as soon as she was free. Her skin was pale, her red hair matted and dirty. The dress she wore must have been beautiful once, but no more – now it was soiled and filthy. Behind her climbed out a second woman, who looked to be her lady-in-waiting.

"Are you okay?" Elisa asked. "Are you hurt?"

"Thank the Virgin Mary, we're fine," the woman said, blinking and averting her eyes from the sunlight. "Just hungry and thirsty."

"Who are you?" Elisa said. Her heart skipped a beat. Could she be back in the Catholic lands?

"I'm Princess Maleen," the woman replied. "This is my lady-in-waiting, Greta."

Greta curtseyed.

"What happened to you, Your Royal Highness?" Elisa asked. "I've never seen a tower like this before...and you were walled in..."

"I disobeyed my father," Princess Maleen said. "He decided to teach me a lesson."

Elisa stared at her in shock. "Your Royal Highness...he walled you up in a tower for *disobeying* him?"

"He wanted to marry me to the son of a prince with an army so that we might resist the French," Princess Maleen stated, looking at her sleeve and shaking her head. "I had already betrothed myself to another, whose father had wealth and resources but no army. I refused to break off my engagement. And, just call me Maleen. You helped me escape, after all."

Elisa realized her mouth was open and closed it. "All that because you wouldn't break an engagement...that's horrible!"

"I'm not going to marry someone I don't love," Maleen stated. "Anyway, my father has this tower built to punish me, and sentenced me to seven years in darkness. At first the food came regularly, but then it stopped...and that's when we realized we had to escape or starve to death."

"I've got some food left," Elisa said. "Not a lot, but I'll share what I have. And then, I guess I'd better get you two across the Rhine, where it's safe."

Maleen stared at her. "What do you mean, 'where it's safe'?"

"I came from the direction of the Rhine, and everything within a day of here has been razed." Elisa took a deep breath. "There were a lot of bodies."

Maleen cursed. "I need to see my father's castle. I'm afraid my path takes me away from the Rhine. Thank you...I'm sorry, but what is your name?"

"Elisabeth Beichtkind," Elisa replied. "But everybody calls me Elisa."

Maleen shook her head. "'Elisabeth Penitent'. Your father or grandfather didn't consider his children very well when he chose that family name, did he?"

"Actually, I chose it. I am a penitent."

Maleen shrugged. "Can't fault you for dedication. What's your penance?"

"Wandering around and helping people in need."

Maleen chuckled. "Some people just go on pilgrimages, you know."

"I'm not one of them. Forgive me for asking, but are you Catholic?"

Maleen nodded. "Our principality is of the True Faith."

Elisa breathed a sigh of relief. "I've spent so long in the Protestant lands...I can go to church again!"

"Anyway, thank you for your help," Maleen declared. "You get to safety, and save your food for yourself. We'll manage."

Elisa took a deep breath. "Is the castle far?"

Maleen shook her head. "Only an hour or two."

"Then I'd like to come with you, if you'll let me," Elisa said.

Maleen shrugged. "If you wish."

Elisa followed Maleen and her lady-in-waiting southwards, finally cresting the rise of a tall hill. In the distance, the ruins of a castle were still smoking.

"Your Royal Highness..." Maleen's lady-in-waiting began, starting to cry.

"I know, Greta, I know," Maleen said, taking a ragged breath. "It happened here too."

"*What* happened here?" Elisa asked. "All anybody tells me is that it's the French."

"His majesty the King of France did not approve of the new Elector of Cologne," Maleen replied through gritted teeth. "As you can see, he expressed his displeasure with his army." She turned to Greta. "We need to go see about Franz. I need to know if he's still alive."

"Sorry, who's Franz?" Elisa asked

"My fiancé."

"I'll help," Elisa said.

"You've done enough," Maleen stated. "Please get to safety."

"I need to stay and help," Elisa pressed. "That is my penance."

Maleen rolled her eyes. "Oh, very well. Greta, let this be a lesson to you – never try to dissuade a penitent. They can be quite stubborn."

Elisa curtseyed. "Thank you, Your Royal Highness."

"I told you not to call me that," Maleen said. "Well, if you're determined to help anyway, might you have some spare clothing we could use? These are no longer fit for wearing."

Elisa's breath caught in her throat. The only women's clothes she had that might fit them had been her mother's. *I'm a penitent*, she reminded herself. *I must sacrifice to help those in need.*

Elisa reached into her bag, pulling out her mother's dresses. She took one last look at them, stroking the fabric, and then handed them to Maleen.

"These belonged to somebody dear to you," Maleen observed.

Elisa nodded. "My mother."

"We shall have to take good care of them, then," Maleen said. She examined the fabric. "They're old, but quite serviceable. You have our eternal gratitude."

"You can keep them if you need to," Elisa forced herself to say.

"Thank you, Elisa," Maleen said. "Greta, let's get changed and on our way."

Greta stared at Maleen, holding the dress she had been

handed, and then changed into it. Once she was dressed, she swallowed and said, "Your Royal Highness, I...I..."

Maleen gave her a knowing glance and a kind smile. "You want to know if your family is still alive."

Greta nodded. "They lived south of here."

Maleen sighed. "Very well. I release you from my service. Go do whatever you need to find your family. If once you have, you wish to return to my service, I will welcome you with open arms."

Greta curtseyed. "Thank you, Your Royal Highness."

Elisa concentrated. Greta's wish was that her family had survived. She pulled on the thread and granted it. Reality shifted.

"I hope they're alive, and I'll pray for your safety and their souls," Maleen said. "And for yours."

"Thank you, Your Royal Highness," Greta said, curtseyed, and began making her way south.

Maleen watched as she walked away, and then said, "Well, if you're coming along, we'd best be on our way too. We're heading east."

They walked until sundown, Elisa trying not to think about how Maleen was wearing the last thing she had of her mother. Then they sat and ate the last of Elisa's food.

"How far do we have to go?" Elisa asked.

"Just a couple of days," Maleen replied.

Elisa took a deep breath. "Even with what your father did to you, I know you just lost your family...and I know how that feels. You can mourn, if you want."

Maleen shook her head. "Not in front of you. In a time of war, a royal must be strong."

Elisa gave her a kind smile. "I think I saw something over that hill. It will take me a while to check it out. Are you okay waiting here for me?"

Maleen took a deep breath. "I am." She looked at Elisa with gratitude in her eyes. "Thank you."

"It's the least I can do, Elisa said, and headed over the hill. She walked for a while, and then sat and watched the stars rise in the sky. Then she prayed for the souls of all those the French had killed.

Finally, she stood and made her way back to Maleen. She could make out in the darkness that the princess was wiping something from her eyes and cheeks.

"So," Maleen said, her voice hoarse. "Did you find that thing you were looking for?"

Elisa shrugged. "It turned out to be nothing of interest."

They slept under the stars, Elisa's back aching when they woke with the dawn. By midday their stomachs were both growling. The only village they had passed by was nothing but charred remains.

"I don't have the foggiest idea of how to hunt," Maleen declared as they crested a ridge. "So, unless you know how to catch a rabbit, I think we'll need to start eating nettles."

Elisa grimaced. "That won't be pleasant."

"Do you know how to catch a rabbit?"

"I don't have a clue," Elisa replied. "I walk from village to village – I've never lived off the land."

"Then this will be a new experience for us both," Maleen declared.

They made camp at sundown under a tree, both of their hands blistered and itching from the sting of the nettles they had picked and eaten. Elisa tried to concentrate on something else as she settled down to sleep.

"So, you're a penitent," Maleen said. "What was your sin?"

Elisa stared at the stars. A dark cloud passed over, covering some for a few minutes before it moved along. "Pride," she said.

"You don't seem to be very prideful to me now," Maleen stated.

"My pride hurt a lot of people," Elisa said.

"Including your parents."

"Yes. I find it very hard to be prideful after that."

"If you tell me their names, I shall pray for their souls."

Elisa took a ragged breath. "Thomas and Helena."

"What did your father do?"

"He was a bookbinder."

"Now that's a good profession to have. The world needs more books."

"My father felt the same."

"I will pray for his soul."

Despite the itching on her hands, Elisa finally fell asleep.

They woke with the dawn, said their morning prayers, and continued on their way. As they walked, a soft rain began to fall. They took shelter under a copse of trees.

"Can I ask you something?" Elisa said as they waited for the rain to stop.

"Whatever you want," Maleen replied.

"In the last few months, or perhaps couple of years, did you hear of any miracles or magic happening nearby?"

Maleen blinked and stared at her. "What do you mean?"

"Animals acting strangely, things happening that shouldn't, that sort of thing."

"I can't speak for when I was in the tower," Maleen began. "And I have no idea how long I was in there. Time just...it felt like it didn't exist anymore. But, before then...I can't think of anything, I'm sorry. Why do you ask?"

"I'm looking for somebody," Elisa replied.

"Do you know their name?"

Elisa shook her head. "I don't even know if it's a man or a woman. I didn't get a close enough look. All I know is that they can...well, do magic."

"Did they hurt you or somebody close to you?"

"Not quite," Elisa said. "But, they blinded three people in front of me by making pigeons attack their eyes."

Maleen lay back on the ground. "That is not a thing pigeons are known for, that's for certain. Did those three people deserve it?"

Elisa shrugged. "I guess? They mistreated my friend, and one of them nearly killed her. But...I don't know. I just need to find them and find out who they are, and why they did it."

"I wish I could help you," Maleen said. "But, outside of the French invading the Reich, I haven't heard of anything happening that shouldn't otherwise be happening. And the French king doesn't need a witch to be an evil bastard who burns down principalities."

"The rain's stopping," Elisa noted.

"Then let's be on our way," Maleen declared. "We've still got at least a day to go."

They took shelter at night under a tree within sight of another burned village. Elisa resisted the urge to scratch at the fresh rash from the nettles they had scavenged to eat earlier in the day. Her stomach growled at her.

"I want a beer and a good meal," Elisa grumbled as she tried to make herself comfortable on the ground.

"Me too," Maleen declared. "If Franz is alive, as soon as we get to the palace, I'm going to have him throw us a feast."

Elisa sighed. "I wish I could join you for that, but I can't."

Maleen nodded. "Right. You're a penitent."

"I'll just find a decent tavern," Elisa said. "Don't worry about me."

"Well," Maleen declared, "I will tell Franz about how you helped me. At least allow us to show our gratitude in some manner."

Elisa sat up. "Please, Maleen, I would ask that you not

167

mention me at all. A penance is not a penance if one is receiving rewards or gratitude for it."

"I think you're taking this penitent thing a bit far," Maleen grumbled. "I might have starved to death if you hadn't come along. Fine, I'll tell him that I made it here on my own, or with Greta."

Elisa lay back down. "Thank you, Maleen."

The itching kept her awake, but eventually sleep came.

They woke up with the dawn again. The sun was bright as they rose and continued their journey.

As noon approached, they came to a refugee column on the road, all heading east, stretching as far as the eye could see. They walked alongside the column at a quick pace, Maleen taking a look at each family. Finally, she stopped in her tracks and closed her eyes.

"I don't see a single person from my principality," she said. "Not one person I recognize."

"Did you get out among the people often?" Elisa asked.

Maleen nodded, her eyes still closed. "Whenever I could. I got to know a lot of families. I'm going to need a moment to collect myself, Elisa."

"Take all the time you need."

Maleen took a deep breath, opened her eyes, and said, "Okay, let's get to the city."

Elisa blinked. "Sorry, did you say a city?"

Maleen nodded, an amused smile crossing her face. "Never been to one?"

"The island I'm from had a town, but..."

"You'll like it," Maleen declared. "Plenty of churches, taverns, and other things to see."

The first thing Elisa saw as they followed the column to the city were the steeples. Elisa's eyes widened – there were so many of them! Beside her, she heard Maleen chuckle and say, "I told you."

The walls of the city came into view, the column stopped in front of it. "There's another gate this way," Maleen said. "And, if we're lucky, I'll know the guard."

As the gate came into view, a much smaller line of travellers before it, Maleen smiled. "I'm lucky. It's Anton."

They got into line, Maleen taking a deep breath. "Elisa, even if you won't let me thank you some other way, please know that you will always be in my prayers for having helped me."

"Thank you, Maleen."

Maleen smiled. "We're around other people again. I think appearances will matter. Better go back to 'Your Royal Highness'."

Elisa curtseyed. "Of course, Your Royal Highness."

The line advanced, and finally it was their turn. Maleen looked at the guard and gave him a smile. "Believe it or not, Anton, it's me. I'm Princess Maleen."

Anton stared at her for a moment, and then his eyes widened. "Your Royal Highness! We thought you were dead!"

"Happily I'm not," Maleen declared. "Have you heard of anybody else..."

Anton shook his head. "I'm sorry, Your Royal Highness – as far as I know, you are the first from your principality to make it here."

Maleen closed her eyes and took a deep breath. Then she opened them again. "The French must have come very suddenly."

"That was what we heard, Your Royal Highness."

"This is Elisa, she's a fellow traveller. She's been very kind to me."

"We will of course let her in, Your Royal Highness."

Maleen smiled and nodded. "Thank you, Anton. Now, how about you tell me what is wrong."

"Your Royal Highness, when you were locked in that tower all those months ago, we prayed for your escape. But then your principality was destroyed, and his Royal Highness Franz lost all hope. He is now betrothed to somebody else...somebody whose father has an army."

Maleen closed her eyes and took a deep breath. "I see."

"I will tell him you are alive, Your Royal Highness, I will–"

"You will do no such thing," Maleen declared. "My beloved is alive, and that is what matters. If this marriage will keep him safe, how can I deny him that? Just mark us down as refugees from the south, and I won't make any trouble."

Anton's eyes glistened. "But, Your Royal Highness–"

"No 'buts'," Maleen said with a kind smile. "A princess must put the safety of her subjects first. My sin was that I failed to do that out of love, and now my family and those we were sworn to protect are gone. I am a princess no longer – if you have to call me anything, just call me 'Maid Maleen'."

"You'll always be a princess to me," Anton said.

"Thank you for that," Maleen said. "Now, we shouldn't keep the line waiting any longer."

Anton waved them through. They walked into the city, the sights and sounds overwhelming. Elisa resisted the urge to cover her ears.

"There's always something happening here!" Maleen declared. "Jugglers, conjurers, festivals. I think I'll find employment here somewhere and stay." She frowned. "Perhaps the palace will take me as a serving maid. I could learn to do that."

"Maleen, I'm so sorry," Elisa said.

Maleen reached out and squeezed her shoulder. "Thank you, for everything."

"Let me buy you some food and some proper clothes," Elisa said. "I have money."

"Use it for your penance," Maleen declared. "We will go to the nearest church, and I will get some cast off dress that somebody has donated there, and then I will return this one to you. It's the least I can do."

They made their way to a church, Elisa marking its location in her memory for later, as well as the time of the next Mass. Maleen emerged from a discussion with the priest with a ragged but clean dress. "Let's get somewhere I can change, and then I can return this to you."

"Thank you," Elisa said. Maleen talked to the priest again, who led her into a back room. She emerged a couple of minutes later, clad in the ragged dress.

Maleen handed Elisa her mother's dress. "Thank you for letting me use this."

"It was the least I could do," Elisa said, packing it back into her bag. They made their way out onto the busy street.

"Make way for Prince Franz and his betrothed!" a herald shouted. The crowd parted, making a path down the street. Elisa watched as an ornate carriage passed, a tall and handsome man sitting beside a veiled woman.

Elisa stared at Prince Franz. His wish came into focus, clear in her mind – *I wish I was marrying Maleen*. Elisa allowed herself a slight smile as she shaped the form of the wish, and granted it. Reality shifted. Maleen would find employment in the palace, Prince Franz would recognize her before the wedding, and their marriage would not jeopardize the safety of the city.

Maleen stared at her. "What was that about?"

"Just a thought on how to help somebody," Elisa replied. "Nothing important."

"Well, then," Maleen said. "This is where we part ways. I'm going to go to the palace and see if there might

171

be a job for me – something that would let me be close to Prince Franz, even if I can't marry him. Thank you for everything, and I will pray for the safe completion of your penance."

"You will be in my prayers," Elisa promised. Maleen curtseyed with a smile, and disappeared into the crowd.

Elisa sighed and looked around the street, trying to find something that would bring order to the chaos and reveal the location of somewhere she could find something to eat. Nothing emerged. *I suppose I could just ask the priest for directions, and–*

"Elisa the Penitent!" a familiar voice cried out. "How wonderful to see you again!"

Elisa turned to find the gentleman from Prince Johann's festival regarding her just down the street, his eyes bright and friendly. He waved. Elisa couldn't help herself – her face broke into a grin.

"How long has it been since you've seen a familiar face, if you're that happy to see *me*?" the gentleman wondered with a laugh as he approached.

Elisa chuckled. "It's been a while. Would you know anywhere to eat, and anywhere I can stay?"

"I know just the place," the gentleman said.

The inn was just around the corner from the church. Elisa and the gentleman sat at a table by the window in the attached tavern, enjoying their beers while they waited for the food to arrive.

"So, what have you been doing all this time, 'Elisa the Penitent'," the gentleman asked with a mischievous smile.

Elisa set down her beer. "My penance. Wandering around, helping whoever I can. You?"

"I'm *not* helping whoever I can," the gentleman chuckled. "But I am wandering around and seeing what diversions the world has to offer."

Elisa nodded. "It would be nice to do some proper travelling when my penance is done...if it is ever done. See some far off places and be able to enjoy it."

"I highly recommend the experience. So what brings you here on this fine day?"

"Maleen," Elisa replied. She moved her beer to the side as the server arrived with their food. "She was a princess from a few days west of here. Her father had walled her up in a tower after she had refused to break her betrothal. Then the principality was destroyed by the French."

"Ah yes," the gentleman said, cutting off a piece of mutton and popping it into his mouth. "I'm familiar with that king. There's a special place in Hell for him after the treatment he gave his daughter, I'm certain of it. It's a very good honey mustard sauce."

Elisa nodded and swallowed. "I just wish I could get a straight answer from somebody about the war. How could we get another so soon?"

The gentleman chuckled. "His majesty King Louis XIV of France is never shy when it comes to starting wars. In this particular case, his candidate lost the election for the position of Elector of Cologne. It gave him an excuse to invade the Rhineland and claim some of the German lands for himself. He thought that the Reich would just fall into despair and surrender the Rhineland to him. He was wrong – it rallied instead, and started driving him out. So, he decided that if he couldn't have those territories, nobody could."

Elisa swallowed. "How bad is it?"

The gentleman grimaced. "Very. Heidelberg, Oppenheim, and Worms have all been destroyed, and they aren't the only ones. Happily, the French are out for now, so this place is safe. And, the war is widening as we speak, so good King Louis will have far more than just the

Rhineland to worry about. At the very least, Britain will give him a handful."

"That's a lot of souls to pray for," Elisa breathed.

"That's normal for these sorts of things," the gentleman said. "Once you've seen enough of them, you gain some perspective."

A thought crossed Elisa's mind. She frowned.

"What is it, Elisa?" the gentleman asked.

"The prince she was betrothed to thought she was dead after her land was destroyed," Elisa replied. "He had become engaged to another. And I helped Maleen break that engagement so that she could get her prince back."

"Seems reasonable enough."

"But what about that other princess?" Elisa asked. "She is going to lose her engagement, and her principality will lose its alliance in the process. So, did I do the right thing?"

The gentleman leaned back in his chair. "Ah. I'm afraid I may be the worst person in the world to ask about ethics, but I will give you my opinion, if you'd like it."

"I remember your advice being very good," Elisa said.

The gentleman popped a piece of mutton into his mouth, chewed, and swallowed. "It is a difficult one. I am familiar with the princess in question, however. She is a Calvinist."

Elisa blinked. "What's a 'Calvinist'?"

"Somebody so Protestant that even the Lutherans can't stand them. They think that whether you are saved or damned is decided long before you are ever born, so nothing you do in this mortal life matters. You'd think that would make them more fun, but it really doesn't." The gentleman leaned forward. "This particular Calvinist is quite ashamed of herself. You saw the veil, I trust?"

Elisa nodded. "I thought it strange."

"Most would," the gentleman said. "So, I think, would

her fiancé. But all she sees is the shame of her body – an ugly, unworthy princess from a tiny principality that nobody wants to deal with. The only way they could get a match at all is to exaggerate the size of their army...and she knows it. Should she ever get married, all of these lies will come out into the light. She dreads that day, and what might happen when the truth becomes known. I think you did her a favour."

"Without asking," Elisa mumbled. "Is it right to interfere with anybody's life without asking, without them knowing it?"

"Let me answer a question with a question: are you doing it to make their lives better?"

Elisa nodded.

The gentleman finished the food on his plate. "Then I think you need not concern yourself with it overmuch. Your penance and the state of your soul are in no danger."

Elisa sighed. "I guess that is a relief. Can I ask you something else?"

The gentleman smiled. "Of course!"

"In your travels, have you heard of any miracles, or magic?"

The gentleman leaned back. "What do you mean?"

"Pigeons suddenly attacking somebody's eyes," Elisa replied. "Animals acting unnaturally. Things happening that should not happen under the sight of God."

"Well, if you're looking for things that shouldn't happen under the sight of God, you need only step out the door and open your eyes. People do those things all the time, without any prompting from magical forces. Many souls are damned for it, and many souls are saved despite it. But, what you're talking about...let me think..."

The gentleman stared into his beer, and then drank it. "Actually, I think I have heard of some odd events happening to the northeast. So, if that's what you're looking for, I'd suggest searching there. I would warn you – you may not like what you find if you do. Why do you want to know, anyway?"

"I'm looking for somebody," Elisa said. "Somebody who performed one of these…'miracles'…in front of me."

"I had thought the reference to the pigeons was a very specific request," the gentleman said. "Go to the northeast, and I think you will find who you are looking for."

"Back into the Protestant lands," Elisa muttered.

"I'm afraid so," the gentleman stated, finishing his beer.

Elisa scowled. "I only just got out of there."

"You don't need to go back, you know," the gentleman said. "You can continue your penance in the Catholic lands as long as you want. But, I don't think you'll find the person you're looking for if you do. The choice, however, is always yours."

Elisa drank down the last of her beer and sighed. The choice was indeed hers, but it was no choice at all. She would need to go northeast, back into the Protestant lands.

Chapter VIII – The Mad King

Elisa was in her father's workshop, her father showing her how to glue a binding together.

"The amount of glue is very important," her father said. "Too little or too much creates problems."

Elisa looked to the stairs. Her mother was standing, staring at her with a kind smile.

Elisa took a deep breath. "Mother, father, are you in Heaven now?"

"We are, sweetheart," her father said. "Your prayers helped us get there. And we watch you every day."

"We're very proud of you," her mother said.

Elisa wiped away a tear. "Mama, Papa, I miss you."

"We miss you too," her mother said. "We pray for you all the time."

"When I finish my penance and my mortal life is done, I will come to join you," Elisa declared. "I promise."

"I don't think you're going to do that any time soon," her mother said.

"But I've received absolution!" Elisa protested. "All I have to do is finish my penance, and then my soul will be free from my mortal sin!"

Her father sighed. "It's not that. Elisa, how long have you been walking?"

Elisa blinked. "What?"

"It's time for us to go now," her mother said.

Elisa began to cry. "Please don't go! I've missed you so much, and there's so much I wanted to tell you!"

"Elisa, sweetheart," her father said. "We're in Heaven. We're already gone."

Elisa startled awake, tears running freely. She curled into a fetal position and wept. "I'll finish my penance," she cried. "I'll finish my penance and then I'll come to be with you after I die."

She collected herself and got dressed, taking a moment to press her face against the clothes that had once belonged to her parents. After a frugal breakfast, she went to confession and heard Mass in the church. The gentleman was nowhere to be found. Elisa allowed herself a smile, and made a silent prayer that wherever he travelled, he would remain safe.

Then she returned to the inn, checked out of her room, slung her bag over her shoulder, and made her way into the Protestant lands.

She moved from village to village, granting as many wishes as she could as she went, always careful to ensure that they were wishes that would not cause harm. When the seasons turned and the harvest came, she stayed long enough to help out, and then went on her way. At every village she asked if there had been any miraculous events or dark magic.

And at every village, the answer had been the same: no.

In the end, it was a desire for the comfort of God's presence after a cold winter that made Elisa turn and start working her way back towards the Catholic lands. It was a few weeks after she had donated her winter clothes to the village church and set out that she met the prince on the road.

He was tall and well dressed, with light brown hair, and couldn't be more than eighteen years old. He rode a white horse with a spare mount tethered behind him. But what was odd was that he was without an entourage – he travelled alone.

Elisa waved at him as he approached from behind her. "Greetings, your...grace? Royal highness?"

He smiled at her. "I'm a prince."

Elisa curtseyed. "Greetings, Your Royal Highness. I was wondering if you knew whether I am close to the Catholic lands."

"You just passed into them," the prince said. "I had to go through a Protestant principality myself, but the people here are Catholic."

Elisa breathed a sigh of relief. She'd be able to confess her sins and hear Mass.

"What brings you out here, good lady?" the prince asked.

"I'm a penitent," Elisa replied. "My penance is to wander around and help those who I can. Without recognition or reward, of course."

"You look my age," the prince said. "Shouldn't you be going on a pilgrimage or the like?"

"Not for what I did."

"That bad?"

Elisa nodded. "My pride hurt a lot of people."

The prince gave her a kind smile. "I shall pray to the Virgin Mary not to succumb to that sin myself. What's your name?"

"Elisabeth Beichtkind," Elisa replied. "Everybody calls me Elisa."

"I'm Prince Joseph," the prince said. "It is a pleasure to meet you, Elisa."

"If I may ask, Your Royal Highness, why are you on the road alone?"

Prince Joseph chuckled. "There was a prophecy that I would die at the hands of a stag when I was sixteen years old. My father decided to protect me by not allowing me out of the castle. I, on the other hand, decided that I wanted to seek out a wife. So, I snuck out, and here I am."

"And what about the prophecy?" Elisa asked.

"Superstition is for peasants and the elderly," Prince Joseph declared. "I am neither."

"So you're just wandering around looking for a wife?" Elisa said.

Prince Joseph laughed. "Not exactly. There is a Catholic prince I heard about, and it is said that his three daughters are very beautiful, and none have yet succeeded in courting them. And, it's said that all of his sons are now dead because of the war. So, I would try my luck, and see if he and one of his daughters might be receptive."

"I wish you the best of luck," Elisa said.

"Shall we travel together?" Prince Joseph asked. "I must admit, the road is lonely, and I had prayed to St. Christopher for a travelling companion. Perhaps you are the answer to my prayers."

Elisa nodded. "If we're going in the same direction, I would be delighted to, Your Royal Highness."

They walked on, Prince Joseph telling Elisa all about his principality and family. Elisa nodded as he spoke, mostly thinking about hearing Mass once she got to the next village or town, whichever it might be.

It turned out to be a town, with a couple of churches, their steeples tall and stately. Just beyond the town lay a palace on a hill, but it looked old and weathered. As they approached, the afternoon shadows lengthened.

Elisa curtseyed to him as they entered the town. "Thank you for the company, Your Royal Highness. By your leave, I would seek an inn, and make my way to church."

Prince Joseph held up his hand. "I would ask a boon of you, my good lady."

Elisa's breath caught in her throat. "What would that be?"

"A prince should not go courting without an attendant, and I am alone. Would you accompany to the palace as my attendant?"

Elisa blinked. "But I'm a peasant woman."

"And I'm a prince who ran away from his father," Prince Joseph pointed out. "I'm not asking you to do anything other than be present for appearances."

Elisa opened her mouth to refuse, but then stopped. *If I'm at the palace, I can ask them about any magic or miracles...they might know more there than in town.* She curtseyed. "Very well, Your Royal Highness. But, I must ask you to remember that I am a penitent – it would not be appropriate for me to sit at table during feasts, or to present myself as a noble lady."

Prince Joseph smiled. "I would not ask anything of that sort."

"Thank you, Your Royal Highness."

They made their way to the palace, Elisa now holding the reigns of Prince Joseph's spare mount. The prince bowed to the guards.

"I am Prince Joseph, and this is my attendant, Elisabeth. I seek to court his Royal Highness' daughters."

The guards shared a look, and then one said, "That's a bad idea, Your Royal Highness. You should go home."

"I will do nothing of the sort," Prince Joseph declared.

"I am a prince of the *Reich*, and I will declare my intentions!"

The guard shrugged and let him through. "It's your own head."

"Rather impudent, that one," Prince Joseph muttered. "I shall have to have a word with the Prince here about him."

They were escorted into the throne room. Elisa's eyes widened, a sinking feeling in her gut as she glanced around. Stag horns decorated the ceiling, and blood red banners with golden stags covered the walls. On a raised throne, a man with grey hair and a bushy beard smirked at them. A table with several large wooden boxes caught her eye, something about them raising her hackles.

"So this is the princeling who would court my daughters," the man declared. "Just how old are you, boy?"

Prince Joseph bowed. "I am Prince Joseph, and I am sixteen years old, Your Royal Highness. My principality is—"

"I don't care," the man on the throne said with a dismissive wave of his hand. "I am *King* Peter, and you have nothing in your principality that I want."

Prince Joseph blinked. "Your Majesty, I was unaware that you had been elevated by the College of Princes."

"I elevated myself," King Peter stated. "My sons are dead, and if my line is to end with me, then I will end it as no petty prince, but as the *king* of this *kingdom*."

"It need not end with you, Sire," Prince Joseph began. "If you might be willing to wed me to one of your daughters—"

The king laughed, something about the sound of it forcing Elisa to suppress a shudder. "You still wish to court my daughters? Are you willing to stake your life on it?"

Prince Joseph glanced back at Elisa. "I don't understand, sire."

King Peter motioned to one of the guards. "Show him what happened to the last princeling who came a-courting."

The guard stepped over the table and removed the lid from the box closest to the edge. Then he pulled out a rotting head, grasping it by the hair, and brought it to the king.

Elisa gasped and forced down a wave of nausea.

"This one was so confident," King Peter said, looking into the head's eyes and then turning it towards them. "He died screaming for mercy. So much for confidence."

"We need to leave!" Elisa whispered, praying that only Prince Joseph could hear her.

"You amuse me, though," the king stated. "Especially since you brought your peasant whore here with you. You will court my daughters, and if you fail any of my tasks, both of you will be introduced to my headsman. I don't have the head of a woman in my collection yet."

Prince Joseph raised his hands. "Your Majesty, Elisabeth is a penitent I met on the road and who I travelled with to get here. She provided pleasant company and in her kindness listened to me talk, even though she did not care about what I had to say. Nothing untoward happened between us. I convinced her to serve as my attendant for appearance's sake. She is not part of this – please send her away and spare her life."

King Peter laughed and handed the head back to the guard. "Of course I won't! I'm the king here, and if I decide this little penitent girl will die with you, then that is what will happen. You wanted to court the Stag King's daughters – I will grant your wish. Tonight, you will watch over my eldest daughter. On every hour from nine at night to six in the morning, I will come to check on you and call

183

through the door. If you reply when I do you and your little penitent girl will live, and I might just decide to let you have my daughter as a wife. But if you don't, or I hear you violating my daughter...your heads will join my collection." He turned to look at Elisa. "And you, little penitent girl, you will get to wait in your 'quarters' to see whether you will live or die in the morning."

Prince Joseph turned back to Elisa and whispered, "I'm sorry."

"Guards, take them to their quarters and give them something to eat," the King said. "We mustn't be inhospitable to our guests."

Two guards escorted them from the throne room, taking them through the labyrinthine corridors to a small servant's quarters, nothing more than an tiny bed and a dresser for furniture. "I'm sorry," one of the guards said as he closed and locked the door behind him. "It's the best we can do for you. At least it's better than a cell."

Elisa sat on the bed, shaking her head in shock. "He's mad. He's actually mad."

"I'm sorry, Elisa," Prince Joseph said, sitting on the floor and leaning against the wall. "I had no idea that the king was insane. If I had known, I wouldn't have involved you."

"Apology accepted," Elisa said. "By your leave, your royal highness, I think I need to pray."

Prince Joseph took a deep breath. "By your leave, I'll join you."

They knelt on the floor and prayed together for their deliverance. A knock sounded against the door and it opened, a serving girl bringing in a plate with two pieces of bread. She handed the plate to Prince Joseph, curtseyed, and left the room, closing the door behind her. Elisa heard the sound of the door locking.

They ate in silence. While they ate, Elisa concentrated

on the prince's wish, letting it form in their mind. Then, Elisa said, "I think I can help you get out."

Prince Joseph blinked. "What do you mean?"

"I have the ability to grant wishes," Elisa said, lowering her voice. "It's not easy to explain, but let's just say that I can look at somebody, know what the wish dearest to their heart is, and make it happen. And yours is to escape this alive."

The prince stared at him. "I see – that's your penance then, granting people's wishes?"

Elisa nodded.

"And what about yourself?" Prince Joseph asked. "Does granting this wish save you too?"

Elisa shook her head. "I think that only happens if you take me with you."

"If it comes to that, that's what I'll do," Prince Joseph said. "But it hasn't come to that yet."

Elisa blinked. "But the king–"

"The king has set me a challenge," Prince Joseph stated. "I intend to succeed."

Elisa sighed and offered a silent prayer that Prince Joseph would not become the victim of his own sin of pride.

The sun set, casting the room into darkness. The door opened, two guards silhouetted in the dim light of the hall. "It's time," one said, escorting Prince Joseph out of the room.

"Can I please have a lamp or–" Elisa began, but the guard just shut and locked the door.

Elisa fell to her knees again and began to pray. First she prayed for the forgiveness of her and Prince Joseph's sins. Then she prayed for mad King Peter to be healed of his insanity. Then she prayed for all of the subjects under the king's care. Finally, she prayed for the souls of those poor princes whose heads now rested in boxes by the throne of the king.

She rose and lay on the bed, the mattress lumpy and uncomfortable. She closed her eyes and tried to sleep. No sleep came.

Reality shifted.

Elisa's eyes snapped open. A wish had just been granted somewhere in the palace...the wish granter she had been looking for was here!

...and she was locked in a servant's room, waiting to see if her head would be chopped off in the morning.

Elisa suppressed the urge to scream.

She rolled onto her side, closed her eyes, and finally fell into a restless and dreamless sleep.

It was the door opening that woke her up. Morning sunlight streamed into the room as a guard stood and motioned to her. "Do your business, and then come with me. It's time."

Elisa used the chamber pot from under the bed, and then followed the guard, quietly praying as she did. She was led into the throne room, where Prince Joseph was already waiting before the king. She curtseyed. Then her eyes strayed to the table, where two new boxes sat, waiting to be filled.

Elisa took a deep breath, getting ready to grant the prince's wish.

"It seems you get to live another day," King Peter declared. "How lucky for you! Perhaps I should have a penitent at my side too."

"I have passed your test, your Majesty," Prince Joseph stated. "May I now have your eldest daughter as my bride?"

The king laughed. "No! You haven't finished amusing me yet! But, I'll let you watch over my second daughter...yes, you will watch over her, and I will check on you every hour. And if you don't...both of your blood will flow, just like a river..."

"I will not fail, Sire," Prince Joseph stated.

The king smirked at them. "Everybody eventually does. Guards, take them to their quarters."

The guards escorted Elisa and the prince back to the servant quarters. Prince Joseph sat propped against the wall, ceding the bed to Elisa.

"What happened?" Elisa asked. "How did you manage to stay awake?"

The prince swallowed. "I didn't. I fell asleep."

Elisa blinked. "But how are we still alive?"

"It was a miracle," Prince Joseph breathed. "The king's daughter prayed to the statue of St. Christopher in her bedroom, and when the king called, it answered for me."

"We should get out of here," Elisa pressed. "Let me grant your wish. King Peter will never give you any of his daughters, you know that. He's going to find an excuse to execute us, and keep giving you new tests until you fail."

"I know," Prince Joseph said. "But I think we need to stay. I think God wants us to stay."

"What?"

"I've never heard of the likes of this," Prince Joseph declared. "A prince gone insane, declaring himself a king, and murdering suitors? Locking a suitor in a room with his daughter for the night?"

Elisa's eyes widened. "The door was *locked*?"

Prince Joseph nodded. "I shudder to think of what would have happened if I had not been raised to be a pious man. I've experienced grief, and I know what it does – both of my brothers died as children, and I remember what it did to my family – but it doesn't do *this*. This 'Stag King' is a danger to everybody in this palace, including his own family. We need to get to the bottom of this, and then we need to get the word to Emperor Joseph and the College of Princes so that they can intervene, and we can't do that by leaving now."

"We can't do that locked in this room, either," Elisa said. "We need to be able to talk to people."

"There are two people just outside that door," the prince pointed out.

"They're guards. Would they really speak to us?"

"Only one way to find out," Prince Joseph declared. "Excuse me, kind sirs! Might you be willing to tell us why we're locked in this room?"

There was a moment of silence. Then, a key turned in the lock, and a young maiden with reddish-blonde hair who looked to be the same age as Prince Joseph stepped into the room.

"I think I would be able to tell you more than they would," the maiden said. "I'm Princess Henriette."

Elisa rose and curtseyed. "Your Royal Highness."

"Are you the princess I will be attending tonight?" Prince Joseph asked.

Princess Henriette shook her head. "That's my older sister, Juliana. I'm the youngest of us."

"So, what happened here, Your Royal Highness?" Elisa asked.

"I think my father was cursed," Princess Henriette replied. "The death of my brothers brought him to his knees, but he was still himself, and keen on finding good matches for us. He hoped that one would become his successor, and the principality at least would live on after his death. But, with the war, most of the eligible princes were on the battlefield, with little time for courting."

Prince Joseph nodded. "I only just came of age. If the war hadn't ended last year, I would have been expected to take command in the field as well."

"My father was always very selective," Princess Henriette said. "What few princes did come he considered to be unsuitable, either because they were not pious enough, or their lands were too poor, or their principalities

188

didn't have an army – he wanted his lands to be in good hands after he was gone. And then, a couple of years ago, my mother died of an illness."

"I'm sorry for your many losses," Prince Joseph said.

Princess Henriette nodded. "Thank you."

"So what happened after your mother's death?" Elisa asked.

Princess Henriette frowned. "He didn't react the way he should. Mother's health had never been very good, and her illness was nothing out of the ordinary. She was one of many in these lands who were lost to it. But, rather than mourn, he declared that the whole of mother's poor health had been the result of poisoning by the physician, and had him beheaded. That was the beginning of his 'collection'." She shuddered.

"I'm sorry, Your Royal Highness, but I have to ask," Prince Joseph said. "Is there any possibility that the accusation was true?"

Princess Henriette shook her head. "The physician had been hired from another principality in the last days of mother's illness after our family's physician died of the same illness that took her. There's no way he could have poisoned her.

"Father was never this way before my mother died. He should not have been this way after. He hasn't threatened or imprisoned us yet, but...but we all fear that it is only a matter of time."

"Was there anybody new in the court when your mother became ill?" Elisa asked.

Princess Henriette shook her head. "There are no new permanent members of my father's court. But that's not meaningful – there are always petitioners, or those who have some business with the principality...too many to count."

"So if there is a witch, it could be anyone," Prince Joseph said.

"Now I have a question for you, Your Royal Highness," Princess Henriette stated. She pointed at Elisa. "Who is she to you."

"She's a penitent I met on the way here," Prince Joseph said. "I had been travelling alone for some time, and I ached for somebody to talk to. I met her yesterday morning, and talked her ear off. Then I convinced her to stand as my attendant for appearances' sake. There is nothing else between us."

Princess Henriette turned to Elisa, her eyes hard. "And have you ever been to this principality before?"

"No, Your Royal Highness, I have not," Elisa replied.

"What is your penance?"

"I am to walk the land and help those in need, Your Royal Highness."

"And did you come to this principality with a purpose?"

Elisa paused. If word got to the other wish granter that she was here... "No purpose other than the fulfillment of my penance, Your Royal Highness."

Princess Henriette's eyes narrowed. "Had you heard of this principality or my father before coming here?"

"I had not, Your Royal Highness. I had spent a great deal of time in the Protestant lands, and I turned back to find my way to a place where I could confess my sins and hear Mass. This is just where the road took me."

Princess Henriette nodded, her eyes still hard and untrusting. "I see. I will bid you both farewell, and perhaps see you tomorrow."

She knocked on the door. The guards opened it, and Princess Henriette left. The door was closed and locked behind her.

Prince Joseph sighed. "Even if we do find the witch

and break the curse, the damage is already done. A number of princes have lost their children here. The Emperor and College of Princes will have no choice but to place the king under the Imperial Ban."

"So Her Royal Highness' family has already been destroyed?"

The prince nodded. "But that's not the baffling part."

"Oh?"

"There are at least a dozen boxes on that table in the king's 'collection'. Two are for us, and we know the first is a poor court physician. If the rest are princes, at least nine princes have died here. Why have none of them been reported missing?"

Elisa took a deep breath. "I think I need to pray."

"I think I need to join you."

They knelt and prayed, first for the souls of all those whose heads lay in boxes, then for answers, and then for deliverance.

After a while the guards delivered a meal. They ate in silence, and then had nothing to do but wait for the sun to go down and speculate about the nature of whatever curse had been placed on the king and his court. Finally, the guards came to collect Prince Joseph, leaving Elisa alone in the dark.

Reality shifted. Elisa frowned. Whoever the wish granter was, they were still here...and she was still locked in a room.

Elisa knelt and prayed, and then felt her way to the bed, falling into a restless sleep.

She awoke with the dawn, and used the chamber pot. Elisa stared at it for a moment – it was now almost overflowing. She went to open the window to empty it out, only to find it locked.

The door opened. "His Majesty has summoned you," a guard said.

"The chamber pot is full," Elisa said as she rose. "Could you please have it emptied?"

"His Majesty has provided instructions as to your chamber pot. You will have another. Now, please come with me."

Elisa swallowed and steeled herself. She followed the guard to the throne room, giving silent prayers to the Virgin Mary. Finally, she stood in front of the king in the throne room beside Prince Joseph.

"Are you okay?" the prince whispered.

Elisa nodded. "For now."

The king rose from his throne. "You have remarkable resilience! You must be exhausted. But I'm afraid I can't let you have my eldest daughter to wife – she is far too dear to me. However, tonight you will guard my youngest daughter, and I will check on you every hour. If you do not answer me, both of your heads will join my collection in the morning. If you succeed, I will consider letting you take my second daughter as a wife."

King Peter turned to Elisa. "Now, tell me, good penitent – how do you like your accommodations?"

"They are...serviceable, Your Majesty," Elisa replied. "It would be nice to have an oil lamp for the evening."

"I will consider your request," the king said. "I would advise you, however, that I take great pride in the windows of this palace. Should any harm come to any of them, I would add the culprit's head to my collection."

Elisa swallowed, her stomach churning. "I understand, Sire."

"Now back to your room with you," King Peter declared. "The princeling will be fetched when it's time for him to watch over my youngest daughter."

They were escorted back to their room. When the guard opened the door, they both wretched at the smell. The full chamber pot had not been taken away or emptied.

Instead, a second, empty chamber pot had been placed beside it.

After they had grown used to the stench, Prince Joseph said, "This really is getting to be a bit much."

"Was there another miracle?" Elisa asked.

The prince nodded. "She prayed to the St. Christopher statue in her room, and it answered for me."

Elisa took a deep breath. *So, whoever this wish granter is, they are protecting him.*

"Shall I grant your wish, and get us out of here?" Elisa said.

Prince Joseph shook his head. "We're not done here yet."

Elisa glared at him. "How are we not done? We know that there's a witch and a curse, and we've seen enough to bring back help, haven't we?"

"My word alone may not be enough for the College of Princes or the Emperor. I am going to be asking them to depose a prince of the *Reich* for the good of his own family and principality. And the King's representative will almost certainly say that I'm lying because I failed at courting. It needs to be more than just me."

"Then I'll come," Elisa declared.

"What good will that do?" the prince demanded. "Did you *see* me locked in a room with two princesses for the night? Did you *see* the king's physician falsely accused and executed?"

Elisa sighed. "No. I've spent most of my time in this room."

"We need to bring somebody with us who did see it all. And I know just who to ask."

Elisa blinked. "You mean Princess Henriette?"

Prince Joseph nodded. "She seems to be friendly to us, at the very least."

Elisa scowled. "Friendly to you, perhaps. She was staring daggers at me."

"You're an unmarried woman accompanying the prince who has come courting. For all she knows, I've taken you as a concubine."

Elisa leaned back on the bed. "I can see how she would think that, yes."

"I'll be watching over her tonight. I'll try to convince her to come with me to the College of Princes. And I'll convince her that you really are who you say you are."

Elisa chuckled. "Are you sure you're just sixteen years old?"

"Said by somebody who looks my age and talks like somebody's mother. Shall we pray?"

Elisa nodded and got to her knees. Once again, they prayed for the souls of those who had been murdered by the king, and then they prayed for success and deliverance. And then, all they had left to them was to wait in the tiny, stuffy room for a meagre meal and for the guard to fetch Prince Joseph once the sun went down.

After the prince was fetched, Elisa fell to her knees and prayed once more. As she did, reality shifted. Elisa took a deep breath. The other wish granter was still here, but finding out who it was seemed an impossibility. She shook her head, sighed, finished her prayers, and then returned to sleep.

She awoke with the dawn and used the chamber pot. Just after she had finished, the guard opened the door and said, "Come with us."

Elisa blinked. Usually it had taken more time before she was summoned. Had something gone wrong? Was she about to be taken to the headsman?

Elise rose and stepped out of the room. As she was escorted to the throne room, she mouthed silent prayer after silent prayer, begging forgiveness for her sins and that she would be allowed last rights and confession if she was to die. She came into the throne room to find herself standing alone before the king. She curtseyed.

"You're filthy," King Peter said.

"I fear I have not been permitted to bathe or wash my clothes, Your Majesty. I would do both if you would allow it to me."

The king smirked. "A penitent who wants to be clean."

Elisa took a deep breath. "If you're going to have me killed, I would also beg that your mercy would permit me a priest to confess my sins and allow me to hear one last Mass."

King Peter laughed. "I imagine you would! But none of the other princes got that, so why would I give it to you? And these boxes have stood empty for far longer than they should."

Elisa forced herself to remain standing and not collapse into a sobbing wreck.

Two guards entered, Prince Joseph between them. Elisa breathed a sigh of relief. He was still alive!

"My executioner is vexed," King Peter declared. "He expected to have two heads to add to my collection by now, and yet I have to keep denying him. And you, princeling, have passed a third night with one of my daughters. I congratulate you!"

Prince Peter bowed. "Thank you, Your Majesty."

"I'm not going to let you marry my second daughter, however," the king said. "You sleep so little, you would keep her up all night! How can I do that to one of my daughters?"

"I assure you, Sire, that I will sleep very well once I am married."

"Despite that, my youngest does seem to have taken a liking to you. So, I will give you another chance. I have a forest not far from here. We need the wood. So, the two of you can go cut it down. All of it."

Elisa and Prince Joseph exchanged quick glances.

"I'll give you until six o'clock tonight to finish," King Peter declared. "If you fail to finish, then my executioner will finally get his satisfaction, and these two new boxes will gain your heads. Never fear, though – I have provided tools. You'll find them when you get there."

"Very generous, Sire," Prince Joseph said.

"Take them away!" the king ordered. "Oh, and while you're out there, both of you should take a bath in the creek. The stench around you is quite...remarkable."

The guards took Elisa and Prince Joseph out of the palace and placed them onto a wagon. Then, the wagon was driven just over a hill to a large forest. One of the guards helped Elisa down from the cart.

"I'm sorry," he said. "We've been posted around all of the exits to the forest, and our orders are to kill you both if either of you try to escape."

"The king is insane, you know that," Elisa said.

"He's still the king," the guard said. "And before his madness, he was very good to my family. We'll come to collect you at six o'clock. Until then, we'll keep our distance and leave you in peace."

Elisa watched the guards depart over the hill. Then she heard Prince Joseph say, "You have got to be fucking joking."

Elisa turned to see the prince holding up an odd looking tool. Her eyes widened as she registered why it looked so strange.

It was an axe. An axe made out of glass. On the grass lay a wedge and mallet, also made of glass.

"Please tell me the princess agreed to come with us," Elisa said.

Prince Joseph shook his head. "She said she would consider it, and give me an answer later."

"If we try to use any of these tools," Elisa breathed, "the shards would slice us to ribbons."

"You said you can grant wishes," the prince said, staring at the forest. "Can you do anything about this?"

Elisa shook her head. "I can only grant the wish that is dearest to your heart, and that's still to escape. I can make the forest impenetrable so that we can hide in it long enough that they stop looking for us, but that's about it."

"What a choice!" Prince Joseph declared. "We can pray for a miracle, hope that Princess Henriette comes by and tells us she's coming with us, escape now without enough to ensure that the College of Princes and Emperor will act, or go back and get executed."

"Whatever we do, I'm going to the creek and bathing first," Elisa said. "You coming?"

"I may as well," Prince Joseph said. "I promise you that your virtue will be safe."

Elisa chuckled. "Honestly, I'm too tired and scared to care."

It took them about an hour to find the creek. They stripped down and bathed in it, and then washed their clothes, leaving them to dry in the grass. As they sat and rested, waiting, Prince Joseph said, "I think that if Princess Henriette hasn't agreed to come with us by the time the guards come to fetch us, you should grant my wish and we should escape. We'll take what we have to the College of Princes, and pray that is enough."

"I agree," Elisa said, checking the state of her undergarments. They were a bit damp, but wearable. Elisa put them on. The prince followed suit, and by the time midday approached they were both dressed.

"I wish we had been able to find whoever did this," Elisa said.

"Possibly for the best that we didn't," the prince stated. "If that's what she did to the king, imagine what she would do to us."

"You two are hard to find!" Elisa heard a voice call.

She turned to see Princess Henriette walking towards them through the trees, a large basket at hand. "I've brought you lunch."

Prince Joseph looked at Elisa and grinned. "We're starved!"

"Then it's a good thing I brought lots of food," Princess Henriette declared. She sat down on the grass and opened up the basket, parceling out bread and meat.

Elisa devoured what the princess handed to her without even saying grace. Then she closed her eyes and sighed.

"Have you considered what we talked about?" Prince Joseph asked.

"I'm considering it," Princess Henriette said. "I still have a couple of things to figure out."

"We have to escape today," Prince Joseph began. "This task is impossible, and the tools we were given would shatter as soon as we use them. If we return, your father will have both of us executed, probably as soon as we get there."

"I know," Princess Henriette said. "Still, you need to be patient."

Prince Joseph sighed. "Look, we can give you until the guards are about to pick us up, but after that—"

Reality shifted. The prince slumped against a tree, sound asleep.

Elisa's eyes widened. Hundreds of tiny men erupted from the earth all around her, carrying axes. A dozen of them toppled her and held her to the ground.

Princess Henriette knelt down beside Elisa, stroking a handkerchief. "Don't worry," she said. "I'm not going to put you to sleep too. I would have words with you..."

The princess smiled at her, her eyes predatory. "...*wish granter*."

Chapter IX – A Conspiracy of Wish Granters

Elisa struggled against the tiny men, but their grip may as well have been of iron. Princess Henriette stared at her. Around them, the tiny men began to chop at the trees.

"You lied to me when I talked to you before," Princess Henriette said. "I would recommend against it now."

Elisa swallowed. "How did you know?"

The princess shrugged. "Those walls in your 'quarters' are thinner than you think. It's amazing what you can overhear in the room beside it."

"And you're a wish granter too," Elisa said. "You performed the miracles with the St. Christopher statues."

Princess Henriette smiled and nodded. "Indeed I did."

"Why are you helping us?"

"I'm not helping *you*," the princess replied. "I'm helping *him*. Never fear, the forest will be chopped down by the time they come back. Prince Joseph will be safe for another day. You, on the other hand...I haven't decided what to do with *you* yet."

Elisa struggled again, and then collapsed back against the ground. "So why are you helping him?"

"Because every other prince only cared for his own life when he found out the truth about this place. Prince Joseph wants to save as many people as he can. I think that makes him a good candidate for marriage and to continue a family line, don't you?"

"I wouldn't know," Elisa gritted. "Romance isn't a thing I've been concerned about since I started my penance."

"Ah yes, your penance," the princess said. "But that's not why you're really here, is it?"

Elisa took a deep breath. "No."

"Why are you here?"

"I'm looking for you."

Princess Henriette cocked her head in surprise. "And what business do you have with me?"

"You're a wish granter."

"That's true. I came into these abilities about three years ago. They've kept me quite amused, at least when nobody else is around."

"Been to many festivals?" Elisa asked.

"I'm a princess of the *Reich*. Of course I have. I've been to many festivals all over the place."

"And how do you like pigeons?" Elisa snarled.

"I think they're lovely birds," Princess Henriette replied. "Feeding them is wonderfully relaxing. Watch your tone. How long have you been here?"

"I only arrived with Prince Joseph."

"Did you curse my father?"

"Of course I didn't!" Elisa spat. "I'm a good Christian! I would never grant a wish like that! Besides, I can't grant any of my own wishes anyway! If I could, I...I..."

The princess leaned forward. "You *what*?"

"I wouldn't need to be a penitent," Elisa said, a tear running down her cheek.

Princess Henriette sighed. "I guess you're not the one

I'm looking for after all. Why did you ask me about pigeons?"

"Because somebody granted a wish that made pigeons attack the step-family of a friend of mine after a festival," Elisa said. "They tore out their eyes."

The princess' eyes widened in shock. "And you think *I* did that?"

"You're not the one pinned to the ground who spent the last three days under threat of death," Elisa growled.

Princess Henriette sighed and waved her hand. The little men let go of Elisa. "You're right. I've only spent the last two years in fear. I'm sorry."

Elisa rubbed her wrists. "So you didn't blind my friend's step-family?"

"I'm a good Christian too," Princess Henriette said. "I wouldn't do that to anybody."

"But you're a wish granter," Elisa said.

"Yes," the princess said. "And I've spent the last two years trying to protect my sisters from my father's madness."

"So if you didn't do it, who put this curse on your father and blinded my friend's step-family?"

Princess Henriette sat down beside Elisa and buried her face in her hands. "I don't know. All I know is that there's this feeling when a wish is granted, and right before the illness that took my mother's life, I felt it."

Elisa nodded. "I'm familiar with that feeling. It's how I knew there was a wish granter here."

"Whoever it was must have caused the illness, driven my father mad, and made it so that nobody notices that princes of the Reich are disappearing."

"Have you felt that feeling since the wish was first granted?" Elisa asked.

Princess Henriette shook her head. "I thought maybe the person had gone away and would come back to see what had happened. That's why when I heard that you were a wish granter, I thought it might be you."

"I'm sorry for misjudging you, Your Royal Highness," Elisa said.

"Likewise."

"This needs to be stopped," Elisa said. "Can you make your father sane again?"

The princess shook her head. "I've tried, several times. It seems that you can't undo a wish that has been granted. You can just add things to it. I can keep the princes my father puts in my sisters' bedchambers from violating them, but I can't stop him from putting them in there."

Elisa leaned forward. "Then you need to escape with us. With your help, Prince Joseph can get the College of Princes to intervene, and–"

Princess Henriette raised her hand. "And what happens to my sisters once I'm gone? What prevents my father from declaring them to have helped me escape and putting their heads into those two empty boxes?"

Elisa stared at the ground. Around them, the little men continued to clear the forest.

"I'll come with you on two conditions. First, it's my sisters as well or none of us – I won't leave them unprotected. Second, I'm the one who gets to marry Prince Joseph."

"I think we can do the first one," Elisa said. "But, only Prince Joseph can decide the second one."

"You tell him what we've discussed," the princess said. "I'll start figuring out how to get my sisters out as well."

"Why can't you just use your ability to grant wishes?"

Princess Henriette sighed. "Because, truth be told, I'm not that powerful. I barely know how this works. I can do small things that I want to do, and only when it's close to me. Creating a bunch of helpers to chop down a forest I can do, and I'll be paying for this tonight. Getting three of us past a mad king and a bunch of guards and onto the open road without being intercepted? I don't even know where to begin."

"I may have a couple of ideas," Elisa said. "We could claim sanctuary in a church, and have them smuggle you out of the principality to the College of Princes."

Princess Henriette nodded. "Okay then. I'll keep you and the prince alive until we can all escape, and you get us to the church on time."

Elisa nodded back. "Deal."

"I don't know how you did it," King Peter declared, leaning forward on his throne. "I think God must like you, to be providing you miracles like that."

"It was a miracle, Your Majesty," Prince Joseph said. "The tools you provided cut each tree down with a single blow."

The king smirked. "And you think this entitles you to marry my youngest daughter?"

"I would not so presume, Sire," Prince Joseph stated.

King Peter frowned. "Something has changed. I know it. And I will discover it."

"All we have is the blessings of the Saviour and the Virgin Mary," Prince Joseph said.

"Well, we'll see just how much they like you," the king said. "I have a fish pond great in size, but of late it has become quite murky. I will give you tomorrow to remove all of the mud until it is as bright as a mirror and fill it with every kind of fish. And if you fail...well, my executioner has been growing bored these last few days."

With a wave of his arm, the king dismissed them. The guards escorted them back to their room. Elisa steeled herself for the stench as the guards opened the door.

There was none.

The room had been cleaned and aired out, the linens on the bed changed, and a single, empty chamber pot rested under it. Once the guard had locked them in, Prince Joseph began to laugh.

Elisa scowled. "What's so funny?"

"They were so convinced they'd be executing us that they cleaned out our room."

Elisa swallowed. "My bag..."

The prince sighed. "I'm sorry, but they probably disposed of it."

Elisa sat on the bed and began to weep.

"There was something precious to you in there," Prince Joseph said.

Elisa nodded and wiped the tears from her eyes. "It had my parents' spare clothes in it. It's the last thing I have of them now."

"We'll find a way to pay them back for this, I promise."

Elisa closed her eyes and leaned back against the wall. "Let's just worry about escaping. Have you thought about Princess Henriette's proposal?"

"I have," Prince Joseph replied. "I'll marry her."

Elisa opened her eyes. "You're already in love with her?"

The prince shook his head. "I've only just met her. But, she seems like somebody I could come to love in time, and that's good enough."

Elisa took a deep breath. "I will never understand how you can accept something like that. Where I come from, we marry for love, and we wait until we're ready to support ourselves and raise a family."

Prince Joseph sighed. "What a nice luxury to have – to marry somebody you love when you're good and ready! Now I wish I had been born a peasant! I don't have that kind of choice. For a prince, marriage is all about the dynasty. You marry as soon as you're able and can produce an heir. A wife's family and what they have to contribute to the marriage is at least as important as whether you can love her, and if you're very lucky you might have met her before the betrothal, and if you're even luckier you've spent enough time with her to fall in love. If you're supremely lucky, it's love at first sight, although I've never known anybody with that much luck."

Elisa allowed herself a smile. "I have. Their names were Eleonore and Karl."

"Well, they were blessed," Prince Joseph declared. "As for me, the reason I set out in the first place was so that I could find my own wife, instead of having one chosen for me."

"Do you think your family will accept that?"

Prince Joseph grinned. "They'll have to. I'm going to marry her before I get home, so they won't have a choice in the matter."

Elisa looked out the window. It was once again locked, and the sun was getting low in the sky. "We should do our evening prayers."

The prince nodded. They knelt and prayed for the souls of those who had been killed by the mad king, and the deliverance of the princess and themselves. Then, when they were finished, Elisa looked out the window again. The sun was setting.

"We should try to sleep," Prince Joseph said. "It's going to be an early morning. You take the bed, I'll take the floor."

Elisa's eyes widened. "Your Royal Highness! It wouldn't be right for a prince to give a peasant like me the only bed in a room!"

Prince Joseph chuckled. "We've been through enough together that you don't need to call me 'Your Royal Highness', and I insist on being the gentleman."

"But I'm a penitent!"

The prince shrugged. "So don't enjoy it."

Elisa lay back on the bed. "Why do people keep saying that to me?"

Prince Joseph shook his head and took the topmost blanket off the bed, rolling it into a makeshift pillow. Then he lay down on the hard floor. "Has it occurred to you that you can be both a penitent *and* something else? That you can try to live a life of your own alongside your penance?"

Elisa closed her eyes. "Not after my sin."

"How bad could it possibly be?"

Elisa swallowed. "Through my pride I accidentally destroyed the entire kingdom that was my home."

There was a moment of silence. Then Prince Joseph said, "Okay, that's pretty bad. But, my point stands. You can be more than just your penance."

Elisa didn't answer him. Instead, as the last of the daylight faded away, she fell into a restless slumber.

They awoke with the dawn, the guard coming for them only moments later. After using the chamber pot, they were taken out to a small lake.

Once again, the guards were apologetic. "I'm truly sorry about all of this," one of them said. "The tools are right over there. Guards are posted at all the places where you might escape, with orders to kill you if you try." He sighed. "We'll leave you in peace."

Prince Joseph shrugged as he watched the guards head away. "Well, they're loyal. That is a virtue, no matter how annoying it is right now."

Elisa walked over to the tools. A shovel and hoe lay on the grass, both made of glass.

The prince walked up to join her. "At least they're not wanting us to chop down trees with them."

Elisa stared out at the water. It was fetid and murky. "It's a good thing Princess Henriette is helping us," she muttered.

"I suppose we're safe to talk freely now," the prince said. "Nobody listening from the room beside us."

"I wish I knew what Her Royal Highness has in mind," Elisa said. "But, I'm pretty sure that if we can get to a church, we'll be safe. Getting us there is my job."

"*Our* job," Prince Joseph said. "They should have no objections to smuggling us out. My father has been a great friend to the Jesuits." He picked up the shovel.

Elisa blinked. "You can't seriously be thinking of trying to use that thing!"

"I'm just curious," the prince said. "It's not like I'm going to hit a tree with it."

He stuck it in the mud, and then applied a bit of pressure to dig. Then he let go and gingerly pulled it out again. "This would break if I try to shovel anything with it. How long ago do you think they made these things? I mean, surely this couldn't have been created overnight."

Elisa shrugged. "The king might have always planned this for anybody who got past the three nights with his daughters."

The prince grimaced. "And we were the first."

They sat and waited as the sun rose. Once it was high in the sky, Princess Henriette came out to meet them, a large basket in her hands.

"I told him everything," Elisa said. "He's on board."

Princess Henriette glanced at them both. "Then you agree to take my sisters with you and marry me?"

"I do, Your Royal Highness," the prince replied.

"Good," Princess Henriette sighed. "It's not easy for a youngest daughter to get a good match, as you are probably aware."

"I am very aware, Your Royal Highness," Prince Joseph said.

Reality shifted. Thousands of tiny men burst from the ground, carrying shovels, hoes, and buckets. They marched into the lake, submerging themselves completely, but then coming out of the water again, their buckets full.

The prince's eyes widened. "That's quite the thing to see, Your Royal Highness. What are they?"

"I haven't the foggiest idea," the princess replied. "I wished that the lake would be cleared and filled with fish in time, granted my wish, and they appeared."

Prince Joseph frowned, his eyes thoughtful. "It could use a bit of flair, though. You know, wave a magic wand, speak an incantation..."

Princess Henriette sighed, tied a knot in her handkerchief, and then held it out in front of her. "This is all you're getting."

The prince shrugged. "A man can dream."

"Shall we stop wasting time and discuss our plans?" Princess Henriette asked, putting the handkerchief away. "I have sent one of my ladies-in-waiting to the nearest church to let them know that we are coming and to have disguises ready. Tomorrow my father will give you a new challenge – I don't know what, but I'll make sure it gets finished. At the end of that challenge, I will ensure that my sisters and I are present when the guards come to fetch you. And that's all I can do."

Prince Joseph nodded. "Okay then – once we're all together, how do we get out?"

"I'll shape the granting of your wish so that we can all get away," Elisa said. "I'm still working out the details."

The princess blinked. "You can shape the way a wish is granted?"

Elisa nodded. "It takes a bit of practice, but if you concentrate enough, it's easily done."

"I'll need to work on that," Princess Henriette muttered.

"Can we bring their ladies in waiting?" the prince asked.

Elisa shook her head. "I'm sorry, but this is going to be difficult as it is with only five people. The ladies in waiting will have to take care of themselves."

"I don't like that," Princess Henriette said.

"The prince's wish is for his own escape," Elisa stated. "I'm already stretching it thin as it is to get all five of us out."

"Very well," the princess sighed.

Prince Joseph looked at the lake and the stream of little men walking in and out of it. "I wonder how they're going to do the fish."

Princess Henriette shrugged. "We'll just have to wait and see."

It took a couple of hours before the lake was clear. An hour before it, a stream of little men wandered off into the landscape, returning carrying fish over their heads and throwing them into the pond. The fish swam away.

"How did they keep them alive while they were out of the water?" the prince wondered.

"Damned if I know," Princess Henriette replied. "I don't know how any of this works."

"It just kind of...does," Elisa said.

The princess re-packed and picked up her basket. "I should go before the guards return. I'll see you tomorrow."

Prince Joseph smiled and bowed. "And I will marry you as soon as we get to the church."

Princess Henriette smiled back. "I'll look forward to it."

The guards returned, gaping at the crystal clear lake as soon as they saw it. Then they escorted Elisa and Prince Joseph back to the palace, where they were presented before the king.

"Once again, you have succeeded in the impossible!" King Peter declared, his eyes livid with anger. "I would know how you did it."

Prince Joseph bowed. "We prayed to our Saviour and the Holy Virgin Mary, Your Majesty. Our tools received their blessing. The shovel alone did the work of ten men."

The king's eyes narrowed. "And how did you bring all of those fish into the waters without leaving the area of my 'little pond'?"

"Once the water was clear, Sire, we prayed again for a miracle," the prince replied. "Our prayers were answered, and fish sprang from the shovel and hoe into the water."

King Peter leaned forward. "The Lord and his angels must favour you indeed. But I will not allow you to marry my youngest daughter, not yet. You must first put this favour you have with the Saviour and the Holy Virgin to the benefit of this kingdom. You saw the hill full of briars out of your window, no doubt – tomorrow you shall cut down all of the briars and build me a palace, complete with all of the fittings and furnishings befitting a royal palace."

Prince Joseph blinked. "I'm sorry, Sire, but a *palace*?"

"Yes, a palace!" the king snarled. "Other princes have built new and grander palaces, and I would have one too! And I will not drown myself in debt to do it like so many of those other pathetic fools. You will build it for me by six o'clock tomorrow evening...and if it isn't perfect, your heads will join my collection."

Prince Joseph bowed. "We will not fail you, sire."

They were escorted back to their room, the stench filling their nostrils. The chamber pot remained where they had left it, still full. A second chamber pot sat under the bed, waiting to be used.

"I guess this time they expected us to survive," Prince Joseph said. "I wonder what other surprises they have for us."

"I'm trying not to think about it," Elisa muttered.

They ate the meagre meal provided by the apologetic guards, and then they prayed and took to bed, Prince Joseph once again insisting that Elisa sleep on it. In the morning, the guards took them to the base of the hill and left them there.

Elisa stood in the tall grass and stared at the tools. An axe and gimlet, both made from glass, stared back at her. She sighed.

"This really is quite ridiculous, isn't it," Prince Joseph said, picking up the gimlet. "I don't think this will be drilling many holes."

"He wants an entire palace," Elisa muttered. "What's wrong with the one he has?"

"Oh, everybody's done it," Prince Joseph said. "Our palace is only a few decades old. My father told me that his father's Court Jew was against the expense, but we could not allow ourselves to fall behind. Appearances are important, after all, and a prince's court must live up to the Emperor's example. I just didn't realize that he hadn't already done it."

"Perhaps he didn't have the money," Elisa said. "Maybe all his wealth went towards the war."

The prince shrugged. "Well, I didn't see a Court Jew, so maybe he can no longer afford one. Or, maybe he was just a miser before he was insane."

Elisa hefted the glass axe. It was a different one from the axe in the forest. It also looked like it would shatter if she set it down on the grass too hard. She placed it back down on the grass.

"Well, we may as well relax," Prince Joseph said. "We're not getting anything about this done before Her Royal Highness arrives."

They waited, making idle conversation, until they saw Princess Henriette coming up the hill with her basket and something slung over her shoulder. Elisa's heart skipped a beat as the princess grew closer and she realized what it was.

"I wasn't able to save everything when they cleaned out your room," the princess said, handing Elisa's bag to her, "but I was able to save this."

Elisa hugged the bag to her chest. "Thank you. God bless you."

Princess Henriette smiled. "It was nothing. So, shall we begin?"

Prince Joseph gave her a hopeful look. Princess Henriette sighed and rolled her eyes. "Fine!" she declared. "But I'm only doing this because I'm going to be marrying you."

She pulled out the handkerchief with a knot and swung it at the ground. The moment the knot hit the grass, reality shifted. Tens of thousands of tiny men erupted from the earth, carrying tools and starting to hack away at the thorny briar.

Prince Joseph sighed. "I had really hoped you might say something like 'Earth-workers, come forth!'"

Princess Henriette glared at him. "I'm not married to you *yet*."

As the prince and princess sat on the ground and ate lunch, and the last of the briar fell to the little men, Elisa paced, figuring out how to best shape the wish. *Any mistake, and we all die.*

"Will you please stop pacing and sit down?" Princess Henriette said. "Eat your lunch – you're going to need it."

Elisa nodded and sat, taking some of the bread and meat for herself.

"Still figuring out your plan?" the princess asked.

Elisa swallowed the meat she had been chewing. "One or two last details."

"Well, I've received word from the church. They know we're coming and they're waiting for us. It's the Church of St. Lothar. I'll guide us there once we get away."

"And I'll marry you once we get there," Prince Joseph declared.

Princess Henriette started, delight in her eyes. "Really?"

"You're not the only one with difficult parents," the prince said. "Better to marry sooner rather than later."

Elisa looked up at the hill. A wooden framework was going up, stone walls following. "They really do work fast," she said.

Princess Henriette gave her a sad smile. "They do. It's a pity we'll never get to live in it."

"Maybe we can get the College of Princes to declare me the true heir after we're married," Prince Joseph said. "We can live in it then."

The princess took his hand and squeezed it. "I just hope they have some mercy for my father. He used to be such a good man."

They sat and watched as the palace went up. As the second floor was completed, the little men began moving furniture into it. The sun grew low in the sky as the little men put the finishing touches on it, laying down a cobblestone walkway and fountain before the main door. Then, they disappeared back into the earth.

Princess Henriette rose from the grass. "I suppose I should get back before the guards come...make certain my sisters are ready."

"Oh, do stay!" a familiar voice called. Elisa spun around to find the king and his guards coming up the hill, bayonets fixed and muskets levelled at them. Behind them was a cart with a block, a large axe, and a man in a black hood.

Prince Joseph rose. "Your Majesty, we have–"

"You've done *nothing*," King Peter declared. "The job was for *you* to do, not for tiny magical men. Did you think I wouldn't have you observed this time? Did you think I wouldn't figure out your conspiracy with my traitor of a daughter?"

Princess Henriette gasped. "Father, I–"

The king struck her in the face hard enough to knock her to the ground. "To think that after all I've done for you, this is how you repay me! There will be three heads added to my collection today, not two."

The guards drew closer. The headsman dismounted, setting down the block in the grass. Elisa took a deep breath, reaching out to Prince Joseph's wish and shaping it while whispering, "Get onto the cobblestones." The prince helped Princess Henriette up and pulled her back onto the cobblestone path.

"Where are my sisters?" Princess Henriette demanded, rubbing her face.

"Under confinement in their rooms," the king said. "I'll decide what to do with them when I get back." He turned to the guards. "Now seize them and execute them. Take my daughter's head last, so that she can see the consequences of her treachery."

Elisa pulled on the thread attached to the prince's wish. Reality shifted.

The guards stared at them in shock.

"Where did they go?" one guard demanded.

"What did you do?" Prince Joseph asked.

"They can't see or hear us," Elisa stated. "Start walking away. Keep on the path, don't disturb any grass – they might be able to see that."

They made their way down the path. As they did, a gunshot tore through the air, right where Elisa had been standing. The guard lowered his musket and began to reload.

"They must have disappeared," the guard said as he finished reloading.

"They did no such thing," King Peter declared at the

top of his lungs. "I can still *smell* them. Fetch the dogs. Run, little rabbits! My hunting dogs are coming for you!"

"We need to go back and get my sisters," Princess Henriette said. "If we don't–"

"They're bringing out dogs," Prince Joseph pointed out. "We need to get away and to the church."

"But, my sisters!" the princess cried. "If we don't go back he'll kill them! He'll put their heads in boxes! Please, you promised!"

Elisa grabbed her by the arms. "You can't save them," she stated. She reached out with her mind, grasping on to the thread of the princess' wish and shaping it. "But *I* can." She pulled on the thread. Reality shifted. "They'll meet us at the church. Now come on!"

"We need to cut across the grass here," Prince Joseph said.

Elisa stared at him. "They'll see it!"

"Those guns probably won't hit us at this range," the prince said. "We'll have to risk it if we want to get free of the dogs!"

"You'd better know what you're doing!" Princess Henriette cried. "Where are we going? The town is *that* way!"

"We're going to the forest we cut down two days ago," Prince Joseph replied, breaking into a run and pulling her with her. Elisa followed as fast as she could.

Princess Henriette's eyes widened. "Why? There's nowhere left to hide there! We chopped it all down!"

A bullet whizzed past Elisa's head. Others followed, smashing into the earth around them.

"Save your cartridges!" she heard the king shout. "Wait for the dogs!"

"To take a bath!" the prince declared. "I think it's this way!"

They came to a halt in a shallow valley, gasping for

breath. "I think it should be close," Prince Joseph wheezed.

"It's just over that hill," Princess Henriette said as she caught her breath. "What do you mean, 'take a bath'? Why would you want to bathe at a time like this?"

The prince grinned at her. "You've never been hunting, then, I take it?"

The princess shook her head.

The prince took a deep breath. "Let's just say that–"

Dogs howled.

"We don't have time," Prince Joseph said. "They'll be on horseback. Now *run*!"

The three of them crested the hill, the sound of barking dogs closing in behind them. A landscape of stumps lay before them, a wide creek running through the middle of it. Prince Joseph pulled the princess to the bank of the creek. "Now get in and roll around – get everything wet!"

"What – why?" Princess Henriette sputtered.

"It will get rid of our scent!" the prince declared, hopping in, lying in the water, and rolling around. Elisa followed him into the water, soaking herself and the bag she carried.

"You couldn't have said that before?" Princess Henriette demanded stepping into the water. "Shit, this is cold!"

"Quickly!" Prince Joseph called, making it to the other side and holding out his hand. Princess Henriette rolled in the water and then grabbed it, the prince pulling her to the other side. Elisa stepped out of the water, wringing as much as she could out of her dress.

"Now, let's get to the edge of this forest and to town," the prince said. "Their dogs will be useless now."

"Wring out your clothes too," Elisa suggested, starting to do so herself. "That way we're not leaving too much of a trail of wet ground behind us."

The prince and princess wrung out what clothes they could without getting undressed, and then began walking to the edge of the forest. Behind them, the dogs went silent.

Elisa looked back. A group of men on horseback stood at the other side of the creek, dogs milling about around them.

"They've lost our scent," Elisa breathed.

"We still have to get to the church," Princess Henriette declared. "And now we've got to go around the long way."

"You can lead us?" Prince Joseph asked.

The princess nodded.

They made their way down towards the town, the church spires rising above the horizon as they crested a small hill. The sun was setting by the time they made it into the maze of cobbled streets. Princess Henriette led them through the twists and turns until they rounded a corner, and then she stopped, pressing herself against the wall and in the shadows. Elisa turned the corner and did the same.

Two guards stood at the door to the church, muskets in hand and bayonets fixed.

"Are we still invisible to them?" the princess hissed.

"I'm sorry, I don't know," Elisa whispered.

Prince Joseph joined them and sighed. "Of course. And there are probably guards at the back door, too."

"Maybe we could go to another church?" Elisa asked. "I saw more than one spire, and—"

Prince Joseph shook his head. "The king knows we need sanctuary, and there's only one place we can get it. He'll have guards on all of the churches."

"Psst!" a new voice hissed.

Elisa blinked and turned. A priest had joined them in the shadow of the building, carrying a large sack.

"I take it you're the ones we're waiting for," the priest

217

whispered. "It is good to see you again, Your Royal Highness."

Princess Henriette nodded, her eyes teary. "It is good to see you too, Father Francis."

"I have something for all of you," Father Francis whispered, pulling clothes out of the sack. "Put these on. I regret the immodesty, but I'm going to have to ask you put some of your clothes back in so that the sack still has something in it. Otherwise, they might suspect something."

"This bag and everything in it is very precious to me," Elisa said, handing it over. "Would it do?"

The priest nodded. "It would, my child. Please get these clothes on now."

Elisa put on a nun's habit, pulling the wimple over her hair. She turned to see Princess Henriette doing the same. Prince Joseph drew the hood of his monk's habit up, putting his face into shadow.

"Now, follow me, and let me do the talking," Father Francis said. He led them out into the open, towards the guards. Elisa concentrated on keeping her breath steady, each step bringing them closer and closer to the guards' bayonets.

One of the guards held up his hand, stopping them. Elisa's heart skipped a beat.

"Who are they?" the guard demanded.

"They are the people I told you about," the priest replied. "My brothers and sisters from Cologne. They travelled a long way, and their feet are very tired."

"And your bag? It looks lighter."

"I provided them with some food," Father Francis said. "They did not need everything I brought however. May we now enter our church so that my monastic fellows may finally rest?"

"The one's we're looking for won't be dressed like monks," the second guard said to the first, then turned to Father Francis. "Go on, then."

It was only once they'd passed the threshold of the church that Elisa realized she had been holding her breath. She leaned against one of the pews, her arms and legs shaking.

"We request sanctuary," Prince Joseph said.

"And it is granted," Father Francis stated.

"Henriette, you made it!" a voice called. Henriette's two sisters rushed up and embraced her.

"We nearly didn't," Princess Henriette said, shuddering with sobs in their arms. "How did you two escape?"

"The guards at our doors turned against our father," Princess Juliana replied. "They disobeyed orders and brought us here. Then, they left. I don't know where they are now."

"Our ladies in waiting?" Princess Henriette asked.

Princess Juliana smiled. "Safe, and getting some rest...including yours."

"We'll put you up in the attached guest quarters," Father Francis said. "And we'll get you out in the morning." He turned to Prince Joseph. "I understand that you're going to Regensburg?"

Prince Joseph nodded. "The Emperor and College of Princes need to know what is happening here. I'll come back with help."

The priest nodded. "Good. We have been praying for something like this, ever since the prince...the king's madness began."

"I'm not going with them," Elisa said.

Princess Henriette turned to stare at her. "Why not? We wouldn't be here now if it wasn't for you. We need to repay you somehow."

Elisa gave her a sad smile. "I'm a penitent. I need to go on with my penance, helping people...without recognition or reward."

Princess Henriette and Prince Joseph exchanged glances. "Why do I have a bad feeling I know what you're about to ask?" the prince said.

Elisa nodded. "When you tell people about this, please leave me out of it. Make something up if you have to."

"Okay," Prince Joseph said. "We'll do that."

"But we won't ever forget you," Princess Henriette added. "And you can't stop us from keeping you in our prayers."

Elisa smiled. "I wouldn't dream of it."

"So where are you going to go?" the prince asked.

Elisa frowned. "I haven't decided yet. I think I want to pray on it for a couple of days."

"We'll you're welcome here as long as you wish to stay," Father Francis declared.

"Thank you father," Elisa said.

Princess Henriette clapped her hands together. "Now that we've got that sorted out, time for our wedding."

Her sisters stared at her. "What do you mean, 'wedding'?" Princess Juliana demanded.

As a happy chaos descended on the prince and princesses, Elisa made her way to a side chapel, knelt down, and began to pray.

Elisa awoke in a cold sweat from a dream of executioners, axes, and blocks. She took a deep breath, allowing reality to re-assert itself. She was in the guest quarters of the church. She had been here for three days. Prince Joseph, his new bride Princess Henriette, and the princess' sisters had left the morning after their wedding, disguised in monastic robes. The search for the fugitives had ended after the second day. And she had stayed behind, confessing her sins, hearing Mass, and thinking.

Then she realized that she couldn't move anything below her shoulders.

"You spoiled my fun," a voice said. Elisa turned her head to look at where it had come from. A beautiful woman with raven hair sat by her bed, staring at her. Elisa stared back. She had seen this person before, but where?

"I was hoping to get an even dozen princes beheaded," the woman said. "After all the work I put into it – creating an illness that would kill the princess and drive the prince mad, ensuring that no prince who disappeared here would ever be missed – you stopped me at nine! That was rather impolite of you."

"You're the other wish granter," Elisa breathed.

"That's one way of putting it," the raven-haired woman said. "I prefer 'Clever Gretel', myself."

"I've heard that name," Elisa said. "A tale my grandmother told me during my childhood...something about a woman who is the cook for some lord, and she tricks him out of his chickens and eats them for herself."

"Is that all that is told of my feats?" Gretel laughed. "You're missing the best part! I gained the power to make my own wishes come true, and I decided that my lord did not deserve his castle and riches...so it all burned down with him and his family inside. You should have heard them scream – they were louder than the fire!"

A chill went down Elisa's spine. She knew where she had seen this woman before. "You were at Prince Johann's festival...you talked to that gentleman who was there."

Gretel clapped her hands in glee. "Good memory, Elisa the Penitent. Oh, he told me all about you! If you only you knew everything that I did..."

"Why did you blind Ella's stepmother and stepsisters?" Elisa asked.

Gretel shrugged. "Because it pleased me to do it. They were so uppity and arrogant...they needed to be taken down a bit. So, I decided to see how they would do without their eyes. It was a wonderful sight, wasn't it?

Those poor women clawing at all those birds as they pecked and pecked away...delicious, I think."

Elisa swallowed. "What are you going to do to me?"

Gretel stroked Elisa's shoulder. "Well, first I'm going to assure you that you can scream all you like however much you like. Nobody will hear you, so please feel free to scream and scream and scream. And then, I'm going to ask you why you haven't done anything to free yourself. You're not as powerful as I am, but you were able to break through my curse...which means..."

Gretel clapped her hands in delight. "Which means it's not that you aren't breaking free – you *can't* break free! You can't grant any of your own wishes, can you? How delicious!"

Elisa gritted her teeth. "If you're going to kill me, please be quick about it."

Gretel laughed. "I'm not going to kill you! By all rights I should – I should pay you back for those three princes whose heads are now not going to be put in boxes – but it has been so long since I've had a worthy adversary. No, I think I like this game. I want to keep playing with you. So, I'll see you around, Elisa the Penitent. Expect me when you see me!"

Elisa struggled to rise, but her body was held down as though by invisible hands. Suddenly, they were gone, and Elisa leaped of bed. She looked around.

She was alone in the room.

Elisa took a deep breath. She now knew where she had to go.

She began to pack her bag.

Chapter X – Matters of Time

Elisa stopped in front of the palace doors and took a deep breath. They looked just as she had remembered them when she had parted ways with Ella. A bit more worn, perhaps.

She knocked on the door. It creaked open, a doorman getting her name and then ushering her inside. Elisa stepped into the ante-chamber, allowing herself a smile. It was good to be back.

A servant bowed and led her through the hallways to the dining hall. Something was different, though. It took Elisa a moment to put her finger on it – everything seemed...quieter.

The sound of footsteps snapped Elisa back to the present. A woman entered the room from the opposite door, staring at her. She looked to be in her sixties, similar in height to Elisa but a bit more rounded.

Elisa curtseyed. "Hello...Your Royal Highness? I'm

looking for a friend of mine, Princess Eleonore. She's about my size, but about five years older than me. You must be her...grandmother, I guess? It's a pleasure to meet you."

The woman's eyes glistened and she took a ragged breath. "You really don't recognize me, do you? Elisa, it's me – I'm Ella."

Elisa shook her head. "No, that can't be – Ella's only a few years older than me."

The woman gave her a sad smile. "When we met, you looked lost and were staring at a sawmill, wondering what it was. We went to get some beers – you paid for them – and I told you that my stepmother couldn't brew a decent beer to save her life."

"Not that it stopped her from trying," Elisa breathed. "Ella, it *is* you! How could this happen? Were you put under a spell of some sort?"

Ella approached and shook her head sadly. "No, but I think you might have been. You look just as I remember you. How can that be?"

Elisa stared at Ella. Her face was wrinkled, but still elegant, her hair a light grey. "I don't understand, Ella."

Ella embraced her. "Elisa, it's been *forty years*. This is the Year of Our Lord sixteen hundred and ninety-eight."

Elisa shook her head again. "That...that can't be! I wasn't gone that long!"

Ella stepped back and gave her a kind smile. "When you were wandering, did you attend any Christmas or Easter Masses?"

"I couldn't," Elisa replied. "I spent most of my time in the Protestant lands."

"What about something else that marks time – harvests. Did you help out in any harvests?"

Elisa nodded. "Every time I was in a village that was collecting the harvest, I helped out."

"And how many of those were there?"

Elisa opened her mouth to answer and then stopped. The memories of dozens of harvests in dozens of different villages flooded her mind. "A lot," she admitted.

Ella sighed. "I think you lost track of time, my friend." She took a step back. "You look like you've been through hell."

Elisa allowed herself a thin smile. "I guess I have."

"Well, you'll need to tell me all about it. I want to hear *everything*."

"He wanted an entire palace?" Ella laughed, pounding her hand on the table. "In a day? He really was mad!"

Elisa nodded. "And if Princess Henriette hadn't summoned those tiny men, we might not have even had a chance to escape. As it was, even with two wish granters working at it, we nearly didn't."

"That sounded like quite the chase," Ella said, sipping from her cup. Elisa stared down at hers, looking at the steaming brown liquid inside.

Ella chuckled. "It's called 'chocolate'. Trust me, you'll like it. And if it's too bitter, you can just add some honey to sweeten it."

"I've heard of it," Elisa said. "I just never thought I'd get to taste it."

Ella grinned. "But you're *not* tasting it."

"It's a luxury," Elisa stated. "And I'm still a penitent."

"You've been a penitent for *forty years*, Elisa. You can allow yourself this."

Elisa sighed. "I suppose I can just confess it as a sin later." She sipped the chocolate, and then frowned. "I think it needs that honey."

Ella passed a honey pot over. Elisa poured some honey into her cup, and then sipped again. "That's better. I can see why you like it."

"If I were them, I'd worry about the workmanship," Ella declared. "Our new palace took months upon months to build. Theirs might fall down if they sneeze inside it."

Elisa blinked. "You have a new palace?"

Ella nodded. "A couple of years after Karl and I got married, somebody discovered a rich vein of iron running through our entire principality. We're wealthy now. We've even got a Court Jew!"

"And how is Prince Karl?" Elisa asked.

Ella frowned. "He passed away a couple of years ago."

"I'm sorry."

"It's okay," Ella said. "We had almost forty good years together. We had five children, three of which survived. Our son Wilhelm is now the prince. But, once he inherited, I decided to come back and live here. Too many fond memories. Besides, Wilhelm and Louise don't need my help to run the principality."

Elisa smiled and nodded. "They wouldn't. Best to just step back and get out of their way. What about Jakob and Anna – are they still...around?"

"Anna is living off a royal pension in the village," Ella replied. "Being related to a princess has its benefits. Jakob passed about five years ago. Their son came back to run the inn."

"And your father?"

"I'm afraid he passed three years ago."

Elisa nodded, then took a deep breath. "I found the person who blinded your step-family."

Ella leaned forward. "Who was it?"

"She calls herself 'Clever Gretel'," Elisa replied. "She's a wish granter, but she can grant her own wishes."

"I think I've heard of her," Ella said. "There was this story that my mother used to tell me when I was little..."

Elisa nodded. "It's the same person. And she's...well, she's evil. No other way to put it. She blinded your stepmother and stepsisters for entertainment. She was the one who drove Prince Peter mad."

Ella sighed. "She needs to be stopped, then."

Elisa stared at her chocolate, and took another sip. "I'm open to suggestions."

"I wish I had some," Ella said. "Not much you can do against somebody who can grant their own wishes. Turn her over to the church as a witch, and she'll just wish her way to freedom."

"And I can't grant idle wishes," Elisa added. "Only the wish that is dearest to somebody's heart. I've learned how to shape how I grant them, but that only goes so far."

"So, you'd need to find somebody who knows who she is, and hates her enough that their dearest wish to see her dead," Ella stated. "That's not a lot to work with."

"Perhaps there's somebody out there," Elisa said, "and I just need to find them."

Ella shrugged. "Well, we've got time to figure it out. Anyway, it's a good thing you arrived today – I've got a new granddaughter!"

Elisa smiled. "Congratulations!"

Ella grinned. "Thank you! Wilhelm and Louise are holding a celebration in a couple of days, and you should come with me to it. I want you to share in my happiness."

Elisa held up her hand. "I really shouldn't. I'm still a penitent, and I've got a lot more to do before I've finished my penance."

Ella reached across the table and took hold of Elisa's hand. "I insist."

Elisa sighed and smiled. "I suppose it would be nice to spend some more time with you. Forty years is a lot to catch up on."

"It is indeed," Ella said. "And hopefully we can come up with some ideas for dealing with this 'Clever Gretel' while you're here."

Elisa nodded. "I'd like that very much."

"And I think you'll love my granddaughter," Ella said. "I was visiting when she was born. Wilhelm and Louise gave her the most remarkable name."

"Oh?"

Ella leaned back in her chair, a twinkle in her eye. "Briar Rose."

As the carriage made its way towards the new palace, Elisa stared out the window, trying to feel comfortable in the fancy dress that Ella had loaned her and thinking about souls.

If forty years had passed, then at least some of the Protestants Elisa had helped would have died by now. Others would be close. And their souls would now be in Hell.

Elisa frowned. In her travels she had seen good people and bad people, but very few had deserved to spend eternity in torment. Somehow, it seemed a terrible injustice to punish heretics with damnation just because they had become misguided. Shouldn't God be more merciful and forgiving than that?

"You look troubled," Ella said.

Elisa turned to look at her. "I'm just thinking about souls. Did you ever find your way back to the True Faith?"

Ella gave her a kind smile. "I've always been a member of the True Faith. You're the one whose church strayed from it."

"But what if you're wrong?" Elisa pressed. "Karl shouldn't be in Hell just because he was misled, and you shouldn't go there either. Or Jakob. Or Anna. Or your father. I just...I can't bear to think of any of you in eternal torment."

Ella sighed. "God is merciful, and God is just. Let's

say for a moment that you're right and I'm the one who's wrong – would it truly be merciful and just to damn me when I have been the best Christian I knew how to be?"

"But if you're practicing your faith wrong, then you aren't being a Christian."

Ella leaned forward. "You've spent years in the Protestant lands, Elisa. Tell me, are we Christians or heathens?"

Elisa sighed. "I...I just don't know anymore."

"Look," Ella said, "I'll pray for God to have mercy on your soul, and I know you'll pray for mine. If God is truly merciful, then neither of us will have anything to fear."

Elisa shrugged. "I guess that's the best we can hope for."

Something caught her eye out of the window. A preacher stood by the road, shouting something at the carriage. Elisa opened the carriage window to hear what he was saying.

"Oh, don't do that," Ella said. "They're so tiring."

"The Seven Seals will be broken!" the preacher declared. "Turn to the word of the Gospel, for only that shall save you when Leviathan emerges! Israel will be restored to the Jews, and they shall convert to the Word of Christ! The dead shall rise, and all souls will be judged! Turn to the Gospel, lest you be damned to eternal torment!"

Elisa closed the window. "What's that all about?"

"They think that the Year of Our Lord Seventeen Hundred will bring about the end of days," Ella replied. "They think that's the Millennium referred to in Revelations. *I* think they don't know how to count. And, anybody who thinks that the Turks are ever going to give the holy land back to the Jews is delusional."

"It does seem unlikely," Elisa said.

They fell back into silence. Finally, the carriage pulled

up to the front steps of a grand palace, the limestone cladding so white it almost shone. An attendant helped Ella and Elisa out of the carriage, and then led them to the great hall. A small gathering looked up at them as they entered.

"The Dowager Princess Eleonore and Lady Elisabeth Beichtkind," a herald announced. Elisa blushed and curtseyed. "Sorry, I'm not actually a noble lady," she said.

"No," a man in fine clothes stated, stepping forward. "You're just the one who made our family possible. Amazing – you don't look any older than eighteen."

Elisa glanced at Ella in alarm. Ella held up her hand and said, "Don't worry, they know."

"I thought I asked you to keep my involvement secret!" Elisa hissed.

"The truth is only known within the family, and everybody who is told it is sworn to secrecy," Ella said. "As far as the rest of the world knows, it was my mother's spirit who performed the miracle that got me to that festival. This is my son, Prince Wilhelm."

Prince Wilhelm bowed. "It is my great honour to make your acquaintance. There are times I doubted that the stories were true."

"Truth be told, I'd prefer if you thought that they weren't," Elisa said. "I am a penitent. I'm not supposed to be receiving credit for any of my good deeds."

"Within the family, that would be too much to ask," the prince said. "My wife is with our daughter, getting her ready to be presented. This is my court, and this is Malachai, our Court Jew." A man with a long bushy beard wearing a yellow circle on his cloak bowed to her. "He takes care of most of the financial functions of the principality, as well as liaising with the merchant guilds of other principalities and cities. We would not be able to sell our iron without him. We are very pleased to have him."

"It is my pleasure to serve, Your Royal Highness," Malachai said. Elisa focused on him for a moment, his wish for his family in eastern Poland to be safe from pogroms becoming clear. She took pity on him and granted it. Reality shifted.

"Her Royal Highness Princess Louise, and Her Royal Highness Princess Briar Rose," the herald announced. Elisa looked up to see an attractive young woman in her mid twenties, followed by a bevy of ladies-in-waiting, descend the stairs, holding a baby girl.

Elisa smiled. The baby was a beauty.

The procession moved across the room to stand beside Prince Wilhelm. He raised his hand. "Family and dearest friends, I present to you my first daughter, Briar Rose. I am certain that she will grow up to be as beautiful as her namesake."

The room filled with applause and congratulations. Elisa joined the press of people to get a closer look at the tiny princess. She looked around with inquisitive eyes, taking everything in.

"Um, I must announce a late arrival," the herald called out. "Lady Gretel."

A chill went down Elisa's spine. She turned to see Clever Gretel descend the stairs, a broad smile on her face. "I apologize for my tardiness," Gretel declared. "I would have been on time, but somehow my invitation got lost!"

Ella sidled next to Elisa. "Is that..."

Elisa nodded. "That's her."

"And to think, I was here forty years ago when all of this began," Gretel said, crossing the room to look at the baby. "Think of all of the problems that stepmother and those step-sisters would have caused if I hadn't summoned those birds." She turned to face Elisa. "And Elisa the Penitent! So good to see you again – shall we play the next round in our game?"

Elisa shook her head. "Please, not here. Not with them – anybody but them!"

Gretel grinned. "But I *want* to play with them."

Behind her, Elisa heard Prince Wilhelm ask, "Who's she?"

"She's like Elisa," Ella replied. "A wish granter."

"Summon the guards," Prince Wilhelm ordered.

"There's no point," Gretel said. "They're all asleep." She gave the baby an adoring look. "She will be a beauty. But just growing up to be a beauty seems boring, doesn't it? Let's make it more exciting."

Elisa fell onto her knees. "Gretel, please, I'm begging you – don't do this! We can play this game somewhere else, anywhere else!"

"I think that it would be more exciting if..." Gretel looked at everybody and grinned. "...if in her fifteenth year, she pricked her finger on a spindle and died!"

Reality shifted. Elisa pushed down the urge to scream.

"What just happened?" Princess Louise asked.

Elisa rose to her feet. "She just granted that as a wish. Sometime when she's fifteen years old, Her Royal Highness Briar Rose will prick her finger on a spindle and die." She glanced at Princess Louise, reading her wish as she stared at Gretel in horror. "Except that she won't die – she'll fall asleep instead. She'll wake up nice and rested."

Elisa pulled on the thread attached to Princess Louise's wish. Reality shifted.

Gretel clapped her hands in delight. "Nice! You're getting good at this, Elisa the Penitent! You've modified my wish!" She gazed and Elisa and smirked. "But now it's my turn. She won't just fall asleep...she'll fall asleep for a hundred years. Along with the entire palace." Reality shifted. "Your turn."

A servant dashed into the room, nearly slipping on the

232

polished floor. "Your Royal Highness, the guards – they're all asleep! Nothing I do can wake them up!"

"Thank you, we're aware," Prince Wilhelm said through gritted teeth.

Elisa glanced at the prince and read his wish. It would do.

"She'll sleep for a hundred years, or until somebody wakes her up before a hundred years have passed," Elisa declared. "And that will *not* be difficult to do." She pulled on the thread attached to Prince Wilhelm's wish. Reality shifted.

"You are getting good at this," Gretel laughed. "It's so nice to have a worthy opponent. But, my turn again! In order to wake Princess Briar Rose up, her rescuer will have to...make his way through an impenetrable briar. That's suitable – fight your way through a briar of rosebushes to rescue a princess named Briar Rose." Reality shifted. Gretel smirked. "I wonder what state the princess and her family will be after a hundred years. I imagine they'll be quite wrinkled."

Elisa glanced at Ella, reading her emerging wish. It would work. She granted it. Reality shifted.

"They'll be preserved throughout their long sleep," Elisa declared. "They will wake up with the same youth and vigour they had when they went to sleep."

Ella breathed a sigh of relief.

Gretel smiled. "I think we're done. I win this round, Elisa the Penitent."

Elisa blinked. "What?"

Gretel stepped forward to look Elisa in the eye, her gaze triumphant. "Consider what you've just helped me do. Without you, they would have lost a daughter – but they can always have more. Now, they're going to lose *everything* else. They will live in fear of spindles for the next fifteen years. And then, they will all fall asleep and disappear from the world. This principality will return to the *Reich*. They will wake up in a changed land with nothing more than their lives and their palace. Good game – I look forward to round three!"

Gretel spun on her heels and sauntered out of the room. Elisa staggered to the wall and leaned against it, taking a ragged breath.

Ella joined her at the wall. "Are you okay?"

Elisa nodded. "Just tired – and so very sorry. I think she won, and I failed you."

"No, you didn't," Ella said.

"She's right though – I just ended this principality."

Ella took a deep breath. "You haven't lost children, but I've lost two. If somebody walked up to me and said that I could have my son and daughter back but only if I gave up all of this, I would accept the offer in a heartbeat."

Elisa glanced at her. "I'm sorry – I can't do that...not with the wish that is dearest to your heart right now."

"I know," Ella said. "I'm old enough that I just want my family to be healthy and to see my grandchildren happy at play. What you've lost in the past is no substitute for what you have in the present. But, there's something...*wrong*...about burying a small child, and you've just spared them that with Briar Rose."

"We have fifteen years to prepare," Prince Wilhelm added. "And one of the best Court Jews in the *Reich*. We'll make sure that the College of Princes knows about the curse that's been put on our family, and that assets are set aside for us."

Elisa looked to Prince Wilhelm. "When you tell people about what happened here, can you keep me out of it?"

"I don't know that it's going to be possible," Prince Wilhelm replied. "At least, not with the arrangements that we have to make. I'm sorry. But we will keep your name out of it."

"You'll just be a good 'wise woman'," Princess Louise said. "Hopefully that will be enough." She turned to her husband. "Perhaps we could get rid of all the spindles. Briar Rose can't prick herself on a spindle that isn't there."

"With the greatest respect, Your Royal Highness," Malachai said, "this principality has a burgeoning cloth industry with great potential for development. To remove all the spindles would be to strangle it in its crib."

"We'll consider the idea," the prince said. He turned back to Elisa. "If you need anything in the next fifteen years, our family will help."

Elisa gave him a kind smile. "I have money. But, what I could use right now is a place to change back into my normal clothes. I need to find Clever Gretel, and figure out some way to stop her."

"I'll take you to a private apartment," Ella said. "We can talk and you can change there."

Ella led Elisa down the halls to a large apartment, every surface decorated. Ella closed the door behind her.

"These are my quarters," Ella said. "We can talk freely. I had the coachman bring your bag here when we arrived. It's in the corner there."

Elisa nodded and started to strip off the fancy dress. "Any ideas about dealing with Gretel?"

"Now that I've seen her in action, none at all, I'm afraid," Ella said, sitting on an ornate chair. "How do you even approach somebody like that?"

"She has to have a weakness," Elisa declared, pulling her dress out of her bag and putting it on. "Maybe after another couple of rounds in our 'game' I'll figure out what it is."

Ella frowned. "That's assuming she doesn't just decide to kill you."

"I don't think she wants to do that. At least, not yet.

She wants an adversary, somebody she can best. I've got a bit of time before she gets bored of that, I think."

"You...just be careful out there," Ella said. "And there's something else."

Elisa finished putting on her red headband. "Oh?"

"Your penance...how much longer will that go on?"

Elisa shrugged. "I hadn't really thought about it."

"You should," Ella said. "You've been doing this for forty years now. Isn't that long enough?"

Elisa shook her head. "My pride ended the worldly lives of thousands upon thousands of people, most of whom died without confessing their sins or being shriven. How many of them will spend extra decades in Purgatory, or even worse, went directly to Hell when they might have been saved, because of me?"

"I don't know."

"A penance of forty years seems hardly enough time to earn absolution for that," Elisa said.

"Even so," Ella declared, "you can't let this penance consume you. You are a good person, and God is merciful. You deserve to live a happy life too."

Elisa gave her a kind smile. "When I'm done my penance."

Ella sighed. "Just promise me this – when your penance is done, you will find somebody or something that will make you happy, and live a good life."

Elisa shouldered her bag. "I promise. And, I won't stay away as long this time. I'll come back to visit, and let you know how things are going with Clever Gretel."

Ella embraced her. "Elisa, I don't think you will. I think you're going to lose track of time again, and this is our final goodbye. And I'm okay with that."

As Ella let go and stepped back, Elisa wiped a tear from her eye and said, "I'm *not* okay with it."

"But I think it's going to happen anyway," Ella said.

"And you need to concentrate on finding and stopping Clever Gretel, not making your way back to me. Just know that I lived a wonderful and happy life because of *you*. You will always be in my thoughts and prayers, and I will pray for you once I'm in Heaven."

"And I'll pray for you to get there," Elisa said, wiping away another tear.

"And now you need to go, my friend," Ella said. "And I need to spend a bunch of time with my children and grandchildren."

Ella escorted Elisa to the main door of the palace. "Goodbye, Elisa," she said. "Be safe, and remember to live a happy life of your own too."

"Goodbye, Ella," Elisa said. "I'll..." She stared at the ground. "I'll try to visit, one last time."

Elisa steeled herself and walked down the stairs. She made to the bottom before allowing herself to look back. Ella watched her, a kind smile on her face. She waved.

Elisa waved back, turned, and set out on her hunt for Clever Gretel.

Chapter XI – A Drink with the Devil

Some days Elisa wanted to scream in frustration.

The hunt for Clever Gretel had gone nowhere. She had searched every village she could find, granting wishes while asking if anybody had heard of Gretel, or seen any miracles or curses. The answer had always been "no."

Well, almost always. One village leader had pointed her to a witch living a few hours away in the forest. She had followed the path to find a kindly old lady living off of a pension whose husband had been a hunter for the prince. Her wish had been that the roof leaked less often. Elisa had granted it on the way out after the old lady had stuffed her with home-baked pastries and coffee.

The seasons changed, and changed, and Elisa kept looking. In one village, she had spent a week meeting everybody and checking their wishes, and then granted most of them all at once, hoping that it would attract Gretel's attention. The only thing it accomplished was leaving Elisa exhausted and sleeping it off in the inn, with the innkeeper worrying that she had come down with some sort of illness.

Every now and then, Elisa thought of turning back and going to visit Ella. She soldiered on instead. It was on a warm spring morning that she heard a familiar voice for the first time in what had seemed an eternity.

She grinned. She knew that voice well – it was the gentleman from Ella's festival! She found herself breaking into a run towards it. She broke into a clearing where the gentleman was talking to three young men in ragged clothes. And then she stopped short.

"I assure you, I'm not interested in your souls," the gentleman said. "I have no claim on them, nor will I ever. My interest is in another's soul, and his soul is half mine already."

Elisa took a ragged breath and made the sign of the cross. The gentleman was richly dressed, but his legs were covered in shaggy hair and ended in hoofs. Two long horns sprouted from his head. Her eyes widened in fear.

"He's the Devil!" she breathed.

"So what do you want us to do?" one of the men asked.

"Simple," the Devil said. "I want you to answer every question in this way." He pointed at the first man. "You are to say 'All three of us'." He pointed at the second. "You are to say 'For money'." He pointed at the third. "And you are to say 'And quite right too!' – and you are to continue saying this, in that order until you are told you can answer different. I promise that your lives and souls will be protected, and once you have helped me you shall never want for gold or work – you can even buy some titles and become great lords of the *Reich*."

The three men looked at each other. "We can do this," the first man said. The others nodded.

Elisa opened her mouth to speak, but nothing came out. She crossed herself again and again, praying silently that the Devil would leave them alone and go away. Instead, he handed the first man a large and full purse and said, "Now take this money and be on your way. There is a very good inn just down that road. I highly recommend the roast mutton. Oh, and if you happen to answer in any other way than I have instructed, all of your gold and riches will disappear, and you'll spend the rest of your lives as paupers. Now, away with you!"

The three men looked at each other, and then ran down the road. The Devil turned to look at Elisa and declared, "Elisa the Penitent! So good to see you again after all this time! We should go and have some beers!"

Elisa shook her head and backed away, making the sign of the cross. The Devil blinked and then slapped his forehead. "Oh, it's the horns and the hoofs – how absent-minded of me! Let me just get rid of those for you."

As Elisa watched, the horns retracted into his head. The hoofs became high leather boots.

"I'm terribly sorry about that," the Devil said. "About twelve hundred years ago some monks just outside of Athens decided that I looked like a satyr – that's a sort of goat person – and the idea got around. Now, if I don't have the hoofs and horns while I'm about my business, nobody believes that I am who I say I am. Quite annoying, really, but not a lot I can do about it."

Elisa crossed herself. "You're the Devil!"

"I have a name, you know," the Devil said. "It's Lucifer."

"I've been consorting with the Devil!"

The Devil shook his head. "No. You've had some pleasant conversations with me. Consorting with me is an entirely different thing, and not one you would ever do, at least not with me."

"You're after my soul!"

"No. You've been a penitent for decades. I have no claim on your soul, and I never will...not that I would ever seek one."

Elisa shook her head and crossed herself again. "Why wouldn't you?"

"Because you're my friend," the Devil said. "And I have far too few of those. The thought of you bound for an eternity of torment in Hell is not one I would countenance."

"You're lying!"

"You're not a person I would lie to."

Elisa shook her head and crossed herself.

The Devil sighed. "Fine. I swear on the true name of God, of which I am very familiar and you will have never heard, that I mean you no harm and that I will never, ever, lie to you." He glanced up at the sky. "I just attracted His attention with that. Perhaps that gives you an idea of just how much your trust means to me."

Elisa swallowed.

"Look, there's a lovely tavern in a village just south of here. They serve their chicken with the most wonderful sauce. Let's sit down, have some lunch and some beers, and I'll tell you whatever you want to know."

Despite herself, Elisa found herself nodding and saying, "Okay. Just this once."

As Elisa sat across from the Devil and stared at him, he took a drink from his stein, smiling. "They do make a great lager here. Don't worry – I have clouded their minds so that they will not consider anything we say to be important. We can speak about whatever we want."

"Have you ever done that to me?" Elisa demanded. "Clouded my mind?"

The Devil nodded. "Oh yes. But just to make you think my name unimportant enough to never ask for it. You wouldn't believe how hard it is to find a good conversation with a friend these days, and I hardly wanted you running away after our first meeting."

"Why do you say that I'm a friend?"

"Because you are one."

"I imagine with your wealth and power, you could have any number of friends you want," Elisa pointed out.

The Devil shook his head. "None of them could ever understand what you and I do."

"And what is that?"

"What it is to have an endless life," the Devil replied. "What do they know of stopping to watch the seasons pass, and losing years or decades without noticing? What do they know of coming to visit a friend who was young a moment ago only to discover they are now old and frail?"

"Losing track of time," Elisa muttered.

"Everybody like us does it. It's unavoidable. There was a woman once – a good Christian who befriended me even though she knew who and what I was. I think she was trying to save me from my own damnation, as odd as that sounds. First told people she was my sister, and then my mother, and then my grandmother, all in the blink of an eye before she was gone beyond my reach forever. Just like your friend Eleonore."

Elisa swallowed. "She's gone?"

The Devil nodded. "A few years ago."

Elisa stared at the table. "I'm sorry Ella," she muttered. "I lost track of time again, just as you said I would."

"If it's any consolation, she's not in my care," the Devil said. "Neither are your parents, or any of the people you've helped during your penance."

"That's a comfort," Elisa breathed. "What year is it now, anyway?"

"Seventeen hundred and thirty-one, I believe," the Devil said.

"And what did you want with those three men?"

"What, the apprentices? They're a diversion to help pass the time."

Elisa took a drink from her stein. The lager was indeed good.

"Some of us just watch the seasons pass, but that's boring," the Devil said. "I prefer to play games with damned souls. This is a short one, only a few days of entertainment – those apprentices will come in contact with a certain person, and he will commit a certain crime in their presence. The answers they give will falsely incriminate them for that crime. This will, in turn, put the soul I am after in a position where he becomes overconfident and exposes himself, at which point he will be executed in their stead. They will be exonerated, and live long, happy, and wealthy Christian lives, just as I promised."

Elisa allowed herself a smile. "And you're not giving me any details in case I try to warn them."

The Devil smiled back. "Of course. You have your penance, and I have my games. Some last years, and some even last decades, but they're all I have to entertain myself through eternity."

"And that's long and boring," Elisa said.

The Devil nodded. "You have no idea. Let me put it this way – imagine for a moment that you've got a mountain made of diamond that is two and a half miles high, wide, and deep."

"Where's this mountain?" Elisa asked.

"I don't know. Lower Pomerania, the Himalayas, it doesn't matter – it's not a real mountain. Now, every hundred years, this little bird comes, and sharpens its beak on the mountain."

"What kind of bird?"

"Whatever kind of bird you like. It's not a real bird."

"Is it the same bird every time?"

The Devil shrugged. "If you want."

"Why does it need to sharpen its beak?"

"Now you're just being difficult," the Devil said.

Elisa shrugged. "I'm having a drink with the Devil and I need to protect my soul from damnation. I'm allowed to be difficult."

"If you really feel that way, fair enough. The bird has an obsession with sharpening its beak on mountains. It works its way around the world, sharpening its beak on every mountain in turn."

"Now you're being silly."

"Says the difficult penitent," the Devil said. "So, once the mountain has been worn away to nothingness, then the first second of eternity will be over."

"Poetic," Elisa stated.

The Devil smiled. "I'm quite pleased with it. Can't take credit for it, though – I got it from a shepherd boy."

"Frankly, I think I'm mostly impressed by the bird."

"You're the one who decided it had to be the same bird," the Devil said.

Elisa sighed and stared at her beer. Perhaps she had been a bit too difficult...with the Devil. The idea seemed both true and morally wrong in her head. "So what happens if I ask you for help?"

"I'll provide it as best I can," the Devil said.

"And the price?"

"None," the Devil said. "You're my friend. A pleasant conversation is reward enough, even if you do seem to have a strange obsession with birds."

Elisa chuckled. The server brought their food. Elisa

frowned as she saw the vegetable on the plate. It was an odd white vegetable that had been sliced up and fried.

"Excuse me," Elisa said to the server as she put the Devil's plate down on the table, and pointed at the odd fried vegetable. "What is this?"

"It's called a 'potato'," the server said. "It's a food from the New World. The owner thought it would be worthwhile to be the first tavern in the principality serving them, but most of our customers would rather send them back. I can bring out something else, if you wish."

Elisa shook her head. "No, I'll try it."

The server nodded and walked away from their table. Elisa poked at a slice of potato.

"I applaud you for your bravery," the Devil said. "Most people seem to think that those are only good for feeding to animals."

"Are they right?" Elisa asked.

"I don't think so," the Devil said, popping a slice of potato into his mouth. "They're quite good when fried up. So, what is this thing you need help with?"

"Clever Gretel," Elisa replied. "I want to find her. I know that you know her."

"I do indeed," the Devil said. "Quite the little demon in bed...and very enjoyable *to* bed." Elisa scowled. The Devil smiled and continued, "She treats me like some kind of pet, though. It's quite odd."

"Do you know where she is?"

"When it comes to where she is *right now* – no, I don't," the Devil replied. "Omniscience was never one of my gifts. But I do know where she told me she was planning to go after our last little tryst. If you really want to find her, head south-east from here. Your paths should intersect. I'd be careful, though – she's quite insane."

"I know," Elisa said. "And thank you." She popped a piece of potato into her mouth and chewed. The Devil was right – it did taste good.

"I'd rather do more to thank you for the company than just send you into danger," the Devil said. "So, let me tell you a secret – the biggest secret – about what you and I *really* are."

Elisa's eyes narrowed. "And is there a price for this?"

"You've already paid it with the pleasant conversation," the Devil stated, leaning forward. "We don't grant wishes or perform miracles." He gestured to the people around them. "*They* do. They just do it through us."

"I don't understand," Elisa said.

"Human beings have the power to reshape the world into their own image in ways that they can't yet imagine, but they're still figuring that out," the Devil began. "So, instead of taking that power and wielding it themselves, they use people like us as vessels, and *we* grant their wishes using their power.

"The day will come when they realize that they don't need us anymore, and then these gifts of ours will disappear. But, until then, here we are, waiting out eternity. Some of us for longer than others."

Elisa blinked. "I'm not sure I believe that."

The Devil shrugged. "Believe it or don't. It's what I've been able to work out. Regardless, the main thing we need to do is stave off boredom. I have my games, you have your penance, Death looms over sick people, and Yitzak has his...irritability."

Elisa frowned. "I'm not a penitent because of boredom. It's the condition of my absolution."

"If that's what you say, then it must be true," the Devil said.

Elisa blinked. "Wait, did you say that Death *looms*?"

The Devil nodded. "It's what he does. If he's about to take somebody, he stands by the foot of their bed, and if he's not going to take them, he looms over their head.

Sometimes he makes himself visible to a physician so that he has an audience, but he does it even when nobody can see him...except perhaps the dying. Not sure what he gets out of it, but to each their own."

Elisa stared at her drink, and then said, "That is odd. Sorry, who's Yitzak?"

"You'd know him as the 'Wandering Jew'."

"Ah," Elisa said. "I've met him. Didn't like him – all he did was taunt and laugh at me. He did give me some food, however, so I guess that's something."

The Devil's eyes widened. "Yitzak actually *talked* to you? That's amazing! I can't get him to talk to me at all. The best I get out of him is obscene hand gestures – I even learned some new ones from him, and I thought I knew *all* of them."

Elisa chuckled and started in on the chicken. The sauce was indeed good. "There's another wish granter, Princess Henriette. Is she going to have lives like ours?"

"I don't know," the Devil said. "I have recently dead of that name in my care. You're not the first wish granter who has emerged. Some lived very long lives, but then died of old age. Some took their own lives after centuries on this Earth. And some lived a normal human life. I don't know why one wish granter becomes immortal while another doesn't."

"So what now?" Elisa asked, finishing the food on her plate.

"Now, I have a game to finish, and I have to be on my way. We'll meet again, though. And, it's a big and amazing world out there. Just imagine who you'll meet – you might even find some sodomites, although you'd probably have to look rather hard for them. One tends to stay hidden when being true to one's self gets you executed. They're probably best left alone." He finished his beer and rose from the table. "I'll do you the courtesy of not offering to pay for your drink and meal, and just cover my own."

After the Devil had left, Elisa shook her head, finished her drink, and then paid for her meal. Then she made her way south-east, stopping at a small village and checking into the inn. When she got to her room, she sat down on the bed and stared out the window.

It's the Year of Our Lord seventeen hundred and thirty-one, Elisa thought. *That makes me...eighty-eight years old. I've been a penitent for over seventy years.*

She picked up her bag and took a close look at it. It was far more threadbare than she had remembered, with several holes, some of which were quite large. She allowed herself a smile. She and this bag had been through a lot – they'd weathered snowstorms, rain, and even an emergency bath in a stream together. She opened it up and reached in to pull out her father's change of clothes.

The fabric ripped as she pulled at it.

Elisa swallowed, gingerly pulling out first her father's changes of clothes, and then the one remaining dress of her mother's. They were threadbare to the point that they were almost in pieces. The fabric on her mother's dress was so fragile that it tore just from her stroking it with her finger.

Elisa buried her face in her hands and wept.

Chapter XII – Huntsmen in the Forest

Elisa had lost track of time again, she was sure of it. The new travelling bag she had bought to replace her old one was ragged and had small holes in it, and the last of her parent's clothing had disintegrated.

She hadn't cried over that, though. She'd already run out of tears to shed.

Elisa walked down a rough-hewn road towards the next principality. On both sides of the road, the forest was dark, thick, and impenetrable. As she walked, she imaged Ella's voice in her head, chiding her.

You could just ask somebody what year it is, you know, Ella said.

Elisa smiled. She liked imagining Ella's voice in her head. It took her mind off how little she had left of everybody else she had cared about. *That would make me look like a crazy person*, she replied.

She imagined Ella laughing. *You're on a penance to*

do good deeds around the Reich *instead of just going on a pilgrimage – you* are *a crazy person.*

Remember the gingerbread house? Elisa asked. *And those two kids we had to help rescue?*

Ella chortled. *That was* bizarre *– who in their right mind builds a house out of baked goods?*

Elisa stopped and peered down the road. Had she just heard something?

Birds twittered overhead. A small animal rustled somewhere in the brush behind her. Elisa shook her head. It must have been her imagination. She resumed walking.

You still haven't answered my question, Ella pressed. *When are you going to stop?*

When my penance is done, Elisa replied.

You've been a penitent longer than most people will ever be alive, Ella pointed out. *You've granted more wishes by now than there were people on your island. You earned your absolution long ago. You could stop right now, and your soul would be fine.*

I haven't found Clever Gretel yet, Elisa said.

Ella sighed. *You don't need to be a penitent to find her.*

Elisa smiled. *Maybe I just like your company.*

I'm just your mind giving words to your memory of me, Ella said. *I went to Heaven decades ago. You need somebody* real *to share your life with.*

Elisa shrugged her off. She liked Ella's company in her mind, but sometimes she could be annoying. And despite the Devil's tip and spending days in every single village she came across, she hadn't seen so much of a hint of Clever Gretel in any of the principalities she had visited.

A man about Elisa's height stepped out from the forest in front of her and levelled a long musket at her. He wore a dark green military coat over his white waistcoat. She heard footsteps behind her and turned. Three more men in uniforms, slightly built, stood behind her and took aim.

"State your business here," the man in front of her ordered, his voice a bit higher pitched than she expected.

"I'm a penitent," Elisa replied, raising her hands in the air. "I'm here as part of my penance."

"There are no pilgrimage sites in this principality," the soldier in front of her stated.

"My penance isn't a pilgrimage," Elisa said. "I'm to wander the Reich doing good deeds and helping people."

"She's a spy," one of the men behind her said in a voice that was strangely sing-song. "We should just kill her and be done with it."

Elisa shook her head. "Please, I'm not a spy! I'm just a penitent! I chose this penance myself, and my confessor said that it was appropriate!"

"What was your confessor's name?" the soldier in front of her demanded.

"It was," Elisa began, and then winced. "I'm sorry, I don't remember – it was too long ago."

"Too long ago?" the soldier sneered. "What did you do, start when you were ten years old?"

"I started when I was fifteen," Elisa said. "I'm just...I'm older than I look."

"Why are we humouring her?" one of the soldiers behind her asked. "We could be on our way home if we just killed her now."

"I like seeing spies squirm," another soldier behind her said.

"Please," Elisa begged. "I'm not a spy! Who would I even be spying for?"

"The Kingdom of Prussia," the soldier in front of her declared. "The King of Prussia, Frederick II, has invaded Saxony. He has been placed under the ban of the Emperor, and declared an enemy of the *Reich*! How can you not know this?"

"Please," Elisa said. "I've...I've been in the countryside for a long time, I don't get any news...I...I don't even know what year it is!"

"You expect us to believe that?" said one of the soldiers behind her.

"It's true!" Elisa cried. "I just wanted to visit the villages and help where I could! And if this is one of the Catholic lands, I wanted to confess my sins and hear a Mass! That's the truth!"

The soldier in front of her scowled. "This is one of the Catholic lands. But what does that matter? Just go to a Catholic church in a Protestant land if you need to."

Elisa blinked. "But...those are heretic lands!"

The soldier's face curled into a scowl of rage. "'Heretic lands'? Is that how you think we Catholics speak?" He reversed his musket and struck her in the chest. Elisa hit the ground hard, gasping. "My *grandmother* spoke like that! Do you really believe that we think Protestants are anything other than fellow Christians, *spy*?" He turned to the others. "Fix bayonets. We'll execute her with them – can't have any gunshots, just in case there are more Prussian scouts nearby."

"No, please, wait!" Elisa screamed. "I'm not a spy! I'm just...I'm just old fashioned! I committed the sin of pride and hurt a lot of people, and I've been a penitent ever since!" She began to weep. "I don't even know what year it is! At least tell me what year it is! If I'm going to die...I just want to know how old I am."

"It's the Year of Our Lord seventeen hundred and fifty-seven," a soldier behind her said. "I think...I think I believe her. Who would make this up?"

The soldier in front of her sighed. "A spy would have a better story than *this*." He kneeled down in front of her. "Do you swear on the Virgin Mary that you are a Catholic?"

Elisa nodded. "I am. I swear it."

"I suggest you get your head straightened out," the soldier said. "Our grandparents calling Protestants 'heretics' is something we are *ashamed* of. The sooner you realize that they're just Christians like us, the better it will go for you."

Elisa nodded again. "I understand sir, I'm sorry for my ignorance, and I–" She blinked. The faces, the build, the voices of all four of them...

"You're women," she breathed.

"We are the prince's *Jäger* company," the lead soldier said. "His hunters and scouts. I am its commanding officer. There were fourteen of us when we put ourselves in the prince's service two years ago, but we lost two in a skirmish with Prussian scouts, so there's only twelve of us left. Those two we lost were dear friends."

"But you're also women," Elisa said, grimacing in pain as she pulled herself up off the hard ground. "How is this?"

She heard a chuckle from behind her. "She's got us, sir," a soldier said.

"We put on uniforms and we volunteered," the lead soldier replied. "That's all you need to know. We do not permit you to enter this principality. You will turn back, and if we catch you entering this land again, we will kill you on sight."

Elisa focused on the soldier's wish – she wished that the prince who had broken their betrothal and to whom she had sworn her life in service would remember their love and marry her. "I'll go," Elisa promised. "Just, please, give me a few moments to catch my breath."

"Be gone by sundown," the Jäger commander said. Elisa looked down, taking a ragged breath. Her chest still hurt. She heard a rustling, and then silence. Elisa looked around. She was alone on the road.

Elisa turned around and began walking back.

You didn't grant her wish, she imagined Ella saying.

She doesn't want my help, Elisa replied. *I don't think she wants anybody's help.*

I think she'd scare the Devil himself, Ella's voice said.

Elisa chuckled at that, and then winced. Her chest still hurt.

By sundown, she was in the village she had left just that morning. She opened the door to the inn, the innkeeper's eyes widening when he saw her.

"You look terrible, Elisa!" he declared. "What happened?"

"They weren't very welcoming," she replied. "They thought I was a Prussian spy."

The innkeeper blinked. "I didn't think you were capable of making a first impression *that* bad."

Elisa gave him a weary smile. "Apparently I am. Is my room still available?"

"Of course it is," he said. "I'll have my wife turn down the bed for you."

Elisa nodded. "Thank you. Is there any food left?"

The innkeeper gave her a kind smile. "We'll find something for you in the kitchen."

She began to make her way to the dining area, and then stopped. "I'm...I'm Catholic. Is there a place I can go to church and hear Mass?"

He nodded. "There's a village a day south of here. They're Catholic."

Elisa nodded and made her way to a table. Then she sat down and sighed.

You've been to that village, Ella's voice said.

I know, Elisa replied. *I never even considered that they could be anything but Protestant.*

It's good news then, Ella said.

Elisa closed her eyes. *Is it? That woman was ashamed*

254

of me for my ignorance. Am I really that backwards and old fashioned?

And what if you are? Ella asked. *What are you going to do?*

Elisa sighed. *Get my head straightened out, I guess.*

That's my girl, Ella said, a smile in her voice.

Did I just live too long? Elisa asked. *Am I even capable of understanding what this world has become?*

Maybe you have, Ella said. *There aren't a lot of hundred-and-fifteen-year-olds out there. But, you know what I think?*

What? Elisa asked.

I think you're lucky, Ella replied. *I think the world became a better place while you weren't looking, just like Jakob and Anna hoped it would, and you got to live long enough to see it.*

I guess it was nice that they were right, Elisa said. *And I wish they'd lived to see it.*

And whatever this world becomes, you'll adapt, Ella's voice declared. *I know it.*

"I guess," Elisa muttered. The innkeeper's wife came with a plate of food.

"It's a bit cold," she said as she put it down in front of Elisa, "but we can make some more if we need to."

Elisa gave her a smile. "Thank you so much."

"It's our pleasure," the innkeeper's wife said. "Just let us know if you need any more."

Elisa ate what was on her plate, and then staggered up to her room. She fell onto the bed and into a deep and dreamless sleep.

Chapter XIII – Missing Princesses

"I don't understand," Elisa groused, making her way through the forest path. "We should have found her by now, Ella!"

Maybe she lost track of time, Ella's voice said. *Just like we keep doing.*

Elisa sighed. "It's possible, I suppose." She looked around. "What year do you think it is?"

How would I know? Ella replied. *I'm just the voice you've given to your memory of me, remember? I only know as much as you know.*

Elisa shrugged. "Fair point."

You've been alone too long, Ella said.

"That's your opinion," Elisa declared.

She could hear the frustration in Ella's voice. *You're talking to yourself out loud. Anybody who sees you will think you've gone as mad as that prince we had to escape – you remember running away from those dogs, right?*

Elisa grimaced and wished that Ella wouldn't be this way. "I'm fine. I'll just not talk to you aloud when other people are around. Problem solved."

Elisa, Ella stressed, *you're not going to get better unless you stop running away from this. You are* unwell.

"I'm not running, I'm walking," Elisa declared. "Look, we'll find Clever Gretel, stop her, and then we'll end our penance. Will that make you happy?"

That might be too late, Ella said.

Elisa smirked. "Not if we stop her soon."

It's been decades since we last saw any sign of her.

"That just means we're due."

And what if we can't find her because she's dead? Ella pointed out. *What if she fell off a cliff, or got shot during a war?*

"I'd know if that happened."

Somebody's close, Ella said.

Elisa stopped and listened. Soft footsteps sounded behind her, and then stopped, followed by somebody cursing.

"Well, she heard you, Hans," a male voice said. "We may as well show ourselves."

Three men in rough uniforms with a grey jacket emerged from the trees, muskets slung over their shoulders. One was considerably younger than the others, looking like he couldn't be any older than seventeen. The other two looked like they were in their late thirties or early forties. "Please forgive us, kind young lady," the oldest one said. "We're trying to teach Hans here how to approach with stealth, and we thought you would be good practice."

"I did everything you told me to!" Hans said. Elisa revised her estimate – he was probably only sixteen.

"You *really* didn't," the second oldest man stated. "And she was even talking to herself!"

"We've all been lost in our own heads before," the oldest man said. "No need to bring that up now."

"Who are you?" Elisa asked.

"I'm Franz," said the oldest man, "and my friend here is Peter. And as you've probably guessed, this young man is Hans."

"Stupid Hans," Peter grumbled.

"Not here," Franz warned. "We were skirmishers in the war over Bavaria about ten years ago. We stayed on after the war ended, but eventually the Prussian army decided it no longer needed us, and let us go to seek other employment. Hans here joined us right before we left."

"I won't see any action at all!" Hans complained. "How am I supposed to make a name for myself without a war to fight?"

Peter scowled. "One day you'll understand how much that's a *good* thing."

Franz sighed. "We've been taking care of him and trying to teach him our trade. Sadly, he doesn't seem to have a talent for it."

"I'm learning!" Hans declared.

Peter opened his mouth to speak, and then just rubbed his temples instead.

"You'll have to forgive our impatience with our young colleague here," Franz said. "We spent most of our war hungry while foraging for potatoes and shooting at half-starved Austrians trying to do the same. Hans still thinks there's glory to be had."

"It's true!" Hans declared.

"Stupid Hans," Peter muttered.

"So you're here to find a prince to serve?" Elisa asked.

Peter grinned. "We're here to *become* princes!"

Elisa blinked. "I don't understand."

"The ruler of this principality has three daughters," Franz began. "Actually, I should say, *had* three daughters.

They disappeared into thin air. He has made it known that anybody who finds them will get to marry one of them."

"So far, nobody has succeeded," Peter added. "But, they're not us."

Elisa stared at them. "They vanished without a trace, you say?"

"That's the story, anyway," Franz replied. "They probably just ran off, or got themselves kidnapped. You know how teenaged girls can be. Why do you ask?"

"I'm looking for somebody," Elisa said. "Somebody who can make people disappear without a trace if she wishes."

"You mean a witch?" Hans asked. "You seriously believe in witches in this day and age?"

"Hans, let the young lady speak," Peter warned.

"It's a long story," Elisa said. "Finding her is part of my penance. My name is Elisabeth, but everybody calls me Elisa. Would you mind if I accompanied you?"

"You're a penitent?" Hans asked. "Who goes around as a penitent in this day and – ow!" He rubbed the back of his head.

"Treat the lady with respect, or I'll slap you again," Peter said.

Franz looked at Hans and Peter and shook his head. "Of course you can accompany us. The least we can do is protect a young lady like yourself on these dangerous roads."

Elisa chuckled. "I'm older than I look."

"You do have a poise that many young ladies lack," Franz said. "Either way, please consider us at your service. We saw an old castle just down the way, and it looks abandoned. We were thinking of using it as our base of operations. We should be there in time to do some foraging for food."

"Well, then," Elisa said. "We shouldn't delay."

The castle was old and crumbling, but enough of the keep remained intact that they were all able to find rooms and a place to eat. The three soldiers went out after they arrived, leaving Elisa to clean up the main hall so that they'd have a place to eat.

They seem nice, Ella's voice said as she cleaned out the fireplace. *Perhaps you should see if one of them would make a good husband.*

"I'm a penitent, remember?" Elisa grumbled. "I don't have time to look for a husband."

Sure you do, Ella said. *Your penance ended years and years and years ago. You just won't admit it.*

"Gretel's still out there," Elisa pointed out. "Three missing princess sounds just like her."

It also sounds like rebellious teenagers getting into trouble, Ella said. *Remember what Charlotte was like? Remember what* we *were like?*

Elisa frowned. "Charlotte's long gone."

And probably up in Heaven worrying about how her best friend has spent years talking to herself.

The door opened and the three soldiers strode in, carrying a brace of rabbits. "We've got meat," Franz declared. "Do we have a fire?"

"We will," Elisa replied. "Just give me a moment to light it."

"I could have done more," Hans protested.

"You managed to catch a *tree branch* in a rabbit snare," Peter said. "Look, you're a good kid, but being a skirmisher or a *Jäger* just isn't for you."

"It is!" Hans declared. "I'll prove it!"

Elisa lit the fire in the fireplace, and soon the hall was filled with the smell of cooking rabbit flesh. As they sat down at the hoary old table, Franz leaned forward and said, "So, Elisa, tell us your story. You say you're looking for a witch?"

Hans rolled his eyes. "Everybody knows that there's no such thing as witch– ow!" He rubbed the back of his head.

"Let the lady speak," Peter warned.

Elisa took a deep breath. "The woman I'm looking for calls herself 'Clever Gretel'. She can grant her own wishes. I've seen her drive a prince so insane that he had declared himself a king and was killing all of his daughter's suitors. I helped a prince and the three princesses escape. Last I heard, they were taking their case to the College of Princes."

"That sounds like something out of a folk tale," Peter said.

Franz blinked. "I think I remember hearing about something like that from my grandfather. Some mad prince who had to be deposed by the Emperor that he had heard about when he was a child. But that had to have been at least eighty, ninety years ago."

"I'm not very good at keeping track of time," Elisa said. "Frankly, I'd be quite grateful if you'd tell me the year."

"It's seventeen hundred and eighty-eight," Hans said.

Franz's eyes narrowed. "So you're chasing her and were able to help those princesses escape because..."

Elisa took another deep breath. "Because I'm also a wish granter. I can only grant other people's wishes, though."

"So you're saying that you're a wish granter who saved a bunch of princesses almost a hundred years ago while looking like an eighteen year old girl?" Peter said. "I hate to say it, but I think I'm with Hans on this one. Believing this is too much to ask."

Elisa focused on each of their wishes, and then said, "Franz, your deepest wish is that your joints would stop hurting. Peter, you wish that your ears would stop ringing.

Hans, your wish is for glory." She granted two of the wishes. Reality shifted. "Franz, get up and walk around the room and you'll have your proof. Peter, I think, already has it."

Franz's eyes narrowed. He rose from his chair and walked a single circuit around the room. Then he stared at Elisa, his eyes wide.

"I haven't felt this good in years," Franz declared, sitting back down. "So you're some sort of, what, fairy godmother?" He frowned. "At least, I think that's what the French call somebody like you."

Elisa scowled. "I'm not a fairy, nor anybody's godmother. I'm just a penitent who can grant wishes...and even then, only the most dearly held wish of another person."

Hans grinned. "Did you grant my wish too? What will happen?"

Elisa shook her head. "You don't need my help to find glory."

Hans frowned.

Peter laughed. "Kid, glory isn't what it's made out to be. Believe it or not, she just did you a favour."

"Right, we still have a job to do tomorrow, and an early start," Franz said. "Once the rabbit is ready, we'll eat and get to bed. And then...well, then we've got a lot of work to do."

Elisa chewed on some stale bread the three soldiers had brought with them as she watched them draw lots. The early morning sunlight streamed in through the cracked glass of the hall windows.

"Alright," Franz said. "It looks like I'm staying behind with Elisa to guard the fort. You two, canvas the villages nearby – see if they've seen or heard of anybody travelling incognito or of anybody acting suspiciously, and if there's any sign of this 'Clever Gretel' Elisa told us about."

"Are you sure I can't go with you to help?" Elisa asked.

Franz nodded. "They'll be much faster on their own, and we've had to look for hidden things and people before. We know what questions to ask."

"Come on, Stupid Hans," Peter said, heading out the door. "Let's see if you can actually learn something new this time."

"I'll learn everything you have to teach me!" Hans declared.

Elisa could almost hear Peter rolling his eyes as he said, "So you say."

Franz chuckled as they closed the door behind him and sat down at the table. "So, you're a fairy godmother."

Elisa sat down across from him. "That a terrible name for what I am."

"Did you know Cinderalla?"

Elisa winced. "Her name was Eleonore – Cinder-Ella was what her step-family called her to taunt her. And how does anybody know I was involved at all? They were supposed to keep it secret."

Franz shrugged. "Somebody talked, I guess – they must have just done it in France. Some Frenchy told us the story. Apparently there was a glass slipper, and a pumpkin transformed into a golden carriage that turned back at midnight."

Elisa rubbed her temples. "None...none of that is right. Ella...Eleonore's aunt and uncle had a carriage that somebody had left at their inn, and had it fixed up. We used that. Eleonore had to be back home before her step-family because if she wasn't, they'd realize that she was at the festival. And the slipper was gold, not glass. How could anybody dance on a glass slipper?"

"And the wicked step-sisters, were they really blinded by birds?"

Elisa nodded. "And their step-mother. That was my first encounter with Clever Gretel, not that I knew it was her at the time."

Franz chuckled. "I never thought I'd be sitting next to a legend."

Elisa sighed. "Please don't call me that. I'm doing all of this as a penance – I can't be receiving recognition or reward for it."

Franz raised his hands. "Okay. Your secrets are safe with me...and all of us. Even Hans...somehow."

Elisa laughed. "Don't make promises you can't keep."

Franz uncorked a canteen and drank from it. "Hans does have a brain, it's just hard to reach sometimes. We'll hammer it into his skull." He grinned. "Don't worry – we'll resist the temptation to use a real hammer."

Elisa grinned back and relaxed, enjoying the conversation as they talked of tiny, insignificant things.

It was at midday that they heard a soft knock on the door.

Franz and Elisa glanced at each other, and then Franz rose to open the door, musket in hand. Elisa's eyes widened as she saw who stood before him.

He had to have been a dwarf of some sort – he couldn't be more then two feet tall. He had a bushy dark beard, and his skin was pale. In his right hand was a short but stout walking stick. He looked up at Franz and said, "I'm starving. May I come inside and have some bread?"

Franz blinked. "Of course. Please, come and join us at the table."

The tiny dwarf-like man waddled into the hall and up to the table. Franz tore off a piece of bread and handed it to him. "Here you go, kind sir."

The bread slipped out of the dwarf's hand and onto the

floor. He looked up at Franz. "Might you be so good as to pick that up for me?"

Franz shrugged. "Um, okay." He knelt down to pick up the bread.

As soon as Franz's head was within reach, the dwarf grabbed his hair and slammed Franz to the floor. Elisa gasped. Before she could react, the little man delivered a beating to Franz's head and shoulders with his walking stick, then he gave both of them a look of contempt and said, "You're not the one."

Then, as Elisa watched in disbelief, the dwarf waddled to the door and back out into the wilderness.

Franz winced. "What the hell just happened?"

Elisa knelt beside him. "Are you hurt?"

"Just a bit bruised," Franz said, getting back up on his feet. "You try to be charitable..."

"None of that made any sense," Elisa said, checking out the red welts on Franz's neck. "What did he mean by 'You're not the one'?"

"I don't know," Franz said, sitting back down in his chair. "We'll have a story to tell when Peter and Hans get back though – not often that you receive a beating from somebody the size of a toddler."

Elisa could only laugh at the absurdity of it all.

The next morning, Peter drew the lot to stay back at the castle. As Franz and Hans got ready to leave, Franz said, "Now, just let me do the talking, and listen and learn."

"I'll impress you, don't you worry!" Hans declared.

Franz sighed. "Don't worry about impressing me – you don't need to impress me. I just want you to *learn* from me. Loosening the tongues of strangers is an art, and part of it is knowing how to *listen*."

"I listen just fine!" Hans protested.

"Then why do you keep trying to get the last word in?" Franz demanded as they stepped out of the hall and he closed the door behind them.

Peter chuckled. "At least he isn't my problem today."

Elisa sat down at the table. "He seems quite a handful."

"He's a good kid," Peter said. "He's eager, and brave, and he's got a good head on his shoulders. He reminds me of my kid."

Elisa blinked. "You have children?"

Peter nodded. "I had just one. It started off as a 'May marriage', but by the time the campaign was done, she was carrying my child. So, we stayed together."

"Sorry," Elisa said, "but what do you mean by 'May marriage'."

Peter gave her a kind smile. "Ah. You haven't spent a lot of time around soldiers. Good for you. We call it a 'marriage', but really it's more of an agreement to be somebody's whore for the duration of the campaign. Well, a bit more than a whore, I guess – we did live as husband and wife until we got married properly. And she and my son...they were great, just great. I loved them to bits."

Elisa swallowed. "What happened?"

"Smallpox took them about three years ago," Peter replied.

"I'm sorry," Elisa said.

Peter shrugged. "I'm a soldier. We soldiers are old friends with death. Besides, they're in Heaven now, so I'm the one stuck in a worse place."

"And what's the story with Hans?"

Peter leaned back. "I think Franz and I must have adopted him, really. He's the youngest of three brothers – well, of the three who survived, anyway. I understand there were at least two more who didn't make it out of childhood. His brothers both served in the war and actually managed to come out of it with some plunder and awards for valour. So, Hans measures himself against that." Peter sighed. "The thing of it is that he'd be a great infantryman. He's brave enough to stand in a firing line, and his aim with a musket is good – better than mine, in fact. But, he's obsessed with being a skirmisher or *Jäger*, even though he can't do anything right other than march in a line and shoot. If he doesn't learn how to do things properly or give up this dream of his, he's going to get himself killed as soon as he's facing an enemy who shoots back."

"Maybe you'll find those princesses and he'll become a prince," Elisa said.

Peter chuckled. "That would get this skirmisher nonsense out of his head."

There was a soft knock at the door. Elisa looked out the window – by the position of the sun, it was close to midday.

Peter glanced at her. "You don't suppose..."

"It could be," Elisa said. "Whoever or whatever he was looking for, he didn't find it yesterday."

Peter stepped over to the door and opened it. The dwarf stood in front of him, leaning on his walking stick. "I'm starving," he said. "Can I have some bread, please."

"You know it's the same bread as yesterday, right?" Peter asked.

"I'm starving," the dwarf repeated. "Any bread will do."

Peter glanced at Elisa and said, "Come on in, then."

The dwarf waddled to the table, supporting himself on his walking stick. Peter tore off a piece of bread and handed it to him. The bread fell out of the dwarf's hand and onto the floor.

The dwarf looked down. "Could you please pick that up for me?"

Peter's eyes narrowed. "When my friend did that, you gave him several welts with your stick."

"Your friend offended me," the dwarf stated. "You haven't."

Elisa realized that she was holding her breath, and then exhaled.

Peter shrugged and knelt down. "Fine, if you're so hungry that you can't pick it up for yourself–"

The dwarf grabbed his head by his hair and slammed it to the ground. Then he beat Peter several times with the stick.

"What the hell is wrong with you?" Elisa demanded, bolting out of her chair.

The dwarf let go of Peter's hair and stared at her.

"What, you think that because you're a dwarf you can just attack people who help you?" Elisa shouted. "You asked *us* for charity!"

The little man scowled at her. "I'm not a dwarf, you idiot girl."

Elisa blinked. "What?"

"He's not the one either," the little man said, and waddled out of the hall.

Peter shook his head and got back to his feet. Then he turned to Elisa and said, "I'd give my eye teeth to know what this is all about."

Elisa sighed. "So would I."

"If he's not a dwarf," Peter asked, "then what the hell is he?"

"You didn't even pick lots!" Hans protested as Franz and Peter got ready to leave on their third morning in the castle. "Why do I have to stay behind?"

"Because every time you open your mouth, we lose any chance of getting information at all," Franz said. "We need people to actually *talk* to us."

"There are at least three villages we can never go again

because of you," Peter declared. "You and I barely made it out of one of those villages with our lives!"

"Ladies like being flirted with," Hans said. "And once you've got them liking you, they tell you things!"

Peter rubbed his temples. "You complemented the ass of a married woman in front of her husband, you damned idiot! Look, the peasants here are very traditional – you can tell if a girl is unmarried by the headband."

"I know that!" Hans said. "If they've got a red headband, they're married."

"*Un*married," Franz stressed. "*Un*married. See Elisa over there? You're wearing a traditional headband, right?"

Elisa nodded. "I'm not married. That's why I wear mine."

"Look, Hans, just try to make sure that the castle doesn't burn down, and do what Elisa tells you," Franz said. "She's in charge. Maybe spending time with an actual woman would be good for you."

"And if that odd dwarf person shows up, try to figure out what he's about," Peter added.

"And Elisa," Franz said, "Don't let him give you any white hairs."

Franz closed the door behind them, leaving Hans slumping down at the table. "I'll never prove myself at this rate."

Elisa stepped over and gave his shoulder a supportive squeeze. "I remember being your age. Part of growing up isn't so much proving yourself as realizing that most of the time you don't have to."

"You talk like my mother," Hans groused. "Or my grandmother."

Elisa sat down beside him. "I've heard that before. Let me ask you something. Why do you want glory?"

"Because I...I..." he said, and then frowned. "Because with the world so full, how else can I make a place for myself?"

269

"The world is always bigger than you think," Elisa pointed out.

"My brothers came back rich, and with medals," Hans said. "They could do it, but by the time I was old enough to try, the war was long gone. Russia has gone to war with the Turks, and I've heard Austria might be following, but we're not going anywhere near either of them. I know Franz and Peter want the best for me, but they don't want to fight any more wars."

"What happens if you find those princesses?" Elisa asked. "You would become a prince."

Hans sighed. "We're not going to find any princesses. Dozens of people have been here before us looking for them, and the three of us will be the ones who succeed? Franz and Peter are dreamers, and it's wonderful, but you haven't been in those villages. They're baffled. They're not hiding anything, there isn't any secret waiting to be unlocked with the right words – nobody has seen a thing. You can tell by the look in their eyes." He looked at her. "Why are you smiling?"

"Now *there's* the real you," Elisa said. "I was wondering if I'd ever see it."

"Pathetic, isn't it?" Hans asked. "The youngest and least of three brothers."

"Actually, I think it's impressive," Elisa said. "If you'd just drop the bravado more often, I think you'd really start to shine."

Hans chuckled. "Should I start to flirt with you?"

"Honestly, you just being you is better than your flirting ever will be."

A soft knock sounded at the door. Elisa looked at the window. It was around midday.

"Here we go again," Elisa muttered.

"Well, let's see what this little dwarf thing has to say for himself," Hans declared, striding forward and opening the door.

The little man stood, propped against his walking stick. "I'm starving. Please give me some bread."

"Sure," Hans said. "You can pay for it with an explanation. Come on in."

Hans walked back to the table, not even trying to let the little man catch up. Then he sat down, tore off a piece of bread, and handed it to him. The little man let it fall from his fingers. "Could you pick that up for me?"

"No," Hans said. "Pick it up yourself."

The little man's brow furrowed in anger. "What did you just say to me?"

"I said, 'pick it up yourself'," Hans repeated. "If you come begging for food and then can't be bothered to do at least that, you don't deserve it."

"You'll pick it up for me, or I'll give you a good thrashing!" the little man declared.

Hans rose from the table and stood before him. "Really? And how do you plan to do that?"

The little man raised his walking stick to strike, only to have Hans catch it in midair. Hans kicked him in the stomach, sending him sprawling on the floor. Elisa found herself gasping.

"Finally!" the little man roared. "Somebody with some fucking backbone!"

Elisa realized that her mouth was open, and closed it. Then she focused on the little man's wish. She closed her eyes and cursed herself for not checking it sooner. What he wished for most of all was help.

"You could have found a less painful way to test us, dwarf," Hans said.

"I'm not a dwarf, I'm a gnome," the little man said. "There are a thousand more like us in the caverns under this land. And when you've seen what I've seen, you make damned sure you've got the right man for the job."

Elisa shook her head. "Wait – you knew this was a test?"

271

"I figured it out after hearing about his second visit," Hans replied. "If I wanted to make certain that somebody would stay the course, the first thing I'd do is check to see if they'd back down from something small."

"You might be wise beyond your years," the gnome said.

Hans shook his head. "I just had two older brothers and grew up around soldiers."

"So, you need help?" Elisa asked. "What happened?"

"We've been enchanted," the gnome said. "It happened about half a year ago. A woman with raven hair came to us and insisted that we show her our riches. We refused, and she cursed us. Now, we have to hold three princess hostage – and no matter what we do, we can't just release them."

Hans and Elisa traded glances. "Wait, you know where the three princesses are?" Hans said.

The gnome nodded. "We thought that if we could find somebody of strong enough mind, they could break through the curse and rescue them, and then we'd be free of that wicked woman's enchantment. That's why I was sent up here."

"This woman who did this to you," Elisa asked. "Do you know her name?"

"I'll never forget it as long as I live," the gnome spat. "She called herself 'Clever Gretel'."

Elisa found herself taking a deep breath, her heart racing. Beside her, Hans said, "I think we've found your evil fairy godmother."

Chapter XIV – A Fairy Godmother's Defeat

"Let me get this straight," Franz said, sitting at the table with Peter, Hans, the gnome, and Elisa. "This evil fairy godmother that Elisa has been looking for showed up in your caverns and cursed you. This curse forces you to guard the three missing princesses, and stop anybody from taking them away."

"That's correct," the gnome said.

"And each of the princesses has to care for a small dragon with multiple heads," Franz added.

"That is also correct."

"And you were sent to the surface to find somebody who wouldn't allow themselves to be stopped from breaking the curse and rescuing the princesses."

"Again correct."

"And you got here using a nearby well," Franz said.

The gnome nodded.

"And your name is 'Erik'?"

The gnome winced. "That's close enough."

Peter shrugged. "Seems obvious enough. We go down this well, rescue the princesses, and break the curse."

Erik shook his head and pointed at Hans. "Only him. He's the one who passed my test."

Franz and Peter exchanged a concerned look. Hans sighed and said, "Don't worry. I'll be careful, and I'll make sure to use my bayonet so that I don't wake up the other dragons."

Franz and Peter shared an amazed look, and then Franz turned to Elisa and asked, "What did you do to him while we were gone?"

Elisa shrugged. "I convinced him that he could just be himself."

Peter grinned. "And you're sure he's not a changeling?"

"I could go right now," Hans said. "We've still got a couple of hours of light left, and–"

"He's not a changeling," Peter chuckled. "Boy, think it through. You don't know how long it will be to get to the well, and you don't know how long it will take to find and kill these dragons. And then, you'll need to get back up the well with the princesses, and *then* you'll need to get them to the palace, which is at least half a day away. The only way we can be sure that there will be enough daylight is to leave at first light."

"I can return at first light to collect you," Erik said. "My eyes are very good in the dark."

"I'll need to come down with Hans," Elisa said.

Erik's eyes narrowed. "You didn't pass my test."

"You didn't test me," Elisa stated. "And even if you had and I'd failed, you still need me. I'm a wish granter, like Clever Gretel. You may need me to break the curse."

The gnome scowled.

"It's better than having Hans slaughter his way

through your people to get to the princesses," Franz pointed out. "Are you here to save your people, or get them massacred?"

"Fine, you can come," Erik spat. "But you'd better not curse us."

"I don't curse people," Elisa said.

"We'll see," the gnome said, hopping off his chair and heading for the door. "I'll be here to collect you at first light – be ready for me!"

"We will," Franz said.

Elisa barely slept that night. She's had plenty of nights on less than comfortable bedding, but this night was different. Her mind twisted itself into pretzels to find a way to stop Clever Gretel...and other than trying to find somebody who would wish away Gretel's power, she had nothing.

It felt like she had only just fallen asleep when she was roused by a knock on her door. No daylight streamed through the window. Peter stuck his head into the room, his face illuminated by an oil lamp, and said, "It's almost time."

Elisa used her makeshift chamber pot, tidied herself up as best she could, and then made her way into the great hall. She found the three soldiers already packed up. Franz gave her a kind smile and said, "You should grab your bag. Once we rescue the princesses, we're going straight to the palace."

Elisa nodded and headed back for her bag, slinging it over her shoulder. She returned to find Franz greeting the gnome, the dawn light visible through the open door. Erik looked at her and then said to all of them, "Let's be on our way. My people will be forever grateful to you for this."

"Be grateful to them," Elisa said. "I'm a penitent. I don't do this for recognition or reward."

Erik shrugged. "However you'd like it. Come along."

It took about an hour for Erik to bring them to the well. As soon as they saw it, Franz and Peter shared a surprised glance. "Erik," Franz said, "the caverns your people live in – were they once a mine?"

"I think so," Erik replied. "What does it matter?"

"This isn't a well," Peter declared. "It's a *lift*."

Elisa blinked and took a closer look. The basket was large enough to fit at least two people, and opened in the front. The housing itself was tall, with a rope and pulley attaching it to the top. By the looks of it, the lift could be raised and lowered from the inside.

Beside her, Hans took a deep breath and stepped into the lift. "I never thought I'd get to be a dragon slayer – let's do this!"

Elisa chuckled and stepped into the lift. The gnome followed. Hans reached up to the rope, only to have Franz say, "Don't – save your strength for those dragons. Let us do it."

The trip down felt as though it took hours. As they descended, Hans used a striker to light an oil lamp. Finally, the lift reached the bottom.

"We're at the bottom!" Hans called. "Can you hear us?"

"We can," Franz's voice called back, quiet but audible. "Good luck!"

Elisa glanced around. The cavern was more of a human-sized tunnel, the walls scored with the remains of pickaxe strikes. Their oil lamp was the only illumination.

"We're this way," Erik said, motioning down the passage. "Follow me."

Elisa and Hans followed the gnome down the passage to a gallery. The space was full of gnomes, all waiting with expectation in their eyes. One, wearing a golden crown, stepped forward.

"Is this the one who passed your test?" the gnome in the crown asked.

"He is, Sire," Erik replied. "This is Hans, of the surface world."

"And who is the woman?" the gnome in the crown asked.

"This is Elisa," Erik replied. "She claims to be a fairy godmother."

"I'm a wish granter, Your Majesty," Elisa said. "I'm not a fairy, and I'm nobody's godmother."

"She thinks she can help," Erik said.

The king of the gnomes shrugged. "We'll take all the help we can get."

"If you show us to the princesses, Your Majesty, we can get started," Hans said.

The king of the gnomes nodded. "Come with me."

He led them down a passage to another gallery, Erik following. On the far wall of the gallery were three chambers, a trio of gnomes guarding each one with a sword and shield.

"It's a compulsion," the king said. "Every few hours, nine of us take up arms and go to guard the these rooms. There is no rhyme or reason as to who is chosen – it has even happened to me. While they're standing guard, they're in a trance. One poor soul's wife and children tried to reach him in the first week of our curse – he slaughtered them without even knowing who they were."

"What happens if somebody tries to fight their way through?" Hans asked.

The king of the gnomes shrugged. "Nobody has ever tried."

Hans put his oil lamp on the floor, un-slung his musket and attached the bayonet. "Better prepare for the worst, I guess."

"My turn to help," Elisa said, focusing on the king's

wish. She smiled. It would work perfectly. She shaped and granted the wish. Reality shifted.

"They are now only guarding the princesses against other gnomes," Elisa announced. "And as soon as they have nothing to guard, the curse will be broken."

The king blinked. "Just like that."

Elisa nodded. "Your dearest wish was to be free of this curse. I can't erase a wish that has been granted, but I can modify it. So, I just changed who the princesses are guarded against, allowing Hans to pass and save them."

"You'll forgive me for saying that I'll believe it when I see it," the king said.

"I've seen it," Hans declared, moving towards the leftmost room. "I believe it." The gnomes guarding it stepped aside, allowing him to pass. Hans stepped into the room, musket and bayonet at the ready.

Both the king and Erik breathed sighs of relief. "We've waited so long for this," Erik said. "Thank you for coming to save us."

"There's no need to thank me," Elisa replied. "I'm a penitent. Helping people is my penance."

Hans emerged from the room, a half-starved princess in her late teens in a ragged dress that had once been regal supported on his arm. His bayonet was slick with blood.

"That's one," Hans said, turning and moving to the middle room. The gnomes guarding it stepped aside.

"One moment," Elisa said, stepping towards the rightmost room. The guards stepped aside. Elisa poked her head in. A princess in ragged clothes, looking like she couldn't be older than sixteen years old, sat on the ground, a four-headed dragon sleeping in her lap. On the wall was an oil lamp, casting a flickering light around the room. The princess looked up at Elisa, her eyes widening. Elisa put her finger to her lips. The princess nodded.

Elisa stepped back as Hans was leading the second

princess out of her prison. Hans looked at her with a raised eyebrow. Elisa shrugged. "I've never seen a dragon before."

"One left to go," Hans said, and headed into the final chamber.

"As soon as he's done, we're leaving," the king of the gnomes said. "Please thank the young Hans for us, and ask him to forgive our haste."

Elisa blinked. "Why?"

"We've been enslaved and cursed by an evil witch," the king replied. "It was a mistake to come this close to the surface. We don't intend to repeat it. I think this is the last any of you will ever see of our kind."

"Thank you for everything," Erik added. Out of the corner of her eye, she caught the guards snapping awake and looking at each other. Then, they ran from the gallery. The king followed. Erik bowed to her and the princesses, and departed as well.

Hans emerged with the final princess and blinked. "Where did they go?"

"They left," Elisa said. "Deeper into the earth. They wanted me to give you their gratitude."

Hans shrugged, shouldered his musket, and picked up his oil lamp. "Well, I remember the way back to the lift. Let's go."

As they made their way though the tunnel, Elisa asked, "What happened, Your Royal Highnesses? How did you get down here?"

The eldest princess shrugged. "We ate apple from father's favourite tree. And then we were here. Any time the dragons stirred, they threatened to eat us, so we had to calm them to sleep."

Elisa shook her head. "Clever Gretel has a lot to answer for."

The eldest princess stared at her. "Who's Clever Gretel?"

"She's the one who made all of this happen," Elisa replied. "She – you know what? It doesn't matter. I'm going to find a way to stop her, and that's all there is to it."

They reached the lift. "We did it!" Hans called up. "We've rescued them."

"That's great!" Franz called back down. "Are you both okay?"

"We are!" Elisa called up. "I was able to dispel the curse. The only ones that died were the dragons."

"Well, that's good," Peter called down.

"We're sending the princesses up first," Hans declared. "Your Royal Highnesses, please get into the lift."

"Thank you so much for rescuing us," the eldest princess said as she got in. The other two followed.

"You can bring them up!" Hans called.

With a creak, the lift began to rise. Hans began to chuckle.

Elisa stared at him. "What is it?"

"I wanted to make a name for myself," Hans laughed. "Today I slew three dragons, rescued three princesses, and broke a curse enslaving thousands of gnomes – the sort of thing a hero of legend would do. But who would believe me if I ever tried to tell anybody about this?"

Elisa chuckled. "I see your point."

With an anguished creak, the lift came back down, empty. Elisa and Hans were about to step into it when she heard the voice from above – a voice she could never forget.

"What do we have here?" Clever Gretel asked. "Two strong men and three rescued princesses standing around the rear entrance to an abandoned mine! It must have been quite a morning!"

Reality shifted. Elisa stiffened, a chill going down her spine.

Hans looked at her. "What happened."

"Clever Gretel is here," Elisa whispered. "Whatever you do, don't step into that lift."

"We're just waiting for you two now!" Franz declared.

Elisa shook her head.

Hans swallowed and called up, "The gnomes are all gone. Do you think it's worth searching the caves for treasure?"

Elisa stared at him in disbelief. Hans looked back and shrugged.

"Forget treasure!" Franz called back. "We'll have more than enough once we return the princesses to the palace. Let's just get you two back up here, safe and sound."

"They sound like themselves," Hans whispered.

"They're not," Elisa hissed. "It's a trick – Gretel has already turned them against you."

"They took care of me when nobody else would!" Hans whispered. "They're my brothers in arms!"

"Not any more," Elisa hissed. "Fill it with rocks, as quietly as you can. Trust me – our lives depend on it."

"Will you two hurry up?" Peter asked. "Everybody wants to get going!"

"We just need to...um...do something!" Hans called up. "Give us a moment!" He turned and grabbed a large rock, placing it in the lift. Elisa joined him. Soon the bottom of the lift was filled with rocks.

"Are you ready *now*?" Franz called down.

"We are!" Hans shouted. "Lift us up."

As they watched the lift rise, Hans shook his head and muttered, "This is ridiculous."

"If I'm wrong, you can blame wasting their time on me," Elisa said under her breath. "But I'm not wrong."

Hans glared at her. "You really think that this 'Clever Gretel' person can–"

The lift crashed to the ground in front of them, the rocks spilling out. The rope fell into a coil on top of it, the end cut clean through.

"Was that Elisa I heard down there?" Clever Gretel called down. "I do hope you're okay! It would be a pity for this round of our game to end here like this!"

Hans stared at Elisa. Elisa shook her head and put her finger to her mouth.

"Well, if you are still alive down there, I'll see you at the palace!" Gretel declared. "Or not!"

They waited a few minutes, and then Elisa collapsed against the gallery wall. She stared up at the shaft and took a deep breath.

"So that was Clever Gretel," Hans said.

Elisa nodded. "She wished that your friends would betray you. And so they did."

Hans sighed. "And here I thought just a few days ago that witches and curses didn't exist."

"I wish you'd been right about that," Elisa said.

"So what now?"

"This used to be a mine," Elisa said. "It stands to reason that there's a front door somewhere. We start walking, and try to make our way upwards."

Hans nodded, stepping forward and leading the way. As they walked, the tunnels and galleries seemed endless. Finally, Hans asked, "If you're a fairy godmother, can't you just grant my wish to get out of here?"

Elisa shook her head. "It wouldn't work. You know I'm a wish granter."

"What difference does that make?"

"I can only grant the dearest wish of another person," Elisa explained. "Since you know that I can grant wishes, you also know that I can get us out of here. Since you know that, your dearest wish is not to escape. Therefore, I've got no wish to grant."

Hans looked back at her and frowned. "Are you seriously telling me that in order to grant my wish to get out of here I have to lose any hope of you ever being able to grant my wish?"

Elisa nodded, stepping over a small rockfall. "That's exactly it."

"And this Clever Gretel person..."

"She can grant her own wishes, no matter how unimportant. I think."

"So, what, she decided she wanted the gnomes' gold, and then punished them for not giving it to her?"

Elisa shook her head. "I don't think she had any interest in the gold at all. All she cares about is amusing herself. I think she wanted to see the gnomes suffer, the princesses live in fear, and try to get as many rescuers killed as possible. It's how she passes the time."

"That's sick," Hans declared.

"It is indeed," Elisa agreed. They walked on in silence, finally coming to a dead end.

"We could be down here for days," Hans muttered.

"We should go back to the gallery with the chambers," Elisa suggested. "Fetch the oil lamps from the princesses' cells. We might need them."

"It would be easier to just ask for help," a familiar voice said. Elisa turned to see Erik standing behind them.

"Where are the others?" Hans asked.

"Gone," Erik replied. "Headed back into the deep depths. I'll be joining them soon. But first, one good turn deserves another – the way out is this way."

Erik led them through the maze of tunnels into a large gallery. At the end was a large pair of doors, reddish sunlight shining through the gaps in the wood.

"The rest is up to you," Erik said. "Thank you for helping us."

"You're welcome," Hans replied, but then stopped.

Erik was already gone. He shook his head with a smile. "Not big on sticking around, is he?"

"I guess not," Elisa said, pushing on the door. "I think it's locked from the outside."

Hans removed the bayonet from his musket, then aimed it at the door. "Step back and cover your ears."

Elisa stepped back and put her hands over her ears. Even with her ears covered, the gunshot was deafening. Hans gave the door a quick kick. It bulged, but didn't open. He shook his head and began to reload.

Elisa covered her ears again as he aimed at the door. Splinters of wood flew by after the deafening shot. He pushed against the door again. It bulged again, but didn't open.

"I think I've almost got this," Hans declared, reloading again. Elisa covered her ears. The gunshot rang out. The doors swung open.

"So, we just need to spend the night here, and make our way to the palace in the morning," Hans declared. "Seems simple enough."

Elisa slumped against the wall, breathing in the fresh air from the door. As the sun finished going down and the stars came out, she drifted into a dreamless sleep.

She awoke to Hans shaking her by the shoulder. The sun was already high in the sky. "I've found the palace," he said. "It isn't far."

Elisa stretched and got to her feet. "You didn't need to let me sleep that long."

"You looked like you needed it," Hans said.

Elisa sighed and nodded. "It hasn't been the easiest week."

"Let's go."

Elisa shouldered her bag. Then, she followed Hans down a cobbled path to a larger road. The palace loomed in the distance.

"I told you it wasn't far," Hans declared.

"I'm glad," Elisa said. *Now, we just need a way to stop Gretel if we meet her*, Ella's imagined voice said.

They came to the gates of the palace around midday, two guards standing watch. "State your business," the first guard demanded.

"We're here about the princesses," Hans said. "I'm Hans, and this is Elisa."

"The princesses have been rescued," the first guard stated.

Hans nodded. "I know. We're the ones who rescued them."

"He did the actual work," Elisa added. "I just helped a bit."

The guards stared at each other for a moment. Then, the first guard shook his head and said, "Come with me."

They followed the guard through the palace, into the throne room. On the gilded throne sat a grey-haired prince with a close cropped beard in regal robes. Beside him was his queen and three daughters. On the other side of the hall stood Franz and Peter, both now wearing fine clothing. Both of them averted their eyes from Hans.

Hans bowed and Elisa curtseyed. The guard said something quietly to the prince. The prince stared at him, and then at Hans and Elisa. The princesses also stared, their eyes wild with fear.

"It seems I have a conflict here," the prince said. "These two fine men claim to have rescued my daughters, and have been award my eldest and second eldest's hands in marriage. But you are claiming that it was you who rescued them."

"We are comrades, Your Royal Highness," Hans explained. "I went into the mines and killed the dragons. They waited above."

The prince turned to Franz and Peter. "Is this true?"

Franz shook his head. "He's a braggart, Your Royal Highness. He followed us around despite our many efforts to rid ourselves of him, and has often claimed credit for what we have done."

"Frankly, we should never have paid any attention to him in the first place," Peter added. "We are the ones who killed the dragons."

Elisa sighed. Clever Gretel has been thorough. She glanced around – there was no sign of her.

The prince turned to his daughters. "Who is telling the truth?"

The three daughters stared at each other. Then, the eldest said, her voice trembling, "We can't tell you. I'm sorry, father."

Elisa suppressed a smile as an idea emerged. "Can you tell the wall, Your Royal Highnesses?"

The eldest princess' eyes widened. "We can!" She turned to the wall and said, "The young man is speaking the truth. He slew the dragons. The other two waited above, and betrayed him when it was his turn to come back up. Peter raised and held the lift, while Franz cut the rope."

"We filled the lift with stones," Elisa added. "That's why they thought we were dead, and why we could escape."

The prince stared at them. "I see." He pointed at Franz and Peter. "Have them arrested and hanged, at once."

As the guards seized Franz and Peter, the two barely struggling, Elisa cried, "Your Royal Highness, please spare them! They are good and honest men, and they were not in their right mind. They were cursed by an evil witch, and–"

The prince rolled his eyes and sneered. "Cursed by an evil witch? What nonsense! This is an age of *reason* – of *science*! There's no such thing as witches and curses!

286

They were dishonest scoundrels who betrayed their charge as soon as he was no longer useful, and they'll hang for it within the hour. This is no place for peasant superstitions."

"Elisa, please," Franz said softly. "Don't do this on our account."

"Don't worry about us," Peter added, a wry smile on his face that didn't reach his eyes. "We're old friends with Death. It's about time we got to spend some quality time with him."

As the guards took them away, Elisa watched the prince turn to Hans. "As for you, you have quite a future here – Hans, was it?"

Elisa resisted the urge to scream and curtseyed instead. "Your royal highness, I would take my leave."

The prince stared at her and then said, "Fine, leave and go wherever you want, you stupid peasant. Guards, escort her out."

Elisa followed the guards to the gates of the palace grounds and then walked down the cobbled road, trying not to think of Franz and Peter dangling at the end of a rope.

"I couldn't save them, Ella," she said.

You can't save everybody, Ella's voice pointed out. *And three princesses and thousands of gnomes are now safe because of you.*

"Doesn't feel like much of a victory," Elisa groused.

Of course it doesn't. You didn't spend any time getting to know the gnomes, or the princesses. You got to know Franz, Peter, and Hans.

"Franz and Peter are dead by now, aren't they?" Elisa asked.

Probably, Ella replied. *It didn't seem like the prince planned to delay.*

"So–"

Reality shifted. Elisa blinked. The roads, the trees,

everything was different. And standing in front of her was Clever Gretel.

Before Elisa could react, Gretel took hold of her shoulder and drove a long knife into her gut, just below her breasts. Elisa gasped in shock and pain.

"I was thinking to myself that I really didn't want to spend any more time in that boring old court," Gretel declared, her eyes sparkling. "So I wished that I wasn't, and brought myself here. Then, I thought to myself, it's a pity Elisa isn't here – so I wished you were here, and here you are!"

Gretel twisted the knife. Elisa screamed, grasping at her Gretel's hand, her fingers slipping on the blood.

"I've been giving it some careful consideration," Gretel began, twisting the blade again. "And while I've really enjoyed this game of ours – leading you across the German lands and back again, clouding your mind so that you forget leads as soon as you start following them, and this round we just played – I think it's time to take a break. You understand, of course." She pulled the knife out. Elisa collapsed to the ground, clutching at her gut as the blood flowed.

"Besides," Gretel declared as she began to walk away, "I hate to tell you this, but this whole penitent thing has gotten really boring. You're just not that fun anymore. See you around...or not."

Elisa gasped, trying to force down the pain and failing as she lay on the ground, the blood pooling under her.

You need to move, Ella's voice said.

"What's the point?" Elisa rasped. "There's no way to beat her!"

That doesn't matter now, Ella stressed. *You need to move forward. If you move you live, if you stay still you die.*

Elisa gasped as a wave of pain overwhelmed her.

Just move a bit forward, Ella begged. *Just a bit. That's all that you need to do. Just* move!

Elisa reached out, her vision darkening. She grunted in agony as she pulled herself a tiny bit forward.

Good, Ella said. *Now they know you're still alive.*

"What?" Elisa tried to say, but nothing came out. She thought she heard people running towards her as darkness took her.

She opened her eyes to find herself on a bed inside a house of some sort. Everything was blurry except for a single figure standing at the foot of her bed, looming over her. The bleached white bone of a skull peered out from a shroud, watching her.

It's Death, Elisa realized. *He's standing at the foot of my bed – I'm going to die.*

"Don't worry, Elisa," the Devil's voice said, close by her ear. "Everything is going to be okay."

No! I'm going to die and the Devil is here to take my soul to Hell! Please, don't let the Devil take me to Hell! Please, somebody save me from Hell!

"Just close your eyes and relax," the Devil said.

Darkness took her.

Part III
Once Upon a History

Chapter I – Seven Dwarfs

Elisa opened her eyes and took a ragged breath. She blinked, willing her eyes to focus. A wooden ceiling emerged from the blur in front of her.

So this is Hell, she thought. *I wonder when my torments begin.*

"She's awake," an unfamiliar voice said.

"Thank you," she heard the Devil reply. "Can you give us the room, please?"

"Of course, good doctor," the first voice said.

It was all Elisa could do to turn her head. She seemed to be lying on a bed of some sort in a homely room. She tried to rise out of the bed, but her strength gave out. That's when she noticed the furniture. Everything about it was ordinary for a normal peasant household except for its size – it was half the height that she would expect.

"Okay, let's take a look at you," the Devil said, pulling

the bedsheet off her. Elisa swallowed and closed her eyes, steeling herself for the torments to begin. She felt the Devil lift her shift off her belly.

"It seems to be healing nicely," the Devil said. "No sign of infection. Good."

Elisa opened her eyes and looked at him. "I'm not in Hell?"

The Devil chuckled. "I should hope not! Hell would be a terrible place to recover from a wound like this. Never fear, Elisa, you are quite alive."

Elisa rested her head back on her pillow. "I thought you had come for my soul."

"I told you before, I have no claim on it," the Devil stated. "Besides, I'd much rather have you among the living. Not that it was easy after this."

Elisa tried to swallow. It took two attempts.

"Ah, have some water," the Devil said, placing the rim of a cup to her mouth. "Drink slowly, take your time."

Elisa drank the water down, and then said, "Death was standing at the foot of my bed. He was going to take me."

"I explained to him why that would be a grave error," the Devil said. "If there's one thing I can be, it's convincing."

"Why did you save me?"

For the very first time, Elisa saw the Devil's charming demeanor drop and a hurt look enter his eyes. "Because you're my friend, and I have so few. If you were to die, you would go to a place I could never follow. Call it selfish if you wish, but I'd rather have somebody walking the Earth who I can talk to."

Elisa swallowed again. This time, it was easier. "There were these two soldiers," she said. "Clever Gretel enchanted them. I tried to save their lives, but the prince didn't believe me. All I did was tell him the truth."

"Ah, yes," the Devil mused. "Science and religion

seem to have so little ability to share these days. It's either one or the other. There's probably nothing you could have done to convince the man, short of performing a miracle, and even that might not have done the trick."

"Franz and Peter, are they in your care?"

The Devil paused. "One is. The other went to join his family."

Elisa frowned. "They were good men. They didn't deserve damnation."

"When you met them, I have no doubt that they had become very good men," the Devil said. "But they didn't start that way. They both did terrible things that damned their souls. In the end, Peter's soul was saved by his family. Franz had no such benefactors. Perhaps if he had lived a few years more...but, perhaps not. I'm sorry – I wish I had better news about that, but I did promise never to lie to you, and I keep my promises."

"So, where am I?"

"You are in the home of seven miners and their ward. You are right now in their ward's bed – it was the only one big enough for you. Don't worry, they're all good men. I wouldn't leave you in this weakened state with those who would take advantage of you or harm you."

"What happens now?" Elisa asked.

"Today, you rest and recover your strength," the Devil said. Tomorrow, we'll see about getting you out of that bed and starting to walk again."

Elisa saw the dwarf the next morning. He was short, with stubby arms and legs, and a grey beard. He carried a bowl of porridge on a wooden tray.

"Good, hearty food to help you regain your strength," he said, sitting down beside her. "Let's see if we can get you upright."

He helped her rise so that she was sitting in the bed, and then placed the tray on her lap. "Now, you eat all of this, Miss Elisa."

Elisa gave him a grateful smile. "It's just 'Elisa'. What's your name?"

"I'm Gunther," the dwarf replied. "I suppose you could call me the head of this household. I'm also a foreman at the mine." He pointed at his grey hair. "I'm old enough that they only call me in every now and then, I'm happy to say."

"Thank you for taking me in," Elisa said.

Gunther nodded. "You're welcome. You're not our first stray – hopefully later today you'll meet Snowy. Tomorrow, we should have a new bed for you, so that you can get out of hers."

"Who's Snowy?"

"Don't worry about that for now," the dwarf said. "Your friend the surgeon will be coming to check on you in a bit. You just eat up."

Elisa thanked Gunther again and began to eat. The porridge was plain, but filling. Once she was done, Gunther took the tray and left the room. Peering behind him was a little girl, no more than eight years old, with very fair skin and dark hair.

"You must be Snowy," Elisa said. "I'm sorry I'm taking your bed."

The little girl nodded at her, and then fled the doorway.

She lay back and dosed off. When she opened her eyes, the Devil was already in her room, his finger against her neck.

"Pulse is good, still no signs of infection...and you're awake! Wonderful!"

"How long did I sleep?" Elisa asked.

"Only a couple of hours," the Devil said. "Now, let's get you out of this bed."

He helped her up, and then to her feet. Elisa's head swam.

"Take it easy," the Devil said. "We're just doing baby steps today. We're going into the next room, and then back to bed. Put your hand on my shoulder."

Elisa placed her hand on his shoulder, and the Devil led her through the doorway. She found herself in a large main room, with long table next to a small kitchen. Gunther puttered away at the stove, teaching Snowy how to cook something. Eight small chairs stood beside it, with one new chair added to it.

"Are they all dwarfs?" Elisa asked.

"Except for their ward, yes," the Devil replied. "Their ward is a normal sized child."

"How did they get a little girl as their ward?" Elisa asked.

"That a story for them to tell," the Devil said. "For now, it's time to get you back to your bed. Tomorrow, we'll get you to sit in your chair for lunch, and the day after, we'll get you outside for a while."

Elisa chuckled. "Baby steps?"

The Devil nodded. "Indeed."

The weather had been too poor to go outside when they planned, but Elisa's health did recover. After a couple of weeks, she was able to help out in the kitchen, and a couple of weeks after that, she was able to go outdoors.

The other six dwarfs were boisterous but kind, and their wishes were for Snowy to have a good and happy life. It took her a while to get everybody's names right. Gunther was the oldest of them, and the one who was most often in the house, outside of Snowy. He loved these things called 'newspapers', and he had somebody bring them in from town for him to read – Elisa had glanced at one out of curiosity, but found nothing to interest her. Christof was the youngest, and the one most likely to send the others into fits of laughter at the dinner table. Harald and Eric were a pair of brothers, and the most recent additions to the household, as least as far as the dwarfs went. Albert was almost as old as Gunther, with a nasty cough that never seemed to go away. Freidrich and Fritz were another pair of brothers, who seemed to be forever pulling pranks on each other.

And then there was Snowy, who Elisa now shared a room with. The little girl was shy, but never failed to help out with the household chores. After a couple of days of trying to get Snowy to talk to her, Elisa finally asked Gunther about her while she helped wash dishes.

"Snowy?" Gunther replied. "Well, we all call her 'Snowy' – her given name is 'Snow White', of all things. She's been with us for about two years. We found her fleeing through the forest, terrified out of her skull. As best we know, the princess wanted her dead for some reason, and ordered a huntsman to take her out into the woods and cut out her heart."

Elisa frowned. "That's insane."

"Definitely not the act of a sane person," Gunther agreed. "Anyway, the huntsman took down a deer and used its heart instead, and told her to run. We don't know who her family is, or what her relationship is to Her Royal Highness."

"That would explain why she's so shy around strangers. Has the princess always been this...homicidal?"

Gunther shrugged. "There are rumours that she poisoned her husband so that she could take the principality for herself, but none of those have ever been confirmed. Besides, there would have to be a male heir somewhere, or the principality would be returned to the *Reich*. She doesn't seem to care very much about folk like us, so we think Snowy will be safe. Anyway, she's like a daughter to all of us."

"Well, so long as she's safe," Elisa said, and went back to washing.

Eventually, Snowy did open up to her, and Elisa found her to be a bright and happy girl, although not one with very much to talk about.

When the weather was good, Elisa came to enjoy walking about. The village was only a couple of hours away, and there were enough Catholics in it that she had a place to worship. Seeing the Catholic church and a Protestant church in the same village still left her feeling odd, as though the world was out of joint. Sometimes, she wandered the hills around the house, coming to particularly enjoy the view from a cliff, a small river streaming below.

She was sitting on the grass, plucking at flowers and looking over the edge one day when she heard the Devil say, "They told me you were out here. Mind if I join you?"

Elisa shrugged. "Go ahead."

The Devil sat down beside her. "You seem to be recovering well."

"My wound hasn't hurt in quite a while," Elisa reported.

"Good," the Devil said. "I think I can say that you have healed, at least your body has."

Elisa frowned. "What's that supposed to mean?"

"When I met you, you were sharp and driven," the Devil replied. "Now, you're just...treading water, I suppose. So what happened to the penitent who was once terrified that I'd take her immortal soul?"

"I'm now pretty certain you're not going to," Elisa answered.

"That's not what I mean, and you know it."

Elisa brought her knees up to her chest and wrapped her arms around them. "I...I don't understand this world. Not anymore. Every now and then I feel like I know how to be a part of it, and the Mass is what I'm used to, more or less, but then the priest starts his sermon, or I overhear somebody in the village saying something to somebody else, and I realize just how lost I am here. It's like they've all forgotten God's true place in their lives." She sighed. "My world is gone."

"Ah," the Devil said, leaning back. "I know that feeling all too well. I wish I could tell you that it will ever go away, but that would be a lie."

"People used to care about whether their *faith* was right," Elisa declared. "They cared about getting it wrong, because they feared damnation. And now – everybody's a true Christian no matter what they do. They care more about 'science' than the fate of their souls."

"The road to damnation has never been that simple," the Devil said.

Elisa chuckled. "And who would know better than you?"

The Devil smiled. "Precisely. This 'science' thing isn't too bad – we live in an age of marvels. Have I told you about the balloons?"

Elisa shook her head. "What about balloons?"

"There are these brothers in France who have managed to make a balloon big enough that they could fill it with hot air and take people aloft. Human beings, sharing the air with birds!"

Elisa chuckled. "That is quite a thing."

"Humanity is learning to reshape the world on their own. It's quite amazing to watch it happen."

"And leaving my world behind."

The Devil took a deep breath. "A long time ago – so

long ago that the continents were in different places entirely, there were these magnificent beasts. Some of them were big as buildings – bigger even! I loved watching them. I loved watching them forage, and hunt, and struggle, and live. And they lasted for so long...mountains rose and fell, and still this world was *theirs*. I could have served them for eternity, and been happy every moment of it. And then, one day, a giant rock fell from the sky and ended it all. It wasn't an act of God, just an unhappy chance – a giant space rock hitting the planet instead of missing it. But, in the blink of an eye, that entire world was gone, and now I'm the only one walking the Earth who remembers it. You lot, you find their bones in the rock and call them 'dragons', but they were so much more. Who knows – maybe one day you'll have a proper name for them, something that does them justice." He sighed. "It's not the first time I saw the world change into something else, and it wasn't the last, but that was the world I miss the most. Nothing can bring it back, just as nothing can bring the world you were born into back. You just have to mourn what was lost and move on."

"And find a way to live in this one?" Elisa asked.

The Devil nodded. "It's the one you're in. Besides, don't you have that penance to finish up?"

"I'll get back to it when I'm ready," Elisa said.

"Don't take too long," the Devil said. "The world's about to change again."

"Oh?"

"Things are happening in France," the Devil replied. "The French have overthrown their king and declared a republic. I think the world's about to become a very exciting place."

Outside, the world might be getting exciting, but Elisa's

world remained the house of the dwarfs and Snowy, and the village nearby. She wasn't happy, but at least it kept her busy while she figured out what she wanted to do.

In the meantime, she helped Snowy with the chores, and wherever she could around the village. It was on a midsummer's day that Gunther finally took Elisa aside while she was cleaning and said, "I think we need to talk. Please, have a seat."

"What is it?" Elisa asked, sitting at the table.

Gunther sat across from her. "You know, back during the war against Prussia – the one that involved all the other nations by the end – I served as a sapper. They liked people like me doing tunneling – we fit in small spaces."

Elisa chuckled.

Gunther smiled. "Well, it's true – it's the same reason all of us ended up working in mining." His smile faded. "During that war, I saw my share of wounds, including some like yours. What I never saw was anybody *survive* a wound like that. Now, I've respected your privacy, but you've been with us now for long enough that we consider you part of our little family, and I think it's time I knew the truth. All of it."

Elisa sighed. "I've only been here for a few months. I'll just figure out what I'm going to do, and then–"

"Elisa, you've been here for *seven years*," Gunther said. "Snowy is old enough that she has a young man in the village now – a cobbler's apprentice. She's already talking about marrying him once he finishes his apprenticeship and can support them both."

Elisa cursed under her breath and muttered, "I lost track of time again."

"And who are you that losing track of time involves years instead of hours?"

Elisa frowned. "You wouldn't believe me if I told you."

"Try me."

Elisa took a deep breath. "I'm a wish granter," she said. "I can look at somebody and know what their wish is, and make it come true. I'm told that the French would call me a 'fairy godmother', but that's a terrible name for it."

"How old are you?"

Elisa shrugged. "I stopped keeping track a long time ago."

"Do you remember the year you were born?"

Elisa nodded. "Sixteen hundred and forty-three."

Gunther took a deep breath. "That's quite a thing."

"You believe me?"

"I don't know," Gunther said. "But I've never met anybody who could lose track of entire years, or survive the sort of wound you took. Who gave you that wound?"

"Her name is Clever Gretel," Elisa replied. "She's like me, but she can grant her own wishes. I can only grant the wishes of other people."

"And you were wandering the world, granting wishes?"

Elisa nodded. "It is my penance. I've been trying to find and stop her."

"When did your penance start?"

"When I was fifteen."

Gunther closed his eyes for a moment, and then opened them again. "So you have been a penitent for *a hundred and thirty-seven years*?"

Elisa shrugged. "I suppose."

"Why?"

"What I did was very bad."

Gunther crossed his arms. "No. No penance lasts that long. I may not be Catholic, but I've known enough of them to know that. What's the real reason?"

It's time to tell the truth, Ella's voice said in her head. *You know what it is. You've always known.*

Elisa frowned. "I...I..."

Say it! Ella's voice demanded. *Speak the truth – you can do it. You need to admit this to yourself at last!*

She closed her eyes and began to weep. "I...*I don't know how to be anything else*."

There, Ella's voice said. *Was that so hard?*

"Well, we'll help you as best we can," Gunther said. "We may be an odd family in this house, but we are a family, and we look after our own."

Elisa wiped the tears from her eyes. "Thank you."

Christof burst in through the door. "We've got a problem, Gunther!"

Gunther turned to face him. "What is it?"

"Her Royal Highness has executed her huntsman for treason," Christof reported. "She's having it announced throughout the principality."

Gunther sighed. "Then we now have to assume that she knows Snowy is alive, and that she's in danger."

Chapter II – Innocence Lost

As Elisa looked around the table, she was reminded of a conference long ago, in which they had made plans to rescue Ella from that terrible step-family. Today, the quandary was similar, but there were more people – and most of them were shorter.

Snowy sat beside her young man, Max, a flaxen haired youth who looked to be the same age that she was. From the way they were sitting, Elisa guessed that they must be holding hands under the table. All of the dwarfs were present as well, their beers sitting untouched as they discussed what to do.

"We don't know that Her Royal Highness knows Snowy is alive," Albert said, coughing. "All we know is that she executed her huntsman. It could have been for any transgression."

"The same huntsman who spared Snowy's life,"

Gunther retorted. "And why announce it to the entire principality, other than to send a message that she knows and that she's coming?"

"Max will protect me," Snowy declared. Beside her, Max nodded, dedication in his eyes.

"That may not be enough," Harald pointed out. "One cobbler's apprentice against a company of soldiers makes for a dead cobbler's apprentice."

"We can bring the entire village in," his brother Eric said. "They all love Snowy as much as we do – they'd protect her."

"And how many muskets and bayonets does the village have?" Harald asked.

"How many muskets and bayonets does Her Royal Highness have?" Eric replied. "This principality has no army."

"That's assuming that she doesn't come after Snowy using subterfuge," Freidrich said. "It doesn't matter how many times we go around the table, we still don't know if she has really discovered that Snowy is alive, and if she does know, we don't know how she'll come after her – or if Her Royal Highness even knows that Snowy is here."

"So take it to the courts," Freidrich's brother Fritz suggested. "People like us have won against their princes. We have legal rights within the *Reich* – let's exercise them."

"With what proof?" Gunther asked. "It will be our word against hers. Would you believe it if somebody came to you with our story? A princess goes mad and decides to eat some young girl's heart, but a friendly huntsman takes pity on her and uses a deer's heart instead? We'd be laughed out of the court. We don't even know who Snowy's family is, or what their relationship is to Her Royal Highness."

Snowy took a deep breath. "She's my stepmother," she said.

The table went silent.

Max blinked. "You're a princess?"

Snowy nodded. "I'm sorry I didn't tell anybody. I was so happy and safe here, and I thought that if anybody knew–" She turned to Max. "Please tell me you still love me!"

Max kissed her. "Of course I still love you."

Snowy smiled and snuggled into him.

Gunther sighed. "Then there's a succession issue as well."

"That gives us standing in the court," Fritz said.

"It still leaves us with an unbelievable story. And we all know what Her Royal Highness will say – that Snowy ran away and made up the story, and that she should have custody. It makes our situation worse, not better. We're dwarfs, remember? As far as most of the rest of the world is concerned, we're tumblers, jesters, or miners."

"Fine," Christof declared. "I'm with Snowy. I say we fight."

Gunther shook his head. "That's suicide, and we all know it. Look, we only have one option, so, let's just say it and be done with it. We raise the money we need for passage, and then we send Snowy and Max to America. I hear there are plenty of Germans there already."

Snowy and Max went pale. "But this is our home!" Snowy cried.

"My apprenticeship isn't even close to over," Max objected. "And until I finish, I have no trade with which to support us."

"I'll talk to Thomas about getting your release from it," Gunther said. "We served together in the war, and he's a good man. I know he'll agree, even if he was planning to retire and hand the business over to you. You can find a new master to apprentice to once you get there. Look on the bright side – the two of you won't have to wait to get married anymore."

"I have money," Elisa said. "I can contribute most of the passage – you just need to let me know how much."

Snowy stared at the table. "I don't want to leave."

"We have no way of protecting you," Gunther said. "Not really. And the only way we can get you out of her reach for good is to get you out of the *Reich*. I'm sorry, but this is the way it has to be."

Albert coughed. "So what do we do?"

Freidrich turned to Fritz. "You can get that...*thing* out of my bed, you jackass."

Fritz grinned. "But it was so lonely after you put it in mine – it missed you! How could I leave it in that state?"

Gunther rolled his eyes. "We return to work, as though everything is normal. My friend Adam is going to town to pick up my newspapers this week – I'll have him make inquiries about booking passage, and I'll talk to Thomas as soon as I can. I trust you two do want to get married first?"

Snowy and Max both nodded.

"I'll talk to the priest as well," Gunther said. "Snowy, until then, we have to assume that Her Royal Highness is coming for you sooner rather than later. So don't trust anybody you don't know. If somebody you don't know knocks at the door, do *not* let them in."

Snowy scowled. "If I must."

Gunther nodded. "The good news is that the border of this principality is just a day to the north, so as soon as we've got the money, we can get you and Max out, and that should protect you long enough to board the ship to America. And once you're there, it should be impossible for Her Royal Highness to ever find you."

Albert grimaced. "So now we just need to pretend everything is normal while we turn Snowy and Max into fugitives from a mad princess."

308

Cristof chuckled. "This week is going to be an interesting one..."

The next morning, after seeing the other dwarfs off to the mine, Elisa watched as Gunther went into a closet and pulled out a long bundle wrapped in cloth. He placed it on the table and unrolled it, revealing a short barreled musket and bayonet, along with a leather satchel.

"Is that a...?" Snowy asked. Elisa turned to find her standing in the door to their shared room, her eyes wide.

"It's from the war against Prussia," Gunther said, starting to clean it. "I had a gunsmith shorten it so that I could use it. I wish I could say I never had to, but I can't. At least I know it shoots true." He finished cleaning the gun and opened the satchel, pulling out a cartridge and looking at it. "The powder is old, but it should still be good." He loaded it into the barrel of the gun.

"You think you'll need it?" Elisa asked.

Gunther shrugged and checked the flint. "I'd rather not need it." He looked at them both. "Guns are not easy to use, and are not to be trifled with. Neither of you are to touch this, even if your lives are in danger. If you don't know how to shoot, don't even try." He put the gun back in the closet, barrel upwards, the bayonet beside it. "I'm going into the village to make arrangements. I shouldn't be too long." He turned to Snowy. "I meant what I said about not opening the door for anybody you don't know."

Snowy rolled her eyes. "I heard you the first time."

Gunther shook his head and said to Elisa, "Try to take care of her while I'm gone." Then he headed out the door and closed it. Elisa stepped forward and locked it.

She turned to Snowy. "We've got a bunch of chores. We should do them."

"Not like we've got anything better to do," Snowy groused.

Elisa began working on the pots while Snowy cleaned the floor. After a while, Elisa left Snowy to work on the laundry while she went to their room to lie down and think.

Elisa chuckled as she realized that she wished the Devil were here right now. He had always been a good sounding board for ideas. *Some good Christian I am*, she thought. *Wishing I was in the company of the Devil. I guess I'll have a new sin to confess on Sunday.*

That was when she realized she was hearing more than one voice from the main room.

"It's so lovely!" Snowy said.

"It's silk of the best quality," the voice of an elderly woman declared. "You made a great choice. Come, let's lace you up and see how it looks on you."

Snowy let somebody in, Elisa realized, cursing herself for not keeping a closer watch. Then she heard Snowy gasp.

Elisa bolted from the bed and raced into the main room. Snowy writhed on the floor, her face turning purple. Above her stood an old peddler woman, watching Snowy suffocate. The peddler stared at her and then ran out the open door, leaving her bag behind.

Elisa grabbed a knife and dashed to Snowy's side, cutting the lace. Snowy gasped for air, the colour returning to her face.

"She was just an old peddler," Snowy panted. "How was I supposed to know?"

Elisa just stared at the ceiling, wondering how she'd explain this to Gunther when he got back.

"I'm sorry," Elisa said as Gunther stared at her. "I just

stepped away for a minute to lie down and think. I know Snowy has a bad habit of not thinking before she acts. I shouldn't have left the room."

Gunther sighed. "You got there in time, that's what counts."

"If I hadn't–"

"Don't beat yourself up for this," Gunther said. "I thought we had at least a couple more days before something happened."

"She was just a peddler," Snowy grumbled. "And if I'm getting married soon, I want some nice lace."

"She was a peddler *you didn't know*," Gunther growled. "The princess wants you dead, and this is her first assassin. And since she knows she failed, there will almost certainly be more."

Snowy stared at the floor. "This isn't any way to live."

"I agree," Gunther said. "That's why we're sending you to America." He looked at the bag the peddler had left, now sitting on the table. "Let's take a look at what she was carrying."

He emptied it out onto the table. Most of the contents were nothing extraordinary – a half eaten lunch, a blanket, the usual things that one brings when travelling. The silver comb caught Elisa's eye...and Snowy's too.

"Oh, I'd love to have that," Snowy said.

"Look at the table," Elisa breathed, staring at the comb. Where the sharp teeth met the table, a thin smoke rose.

"That must have been her backup plan," Gunther said. "How sick and twisted can you get?"

"I'll take this out and bury it," Elisa said. "I'll be careful."

Gunther nodded. "Thank you. Snowy, I have good news. Thomas has agreed to release Max from his apprenticeship, and I was able to convince Father Joseph to marry the two of you on Sunday. Now we're just waiting on the price for passage to America."

"I still don't want to go," Snowy said.

Gunther shook his head. "I wish there was another choice, but we've already had one close call. This is a small principality – the palace is only a couple of days away, less on horseback."

"Maybe I should go stay with Max," Snowy suggested.

Gunther shook his head. "Too many strangers go in and out of that cobbler's shop. It will be easier to protect you here. But, this changes *everything*."

"How so?"

"We can no longer act as though everything is normal and hope Her Royal Highness doesn't find you here," Gunther said. "And we only have the one gun."

The next couple of days were some of the busiest Elisa had seen in years. The house became a hub of activity, with villagers coming and going, making their plans with Gunther and the dwarfs. The musket was also out of the closet, now resting against the corner nearest the front door.

Elisa took comfort in the chaos. With this many people coming and going, the princess' assassin would have to be insane to make another attempt. Even Gunther felt able to relax a bit, allowing Snowy to leave the house and take in the outside air, so long as she didn't stray out of sight.

It was on the second day that Gunther got back the price of passage to America. It was relatively quiet in the house, with just Gunther, Elisa, Max, and Gunther's friend Adam, a short man with greying hair, although not as short or grey as Gunther.

"So, that's what it will cost for the two of them," Adam said. "Now we just need the money."

Elisa reached into her magic coinpurse and pulled out the exact amount, placing it on the table. "And there it is."

Max stared at the table. "We'll need some money for when we get there as well."

"How much?" Elisa asked.

Max told her. Elisa took it out of the coinpurse and put it on the table.

Gunther, Max, and Adam stared at her. "Just how much money do you have?" Gunther asked.

"Enough," Elisa replied, turning to Max. "Now we just need to get you two to the church."

"Well, this will be a lot easier than I hoped," Gunther said.

The door burst open, Christof panting. "Gunther, come quick – it's Snowy!"

Gunther cursed, grabbed the musket and raced out the door, Elisa, Max, and Adam following. Snowy lay on the ground, her face pale, not moving or breathing. An apple lay beside her, a bite taken out of it, the flesh discoloured.

"I looked away for just a moment," Christof said. "When I looked back, she was standing with some old woman...and then she fell down."

Gunther gritted his teeth. "Did you see where the old woman went?"

Christof grabbed an axe off a tree trunk. "She fled towards the river."

"She's not getting away," Gunther swore, shouldering his musket and running as fast as his short legs could carry him. It wasn't long before he was joined by the rest of the dwarfs, Elisa, and a not small number of villagers who had been nearby when Snowy had fallen. Max stayed behind, cradling Snowy's body.

They caught up to the old woman near the edge of the cliff that Elisa had spent so much time in contemplation. Gunther un-shouldered his musket and took aim. Cristof and many of the others brandished axes and clubs – whatever they could grab to use as weapons.

"You may as well give up," Gunther declared. "We have you surrounded."

The old woman sneered and pulled off her hair. A white wig fell to the ground, revealing long auburn hair. The woman brushed at her face, the wrinkles falling away into a mess of smeared makeup. "You would raise arms against your princess?"

"You killed our daughter," Gunther growled. "I don't care if I hang for it, you will pay for what you did."

"Oh guaaaards!" the princess called. Elisa turned to see a handful of soldiers crest the hills around them and raising muskets, bayonets fixed. "Did you really think I wouldn't have my palace guards nearby?"

"It won't save you," Christoff said. "There are a lot more of us than there are of you."

"But not that many guns," the princess declared. "If you're smart, you'll let me pass, and I might show mercy."

"We'll take this to the court!" Fritz said. "We have rights!"

"This isn't a Protestant principality!" the princess declared. "You're *serfs*! You only have the rights I give you! And the longer you stand there threatening me, the more likely I'll be to have you all drawn and quartered, just like in the old days!"

"Well, this is getting interesting," a quiet and familiar voice said. Elisa turned to find the Devil standing beside her. "I wonder what will happen next."

"Do something," Elisa hissed.

The Devil looked at her with bewilderment. "I don't stop people from sinning."

"You won't get away with this!" Christof declared.

"Why?" Elisa demanded, staring at the princess. "Just tell me why! Why do you want your stepdaughter dead this badly?"

The princess sneered at her. "Because there can only be one great beauty in the land, and it has to be me!"

Elisa realized that her mouth was open in shock. "*That's* what this is about?" she cried. "You killed her because you think she's going to be *prettier* than you? That's insane!"

"That's *power*," the princess stated. "There will be no Jacobins here! There will be no revolutionaries, or guillotines! The French republican poison will not come to my lands! There will be only one ruler, and it will be me! And that means that I will have the most wealth, the most power, and the most beauty, and none will stand against me!"

"You're mad," Gunther breathed.

"There's been enough talking," the princess announced. "Guards, open fire at my command."

Elisa gritted her teeth in fury. She read the princess' wish: to escape. Elisa shaped the wish and granted it.

Reality shifted. The princess began to dance.

"What's happening?" she demanded. "Why am I dancing?"

Her feet began to move faster and faster, carrying her towards the edge. "Somebody, stop me from dancing! Please!"

Gunther stared at Elisa. "Are you doing this?"

"She made her wish," Elisa stated quietly.

"A thousand Thalers to whoever can stop me from dancing!" the princess shrieked, coming ever closer to the cliff. With a scream, she leapt over it. A sicken crunch of broken bones sounded from the bottom, followed by silence.

Elisa turned away. The Devil gazed at her with appreciation. "I never knew you had it in you," he said. "Good on you, my friend! I will make sure that she receives the appropriate treatment now that she's in my care."

"It's nothing to praise," Elisa declared. "Did Clever Gretel have anything to do with this?"

The Devil shook his head. "Last I heard of her, she was in the eastern *Reich* looking for a principality of her own to rule. I imagine she's found one by now."

Elisa began walking back to the house. As she did, the crowd dispersed, the other dwarfs following her to where Snowy lay dead on the ground before the house, Max still cradling her. Elisa stared at Snowy's body, and then took a deep breath and closed her eyes.

"Can you do something about this?" Gunther asked.

Elisa opened her eyes and nodded. Gunther's wish was clear, and she could use it.

"What can she possibly do?" Albert asked.

"Ever heard of what the French call a 'fairy godmother'?" Gunther asked. "Elisa happens to be one."

Albert coughed and scowled. "That's a bit hard to believe."

Elisa granted Gunther's wish that Snowy was still alive. Reality shifted. "I'd prefer that when you tell people about this, you leave me out of it."

"Your penance?" Gunther asked.

Elisa shook her head. "My penance has been over for years. I just don't want to be remembered for dancing somebody off a cliff."

Gunther stared down at Snowy's still form. "So, when are you going to do your...thing?"

Elisa blinked. "I already did. She should be waking up right now."

Max stared at her. "She's not breathing."

Elisa stared at Snowy. "I don't understand. This has never failed before."

Gunther reached up and patted Elisa on the shoulder. "Perhaps the world is becoming less welcoming to good wishes." He wiped away a tear, but more came.

"She should be breathing," Elisa declared. "I granted the wish. She can't be dead."

"I'll contact the priest," Harald said, tears of his own running down his cheeks. "She'll get a proper Christian burial."

"She can't be dead!" Elisa cried.

Max held Snowy in his arms, weeping. "I'm sorry! I should have been there beside you!"

Elisa knelt down, grabbing Snowy's body and shaking it. "She can't be dead – I granted the wish!"

Gunther glanced at the other dwarfs. "Elisa..."

"She can't be dead!" Elisa screamed. "Wake up, Snowy, wake up!"

Albert grabbed her and pulled her away. Snowy's body fell to the ground. "Enough, Elisa! She's gone." He coughed.

Snowy stirred.

Max and the dwarfs stared at Snowy, and then at Albert.

"Did you make his cough magic?" Harald asked.

Elisa shook her head. Then she spotted the piece of apple that had fallen out of Snowy's mouth.

"Of course," Elisa breathed. "The wish brought her back to life, but the poison was still in her mouth killing her. That's why it took so long."

"What happened?" Snowy rasped. "Why am I on the ground?"

"The danger's over," Gunther said. "The princess is dead."

"You might have a claim to the principality now," Fritz said. "You could go back to the palace."

Freidrich shook his head. "That's only for male heirs. In the absence of one, the principality still goes back to the *Reich*."

"Suppose she marries Max - then he becomes the male heir."

Elisa stood and made her way back into the house. Then she started to pack up her belongings.

"You're leaving us?" Gunther asked. Elisa turned to see him in the doorway. "We'd all rather that you stay."

Elisa gave him a sad smile. "This has been a wonderful place, and I wish I could live here and see what happens to Snowy and Max...but I can't. I have a job to do – Clever Gretel is somewhere out there, and I need to find a way to stop her."

"Because of your penance?" Gunther asked.

Elisa shook her head. "Because it needs to be done, and I may be the only one who can do it. Besides, now that I'm no longer a penitent, I don't know what I am, and I want to spend some time finding out."

Gunther stepped forward to embrace her. She knelt down so that he could. "You be safe in your travels, and remember us."

"You'll all be in my prayers," Elisa said. "And I'm old enough that I pray a *lot*."

"Will you at least stay long enough for us all to give you a proper goodbye?"

Elisa wiped away a tear. "If I do that, I think I'll never leave."

Gunther gave her a sad smile. "I may have to insist, then."

"But you won't," Elisa stated. "You're too good a man."

"Don't lose yourself again," Gunther said.

"I won't," Elisa promised. She stood and threw her bag over her shoulder. "Please give my love to all of the others."

"I will," Gunther promised.

Elisa made her way out the door. The others were still arguing over whether Snowy should try to claim the principality after she had married Max. She smiled as she watched them, and then forced herself to turn away. She took a deep breath and began walking down the road, tears running down her cheeks.

Chapter III – A Soldier's Wish

Elisa hardly ever granted wishes anymore. Instead, she hunted for them.

Somewhere out there was a wish she could use to stop Clever Gretel. All she had to do was find it. That, on the other hand, had proven harder than she had ever imagined. None of the wishes she found could work.

It was as just after she had crossed to the western bank of the Rhine that she first encountered the French. They patrolled the roads, travellers often giving them a wide berth. It was close to a village in the autumn that she saw why. A group of French soldiers had stopped a cart, and were taking it away from its owners at gunpoint. She couldn't understand what they were saying, but their meaning was clear. The owners of the cart walked away, dejected but alive.

It was long after she had passed them by that she

realized that she was clutching her magic coinpurse for dear life.

Elisa stopped in the inn for the night. The first thing she did when she approached the innkeeper was ask if there were any newspapers.

"It's a bit old, but we have one," the innkeeper said, handing it over. The first thing Elisa looked at was the date. It read August 20, 1797. The front page story talked about the new rules the French would be imposing in the Cisherian Republic.

"They're just robbers if you ask me," the innkeeper declared. "For all their talk of liberty and fraternity, the only thing they've really liberated is our belongings."

"That's what I've been hearing," Elisa muttered. Then she looked up and said, "Is there a room available tonight?"

"We've got a couple," the innkeeper replied. "I'll make sure you get the nicer one. We've got some decent food in the dining hall. It's not much, but it's well cooked."

Elisa gave him a smile as he handed her a room key. "Thank you."

She made her way to the dining hall, and then sat down and scanned the room for wishes. There was nothing out of the ordinary, and nothing that needed to be granted, either. There was also nothing she could use. She sighed as a serving girl placed a plate of food in front of her. Almost all of it was potatoes.

Maybe I should head back out of occupied territory, Elisa thought. *Nobody's going to be wishing for bigger things while the French are here...at least not that I can use.*

The door slamming open and four French soldiers marching into the dining hall, muskets un-shouldered and bayonets fixed, snapped her back to the present. They said something in French, and then one of them repeated in German, "In the name of the First Republic, all food supplies, including the harvest, are hereby commandeered by the army."

"But the winter is coming!" the innkeeper protested. "The entire village will starve!"

The German speaking officer just sneered at him. "You're farmers. Grow some more food."

Two of the soldiers strode back into the kitchen. Elisa closed her eyes as she heard the sounds of a struggle and then a hoarse screaming from the open doorway, failing not to think about what had to be happening. When she opened her eyes, she saw that most of the room had been doing the same, fear in their eyes of what would happen if any of them tried to stop it. After a few more minutes, the soldiers emerged, both with their muskets shouldered and large bags of food. Then they departed.

The room went silent. Elisa scanned the wishes again. One was that the rapist would die. She shaped the wish and granted it. Reality shifted. That soldier would suffer a terrible and fatal accident after he had left the village, far enough away that the French wouldn't come back for reprisals.

Most of the other wishes were for enough food to survive the winter. She picked one, shaped it, and granted it. Reality shifted. After the French left with their harvest, the village would discover that enough had been missed to survive.

She spent the night, before she went to bed praying for her soul and for the souls of all of the lives she had touched. Then, in the morning, she turned back east, returning to the unoccupied German lands.

As Elisa continued her long search, whenever she remembered, she would seek out a newspaper, just to check the date. When she saw that it was April 14, 1803, she smiled and thought, *I only lost track of three years this time.*

But a wish she could use to stop Clever Gretel remained elusive.

It was a chilly day in October as she walked along the bank of the Danube river that she heard the firing in the distance in front of her. Elisa stiffened, listening as the sound of battle intensified.

I should turn back, she thought, but didn't. Instead, another idea emerged.

I've never looked for a wish I could use on a battlefield before.

She took a deep breath. Battlefields meant death, but she'd already seen plenty of that. It also meant soldiers, at least some of whom might be French.

I've been looking for at least eight years everywhere else and I've found nothing, Elisa thought. *What have I got to lose?*

She sat down and waited for the firing to stop. No point in getting caught in a crossfire looking for wishes. She could try to find the survivors once it was done. She sat down and waited.

The sounds of fighting lasted throughout the day, only dying down as the sun grew low in the sky. Elisa stood and took a deep breath, making her way forward. She saw the bodies before she saw the wreckage of the bridge or the town on the opposite bank.

Elisa swallowed. Flies were already buzzing over the corpses, some in the blue uniforms of the French, some in light grey uniforms with red trim. The bridge they had been fighting over was little more than rubble.

Elisa braced herself, and began to make her way through the battlefield. *I need somebody alive.*

"Hey!" a voice called with an Austrian accent. "You loot a single thing, and I'll shoot you where you stand!"

Elisa turned to see a white-clad soldier at the edge of a building crew, musket leveled at her with fixed bayonet. She raised her hands. "I'm not looting. I'm just looking to see if there's somebody I know."

"You won't find any Bavarians here," the soldier stated. "If you want the Bavarians, they're fighting alongside the French."

"I'm not from Bavaria," Elisa said. "And I have no love for the French."

The infantryman scowled and shouldered his gun. "Well, you sound like a Bavarian. Go find who you're looking for and stay out of our way. We have a bridge to rebuild."

Elisa nodded, taking in all of their wishes. Nothing she could use. She looked around the field. Nobody was moving, outside of the crew approaching where the bridge had once stood. She sighed. She'd probably have to look further afield to find survivors.

She left the main mass of dead and made her way away from the Danube. The dead still littered the ground, but in smaller numbers. It was on a small hill under a tree that she found him, clutching at the hole in his belly, his white uniform soaked with blood. The soldier looked up at her with the gaze a man has when he knows he's dying.

Elisa read his wish and then swallowed. *I wish somebody would just listen to me for once.*

Elisa knelt down beside him and said, "Hello. I'm Elisa. Tell me about yourself."

"We were trying to get away from Ulm," the soldier rasped. "We tried to cross the bridge here at Günzberg, but the French were faster than we were. We thought we had a chance, but...we didn't." He stared at the ground. "Ulm will be surrounded. Napoleon will win."

"Do you have somebody special waiting for you?" Elisa asked. "A sweetheart?"

The soldier smiled. "Maria...she's the baker's daughter. She makes such wonderful bread for me. We were planning to have so many children."

"She must be very special,"

"She's the most beautiful woman in the world."

"And what about your family?" Elisa asked. "Who are they?"

The soldier winced in pain. "My father is a stonemason. He works on the church...it always needs work. My mother makes wonderful beer...better than the tavern's. But...they don't like me very much. They were always disappointed in me. I thought if I joined the army...they'd finally respect me."

"I'm sure they're proud of you now," Elisa said, her voice barely a whisper.

The soldier looked out to the distance. "I hope so." He turned his head to stare at her. "Why are you here?"

Elisa took a deep breath. "Would you believe I'm a...a fairy godmother? I came to grant your wish." She wiped a tear from her eye.

"What, like in Cinderella?"

Elisa chuckled. "Her name was Eleonore, and she was a good friend. I wish I'd appreciated her more. The French are wrong, though – there was no pumpkin, or glass slipper."

"Why are you really here?" the soldier asked.

"Your wish is to be listened to," Elisa said, wiping more tears from her eyes. "You tell me whatever you want, and I'll listen, for as long as you want me to."

"Listening to somebody else is nice too,"

Before she knew it, Elisa was pouring her heart out. She told him about Clever Gretel, and about her long hunt to find her. She told him about the Devil, and how he had saved her after Gretel had stabbed her. And then she told him about her search for a wish she could use to stop Gretel once and for all.

The soldier chuckled, wincing at the pain as he did.

"You make it so complicated," he said, his voice reedy. "You should just shoot her."

Elisa blinked. "What?"

The soldier motioned to his blood soaked gut. "People die when you shoot them."

Elisa shook her head. "I...I actually had never thought of doing that."

"Maybe that's why you're here," the soldier suggested. "Maybe God sent you to speak to me." He smiled, then asked, "Are you Catholic?"

Elisa nodded. "I am."

"I'd like to pray, one last time. Could you pray with me?"

Elisa nodded, the tears flowing freely down her cheeks. She knelt and began to pray with him. She had barely finished the "Our Father" when he let out a final, ragged breath, and was still.

Elisa sat beside him and wept. The sun set, the shadows turning to darkness. From the Danube, she could hear the men working quietly on the bridge. She looked down at the outline of the soldier's musket on the grass in the faint starlight.

Gunther's words came unbidden to her mind. *"Guns are not easy to use, and are not to be trifled with. If you don't know how to shoot, don't even try."*

"Can I even stop her as I am?" Elisa wondered aloud. Everything she had tried had failed. Years of searching had provided no wishes that she could twist into a shape that could end Clever Gretel. All she had ever succeeded in doing was stopping whatever "fun" Gretel was having.

Elisa sighed and rose to her feet. She could not stop Clever Gretel as a fairy godmother. It was time to try something else.

Perhaps, she reflected as she made her way away from the battlefield and the men repairing the bridge, it was time to find somebody who could teach her how to shoot.

Chapter IV – A Soldier's Wife

Deciding to find somebody to teach her how to shoot was one thing. Actually finding one proved to be far more difficult.

Walking across one battlefield was enough to make Elisa decide to head away from the fighting. She found herself making her way deeper into Bavaria, looking for soldiers or hunters who would be willing to teach her how to use a musket. After a few weeks, she began to feel as though she was banging her head against a wall.

The soldiers were all at war. Before long, she stopped looking for hunters – they were all too old, too unwilling to teach a woman, or gone to war as well.

She found herself at an inn in the town of Vohburg, just east of the city of Ingolstadt, waiting for the war to end.

The snow had begun to fall when news of a French

victory at a place named Austerlitz arrived. It was a such a crushing victory, in fact, that the patrons around her in the dining hall were already speculating that the war had to end soon. Elisa added that to her evening prayers. She needed the soldiers to come home.

As the weather grew colder, she made her way into the town centre to get some warmer clothes. She found herself stopping in front of a store, a fur coat in the window. *I'm not a penitent any more*, she reminded herself, and then went inside and bought it, along with some other nice clothes.

This must be what a successful merchant's wife feels like, she thought as she stepped out onto the street. The one thing she hadn't replaced was her red headband. She was still an unmarried woman – it felt wrong to ever take it off when she was outside.

It took Elisa less than two blocks to feel self-conscious, head back to the store, and return most of it. She emerged the second time with clothes that were nice, but still very much what a peasant would wear, albeit a peasant with enough money to pay for quality.

It was after Elisa attended the New Year's Mass and welcomed in the year eighteen hundred and six that word reached Vohburg that the emperors of Austria, Russia, and France had signed a peace, and the war was now over. Elisa took a deep breath and thanked God. Then, she settled in and waited for news that the soldiers were returning.

It was the middle of January before that news finally arrived. The soldiers were at Pullach to the south. She caught the first carriage there, emerging with excitement to ask where the soldiers were.

"I'm sorry," a passer-by told her. "They left two days ago. I think they were going to Ingolstadt."

Elisa cursed under her breath. Happily, there was a

carriage headed to Ingolstadt in a few hours, and she caught it. As the carriage entered the city, Elisa marvelled as the Medieval city walls gave way to a maze of red roofs and churches. She stepped out once it stopped, wondering how travelling by carriage had somehow managed to be as exhausting as walking. She found an inn, took a room, and flopped down on the bed. She'd find the soldiers in the morning.

"I'm sorry," the innkeeper told her the next morning, "I'm pretty sure they went to Neuberg."

"And where's that?" Elisa asked.

"It's about half a day to the west by carriage."

Elisa caught the next carriage heading west, watching as she approached a walled town on the shore of the Danube, a large white palace overlooking the river. As the carriage stopped and she stepped off, she offered a quick prayer that the soldiers would still be here.

"You mean the Seventh Infantry?" a passer-by replied when she asked about soldiers. "I think they're garrisoned down that way."

Elisa found herself breathing hard as the man walked away, waving to a woman who appeared to be his wife. At last, she'd found them!

She forced herself to start walking towards the garrison, her heart pounding. Her mind churned, trying to figure out how to present herself and what to say. She emerged into a large square, soldiers in sky blue coats with muskets shouldered milling about.

This is it, Elisa thought. *I need to just walk up to one, and ask if there's somebody who can–*

"Hey, you want a beer?" a woman's voice called out to her.

Elisa turned to find herself facing a young woman in a makeshift stall, waving her over. Elisa blinked and stepped over.

"I'm sorry?" Elisa said.

"I asked if you wanted a beer," the woman said. "It's nice and cheap. Besides, you look lost."

"Sure," Elisa said, paying the woman and taking a sip from the stein placed in front of her.

"So, what do you want with the Seventh Infantry?" the woman asked.

"I'm looking for somebody to teach me how to shoot," Elisa replied. "I can pay for it – I have money."

The woman chuckled. "I can't say I've heard that one before. I think our best sharpshooter is Karl Mueller – he's the corporal over there." She pointed to a tall man with dark hair, broad shoulders, and a moustache. The gun on his shoulder was shorter than the others, and his uniform had a green plume and tassels. "He's one of the light infantry specialists. If anybody can teach you how to shoot straight, it's him."

Elisa finished her beer. "Thank you."

"He's unmarried, you know," the woman added. "And a good catch. If I wasn't already married to an officer, I'd be sorely tempted."

Elisa blinked. "I'll try to keep that in mind."

She took a deep breath and began towards the corporal. He noticed her approach and raised an eyebrow. "Can I help you, miss?"

Elisa curtseyed. "My name is Elisabeth Beichtkind. Might I talk to you for a moment in private, mister, er, corporal Mueller?"

Corporal Mueller gave her a kind smile. Elisa found her heart fluttering. "Of course," he said. "There's a little park just over there that I think we can use."

Elisa nodded. "That would be wonderful, thank you."

He escorted her to a small park by the Danube, where they sat on a bench overlooking the river. A handful of couples walked along the riverbank, but otherwise the park was empty.

"So, what can I do for you, Miss Elisabeth?"

Elisa smiled, feeling shy for the first time she could remember. "It's Elisa, please. I'm looking for somebody to teach me how to shoot. I can pay for lessons – I have money."

The corporal looked surprised. "I can certainly do that, but it is irregular. Why do you want to learn how to shoot? It is to hunt?"

Elisa took a deep breath. "Something like that. And I need to be able to kill with the first shot."

Corporal Mueller's eyes narrowed. "There's a lot more you aren't telling me."

"Yes. But, I assure you, I'm...I'm not some evil woman."

"Oh, I believe you," he stated. "I've met some truly evil people before – they're not shy about asking for what they want."

"As I said, I can pay, Corporal Mueller – I have plenty of money."

Corporal Mueller held up his hand. "Please, just call me Karl. And I don't want your money."

Elisa sighed. "Then the answer is no. I'm sorry I wasted your time."

"I didn't say that," Karl said. "I'll teach you. I just don't want your money. I want something else."

Elisa blinked. "What's that?"

"I want you to marry me."

Elisa realized that she was holding her breath, and forced herself to exhale. "I'm sorry, I don't think I understand. Are you asking for a 'May marriage'?"

Karl shook his head. "I don't want a whore for the next campaign, I want a *wife*. And I want you to be her."

"And you'll teach me how to shoot."

Karl nodded. "Yes." He leaned forward. "But, be aware – the life of a soldier's wife is not easy or safe. It

331

can be quite dangerous when you go on campaign, and very hard. I'm talking about long marches in bad weather, digging trenches, and possibly being shot at or captured by the enemy. I thought you should know all of that before you answer."

Elisa's heart pounded so hard she was amazed Karl didn't seem to hear it.

"So," Karl said. "Marry me, and I'll make sure you know how to shoot. Will you be my wife?"

Elisa looked at Karl and focused on his wish. *I wish I wasn't lonely anymore.*

She closed her eyes for a moment and granted his wish. Reality did not shift.

"Yes," she said.

Elisa stood beside Karl as he faced the lieutenant, who stared at them as though they had crawled out from under a rock.

"Karl, is this just a ploy to get a partition for your bed in the barracks?" he asked.

"No sir," Karl replied.

"You know that the army frowns upon non-commissioned officer marriages," the lieutenant said.

"Even so, sir, we have not yet met our allotment of six wives to the company. I would add Elisabeth as mine."

He turned to Elisa. "And you consent to this arrangement?"

Elisa swallowed and nodded. "I do, sir."

"Do you understand what that means?" the lieutenant asked.

Elisa blinked. "Um...I think so."

The officer sighed. "That's a 'no'. If you marry Corporal Mueller, you will become a member of the Seventh Infantry, light infantry section baggage train. You will be subject to military discipline and military law. You will be provided duties for the company, and you will be expected to fulfill them. This may include anything from laundry to cooking to digging trenches. You will carry your husband's gear, and march alongside him. You will provide him with support in the field, including under fire. Should you be captured, you can expect to be treated harshly, and that includes being raped or killed. You will be lodged in the barracks with your husband and the rest of the company, with only a partition for your privacy. In the field, you will share whatever accommodation that may be. This will be your life until your husband is killed, discharged, or furloughed. Should he be wounded, you will nurse him, as well as assist in nursing the other wounded of his company. Should he be killed, you will inherit his belongings. Now, taking this into consideration, do you consent to this arrangement?"

Elisa took a deep breath. "I do."

The lieutenant nodded. "Very well." He turned to Karl. "You know there's a fee for being permitted to marry."

"I can pay it," Karl said.

The lieutenant sighed. "Fine. Take forty-eight hours leave, say your vows, and have your wedding night. That will give us time to set up your partition in the barracks."

Karl saluted. "Thank you, sir."

Elisa frowned. "Should I, um, salute?"

"You're not a soldier, so no," the officer replied. "Now get out of my sight so that I can deal with more important things."

They got married at the closest church. When Karl gave his age as twenty-eight, Elisa gave hers as twenty-five. As the priest pronounced them man and wife, it was all Elisa could do to keep her legs from shaking. *Is this what Ella felt like when she married her Karl?*

333

Once the ceremony was over, Elisa removed her red headband, staring at it for a moment, before donating it so that some other unmarried woman could use it. *I'm Elisa Mueller now*, she thought, running the name through her head. *I'm a married woman.*

When they left the church, Elisa and her new husband went to an inn that Karl had heard was a very good one, and rented a room for a couple of days. There they undressed and consummated their marriage. As they lay naked on the bed after, their bodies covered in sweat, Elisa turned to look at Karl and asked, "Why did you ask to marry me?"

"I was tired of being alone," Karl replied.

Elisa ran a finger down his chest. "But why me?"

Karl kissed her. "Because you're beautiful, and I can tell just by looking at you that you're a good woman, and that you needed help. Why did you say 'yes'?"

Elisa leaned her head back on the pillow. "Because I'd been alone for a long time. Too long. And I'd seen so many others find happiness...and I wanted some for myself at last. And I think you're somebody I can easily love."

She felt his finger caress her, coming to rest on the scar below her breasts where Clever Gretel had stabbed her all those years ago. "You were wounded once."

Elisa pressed his finger against her. "It was a long time ago."

"The person you want to shoot, did they do this to you?"

Elisa nodded. "I'm...I'm not quite ready to talk about it yet."

He kissed her again. As he did, she felt her body respond, and they made love, this time without the pain of her first time. They fell asleep in each other's arms.

The next morning, she woke up before Karl. She watched him sleep, studying his features in the sunlight.

There was something about looking at him that just made her heart feel lighter. *Is this what happiness feels like?* she wondered.

The she chuckled. *I got a Karl of my own, Ella. I wish you could have met him.*

Karl stirred, as though he had felt her watching him. She smiled as he looked up at her, but didn't kiss him. His morning breath was atrocious.

They never tell you about that in the stories, Elisa thought.

"We have another day before we have to be back at the barracks," Karl said. "What do you want to do?"

Elisa thought for a moment, and then said, "Can you show me the town?"

"Of course," Karl replied. "Anything for my lovely wife."

Once they had dressed, he took her to see the Town Hall and the churches of St. Ursula and St. Peter. It was after they had finished looking at the churches that they walked, arm in arm, Elisa enjoying the feeling of being close to him, that he asked, "So, where are you from?"

"The north," Elisa replied. "Not a place anybody would have heard of – it was this island on the Baltic Sea. My father was a bookbinder, but he and my mother died when I was fifteen. You?"

"I come from Munich," Karl said. "My father was a gunsmith – he made my rifle for me when I decided to join the army. 'If you're going to go to war, you should at least have something that can shoot straight,' he told me. He and my mother died a couple of years ago. Smallpox."

Elisa frowned. "I'm sorry. Any brothers or sisters?"

Karl shook his head. "You?"

"Not that survived."

Karl took a deep breath. "Come on – there is this wonderful spot on the Danube that gives you a good view at the castle. Let's go and think of happier things."

335

By the time they got there, Elisa was certain she had married a man she would fall in love with.

Elisa stared at the barracks in disbelief.

"It's not so bad when you get used to it," Karl said.

"Are you sure we can't rent a house?" Elisa asked. "I've got money."

"Renting houses is for officers. The noncoms need to stay with the men."

Elisa hadn't known what to expect when she walked into the barracks to see where they would be spending the next few months of their married life. She hadn't expected to find out that the unmarried men were sleeping two to a bed to save space. Or that the partition she had been told about was a makeshift wall of wood covering up a space that was barely big enough for one person, much less two.

Karl gave her a squeeze on the shoulder. "We're only going to be sleeping here."

Elisa gave him a fragile smile. "I guess I just wasn't prepared for the reality of what I'd been told."

"You'll be amazed at how quickly you'll adjust," Karl said. "My first night in barracks, I barely slept – all the other men's snoring kept me up. A couple of weeks later, I slept like a baby no matter how much noise they made. Anyway, you can put your belongings in that chest here."

Elisa chuckled, and put her back into the chest. "It's a good thing I spent most of my life traveling light. Now what?"

Karl reached into his chest and pulled out one of his jackets. "You'll want to wear this."

Elisa blinked. "Why?"

"Mainly, it prevents misunderstandings. It tells anybody who sees you that you're with the regiment, and that you're my wife."

Elisa smiled and pulled it on. The sleeves ran long enough to cover her hands. "I think I'm going to like this."

Karl smiled. "You look great in it. Still, you'll probably want to alter it to fit you a bit better."

She chuckled. "I'll take care of that."

"And now, you talk to the Provost," Karl said. "He'll tell you what your duties are. I'll take you there."

Karl took Elisa across the compound to the administration building, where the Provost occupied a small office. "So you must be Corporal Mueller's new wife," the Provost declared as they entered. "Welcome to the regiment!"

Elisa curtseyed. "Thank you, sir."

"I'm a sergeant," the Provost said. "You don't need to call me 'sir'."

"I'm sorry," Elisa said.

"So, do you have a profession?" the Provost asked.

"Not really," Elisa replied. "I spent most of my life as a penitent helping people."

The Provost nodded. "I see. Can you cook?"

"Not really," Elisa replied.

"Can you sew?"

"My father was a bookbinder," Elisa said. "He taught me how to sew bindings, and my mother did show me how to do basic repairs."

"I'll assign you to laundry duty, then," the Provost declared. "You'll work repairing and cleaning clothes for the regiment. They'll let you know when the meals and breaks are."

"Karl promised to teach me how to shoot," Elisa said.

"The two of you can do that on your own time," the Provost stated. "While you're on mine, you'll help with the laundry, and whatever else I need you to do for the regiment."

Elisa nodded. "I understand."

"Now, let's take you to meet the other wives," the Provost said. "Corporal Mueller, you have better places to be, I assume?"

Karl nodded and saluted. "I do." He gave Elisa a kiss, and then headed out of the office.

The Provost gave Elisa a warm smile. "It's a bit to get used to, but it's a good life, for all of its hardships. We take care of our own, and you are now one of our own." He stood. "Follow me."

He led her to the laundry, where she found three other women working and talking. One was sewing, and the other two were washing.

"Ladies," the Provost announced, "I've brought you some help."

They stopped and stared at her. Elisa swallowed.

"This is Corporal Mueller's new wife, Elisabeth was it?"

Elisa nodded. "Everybody calls me Elisa, though."

"Well, she's going to be working here with you," the Provost said. "Anna, I leave her in your care."

A robust woman with red hair put down her sewing and grinned at her. "Welcome to our little corner of the regiment. I'm Anna, and I'm Lieutenant Ritter's wife. I'm in charge."

Elisa nodded. "It's a pleasure to meet you."

Anna pointed to a dark haired waif. "That's Helena – she's married to Sergeant Weber."

"So you're the one they put in the new partition for," Helena said, scrubbing at a jacket. "Karl has good taste."

Elisa blushed. "I'm really nothing special."

Anna pointed to a flaxen haired beauty. "And that is Louisa. Somehow, Private Hofmann managed to capture her heart."

"You're lucky," Louisa declared, setting one jacket aside and starting to wash another. "We just get a curtain."

"And a corner," Helena pointed out. "You're not in the middle of the barracks, at least."

"One day, Franz will get promoted," Louisa said. "And then we'll get a partition of our own."

Helena laughed. "That would be terrible! What would the men do without the entertainment of listening to you and your husband at night?"

"Tear down your partition and listen to *you*!" Louisa replied with a grin.

Elisa smiled and tried to figure out whether she should laugh.

"Sit down, grab a jacket and needle, and let's see what you can do," Anna instructed. As Elisa sat, she added, "And tell us *all* about you!"

It was an exhausted Elisa that ate dinner with her husband at the mess hall, who then took her out to the firing range.

"Time for your first lesson," Karl said. "Today, you're learning how to load. I take it you've never used a rifle before?"

"I've never used any type of musket," Elisa replied.

"This isn't a musket," Karl stated. "It's a rifle. That means the barrel has grooves in the barrel called 'rifling', which makes it more accurate. A musket is made to send a ball in the general direction you are aiming. A rifle is made to hit what you're aiming for."

"Do I need to worry about a bayonet?"

Karl shook his head. "Rifles don't use them." He held out the gun to Elisa. "Don't worry – it's not loaded. It takes time to load a rifle – more than it takes to load a musket – but it's worth the extra time to hit what you're shooting at. So, first, check your flint – it should be nice and sharp."

As Karl ran Elisa through the parts of the gun, she

tried not to feel overwhelmed. She failed. It wasn't as simple as aiming the rifle and pulling a trigger. She had to worry about putting just enough gunpowder into the priming pan, and then putting enough into the barrel before she loaded the ball. To make matters worse, she couldn't use the cartridges that the rest of the infantry used – she had to measure out the gunpowder herself.

Finally, Karl told her to put the rifle to her shoulder. "Now, aim down the sights. Don't worry about whether you're going to hit the target – you probably aren't. Just worry about not dropping the gun. Exhale, and then pull the trigger before you take your next breath."

Elisa followed Karl's instructions. The loudest sound in the world went off beside her ear, and the stock of the rifle slammed into her shoulder.

"Good!" Karl declared. "You didn't drop it!"

Elisa realized that she was staring with her eyes wide open, and forced herself to blink. "Is it always like that?"

Karl chuckled. "Good heavens, no. I started you with a half charge. Usually, it's louder and hits your shoulder harder. Now, reload, and you're going to fire again. Don't worry – we'll use the same charge. I want you to get used to a half charge before we move you up to what you'll *really* be shooting."

"Can I take a moment to rest before I try this again?"

Karl shook his head. "I don't know exactly who this person is you're after, but if you miss the first shot, you're going to need the second ready. So, you need to practice loading, and to practice doing it right after you've fired. Now, load."

By the eighth time Elisa had loaded and fired the weapon, Karl was no longer having to correct her on loading. The tenth time, Karl told her it was time to stop.

"You did well," Karl said. "That's it for tonight."

"So what's next?" Elisa asked.

"Next, we go back to the barracks and get a good night's sleep," Karl said, picking up and cleaning the rifle. "Then we've both got an early morning and lots of work to do."

"And then we're going to work on aiming?"

Karl shook his head. "Then we're going to work on loading a three-quarters charge."

Elisa sighed. "This isn't easy to learn, is it?"

Karl shook his head. "Not if you want to be good at it. The infantry in the line can afford to send balls flying all over the place, since they're all firing at once and filling the air with lead. But, a skirmisher doesn't have that luxury, and a skirmisher's wife who can shoot has to learn to be a skirmisher too."

"This gun of yours," Elisa said. "It looks a bit different from the others I've seen."

Karl nodded. "My father made it for me when he found out that I was joining the army. He thought that if my life was going to depend on my gun, I needed the best gun I could have."

Elisa blushed. "You told me that on our wedding night. He was a wise man."

"The very best."

The routine Elisa life took on was exhausting, but also satisfying. She found herself looking forward to each day in the laundry with the other wives, waking up with eager anticipation to see what stories and jokes they'd all be sharing. And then she would learn how to shoot, with Karl quickly moving up to a full charge and making her practice loading until the process became second nature. It was as the weather turned warm that Karl began working on her aim.

"Get on one knee," he instructed, setting the target two hundred yards away.

Elisa nodded and knelt.

"Now put the rifle butt snug with your shoulder, and concentrate on lining up the sight with your target."

"Doing it," Elisa replied.

"If the target was moving, you'd have to lead it a bit, but you can't do that until you've paid enough attention to how long it takes the ball to hit it. So, when you fire, count in your mind to measure it. Make sure you count *fast*."

"I will."

"The best time to fire is when you're not breathing," Karl stated. "That's when your body is completely still. So, either hold your breath when you fire, or, even better, breathe out and hold, and then fire."

"I understand," Elisa said.

"Now breathe out and fire."

Elisa aimed, slowly exhaled, and then pulled the trigger. As soon as the shot was off, she started to reload. Karl took a few steps towards the target.

"Did I hit it?" Elisa asked.

Karl shook his head. "Don't worry about that. It will take time to get used to aiming and shooting. Just keep practicing, and you'll get there."

Karl was right. Within a week, she was putting shots onto the target, although a bulls-eye was rare.

Sometimes, she found herself with the fifth wife, Sophie von Erfurt the sutler, who ran the canteen just on the outskirts of the barracks. Sophie operated the entire business, trading gossip with a wry humour and a sparkle in her eye.

In the meantime, the weather grew hot and then cool again, the autumn colours beginning to emerge. When they were off duty and not practicing her shooting, Karl took her on hikes through the wilderness, teaching her how to move like a skirmisher as they enjoyed the outdoors. Sometimes they stopped laid out a blanket, and made love with nothing around them but the trees and the birds. As the leaves began to fall, Elisa realized that for the first time since she had left her island, she felt as though she belonged.

So this is what happiness feels like, Elisa thought.

It was in the first week of October that Elisa and the other wives went to get some beer during their break and found Sophie's eyes stern and serious.

"My husband says that France is going to war against Prussia," Sophie said. "We're going to join them."

A chill went down Elisa's spine. "We're going to war?"

Sophie nodded. "We'll be marching as soon as we're ready."

Chapter V – A Little Taste of War

The night before they left, Elisa clung to Karl after their lovemaking, trying to memorize the feeling of his body pressed against her.

"It's not going to be as bad as you fear," Karl said, stroking her hair and then her back.

"All I've seen of war is the dead and dying," Elisa sighed. "I don't want you to die too."

"This won't be my first campaign," Karl stated. "And far more of us survive than die."

Elisa took a deep breath. "I love you."

Karl kissed her. "I love you too."

They were mustered first thing in the morning, Karl helping her shoulder the heavy pack containing both of their belongings while they waited in the line. Beside her, Helena shouldered her own pack and grinned.

Elisa looked at her and shook her head. "How are you this...happy?"

"Campaigning is the best part of this life!" Helena declared. "You get out of the barracks, and when you're not staying in a town, you get to sleep under the stars. But, most of the time, you get to billet with the locals – no barracks, but an actual house! And you don't even have to worry about making the bread or scrounging for the beer – the family hosting you takes care of it!"

Elisa frowned. "Do they have to volunteer for that?"

Helena laughed. "You don't need to worry about that – you just show up at the house you like and present your lodging billet, and they have to put you up. They get paid well enough for it. And then, if we storm a town, there's plunder!"

In the line behind her, Louisa called out, "Don't listen to her. Sharing the plunder is just a tall tale."

"It is not!" Helena protested.

"When have you ever seen a town get stormed instead of just surrendering?" Louisa demanded.

"Just because it hasn't happened yet, doesn't mean it can't happen. If the town gets stormed, we have a right to take plunder."

Ahead of her, Anna shouted, "Silence in the ranks, ladies! We're about to start marching."

The bugle called, and the march north began. Karl gave Elisa a smile as they left Neuberg. "Just keep putting one foot in front of the other," he said. "It will seem tough at first, but you can do it."

He wasn't wrong. By the time they took their first break close to midday, Elisa thought that she might collapse. "You did great," Karl told her. "The longer you do this, the easier it gets."

They broke at sundown in a large clearing by the road. Karl pulled the pack off Elisa's back, and then un-shouldered his own pack. As he made a fire, they were joined by Helena and her husband. It was all Elisa could do to stay awake long enough to eat something for supper.

"Do we get tents?" Elisa asked, rubbing her sore legs and shoulders.

Karl shook his head. "This is a bivouac. We sleep out in the open."

"I'm jealous," Helena declared. "This will be your first time sleeping under the stars with your husband. It's just...magical."

"Better than doing it alone, anyway," Sergeant Weber added.

Elisa slept curled up beside Karl, a heavy blanket over them to keep out the chill. They woke to a bugle call.

As they shouldered their packs and made ready to leave, Helena winked at Elisa. "I told you it was magical."

Elisa chuckled. "It was definitely better than doing it alone."

They marched for another full day. Elisa was stiff at the beginning, but just as Karl had promised, once she was marching for a while, it got easier.

"Do you know where we're going?" Elisa asked as the column broke for lunch.

"If I had to guess, Bayreuth," Karl replied. "You'll like it there. It's a wonderful old town with a beautiful castle and opera house, and some very nice churches."

"How long before we get there?" Elisa asked.

Karl shrugged. "If that's where we're going, we'll probably be there tomorrow afternoon."

They slept under the stars again, Elisa taking the time to enjoy the feeling of it. As the sun rose, the bugles called the muster, and the regiment departed for a third day of marching.

As Karl had suggested, the reached the town of Bayreuth in the late afternoon. As they came to the town square, Karl and the other non-commissioned officers were called up to talk to the officers. The officers handed them a large stack of papers. Then Sergeant Weber bellowed, "Everybody, come and get your lodging billets! We're going in order of seniority."

"This one is ours," Karl said, handing a billet to Elisa. "Don't lose it."

"I won't," Elisa replied.

Helena grinned at her. "It's time to go looking for a house."

Once Karl had finished handing out the billets, he and Elisa began their hunt for lodgings. "We want a place without children if possible," Karl said. "An older couple who will stay out of our way is best."

"And we'll stay out of theirs?" Elisa asked.

Karl nodded. "As best we can. Remember, we're just there in the evenings and for breakfast." He looked up at a house. "This looks good."

"I'm not sure I'm okay with this," Elisa said.

Karl gave her hand a squeeze. "You will be. I promise."

He stepped up to the front door and knocked. An older man opened the door, a look of fear in his eyes when he saw Karl's uniform.

"I'm sorry to do this, sir," Karl said, handing him the billet. "We'll require lodgings for a couple of days."

The old man swallowed. "I'll make sure you get the bread and beer you're owed."

Karl gave him a kind smile. "Thank you sir." He turned to Elisa. "Now, we just need to remember that this is where we're staying."

Elisa thought that she'd have trouble sleeping in a bed that she'd kicked somebody from, but she didn't. She was so tired when they got under the covers that she fell asleep as soon as her head hit the pillow.

In the morning, the regiment mustered in the town square. Elisa watched as the officers consulted with the non-comms. "I wonder what the news is," Helena said.

Elisa nodded. "Hopefully nothing too bad."

Karl and Sergeant Webber returned to their wives, Sergeant Webber declaring, "We've been put under the command of one of the Bonapartes."

"Which one?" Karl asked.

"Jerome," Sergeant Webber replied.

"Not Napoleon, then," Helena whispered to Elisa.

"So, what are the orders?" Karl said.

"The Thirteenth Infantry will be leaving for the siege of Plassenburg as soon as it's organized," Sergeant Webber answered. "We'll be going with the rest of the division to Schleiz...to guard the road to Leipzig."

Karl sighed. "The men won't like that."

Sergeant Webber nodded. "I know. But what can you do? The Frenchies want all the glory for themselves."

Elisa heard Anna calling her name, as well as Helena's. She turned to see Anna hurrying over. "What is it?"

"The march is over, and we've got a couple of days," Anna said. "So, time to set up the laundry and take care of uniforms. I've commandeered a building."

The laundry wasn't the only thing that had been set up – when Elisa and the other wives took her break, she found that Sophie's canteen was also up and running.

"So, what's the news?" Louisa asked.

"We're going to Schleiz," Sophie replied.

Helena scowled into her beer. "We know that. What do you know about Jerome Napoleon? Is he one of the good ones?"

Sophie shrugged. "We're his first army."

Louisa chuckled. "So, he could be good, or he could get all of us killed."

"Hopefully the talent runs through the family," Helena said.

When the day was done, Elisa met her husband back at the house, the old man and his wife eating with them at the table, but saying little. As they made their way into the bedroom, Elisa said, "I still feel terrible about doing this to him."

"That will pass," Karl stated. "This is just part of being an army on the march. You get used to it."

"Still, this was their bedroom two days ago."

Karl shrugged. "And when we leave tomorrow or the day after, it will be theirs again. What matters is that they get paid for their trouble, which they will, and that we are well-behaved guests, which we are. There's nothing to feel bad about."

Elisa scowled. "I hope I never get used to it."

"Trust me," Karl declared, holding and kissing her. "The time will come when you get off a long march, and you don't care what bed you fall into, so long as it's a real bed."

They departed the next day, marching for two full days to reach Schleiz. The town rested among forested hills, with a pleasant looking church and a castle. Once again, lodging billets were passed out, and once again, Elisa found herself on a hunt for a suitable house.

The owner of the home they commandeered was a widow, both pleasant and chatty. Unlike the previous lodgings, Elisa found herself feeling welcome.

"You're such a nice young couple," the widow declared as she served them some lamb in a honey mustard sauce with potatoes on the side. "Do you have plans for children?"

Elisa and Karl shared a bemused glance. "Eventually," Karl replied. "You just need to provide bread and beer, you know."

"I know," the widow said. "I just don't care. I'll feed you whatever I want!"

The next morning, Anna came to find her and show her to the laundry. Then, as soon as the other wives were gathered, she made an announcement.

"Now that our husbands are patrolling the road, we're going to do half days here," Anna declared. "We take care of laundry in the morning, and in the afternoons we'll take provisions to our husbands and their men."

"Your men," Louisa groused. "My husband doesn't have any men of his own yet."

"That's what you get for marrying a common soldier," Helena chuckled. "Don't worry – you're lucky! You can just bring your husband food and relax with him. You could be Elisa or me, or even worse, *Anna*."

"What's so bad about being Anna?" Elisa asked.

"She has to hold court," Helena replied.

Elisa blinked. "I'm sorry, I don't understand."

"When a soldier like Louisa's poor, un-promoted husband has a gripe with the higher ups, who do you think they take it to?" Helena said, and then pointed at Anna. "You and I might get just a bit of it, but Anna married an *officer* – she spends half her time listening to soldiers complaining."

"There's a reason I prefer to run the laundry," Anna declared. "Let Sophie handle all of the grousing. She's the sutler around here – she's supposed to be dealing with other people."

Helena laughed and said, "And every time they try, she tells them to talk to Anna."

The morning passed quickly. After her lunch, Elisa was given a large pack of food and drink, and sent down the road to the checkpoint where her husband waited with a handful of men.

"Anything exciting?" Elisa asked as she un-shouldered the pack.

Karl shook his head and gave her a kiss. "Afraid not. A couple of merchants came through, and that's it."

"So is this what you do when you're standing guard?"

"This is what I do when I'm assigned to the checkpoint," Karl said. "When I'm in the field skirmishing, it's very different."

Elisa stared down the road, shivering with the chill breeze. "I thought war would be a bit more..."

"Fighting battles?" Karl asked with a smile. "Those happen, but they aren't most of it."

Sergeant Webber hailed them, his wife beside him, along with a company of men. "Time for you to get back to town," he called. "His Excellency wants to inspect you, so look sharp."

"Don't get your hopes up," Helena said as Elisa packed up and shouldered her pack. "He's nothing too special – just a kid in a uniform."

They returned to town to discover a young man with curly dark hair in a French uniform examining the men. Karl and his company got into line and stood at attention. Elisa watched as Jerome Bonaparte trotted past her husband, barely giving him a glance. Then, the bugle sounded, and Karl and his men fell out of line.

Whatever Jerome Bonaparte's role was, it didn't seem to involve spending much time with the Bavarian Seventh Infantry. After the inspection, she didn't see him again.

It was when she got to the canteen for lunch the next day that she found out that the war against the Prussians was probably over.

"Napoleon crushed them yesterday," Sophie declared.

"Where?" Helena asked.

"I think the places were called Jena and Auerstädt," Sophie replied. "I can't imagine Prussia will go on for much longer."

While Elisa breathed a sigh of relief over her beer, Helena scowled and said, "We barely got to do a thing!"

The next two days of her Elisa's life was a steady routine of waking up, eating breakfast while the widow talked their ears off, working in the laundry, and then bringing supplies to Karl and his men on the road.

It was at the end of their fifth day in Schleiz that Carl told her, "We're leaving for Dresden tomorrow."

"To guard more roads?" Elisa asked.

Karl shook his head. "To occupy it."

Elisa's eyes widened. "Did Prussia sue for peace?"

"Unfortunately not," Karl said. "But, we've apparently secured Saxony, and now they're worried about what Russia will do."

Elisa frowned. "So this isn't over yet."

Karl shrugged. "It will be over when it's over."

It took two and a half days to make their way to Dresden. As they approached, the sight took Elisa's breath away. Domes and spires rose above the city, rivers running through it. But, once they entered, she found herself being watched by wary, and even hostile, eyes.

"Don't mind them," Karl said. "They may not like us, but they won't try to harm us."

For once, Karl's instinct for finding houses owned by elderly couples failed, and he presented his lodging billet to a young family with three children. The parents watched them with guarded expressions, but the children gushed over Karl's uniform.

Elisa hadn't spent much time around children, but she got used to the chaos after a few days. She found herself getting pulled into story time, with the young wife asking her if she knew any good tales to tell. Elisa began to tell the tales of the people she had helped, always leaving herself out. Instead, she told them that the wishes had been granted by talking animals, or the spirits of loved ones watching in Heaven.

Elisa also took the opportunity to start reading the local newspapers when she had time away from the laundry. She startled when she read the date on the October 20th, 1806, edition of one of the broadsheets.

I didn't *lose track of time*, Elisa realized.

It was after she had come home with the October 30th edition of the newspaper that Karl told her to pack up and get ready to leave in the morning.

"We're heading for the Oder River," he said. "We're forming up there with 'Allied Army' under Jerome Bonaparte."

"What will happen then?" Elisa asked.

Karl shrugged. "I don't know. But, this takes us towards Silesia."

They left in the morning, and marched for four days. Finally, they came to a town named Krossen, which the locals called Krosno.

"The officers say we're moving out as soon as the rest of the army arrives," Karl said as he handed her their lodgings billet. "We're just waiting on the First Division, as far as I know."

They billeted with an elderly couple, Elisa helping out with some of the housework when she wasn't working at the laundry. During the day as she mended and washed uniforms, the main topic of conversation was what would happen next.

"If they're gathering us all up into a big army, that means they're planning to use us," Helena said. "Perhaps there will be a big battle."

"It could be sieges," Anna declared.

Helena cocked her head. "Sieges can be good. We might actually get some plunder from a siege."

"If we live long enough," Louisa pointed out. "They're shooting at everybody in the trenches, not just our husbands."

Elisa blinked. "How bad can a siege be?"

"It depends," Louisa replied, putting down the uniform she was working on. "If we invest the place and they surrender, it's just a bunch of digging and waiting, and it's fine. If they don't, and we have to storm ramparts, well..." She grimaced. "Let's just say we won't be the ones with the advantage."

It took the Bavarian First Division another couple of days to arrive, during which the weather grew colder. Elisa found herself dressing in layers as she bustled to and from their lodgings.

A day after the Bavarian First Division arrived, another group of soldiers made their way into the town square. Elisa, Helena, Anna, and Louisa watched them march in from Sophie's canteen.

"Who do you suppose they are?" Elisa asked.

"Würtemburgers," Sophie replied. "Now that they're here, we'll probably be leaving tomorrow."

"To where?" Helena asked.

"Glogau, I think," Sophie replied. "But I hear the locals call it Glogow. We're to take it from the Prussians."

"That's a siege, isn't it?" Elisa said.

Anna nodded. "Just remember to keep your head down in the trenches, and you'll be fine."

Elisa didn't sleep well that night. She kept thinking back to that battlefield by the bridge, and all of the fallen soldiers, imagining Karl among them.

She marched the next morning in a stupor, her legs carrying her along while she struggled to keep her eyes open. At least twice, she blinked and found herself on a different part of the road.

"You fell asleep while marching," Karl said. "Don't be too worried – we've all done it."

"That's terrifying," Elisa declared. "What happens if somebody catches you when you're doing it?"

Karl shrugged. "Don't know. It's never happened to me. But, I imagine you'd wake up when the rest of the army shoots back."

It was towards the end of the day that the column came to a halt, the town of Glocau standing before them, a river running through it. Facing them was a long line of angular earthwork fortifications and stone walls behind it.

"What now?" Elisa asked.

"Now we find a place and bivouac," Karl replied. "We're out of range of the fort guns here, so it should be safe. We'll have pickets up to intercept any reinforcements."

"The fireworks start tomorrow," Helena gushed.

"Fireworks?"

"The initial bombardment," Karl explained. "Our way of suggesting that it would be wise to surrender before we start digging trenches."

"Best get some rest tomorrow," Helena said. "If they don't surrender, we start digging at sundown."

Elisa swallowed. "All of us?"

Helena nodded. "*All* of us. And they will take shots at us once we're in range."

"Just keep your head down and you'll be fine," Karl said. "Besides, it will take a couple of days before we're in range."

Any concerns Elisa had about sleeping were allayed the moment she lay down beside Karl. She closed her eyes, and the bugle sounded.

It was already dawn.

Elisa rose from the blankets they had laid down to see Karl already awake, watching the fort.

"You'll want to put your hands to your ears," he said. "This is going to get loud."

The first to fire were the rockets, streaking towards the town and exploding inside the walls. Then the guns began to fire. Cannonballs arced overhead, slamming into the ground around the fortifications, with an occasional hit.

"So what do we do now?" Elisa shouted, putting her hands to her ears.

"We wait," Karl said. "You need to rest up – we'll probably be digging tonight. I've got picket duty, so I'll be back in a few hours."

With little else to do, Elisa watched the bombardment. Smoke began to rise from the town as the rockets and artillery hammered it.

"Quite a show, isn't it?" Helena said, sitting beside her.

"It's sobering," Elisa replied. "All those poor people."

"Those poor people could end it all by surrendering," Helena pointed out.

"Would you surrender if you were in their place?" Elisa asked.

Helena nodded. "It beats being pillaged, raped, and murdered."

Elisa stared at the pillars of smoke rising from the town. "I guess it does."

"That said, if they're going to surrender, it will be in the next couple of hours," Helena stated as her husband and Karl rejoined them. "And if they don't, it's time to dig trenches."

The bombardment ended as the sun kissed the horizon. "As soon as it's fully dark, we start working," Karl said. "Don't worry – I'll be right beside you."

Once the sun had set and the stars were out, Elisa found herself fumbling her way alongside her husband to a working party. A couple of engineers directed them in a whisper, a wheelbarrow full of shovels waiting beside them.

"You're going to dig in that direction," he hissed, pointing. "Just match the depth of the trench beside you.

Another engineer is standing by where you'll be stopping – keep digging until you reach him. And for the love of God, no talking! If they hear you, they'll start shooting at you with everything they've got."

Elisa and Karl began to dig. Within an hour, Elisa's arms were so sore she thought they would fall off. She pushed through the pain and kept digging. Time lost any meaning.

A hand on her shoulder startled her. She turned her head to see a shape in the darkness. "You're relieved," Helena whispered. "Our turn now. Go get some rest."

Elisa and Karl stumbled out of their trench and back to the bivouac area. They lay down, covered themselves in blankets, and fell into a deep sleep.

The next few weeks made Elisa fear that she would become a night creature. The laundry duty was gone – instead, she rested during the day, and dug during the night. On the other side of the army, field fortifications went up to protect them. Some nights, she was taken off digging and set to filling sandbags, and then helping deliver them into completed trenches.

It was a couple of weeks into the siege before she saw what happened when somebody made a mistake. A loud coughing broke out from the communications trench a few dozen yards away. And then hell descended upon it.

The ground around the coughing was ripped apart by cannon fire, while small arms fire erupted from the wall, peppering the ground. Elisa covered her ears, knelt down, and suppressed the urge to scream as chunks of earth landed around her. After a few minutes, silence descended on the field once again, broken only by the soft sounds of digging.

Three and a half weeks into the siege, the final trenches were completed and the mortars brought up to shatter Glogau's fortifications. As the snow began to fall, a white flag was raised from the fort.

"The siege is over," Karl said, dark bags around his eyes. "They're surrendering. We've won."

Elisa breathed a sigh of relief. "What now?"

"Now, once the negotiations are completed, we move into the city and get a few days of rest," Karl replied. "Then it's on to the next place."

"I hope this is over soon," Elisa declared.

Karl embraced her. "So do we all, my love."

Helena groused about once again being denied plunder, but they entered the town unopposed. Elisa forced down nausea as she walked down the streets, entire blocks of houses reduced to charred rubble. They finally occupied the town hall, turning it into a temporary barracks.

In the end, they only got two days of rest before the order came to march for Breslau. Elisa discovered new and previously unexplored types of exhaustion as they made their way through the snow, the roads turning to a thick slush under their boots.

A city with handsome white church spires and roofs covered in snow, surrounded by a river, rose before them. Once again, they set up their bivouac out of range of the city guns, this time trying to clear away enough snow that they could stay warm overnight.

"Will this be like the last one?" Elisa asked in the morning as the bombardment began.

Karl shook his head. "I don't think we're that lucky. This is a lot bigger than Glogau."

Breslau did not surrender that night, and the digging began. Once again, Elisa found herself spending most of her nights in the trenches, pray that a mistake wouldn't bring cannon and musket fire down upon her head.

Ten days after they had arrived, the First Division arrived. Elisa and Helena watched them march into the bivouac area through the morning.

"They took their sweet time," Helena said. "The trenches are half done."

"So long as they help dig while they're here, I have no complaints," Elisa yawned. "I'm going to try to get some sleep."

"You rest," Helena said. "With luck, once the trenches are dug, we'll storm the town, and you'll get to experience what it's like to have some plunder."

"No offense, but I hope they surrender instead," Elisa said.

The First Division did help with the trenches, but Breslau did not surrender, even once they were close enough to attempt to storm the fortifications. Five days after the First Division, arrived, Elisa found herself mouthing silent prayer after silent prayer in the dark, standing beside Helena as their husbands issued instructions to their men, the non-commissioned officers of other companies to each side doing the same.

It was time to breach the wall, and the skirmishers were going first. They would launch the attack just before dawn. All they had to do was get past a large, wet ditch.

"It will be okay," Helena whispered. "They won't even know we're coming."

"They'd better not," Elisa hissed. Men with carts brought breaching supplies forward, Karl and Sergeant Webber pointing at them and issuing whispered orders. The men began to take the supplies from the carts and work on crossing the ditch.

Elisa closed her eyes and concentrated on her breathing. The men worked so quietly she could barely hear a thing. Then, the sound of them working stopped.

Elisa opened her eyes. Hundreds of men stood in the middle of the ditch on partially constructed bridges, looking at each other and gesturing in frustration. Across the ditch, men ran back to talk to the soldiers by the carts.

"You have to be fucking kidding," Helena breathed. "They didn't bring enough supplies!"

Elisa glanced at the horizon. The pre-dawn glow filled the horison as the sun began to rise.

"They need to get out of there," Elisa hissed.

The sun had barely started rising when a call of alarm sounded from the fortifications. A moment later, hell descended on the men in the ditch, cannon shot blowing pieces of the bridges off and taking parts of the men off as well.

"Karl!" Elisa cried as the debris from the cannon shot obscured him from view. She tried to step forward, only to feel a firm hand on her shoulder.

"Don't move," Helena instructed.

"But Karl's down there!" Elisa protested.

"So is my husband," Helena stated. "It won't help either of them to find out that you ran in there and got killed."

Elisa glanced around at everybody she could see, reading each wish.

There was nothing she could use. Nothing that would protect the men in that ditch.

The firing hit a fever pitch, the men starting to run back to the trenches, falling as sharpshooters shot them down.

"I don't see Karl," Elisa breathed. "Where's Karl?"

The firing stopped. Dozens of bodies lay across the tattered remains of the bridging in the ditch. Elisa closed her eyes, terrified that if she opened them, she would see Karl's broken body lying in the muck.

"Elisa," Helena said.

"Please," Elisa mumbled. "Please let him be alive."

Elisa felt Helena's hand squeeze her shoulder. "Elisa, we need to get to the hospital. We have work to do. And if our husbands are alive, they'll be there."

Elisa opened her eyes and nodded. She followed Helena to a large tent that had been erected, wounded men lying in front of it, moaning and shivering in the snow. Elisa suppressed the urge to cry when she saw them – none of them were Karl.

She stepped into the tent and stopped. Karl was there, his arm bloody, talking to the surgeon.

"These are my men here," he said. "I'll need to know who doesn't make it."

"Karl!" Elisa cried, rushing forward and embracing him. Tears streamed down her eyes. "I was so afraid that...that..."

Karl kissed her. "It's just a graze, my love. I'm fine."

Helena stared at them. "My husband, Sergeant Webber, is he...?"

Karl stared at her and shook his head. "I'm sorry. He didn't make it out of the ditch."

Elisa watched Helena take a deep breath. "I'd better get to work, then. Elisa, help me with these wounded. I'll show you what to do."

Helena showed Elisa how to nurse the wounded, check bandages, and provide comfort to the dying. When her shift was over and she was relieved, Elisa went back to the bivouac area, and held Karl close throughout the night.

"Is it always like it was yesterday?" Elisa asked after they woke up.

Karl shook his head. "Yesterday was a massive screw up. Most of the time, when I'm in the field, I'm behind cover."

She snuggled into him. "I felt so helpless. I don't ever want to lose you."

"I've been pretty lucky," he pointed out. "This isn't my first campaign. And skirmishers get cover that the line infantry doesn't. I'll be fine."

"When this war is done, can we leave the army?" Elisa

asked. "Make a life for ourselves in a town, or village somewhere?"

Karl gave her a kind smile and kissed her. "Okay. When the time comes, I'll ask to be furloughed."

Elisa frowned. "But not fully discharged."

"For people like me, being furloughed is the best we can ask for. But, it's always possible that I might not be called back up if another war starts."

Elisa chuckled. "That *we* might not be called back up."

Karl grinned. "True. Its both of us or neither of us."

For the next two weeks, Elisa found herself in a new routine. With the trenches no longer requiring the same amount of work, she was shifted to the makeshift hospital, where she served as a nurse. Helena still joined her, and gave her pointers when Elisa needed help, but otherwise didn't talk.

"Are you okay?" Elisa asked Helena during a quiet moment.

Helena shrugged. "I'm surviving."

"If you need anything, Karl and I can–"

Helena held up her hand. "I'll be fine."

Karl also had a new routine, one that left Elisa in constant dread. With the other skirmishers, he was assigned to screen the roads for Prussian reinforcements. Every couple of days Elisa would hear distant firing from the rear, causing her to make the sign of the cross and pray for his safety. But, he always came back, albeit sometimes with new scratches.

"Stinging nettles make terrible cover," he told her at the end of one day, coming back badly scratched on his hands and face. "If you're going to dive behind one, don't get too close."

Elisa chuckled. "Oh, I know. I once had to spend a couple of days living off the things."

Karl raised an eyebrow. "You'll have to tell me that

story one of these days."

"Once we're furloughed and we've got a house of our own," Elisa promised. "Then I'll tell you everything."

At the end of the two weeks, a white flag finally rose from the city's parapets, and the regiment moved into the shattered city as a garrison. Once again, Elisa and Karl found themselves in a barracks, albeit one needing repair from the siege. The sheer number of empty beds gave her pause – a full third of the skirmishers from her company were gone.

Elisa was reassigned to the laundry. But this time, when she showed up to work on the massive pile of soiled and damaged uniforms from the siege, Helena wasn't there.

"She asked to be discharged as soon as the siege was over," Anna explained. "They agreed."

"I wish we could do something for her," Elisa said.

Anna just shrugged. "With luck she'll receive a pension as a war widow. Other than that, she decided to leave, and all we can do is respect that."

Elisa added Helena to her nightly prayers, praying for her safety and that she might find some comfort to relieve her grief.

The snow continued to fall, and with the blockade over, some newspapers finally made it into Breslau. Elisa got her hands on one as soon as they were available, checking the date. It was February 10, 1807.

She smiled. Not losing track of years at a time felt good.

As much as she would have preferred it, the shooting lessons did not resume – the daylight was just too short. By the time she finished at the laundry and made her way back to the barracks, it was already dark. At least the barracks had been fixed with reasonable speed.

It was a couple of weeks after buying the newspaper

that Karl told her new orders had arrived. "We're leaving tomorrow for Warsaw. The French V Corps is waiting for us."

"Can't they wait until the snow clears?" Elisa asked.

Karl shook his head. "Not how this works, I'm afraid."

"Haven't the Prussians had enough?"

Karl sighed. "I don't think it's the Prussians this time. I think we're up against the Russians now."

The trudge through the snow was long and hard, Elisa and Karl bivouacking in larger groups by a large fire, the men taking shifts to feed it through the night. Thankfully, as they marched, the weather began to warm, although the slush this created was more curse than blessing. After two weeks on the road, they finally entered Warsaw and were granted two days of rest.

The first thing Elisa did the next morning was replace her boots and find a newspaper, in that order. Her boots were worn out from the marching, and the unpaved streets of Warsaw had been churned up into a cold and sticky combination of slush and mud. The newspaper told her that it was now March 9, 1807. Then she reported to the laundry.

The regiment left Warsaw the next day, and after a blissfully short march of only a day and a half Elisa and Karl found themselves billeting in Pultusk, a town on the bank of the Narew river. Or, at least they might have, if Karl hadn't lucked into an empty house and used their billet to rent it, with the landlord delivering the required bread and beer.

And then, at least for them, the war went quiet.

During the days, Karl went out on patrol and Elisa worked in the laundry. On her breaks, she enjoyed checking out the long market in the town square. But, while the walk was pleasant, the pickings were slim.

"I'm sorry miss," said one shopkeeper with mostly

empty shelves. "You can thank Emperor Napoleon and his Continental System for this. It used to be that we got all sorts of things from Britain, but now nothing is getting through the embargo."

"That's okay," Elisa said. "I'm sure it will end soon."

"I hope so," the shopkeeper declared. "At this rate, it won't be long before we've got nothing left to sell." The shopkeeper glanced at her jacket. "Are you with the Bavarians?"

Elisa nodded. "My husband is a corporal with the skirmishers."

"Pity, a nice young woman like you getting involved in a war like this."

Elisa chuckled. "I'm older than I look."

In the laundry, the discussion often turned to other parts of the war.

"I heard a story from my husband," Anna said one day. "It's almost impossible to believe. Strange things happen in Italy."

"Oh?" Elisa asked.

Anna grinned. "He got it from a Frenchie artilleryman he met. Apparently, it happened during this very campaign...or the last. He was a bit fuzzy on that."

"So, are you going to tell us about it or not?" Louisa asked, taking the jacket she was washing out of the water.

Anna drew herself up to her full height. "It seems – and my husband has this on good authority – in the campaign in Italy, there were negro soldiers chasing cannonballs."

Louisa blinked. "What's a negro?"

"People from Africa and the Caribbean," Anna replied. "They've got skin the colour of chocolate."

Louisa chuckled. "What, so they smeared chocolate on their faces?"

"No, they were born that way," Anna said. "And, the

negro soldiers were chasing enemy cannonballs on the field."

Elisa blinked as she finished sewing a patch on a jacket. "Why would they do that?"

"Apparently, the Frenchies got short on cannon balls, and offered a reward for anybody who could recover one that could be fired back," Anna said. "The negroes got shot to pieces trying to claim the money."

"I'm not sure I believe that story," Louisa stated. "Who goes running into enemy fire to carry back a cannonball?"

Anna shrugged. "The negroes, I guess."

Louisa chuckled. "I think that Frenchie was pulling your husband's leg."

Elisa frowned. The only time she'd ever met the French was that incident in the inn years ago.

"What are the Frenchies like, anyway?" Elisa asked.

Anna shrugged. "They're like...they're Frenchies. Not quite sure what else to say. They're smooth talkers if you can understand the language, and you probably shouldn't let one near your virgin daughter. And they fight well. And that's all, really."

The snow had melted under the warm April sun when Karl told Elisa over breakfast that the regiment had a new commanding officer.

"His name is Colonel von Stengel," Karl said. "And he comes out of the fourth light infantry."

Elisa blinked. "Wait, does that mean that he's..."

Karl grinned. "A skirmisher, yes. He's one of us."

As the April came to a close and May began, the days grew longer, and Elisa's shooting lessons resumed. This time, she discovered that they had an audience, who watched and talked while Karl ran her through target shooting.

"I wish they'd go away," Elisa said as they headed

back to their lodgings on her fourth day of practice.

"I'm afraid that's not likely," Karl stated. "They're not used to soldiers here, and a soldier teaching his wife to shoot is a novelty upon a novelty."

Elisa scowled. "Is my aim good enough to stop?"

Karl shook his head. "You're getting good, but not good enough to be a skirmisher. And as best I can tell, for what you want, you need to be as good as a skirmisher."

"So just ignore them."

Karl nodded. "It's for the best. Being able to shooting well around distractions is important too."

Elisa's life continued this way for a month before Karl came back with news that sent a chill down her spine.

"It looks like we're going back into action," he said. "We've been ordered to clear the far side of the Narew river and fortify it."

Elisa swallowed. "They'll be shooting at you again, won't they?"

"Probably," Karl replied. "But this time, we'll be the ones behind cover."

That evening, Elisa heard a knock at the door. Karl opened it to reveal Anna, waiting in a light rain.

"I need to speak to your wife, Corporal," Anna said.

Karl nodded and ushered her inside. "She's just in here."

Anna nodded at Elisa as she came into the kitchen. "Sit down."

Elisa sat, Anna sitting opposite to her.

"Sorry to bother you this late," Anna said. "Normally I'd rely on Helena to instruct you for something like tomorrow, but she's gone now."

Elisa nodded. "I understand."

"Tomorrow, you will be supporting your husband," Anna said. "This means you will be doing two things. The first is that you will be a runner for his company – when they need supplies, you will go to the back and fetch them. Don't worry, you won't be the only one."

Elisa swallowed. "And this will be while they're shooting at us?"

Anna nodded. "It's up to you if you want to wear your husband's jacket. If you take it off, they'll know at a glance that you're a woman, but I have no idea of how much of a difference that will make. What's important is to keep your head down and move as fast as you can. That's your best protection against enemy bullets."

Elisa took a deep breath. "I see."

"If it's any consolation, Louisa, Helena, and I have all done it, and we came out in one piece. So, as long as you're careful, your odds are good."

"What's the second part?" Elisa asked.

"You're going to help evacuate the wounded," Anna replied. "Again, you'll have some help. The most important thing there is to wait for a lull in combat. You can't run while carrying a wounded man, so don't risk it, even if it's your husband. You can't help anybody by getting shot."

Elisa sighed. "And people will die while we wait for the other side to stop shooting."

Once again, Anna nodded. "That's unavoidable in war."

Anna stood. "The next few days will be difficult. Get some rest, spend time with your husband. When tomorrow comes, the main thing is to just follow the orders you're given. I don't think a lack of bravery will be a problem for you."

Elisa allowed herself a thin smile as she recalled her escape from the mad king. "I've been in danger before."

"Good luck tomorrow," Anna said. "Hopefully, clearing the other side of the river will be nice and quick, and you'll be able to spend most of the day digging trenches."

With that, she left. Without a word, Karl held out his hand. Elisa took it, and they headed to the bedroom.

The next day started early, Elisa and Karl receiving a loud knock at their door before dawn. They dressed in silence, stopping only to kiss each other as they left the house. Their mustering point was the riverbank, where dozens of small boats were waiting for them. Anna was waiting for them with Louisa, gesturing to Elisa to come over.

"We go over last," she whispered, "once enough of the river has been cleared."

Karl gave her a hug and kiss, and then motioned to his men. They got into the boats and rowed across. On the opposite shore, they un-shouldered their rifles and made their way forward. A single soldier remained with each boat to row it back. Upon reaching their side of the river, soldiers with muskets and bayonets piled in.

The third wave of men were almost to the opposite shore when Elisa heard a distant popping sounded, growing in intensity and then fading, only to start up all over again a few minutes later. She looked down and realized that she was clenching her fist. As she loosened it, she checked the position of the sun. By the looks of it, it was now mid-morning.

The firing died down for a third time. A bugle call sounded from the opposite bank.

"Our turn," Anna said. "Along with supplies."

Elisa, Louisa, and Anna got into the nearest boat, joined by several other soldiers. They were ferried across in silence. She stepped off onto the opposite shore.

The first thing she did was corner a soldier heading back towards the river. "My husband, Corporal Mueller, have you seen him? Is he okay?"

The soldier shook his head. "Sorry Mrs. Mueller, I

haven't seen him."

Elisa forced down a wave of nausea. As she started towards another soldier, she felt Anna's hand on her shoulder.

"Focus, Elisa," Anna said. "We need to find our units."

Elisa and Anna headed away from the river, asking for directions from soldiers coming the other way. A few were helping wounded comrades.

"The skirmishers?" one soldier replied. "They're just that way, with Corporal Mueller." He pointed.

Elisa breathed a sigh of relief. "He's okay, then?"

The soldier stared at her. "Are you his wife?"

Elisa nodded.

"He's okay," the soldier said. "The Russkies got close a couple of times, but that's all."

"Alright," Anna said. "You go to your unit. I need to find mine."

Elisa nodded and rushed in the direction that soldier had pointed. After a few minutes she cleared found Karl and his men, setting up at the edge of a large copse of trees.

"Good, you're here, my love," Karl said. "We need ammunition and powder."

Elisa nodded. "Any wounded?"

"We already sent them back."

Elisa rushed back to the bank of the river, where supplies were being unloaded.

"I need rifle balls and powder for the skirmishers," she told the supply sergeant.

"Those barrels there," the sergeant declared. "Make sure you use one of these bags for the powder."

She filled a large bag full of balls and large leather bag with black powder. Then she slung both over her shoulders and began to trudge back to the skirmishers. After what felt like forever, she made her way back to the treeline.

"Help her with those," Karl ordered. A couple of soldiers relieved her of the bags.

Elisa panted for breath. "Those were really heavy."

Karl handed her his canteen. "Have some water. You'll need it."

Elisa took a swig. "So, what now?"

"Now we wait for a counter attack," Karl said. "We're going to hold here while the line infantry get a bridge and some trenches ready."

"You think they're going to counter attack?" Elisa asked.

Karl nodded. "I'd be very surprised if they didn't."

"So, what do you need me to do next?"

"We'll need provisions," Karl replied. "Enough bread and water to make it through the night. Take a moment before you go, and I'll send a couple of men with you."

Elisa rested against a tree for about an hour, and then stood. "I'm ready to go."

Karl pointed to a couple of the skirmishers. "You and you – go with her."

When they made it back to the bank of the river, a makeshift wooden bridge was almost complete, and hundreds of infantrymen were digging field fortifications.

"What now, Mrs. Mueller?" the supply sergeant asked.

"Enough food to make it through the night, and some more ammunition and powder," Elisa replied.

"There, there, and there," the sergeant directed, pointing at three large barrels.

By the time they trudged back to Karl's position, it was almost mid-afternoon. Elisa helped pass out the food, and then sat against a tree. "Now what?" she asked.

Karl gave her a kind smile. "Now we wait for the Russkies to show themselves."

Elisa took a ragged breath, her muscles aching. Time

passed. The shadows lengthened. As it became dark, and the men divided themselves into watches, she leaned against her husband and dozed off.

Elisa awoke shortly after dawn, every muscle aching. She stretched out, wincing as one of her legs cramped.

Karl gave her a kiss. "I'm glad you're awake. We'll need more provisions. Just food and water this time. Take your time and have something to eat and drink first."

Elisa nodded. "Is this what it's usually like for you?"

Karl nodded back. "This is what it means to be a skirmisher, yes." He smiled. "Still glad you signed up for this?"

Elisa chuckled. "I signed up for *you* and to learn how to shoot. *This* is just the bonus."

She ate some stale bread and gulped down some water, and then she went back for food. The bridge was completed, wagons of materiel being driven across it, and by the looks of it, the trenches were getting close to half-finished.

"Welcome back, Mrs. Mueller," the supply sergeant said. "What do you need now?"

"Just food and water."

"Take all you need."

Elisa filled two bags, slung them over her shoulder, and trudged back to the copse. Two of Karl's men relieved her of the bags, and she sat down to rub her sore muscles.

Once again, time passed. The sun rose high into the sky and then began to descend again. Elisa stared out at the field before them, which continued to remain empty.

Elisa startled as a runner dashed up to their position from the rear. "From Colonel von Stengel," he reported, gasping for breath. "Expect a major enemy assault within the next day, around ten thousand men. Delay them as best you can, and then withdraw to the trenches."

"Thank you," Karl said. "I'll make my plans

accordingly."

Elisa swallowed. Once the runner ran back towards the river, she said, "Ten thousand men...that's a lot."

Karl shrugged. "It just means we have to be careful on our withdrawal. We're skirmishers – we take our shots, and then we fall back. Standing and fighting is for the line infantry and whoever is in the trenches."

"So, what do you need?" Elisa asked.

"More food, nothing else," Karl replied. "Nothing we can't carry away when we withdraw."

Elisa nodded and headed back to the river. The line infantry was out of the trenches and drilling on forming squares. The trenches looked to be at least half complete, and cannons and mortars had been put into place to protect the river bank.

"Hello Mrs. Mueller!" the supply sergeant called, waving. "Here for more food and water?"

"I am," Elisa said. "Enough for the night and tomorrow morning, I think."

"You know where to get them," the sergeant said. "By the way, make sure you get everything you need tonight. After sundown, we're moving back to the other side of the river."

"Thank you for letting me know," Elisa said.

The supply sergeant nodded. "It's my pleasure."

Elisa filled two bags, and trudged back to the copse. Once she had been relieved of the bags, she sat down under a tree and rubbed her sore muscles.

"Have something to eat," Karl said, handing her some bread. Elisa chewed on it, lost in thought. "You okay?" he asked.

Elisa shrugged. "I guess I'll be fine. I wish it was over, though."

"It will probably start tomorrow morning," Karl said. "When it does, the time will come when I tell you to go back. When that happens, you grab whatever you can carry while still running, and you run to the trenches."

Elisa drank some water from Karl's canteen. "And what about you?"

"God willing, I'll be right behind you."

Elisa prayed extra hard that night before she finally drifted off to sleep. The morning came all too soon, Elisa rubbing her eyes as she rose.

"Make sure you stay behind the trees today," Karl said.

Elisa nodded. "Anything yet?"

Karl pointed to the horizon. A cloud of dust rose in the distance. "That's them." He turned to his men. "Okay men, you know the drill. As soon as you can get a hit, fire at will. Aim for the officers first, and then the non-comms. And check your flints now."

Karl checked his rifle, testing the edge of the flint against his finger. Then he motioned for Elisa to get down beside him and lay on the ground in a prone position, resting the barrel of his rifle on a tree root.

Then they waited.

Elisa frowned as the time passed, willing herself not to move. She glanced at Karl. Her husband was staring straight ahead. She glanced at the sky. By the location of the sun, it looked to be about mid-morning.

In the distance, the cloud of dust grew closer.

Elisa swallowed, forcing herself to control her breathing. Beside her, Karl remained still and silent.

The ground began to tremble.

The first Russian soldiers broke into the field before them, marching in an enormous column surrounded by men on horseback. Their uniforms were all dark green, some men wearing red cuffs. Beside her, Elisa felt and heard Karl slowly exhale, hold, pull the trigger, and then begin to reload. One of the men on horseback fell to the ground. Around the copse, Elisa heard the other skirmishers open fire, Russian troops falling where they marched.

The Russians stopped and began to mill around, one of their officers raising his arm and shouting something Elisa couldn't understand. Karl fired again, and began reloading. The officer toppled from his horse. Another took his place, shouting orders, only to be shot as well.

The Russians began to form into a long line, three ranks deep.

"This is what we were waiting for," Karl hissed in her ear. "Gather what you're taking with you. As soon as they fire their first volleys, you go and keep the trees to your back."

Elisa nodded and grabbed Karl's canteen and his spare bag of powder and ammunition. As she did, Russians forming the line collapsed as the skirmishers kept up their fire.

The Russians finished their line and leveled their muskets. Karl put his hand on Elisa's shoulder.

The Russians fired. The discharge of their muskets was so loud that Elisa almost felt it in her chest. Musket balls zipped overhead, impacting the trees and knocking down branches. The first rank dropped to their knees, the second rank leveling their muskets and firing. As soon as they did, Karl tapped her shoulder.

Elisa stood and ran. Behind her, she heard the thunder of another volley, a couple of balls zipping by her. As she approached the field fortifications, she saw the line infantry forming into columns of their own.

"They're coming!" Elisa shouted as she ran by them. "The Russians are on their way!"

She reached the half finished breastworks, somebody rising to help her into the trench. "You're with the skirmishers?" he asked.

Elisa nodded. "Under Corporal Mueller. They should

be right behind me."

She stood and looked over the edge of the breastworks. The volley fire continued in the distance. Some of Karl's men ran across the field, hopping into the trench.

"Where's my husband?" Elisa asked the first of Karl's men to make it over the breastworks.

"He'll be in the last group to leave," the skirmisher said, then grinned. "Can't have the Russkies thinking we dislike their company, after all."

Elisa muttered a prayer for Karl's safety. Then she sighed. There was nothing else to do but wait.

Another group of skirmishers broke into the field before the breastworks and raced to the line. Elisa swallowed. Karl still wasn't among them.

"My husband–" she began as soon as the first was into the trench.

"He's coming," the skirmisher said. "Don't worry, Mrs. Mueller – we've done this plenty of times before. We know how to get away."

A third group of skirmishers raced to the breastworks. Elisa swallowed. Still no sign of Karl.

Elisa muttered another prayer, and looked up at the sun. It wouldn't be long before noon.

A fourth and final group of skirmishers raced to the trench. Elisa breathed a sigh of relief – Karl was among them.

"We held them off as long as we could," he reported as soon as he leapt into the trench. "Once they realize we're no longer there, they'll reform their columns. They should be here within the hour."

Elisa embraced him. "I'm so glad you're safe."

Karl kissed her, and then pulled her down to the breastwork. "Keep your head down. Once they arrive, it will get truly dangerous."

The ground began to tremble. Two massive columns

of dark green jacketed men broke into the field, bayonets fixed. Elisa glanced at the sky. It was noon.

The Russians fired as they advanced. Bugles called out. The line infantry formed into squares and began volley fire at the Russians, and then began to withdraw to the trenches, leaving their dead behind them.

As soon as all the line infantry were in the trenches, the artillery behind them fired. Clouds of musket balls zipped over their heads, blasting holes in the column. Still, the Russians advanced.

"Canister," Karl said beside her as he took aim. "Very good at telling Russkies they're not welcome." He fired and began to reload. All across the trench, the line infantry did the same. The Russians lowered their bayonets and charged, falling before they reached the breastworks.

Elisa stared at the closest Russian body and swallowed. Half of his face had been blown away.

The remaining Russians withdrew.

Elisa took a deep breath. "Is that it?"

Karl shook his head. "They'll be back."

Even as he spoke, another pair of Russian columns began to advance. The artillery resumed its canister fire blasting holes in the line. The Russians yelled and charged with their bayonets, firing as they ran forward. The man beside Karl slumped against the breastwork. Elisa glanced at him. A bloody hole had been blown through his cheek just under his eye.

Karl continued to fire, the sound of his rifle lost in the din of the musketry.

The Russians began to withdraw again. Karl gave Elisa's shoulder a squeeze. "Water," he said.

Elisa nodded him and passed him a canteen. Karl took a deep drink from it.

"Is this done?" Elisa asked.

"We'll know in a moment," Karl replied.

Two more Russian columns broke into the field and began advancing, bayonets fixed. They fired and broke into a run. This time, they reached the breastworks.

Elisa raised an arm to shield herself as Russian lunged at her. Karl fired, taking the Russian in the chest, the man falling beside Elisa, his bayonet ripping into her dress. Karl drew a long knife and stabbed the next Russian into the trench in the neck, sending an arterial spray against the sandbags.

Line infantry pushed both of them aside, striking at the Russians with their own bayonets. The canister fire roared overhead, reducing the Russians hovering over them to a bloody mess.

The battlefield went silent. Elisa glanced over at Karl. He was bloodied, but alive. She took a deep breath and peered over the edge of the breastworks.

The Russians were withdrawing, leaving a field filled with corpses in dark green, matted with blood. This time, they didn't reform and attack again.

Elisa glanced at the sky. By the position of the sun, it was only mid-afternoon. She swallowed. *That had to have been the longest couple of hours of my life.*

"Is that as bad as it gets?" Elisa asked.

Karl shrugged. "Probably not. Hopefully we'll never see worse." He embraced her. "You did wonderfully."

She gave him a fragile smile. "It was my first battle."

Karl smiled back. "I wouldn't have known from watching you."

"I'd best get to the hospital," Elisa said. "They'll need nurses."

"I'll see you back at home," Karl stated. "I love you."

Elisa kissed him. "I love you too."

Since the campaign had begun, Elisa had wondered what

it would look like when it ended. She had her answer within a month.

The battle at the Narew outside of Poltusk was the last time she watched her husband go into battle. She came home from nursing the wounded, expecting the Russians to return and attack again. They didn't.

Instead, she and Karl settled into something resembling a garrison life, Elisa dividing her time between the hospital and the laundry while Karl went out on reconnaissance. In the evenings, Karl continued to teach her how to shoot. A month after the battle, the V Corps left Poltusk – all except for the Seventh Infantry. Karl just shrugged and said, "I guess we get to keep enjoying our house."

Two weeks later, word arrived that the war was over, and they were to begin occupation duties. Elisa went to the church the evening the word arrived and prayed, thanking God for preserving her husband throughout it all. Otherwise, little of life changed. Karl went from patrols to training and inspections. Elisa continued in the laundry.

It was a pleasant autumn day, the leaves beginning to change into reds, oranges, and yellows, that Karl told Elisa about the discussion he had with the officers that day.

"Once we're done here, they're probably going to be furloughing most of us," Karl said. "And I may be eligible."

"Have you asked for it?" Elisa asked.

Karl nodded. "I think I've had enough of war."

Elisa smiled. "Me too."

It was a cold day in November that they finally packed up their belongings and began the long trip back to Neuburg. The snow was falling by the time they returned. Elisa stared at their partitioned space in the barracks, wondering how she would adjust to living there again.

She didn't have to worry for very long. A few days

before Christmas, Karl came to her holding a piece of paper in his hands and a big grin on his face.

"It's official," he said. "We've been furloughed."

Chapter VI – Fairy Godmother No More

First, Elisa and Karl rented a house in Neuburg close to the market square. Then, they went shopping for furniture.

"One of these days, you're going to need to tell me where all this money you have is coming from," Karl said as Elisa paid for a plain but well-built kitchen table.

"I will, my love," Elisa promised. "Soon." But there was one thing she needed to do first. She needed a wish – something she could grant that would both prove that she was a fairy godmother to Karl but would also seem like a lucky chance to the recipient.

There were none. Everybody had wishes, but most of them were mundane, and none required miracles that she could use as proof by performing on command.

Elisa found herself chuckling as she walked back to the house. She'd just have to use the magic coinpurse.

That evening, she sat down with Karl and placed the

purse on the table. "What I'm going to tell you is hard to believe, my love, but it's all true. First, please take a good look at my purse, including the inside."

Karl looked the purse over. "It looks pretty ordinary to me."

"Do you remember how much we'll probably need for some new oil lamps?" Elisa asked.

Karl nodded. "Roughly."

"Now, think about that amount and check the purse."

He opened up the purse and looked inside. His eyes widened.

"I'm a fairy godmother, my love," Elisa said. "Just like in the French fairy tales. That coinpurse was my mother's – her wish was that she would always have the money she needed, and when I granted it, this is how it manifested."

"It beggars belief," Karl breathed, pulling the money out of the purse. He looked up. "So, when you say you're older than you look..."

"I was born in sixteen hundred and forty-three," Elisa began, and then told him everything. She told him about her island, and her great sin. Then she told him about her long penance, and all the people she had helped. She told him about Clever Gretel, and her encounters with the Devil. Karl listened, his eyes widening as she talked about the more outlandish parts of her life.

When she was finished, he leaned back in his chair. "That's a lot to take in." He frowned. "So, all those fairy stories...they're true?"

"At least some are," Elisa replied. "I can't speak for all of them. And the ones that I helped happen...well, a lot of them have been pretty distorted. But that's okay – I was doing it as a penance."

"I'm going to need some time to wrap my mind around this."

"I know, my love," Elisa said. "I wanted you to know

everything, but I didn't feel like I could tell you while we were in the barracks or on campaign. And, the truth is that I haven't granted a wish in years...and I don't really want to anymore."

Karl gave her a kind smile. "So you *were* a fairy godmother."

Elisa chuckled. "I guess now I'm just your wife. I think I'm happier that way too."

"And this Clever Gretel person you need to kill?"

Elisa stared at the table. "I haven't heard of her in years. The Devil said that she was looking for some prince to marry to get a principality of her own, but that was at least ten years ago. And there aren't many stories about miraculous or magical events happening anymore."

"Just old fairy tales."

Elisa nodded.

"But you've never directly killed somebody," Karl said.

Elisa sighed. "No. I've granted wishes that made them die. The first time was by accident, and the second was out of desperation, and then I swore I'd never do it again. But then I danced some mad princess off a cliff, and arranged the death of a French rapist, and both felt so easy and right that it terrified me. But, I've never done shot anybody or the like." She swallowed. "Karl, I don't want to do this anymore. I don't want to hunt Clever Gretel down, or grant wishes. I just want a normal life with you. Does that make me a bad person?"

Karl shook his head. "I think after over a century of helping people without recognition or reward, you're owed a normal life for a change. Besides, anybody with a gun can kill Clever Gretel. It doesn't have to be you."

"I don't know if I can give you children," Elisa pointed out.

Karl shrugged. "Let's keep trying and find out."

Elisa grinned. "I think I'd enjoy that."

The next day, Elisa and Karl began their normal life together. At first they enjoyed being without the rigid structure of the regiment, but it took less than a week for both of them to feel at loose ends without it. Karl began to hire himself out for manual labour, working jobs wherever in the town he could find them. Elisa found work with a local seamstress, repairing and learning how to make clothes.

It wasn't long before Karl began hiring himself out mainly on construction work, only returning to odd jobs when there wasn't a building he could work on. When Elisa asked him about it, he said, "I spent enough time killing and destroying. I want to build and create now."

He also began whittling. One evening he handed her a misshapen lump with four legs. "My first attempt," he declared. "It's a horse...I think."

Elisa looked it over and smiled. "It looks vaguely horse-like, yes."

"I'll get better," he promised.

Elisa kissed him. "I know you will."

For Elisa's part, she found herself collecting a small library. Having missed so much history while she had lost track of time, she began catching up with it in earnest. It wasn't long before they had bought a bookshelf, and volumes on the Nine Years War, the Seven Years War, and the history of several of the major principalities filled its shelves.

But as the weeks turned into months, and Karl's whittling improved to the point that his creations actually looked like what they were supposed to be, and the snow melted with the spring thaw, they remained without child. And Elisa found herself missing Anna and Louisa.

It was a sunny day in May that she decided to head back to the regiment and see if they were still working in the laundry. She only found Anna with a couple of women she didn't know.

"Louisa and her husband were furloughed too," Anna told her. "I've got no idea of where they are now. These are people from town that we hired. I'm the only one of us wives left."

"I'm sorry," Elisa said.

"Don't be," Anna declared. "Everybody furloughed but me means that nobody is going to die on some battlefield or taking some far away town. If another war starts, they'll just call everybody back. But, I'm hoping that won't happen."

"You need an extra hand?" Elisa asked.

Anna grinned and shook her head. "Even if I did, I wouldn't want you back here. Go build a new life away from this with your husband, Elisa. You've earned that – take your reward."

Elisa smiled. "I will. But you have to come visit me in town. We've rented a nice house."

Anna nodded. "I'll do that."

The spring turned to summer, and Anna became a regular visitor during the evenings, sometimes joined by her husband. On quiet days, Elisa and Karl took romantic walks down by the river, or spent time at the theatre. A production of Cinderella had her forcing back laughter throughout.

"How much did they get wrong?" Karl asked as they made their way home.

"All of it!" Elisa laughed. "I don't know where they got the pumpkins from, or why they'd think anybody would name their daughter 'Cinderella'. If Ella could have seen it, she'd fall over in fits of laughter."

It was well into the autumn that she saw the Devil once again.

Elisa was in the market buying some food. She

glanced across the cobbled road to see the Devil checking out some goods at another stall. Her breath caught in her throat. He glanced at her and nodded, giving her a smile. She nodded back.

And then he disappeared into the crowd.

Elisa breathed a sigh of relief.

The autumn leaves fell as the weather grew cold, and the snow began to fall. Karl's whittling had produced an entire barnyard of animals perched on every available surface. Elisa and Karl picked up a Christmas tree that filled half of their main room. The pleasant scent of pine filled the house. After the Christmas Mass, Elisa volunteered to help with a reception for the congregation.

A few days later, they welcomed in the new year. "To our first year of a normal life," Karl toasted, raising a glass of wine.

"May we have many more," Elisa added.

It was as the winter weather was at its coldest that Elisa brought up the matter of children.

"I don't think I can conceive," she said. "Perhaps that's part of the price of being an immortal wish granter."

"You think we should adopt?" Karl asked.

Elisa nodded.

"Let's give it another year of trying," Karl suggested. "If we haven't gotten pregnant by then, we'll adopt."

Elisa nodded. "One more year, then."

At last the weather began to grow warmer, and some of the snow began to melt. But there was still snow on the ground when Elisa heard the knock at the door. She opened it to find Anna, a somber look on her face.

"What is it?" Elisa asked. "Did something happen to–"

"I wanted you to hear it from me first," Anna interrupted. "It looks like we're about to be at war with Austria. Karl's being recalled to the regiment. I'm sorry – I tried to put in a good word for letting him stay out of it, but good sharpshooters are too valuable as skirmishers. The best I could do was arranging for you to come with him again."

Elisa swallowed. "I see."

"You should be receiving the notice in the next couple of days."

Elisa gave her a fragile smile. "Thank you for letting me know."

"Again, I'm sorry," Anna said. "I did everything I could for you both."

Elisa nodded. "I appreciate that. We'll report on time, never fear."

"I'll see you in a few days," Anna said, and left.

Elisa closed the door and leaned against the wall. Then she screamed.

Chapter VII – A Final Taste of War

The day before they were to report to the barracks, Elisa and Karl packed up the last of their normal life and put it into storage.

Elisa had suggested donating their furniture and all those things they couldn't take with them to the church, but Karl had refused. "It's a promise to ourselves," he said, "that we'll come back alive."

They ate dinner at a tavern, and slept that night on the floor. The next morning they returned the keys of their house to the landlord, Karl put on his uniform and Elisa one of Karl's old jackets, and they reported to the barracks.

Elisa frowned when she saw their partitioned space waiting for them. "I already miss our house," she said.

Karl gave her a squeeze. "It's just for one campaign. When it's done, we'll rent an even better house."

Elisa looked around the rest of the barracks. It was

already full. Many of the men watching them arrive were unfamiliar to her.

"Finally, our corporal arrives!" one of the soldiers declared.

The soldier beside him grinned. "And here I thought we'd have to wait another month."

Elisa and Karl glanced at each other. "We must not have all been called up at the same time," he said. He turned to the men. "I'm Corporal Karl Mueller, and this is my wife, Elisa. She'll be helping me and the skirmishers."

"The corporal has good taste," the first soldier declared.

"And the wife needs to report to the Provost," Elisa stated. She gave Karl a kiss. "I'll see you this evening."

Elisa dropped her back on the bed and made her way to the Provost's office. The sergeant looked up as she knocked on his door. "Welcome back, Elisa," he said.

"Just reporting in," Elisa declared. "I take it you want me in the laundry again?"

"Unless you've developed some other skills," the Provost said.

Elisa almost told him that she could read, write, and do sums, but then thought better of it. "I'm quite happy in the laundry."

The Provost smiled. "I thought you would be. You should thank Anna once you get there. She twisted every arm she could get her hands on to delay your calling up as long as possible."

Elisa nodded. "I figured as much when we got teased about arriving weeks late. I'll get over there now, then."

She made her way to the laundry, finding Anna and Louisa already there. Louisa gave her a hug. Anna nodded with a warm smile.

"I'd hoped you'd be back," Louisa declared. "It wouldn't feel right without you."

Elisa turned and embraced Anna. "Thank you for everything."

"You're welcome," Anna said. "If they were calling you up anyway, giving you some extra time was the least I could do."

Elisa and Karl spent the next seven days reacquainting themselves with their old military life. Karl spent his time training and getting to know his new skirmishers. Elisa spent hers in the laundry, hoping for another wife to show up to fill the void Helena had left in their ranks. None did.

After the seventh day, the regiment departed, marching across the Danube. Every single one of Elisa's muscles ached by the time they finished the ten hour march to Regensburg, at which point they piled into another barracks, this time without anything for their privacy.

"No lovemaking tonight, I guess," Karl whispered. Elisa just nodded.

The next day they marched to a village named Pfatter, and the day after to a tiny village named Niederwalting, where they stayed in a makeshift barracks for seven days. As soon as it became clear that the army wasn't going to be leaving the next day, the laundry was set up.

"I'm tired of barracks," Louisa complained. "Why can't they give us lodging billets?"

"We're still in Bavaria," Anna replied. "Everybody's happier if we don't take over their homes. Once we're out of Bavaria, they'll probably give us billets."

"I miss my house too," Elisa said. "But, it gives us something to look forward to."

Louisa sighed. "When this is over, I'm convincing Franz to move us to America. I want a farm to raise our children on!"

"Do you have children?" Elisa asked.

"We had one," Louisa said. "He passed in his crib."

Elisa frowned. "I'm sorry."

Louisa nodded. "Thank you. So long as Franz is alive, we can have others."

"We might have to adopt," Elisa said.

Louisa patted her on the shoulder. "I'm sure if you keep trying, you'll have some luck."

While Elisa worked in the laundry, Karl drilled with his men. On the fifth day of their stay in Niederwalting, he told her, "They're getting into shape. I think we can give the Austrians a run for their money. Some of them still need to get better at working in pairs, though."

On the seventh day, they marched to another improvised barracks, this time in a large town named Dingolfing. The next day, they crossed the Isar River and marched to a village named Neufahrn. The first thing the regiment did was fix the roof. The laundry was set up the next day.

"So, you think the Austrians are ever going to get off their asses and do something?" Louisa asked as she mended a jacket.

Elisa sighed as she set down her own mending. "It would be nice to not feel like all of this time has been wasted."

Anna shrugged. "The Austrians will do what they'll do. After the beatings they took at Ulm and Austerlitz last time we fought, I imagine they're having lots of second thoughts."

They were only in Neufahrn for a handful of days. Most of the snow had melted and April just begun when they marched back across the Isar and returned to Dingolfing. There, they fixed up the barracks while waiting for news.

"Maybe there won't be a war," Elisa mused as she washed an undergarment on her third day in Dingolfing. "Maybe the Austrians will decide they don't want to chance it."

"I don't think we're that lucky," Anna replied.

Elisa was coming back to the barracks with a newspaper she had bought in town when she saw a messenger rush past her. She walked into the barracks to find a purposeful silence.

"What happened?" she asked.

"The war's started," one of Karl's men told her. Elisa glanced down at the date on her newspaper. It was April 9th, 1809.

Elisa knew better than to expect that the fighting would begin immediately, even when Austria invaded Bavaria the next day. She hadn't expected the marching back and forth, however. First, the regiment gathered at Vohburg. Then it marched all night to a village called Langquaid, leaving Elisa and Karl collapsing into their bunk in exhaustion once they arrived. Then they marched to a barracks at the village of Sünching, only to turn around the next day and march back to Langquaid. At least for the first few marches lead to a barracks. The day after arriving at Languaid, they marched through the day to Bachl.

That night Elisa sighed as they stared up at the holes in the barracks ceiling and said, "I wish they'd let us stay in one place for a bit."

Karl chuckled. "It does seem like they're not sure what to do with us, doesn't it?"

Even Karl groaned when the orders for the next march not only had them returning to Vohberg, but they were ordered to go through the night to get there.

Elisa was already on the edge of exhaustion, marching beside Karl with her muscles aching in the cold and damp night air, when the column stopped just before they crossed the bridge over the Danube.

"New orders," an officer announced, walking down the column. "We're to march back to the bank of the Abens River and prepare for battle."

"Are you fucking kidding?" one of Karl's men erupted. Elisa groaned.

"Can't they just let us get some sleep first?" she griped.

Karl sighed. "Okay, you heard the man – turn around!" he ordered. "We'll sleep once we get there."

As they about faced and waited for the column to start moving, Karl whispered to Elisa, "I guess they finally figured out what they want us doing."

Once they arrived near the banks of the Abensberg and bivouacked, Elisa and Karl fell into an exhausted sleep.

As soon as they woke up, they were ordered to break up the bivouac and march to a point near Neustadt, where after an hour of marching they bivouacked once again. As soon as Elisa and Karl had set up their blankets, the bugle called the regiment to attention.

Elisa and Karl traded a glance. "What's this about?" Elisa asked. Karl shrugged and got into a line.

As Elisa watched, the line was called to attention. A white haired Frenchman on a white horse trotted before it, accompanied by a small escort of cavalry.

"Who's that?" Louisa asked, sidling up to Elisa.

"Some Frenchie bigwig, I guess," Elisa replied.

"That's Marshal Bessières," Anna said, stepping up to them. "He's one of Napoleon's marshals."

Elisa blinked. "Are we under his command?"

Anna shook her head. "I think he's mainly cavalry."

"So the Frenchies are just showing up to look impressive at us," Louisa said.

Elisa shook her head. "I'm going back to get some rest. Let me know if anything interesting happens."

The afternoon wasn't even over before they were ordered to move to new positions. As they marched towards the village of Siegenburg, a dull booming sounded from the horizon.

"Artillery," Karl said. "It's starting."

They bivouacked for the night, and then marched for an hour to Allersdorf. As they marched, Karl said, "If something happens to me during this campaign, I want you to take my rifle."

Elisa frowned. "Don't talk like that."

"Elisa, this is important," Karl stressed. "If I'm gone, and you no longer have the life we were building for ourselves, then you need *something*. And if that something is your business with Clever Gretel..."

"It won't come to that," Elisa declared. "Remember our promise to ourselves. When this is over, we're renting a better house and bringing our belongings out of storage."

Karl nodded and gave her a kind smile. "I remember."

By the time they reached Allersdorf and found a place to set up their bivouac, the rumours were already circulating.

"Is Napoleon really here?" Elisa overheard an officer ask his superior.

"That's what I heard," came the reply.

Karl pulled Elisa aside. "I want to make sure we have enough supplies for the next couple of days," he said. "Find the supply sergeant, and make sure he's carrying enough."

Elisa nodded and made her way into the camp, searching for the rest of the baggage train. It wasn't long before it became an exercise in frustration. Every time she asked somebody where the wagons had gone, she was pointed somewhere else.

It was just after she had followed her third lead that she sensed it. A wish. A very powerful wish. She blinked, and began moving in its direction, making her way towards a small collection of tents. That was where she came before him.

He was taller than she thought he might be. His

uniform was plain, but he exuded an absolute authority. He was talking to the man beside him, by the looks of it a crown prince of some sort, in French. But what struck her the most was his wish.

It rippled out from him, almost overwhelming her as it washed over her. A desire for eternal legitimacy and glory, not just for his empire but for his family as well. A wish so powerful that to grant it would shatter the world.

Napoleon turned to look at her, his gaze transfixing her. Then he said something in French. The prince beside him translated it into German. "His Excellency would know who you are."

Elisa swallowed and curtseyed. "I am Elisabeth Mueller, Your Excellency. I am the wife of Corporal Karl Mueller, a skirmisher in the Seventh Bavarian Infantry."

The prince translated what she said into French. Napoleon nodded and replied.

"His Excellency has heard of you and your husband, the most acclaimed sharpshooter in the Bavarian Seventh. It is his honour to make your acquaintance."

Elisa curtseyed again. "Thank you, Your Excellency."

The prince translated her words. Napoleon gave her a kind smile and spoke. The prince translated. "His Excellency wishes to offer you a deal. You take care of your husband off the battlefield, and he will endeavour to take care of him *on* it."

Elisa swallowed and nodded. "That is very kind of Your Excellency."

Napoleon nodded and turned away.

"You should go now, Mrs. Mueller," the prince said.

Elisa blinked and curtseyed a third time. "Of course. Sorry. And thank you, Your Royal Highness."

It was all Elisa could do not to flee. Once she was back in the depths of the bivouac, she stopped, concentrating on controlling her breathing. Then, she resumed her search for the supply sergeant.

When she got back to Karl with the location of the supplies, it only took one look for him to realize something had happened. "My love," he said, "what's wrong?"

"I saw Napoleon," Elisa breathed. "His wish, it was...terrifying."

Karl embraced her. "Great men can be like that."

She had barely finished filling him in on the supply situation when a lieutenant called them all to gather around.

"We have new orders and a message from Napoleon, Emperor of the French, who is with us today," the lieutenant announced. The soldiers erupted in cheers.

"Now we can't lose!" one of Karl's men declared.

"The message of His Excellency the Emperor is as follows: 'Bavarian soldiers! I stand before you not as the Emperor of France, but as the protector of your country and of the Rheinbund. Bavarians! Today you fight alone against the Austrians. Not a single Frenchman is in the first line, they are in reserve and the enemy is unaware of their presence. I have complete faith in your bravery. I have already expanded the borders of your land; I see now that I have not yet gone far enough. I will make you so great that you will not need any protection in any future war with Austria. For two hundred years, the Bavarian flag, supported by France, has fought heroically against Austria. We will march to Vienna, where we will punish Austria for all the evil it has caused your fatherland. They want to divide your land and enroll you in Austrian regiments! Bavarians! This war will be the last one you fight against your enemies. Attack them with the bayonet and destroy them!'"

As the cheering of the soldiers around her reached a fever pitch, a chill went down Elisa's spine. These were the words of a man who would lead them into war after war, until all of Europe was burning...and one who would inspire men to fight every single one of them.

"The orders are as follows," the lieutenant continued once the cheering had died down. "This regiment will proceed in battle order to the heights around the Biburg monastery, where it will support the Royal Bavarian artillery. Skirmishers will harry any Austrians who approach before they reach the lines. We move in ten minutes."

Elisa joined the skirmishers, and they made their way to find cover before the heights of the monastery. As the sun rose in the sky, Karl and his skirmishers settled into a small copse, Elisa taking her customary place beside him.

A rumbling of artillery sounded from the northwest. Elisa took a deep breath, readying herself, but no enemies came. She glanced at Karl.

"They must not have gotten here yet," he said. He turned to his men. "Just because somebody else is catching hell right now, it doesn't mean that we won't soon. Keep your eyes sharp!"

Noon passed, and Elisa made her first run to the supply carts. As she picked up food and ammunition, the supply sergeant told her, "It looks like the Austrians have been driven out of Regensberg."

"A good start, then," Elisa said, grabbing her bags and trudging back to the copse.

After delivering the supplies, she retook her place at her husband's side. "Something's happening," he said. "They're setting up some guns, way back there."

"Are they within range?" Elisa asked.

"Not for us," Karl replied. "But, I think those around the monastery about to catch hell."

It was midway through the afternoon when the cannonades started. The Austrians were the first to fire, sending shot well over the skirmisher's heads. Elisa turned back to look at the Bavarian artillery position. Falling shot threw dirt up into the air all around it. Then it began to fire back.

"Do we do anything?" the soldier beside Karl asked.

Karl shook his head. "If we try to advance, they'll just pepper us with canister fire. We wait for their infantry, and then we start firing."

But the infantry never came. Instead, the cannonade continued for several hours, until both guns fell silent.

Karl turned to Elisa. "While you've still got the light, go back for supplies to get us through the night," he said.

Elisa nodded and made her way back to the supply wagon. A light rain began to fall. As she approached, the ground became cratered, forcing her to pick her way across, the mud sticking to her boots. She turned her gaze away from where the bodies of the fallen were being stacked to get them out of the way prior to burial in a mass grave.

"How bad was it?" she asked the supply sergeant once she arrived.

"Bad enough, but we gave better than we got," he replied. "I've already set aside what you need."

Elisa gave him a smile. "Thank you so much."

She filled her bags and trudged back to the copse. Karl helped her un-shoulder her bags, and then they settled down into a meal.

"What now?" Elisa asked.

Karl shrugged. "Now we set our pickets and rest for the night."

The rest didn't last long. It had only just gotten dark when a messenger arrived. "The Seventh is advancing in battle order across the bridge to take Pfeffenhausen," he said. "You're to screen the advance."

Elisa glanced at Karl. "What does that mean?"

"It means we're now pickets." He turned to his men. "Gather your things and get up. Take only what you need to. We have to cross the bridge before the column does. Divide into pairs. As soon as the column passes you, leapfrog forward ahead of it." He turned to Elisa. "We're an odd number of soldiers, so you're paired with me."

Elisa and Karl took a moment to fill their packs with essentials, and then rose with the rest of the skirmishers. They made a brisk pace over the bridge crossing the Abens River, and then spread out into the countryside. As they did, they heard the sounds of firing behind them. The light rain ended.

"The Austrians noticed the advance of the column," Karl said. "They must have decided to contest the bridge crossing."

The firing stopped, but it was still well past midnight when the Bavarian column passed, Elisa hearing instead of seeing it advance. As soon as the sounds were ahead of them, Karl gave her shoulder a squeeze, and they made their way through the dark until they couldn't hear it anymore. Then they waited for it to pass again.

Elisa sighed. This wasn't going to be a night where she got much sleep.

She got a bit of dozing in each time they waited for the army to pass. The dawn broke with them still on the move, although with rain falling again, it looked more like a grey sky lightening up.

"You think the others got any more sleep than we did?" Elisa asked.

"You mean the column or my men?" Karl replied. "My men are probably as tired as we are. As for the column, half of them were probably marching in their sleep, but they likely stopped for a couple of hours."

"I wish we could," Elisa said.

Karl gave her a wry grin. "That's the life of the skirmisher, I'm afraid."

They continued their leapfrogging alongside the column for the rest of the day, finally coming in the evening to a village named Ludmannsdorf. There, as the evening began, they finally rejoined the main column as part of it went into bivouac. Elisa took a moment to watch part of the column form into a line and fire a couple of volleys into the village. As they did, a stream of Austrians scrambled out on the opposite side, fleeing. Finally, the rain stopped and the clouds parted, revealing the stars.

She returned to the skirmishers part of the bivouac. "Did they take the village?" Karl asked.

"I think so," Elisa replied. She curled up beside him, and fell into a deep slumber.

She awoke with the bugles' call at dawn. Karl was already getting their packs ready. "We're back to screening duty?" she asked.

Karl shook his head. "They're keeping us in reserve this time. This one's a straight-out pursuit towards Landshut."

"So we'll be at the back of the column?"

Karl grinned. "Close to it, anyway. So, take some time to wake up and eat. Today, we've got it."

She watched the column march past as they packed up their corner of the bivouac, and then went to join it. As they joined the column, Karl said, "If we get ordered into the town, I want you to stay behind with the supply wagon."

Elisa blinked. "That's not where my place is."

"You've never seen what street fighting is like," Karl said. "There's no quarter given or taken. The enemy can come around a corner at you at any time, with no warning whatsoever. I can't protect you in the face of that."

Elisa swallowed. "I'll stay behind if you want. But, you have to promise me that you'll come back alive."

Karl smiled. "I'll do my best."

Elisa shook her head. "That's not good enough."

Karl sighed. "Very well, I promise, my beautiful love."

They reached the Isar River in the middle of the afternoon. As they approached, a pillar of smoke began to rise over the horizon.

Karl went pale. "They must be burning the bridge!"

The column broke into a run. The crested a hill overlooking the town, to find troops rushing over a smouldering wooden bridge and through a broken gate. Explosions sounded from within the town.

"Skirmishers in," a lieutenant said behind them. Karl turned and saluted. Then he kissed Elisa.

"You come back to me," Elisa said, embracing him and not letting go.

"I will," Karl said. "I promise."

Elisa let her husband go, and then watched him lead his skirmishers across the bridge. Then she sat on the hill and watched.

The sound of firing became a constant drum roll. Every now and then, a fire would start somewhere in the town. Elisa prayed for her husband's safety.

As the firing became more sporadic, she felt a tap on her shoulder. She turned to see a sergeant standing over her. "Are you Corporal Mueller's wife?" he asked.

Elisa swallowed and nodded.

"When he gets out, tell him that we're bivouacking at a farm at Mariburg." He pointed. "It's just that way."

"My husband...do you know if he's..."

The sergeant shrugged. "All I know is that I was ordered to tell the skirmishers when to go once they leave the town, and that's what I've done. Have a good day, Mrs. Mueller."

The firing ceased. Elisa watched soldiers emerge from the town, bloody and limping. None of them were Karl. She took a deep breath.

The sun grew low in the sky, the faces of the soldiers becoming more and more difficult to see. Elisa fell to her knees and began to pray.

"Karl said you'd probably still be here," a voice said.

Elisa looked up to see one of his skirmishers. "He's a bit bruised, but he's okay and he'll be along in a moment. He wanted you to know."

Elisa breathed a sigh of relief and rose to her feet. "Thank you."

"Least I can do for the man who saved my life three times today."

"We're bivouacking at a farm around Mariburg," Elisa said.

The soldier nodded. "I think I know where that is. I'll let the others know."

Elisa looked down at the town. Small pillars of smoke were still rising from it. A group of men emerged and crossed the bridge, one of them waving to her. Elisa grinned and waved back.

She leapt into her husband's arms as soon as crested the hill, and gave him a deep kiss. He held her tight.

"How bad was it?" she asked.

"Pretty bad," Karl replied. "But, the French came in from the north, and we drove them out of the town. You know where we're bivouacking?"

Elisa nodded and told him.

They set up with the other skirmishers, and curled up together.

She awoke in the morning to find Karl cooking some sausages over a fire. "The news is good," he said. "They're giving us a rest. We're staying in the reserve while another company of skirmishers takes over for a while."

Elisa gave a sigh of relief. "Oh good. Do we have to do anything today?"

"The reserve will be marching out in a bit. We're going to the city of Neumarkt. The rest of the army will be chasing the Austrians to a place called Frontenhausen and trying to take as many prisoners as possible."

Elisa found herself smiling. "Not really a job for skirmishers, anyway."

Karl chuckled. "That's true enough."

After ten hours of marching, they bivouacked just outside of Neumarkt. Once they had set up their blankets, she spent the day resting with Karl. Towards the end of the day, the main column arrived, without a single prisoner in sight.

Karl got up and talked to one of the corporals in the column as they set up their sleeping area. Then he returned to Elisa. "The Austrians were running faster than the column could chase them," he reported. "They came out of it completely empty handed."

"So what's next?" Elisa asked.

"I can't imagine the Austrians are broken yet, so they'll keep us in pursuit. We'd better enjoy being in the reserve while we can."

The next day, they turned back in the direction of Landshut, and marched to bivouac around a town named Vilsbiburg. When they received the order, Karl could only shrug. "I've got no idea what they're doing with us now," he said.

They had barely set up when they were informed that they were to march back to Neumarkt first thing in the morning. Elisa groaned and muttered, "We could have just stayed there and rested."

"At least we're still in the reserve," Karl declared. "We won't be called into action unless we're needed."

They set out in the morning, the sun rising in the sky. Their part of the column had just crossed a narrow bridge over the Rott river when the firing began ahead of them.

Elisa blinked and glanced at Karl. He un-shouldered his rifle. An officer rode down to the end of the column, calling out, "All line infantry, form into lines! Skirmishers, into action!"

"We've been ambushed," Karl gritted, glancing around. "All skirmishers, get to those woods and under cover! We'll make our way forward towards the front lines from there!"

Karl dashed forward, the skirmishers and Elisa following. They reached the treeline and crouched down, moving silently through the brush. Finally, they made their way to the other edge of the trees.

Elisa had never seen a line infantry battle before. The sight of it made her gorge rise. On both sides, the men stood in lines, firing volleys into each other. Those men who fell would be replaced by the man behind him. The ground before the lines was already littered with corpses.

A cannon fired, blasting a hole in the Bavarian line. "Canister," she heard Karl mutter, his voice grim.

Karl handed her his spare powder and ammunition. "Hold these for me. I'll let you know when I need them."

Elisa looked out at the enemy lines. They were far larger than their own.

"Start picking off the officers," Karl ordered, settling into a prone position and taking aim. The other skirmishers did the same.

Karl fired, the skirmisher shots almost a volley of their own. A couple of men on horseback and a handful of men in the line collapsed to the ground. Karl was already reloading.

A bugle call sounded from the Bavarian lines. Karl fired again and grimaced. "That's the retreat. They're ordering the Seventh to cover it."

"How bad is this likely to get?" Elisa asked.

"I may send you back to join the retreat before it's over," Karl replied, reloading and taking aim. He fired and began reloading.

Part of the Austrian line turned towards their cover and levelled their muskets.

"Everybody down!" Karl shouted, going completely prone. Elisa covered her head. The Austrian volley struck around them, shredding some of the branches.

Karl finished loading and fired again. An officer on a horse fell to the ground. As Karl reloaded, the Austrians levelled their muskets towards the skirmishers again. They ducked down as the volley fired, some dirt from a bullet hit in front of her flying into Elisa's eye. Elisa blinked and rubbed the dirt out.

"How long do we have to stay?" Elisa asked.

"We'll be the last to leave," Karl replied. He fired again and began reloading. As he did, the Austrians prepared another volley.

The volley exploded around them, this time kicking dirt up into Elisa's hair.

"They're getting too close. Everybody get ready to relocate and resume fire," Karl ordered.

Karl took aim. As he did, the Austrians fired another volley. The bullets kicked up dirt and knocked branches from the trees, one stinging as it hit Elisa on the arm.

"Karl, let me know when to move," Elisa said.

There was no answer.

Elisa blinked, a terrible feeling sweeping over her. "Karl?"

Karl was completely still. Elisa shook him by the shoulder. Nothing.

"Karl, please say something," Elisa begged.

Nothing.

Elisa pulled Karl back. As she did, she saw the bullet hole in his forehead.

"No," Elisa wept. "Please, God, no!"

The Austrians fired a volley. More branches fell down around her.

"You need to take his rifle and go," the soldier beside her said.

"I can't leave him here!" Elisa cried.

"He's gone!" the soldier declared. "And he made us all promise that if this happened, we would make sure you took his rifle and got to the rear. So, take his rifle and go, and don't make me carry you!"

Elisa took a ragged breath, and gave Karl one last kiss on the cheek. "Goodbye, my love," she said. Then she wiped away her tears, shouldered his rifle and began to crawl back towards the bridge. As she did, the firing only increased in intensity behind her.

She made her way to the back of the tree line, and then broke into a run towards the bridge. A cannonball struck the ground beside the bridge, peppering her with clumps of dirt.

She didn't collapse into tears until she made it with the rest of the army back to Vilsbiburg. Anna and Louisa found her in the skirmisher area of the bivouac, staring into nothing.

"I'm so sorry," Anna said. Louisa gave her a hug, holding her as a fresh bout of crying began.

"He knew," Elisa cried. "Somehow he *knew*. He never talked about what would happen if he died in the last campaign, but this time–" She broke down into uncontrollable sobbing.

"We'll help you get your blankets set up," Anna said. "And I'll talk to my husband and the Provost. Your discharge will be ready tomorrow morning, I swear it. You won't have to stick around for the rest of the campaign. And, I'm pretty sure you can claim a pension after this is all done."

Elisa took a ragged breath and wiped her eyes. "I don't want a pension. I just want Karl back. I don't want him lying in a mass grave just like all the others – it's not right!"

Anna glanced over at Karl's rifle. "That gun, was it issued to him by the army?"

Elisa shook her head. "His father gave it to him."

"I'll make sure they know. They won't try to take it from you."

"Would you like one of us to stay with you tonight?" Louisa asked.

Elisa shook her head. "I'm safe around my husband's men."

"That's not what I mean," Louisa said.

Elisa gave her a fragile smile. "I'll be fine."

Only half of Karl's men returned to the bivouac, each one giving her their condolences and offers of support as soon as they saw her. Once it was clear that nobody else would be coming, Elisa got up and found a quiet corner. Then she knelt and began to pray for the soul of her husband.

As she finished, Karl's words came unbidden to her mind. *Elisa, this is important. If I'm gone, and you no longer have the life we were building for ourselves, then you need something. And if that something is your business with Clever Gretel...*

Elisa sighed. Karl had been right. And now that he was gone, she had unfinished business that needed to be settled.

It was time to find and kill Clever Gretel.

Chapter VIII – Elisa Victorious

Even a year after Karl's death, the nights still felt *wrong*. Every time she went to bed, there was somebody missing beside her.

The first thing Elisa had done was return to Neuburg to sort out their belongings in storage. She stood in front of the door to the space they had rented, willing herself to go inside, but her feet didn't move. The life they had been building together waited for her, but now that Karl was gone the idea of facing it drenched her in a cold sweat.

In the end, she mustered enough courage to step in and claim a couple of Karl's whittled animals – the horse and dog that had been her favourites – and then she told the landlord to sell the rest.

That night, she cradled the two animals and wept. Then, she wrapped them up in cloth, put them in her pack, slung it and Karl's cloth-wrapped rifle over her shoulder, and left Neuburg to begin her hunt for Clever Gretel.

She began in the larger principalities, drawing curious glances as she walked around still wearing Karl's old jacket. Whenever anybody asked her about it, she told them, "I was discharged after my husband died," and showed them the discharge slip if they expressed disbelief. The war that had claimed Karl's life still raged around her, but only for a few months. By the time the leaves had finished turning to ambers and reds, it was over.

But there was no sign of Clever Gretel. Every time she inquired about the local royal family having married somebody named 'Gretel' within the last thirty years, all she got was a shake of the head. Before long, the snow began to fall.

"It didn't happen here," the steward at a palace told her in some tiny principality. "But, have you considered going to Regensberg and asking there? That's where the Imperial Diet was – surely they kept records for the College of Princes."

Elisa gave him a tired smile. "I'll try that, thank you."

And so it was that she found herself spending the new year back in Bavaria, in the Imperial capital she had heard so much about during her long travels. Construction had halted for the winter, leaving pockets where buildings had been reduced to rubble although they were few and far between.

She made her way to the old town hall, still bustling with activity.

"You want the archives," a minor official said, his nose poking up from a large stack of papers in his arms. "Any marriages recorded through the old College of Princes would be there." Then, he gave her directions.

When she got to the archives, she found the archivist to be a middle aged man with a bushy beard. After she had introduced herself, he glanced her over and said, "You were with the army?"

"Until my husband died," Elisa stated.

"I'm sorry to hear that. He must have meant the world to you."

Elisa stroked the lapel of Karl's coat and gave him a sad smile. "He did."

The archivist chuckled. "You remind me of my daughter. I'll help you, but it may take some time. Back in the days of the Holy Roman Empire, principalities would get consolidated with others, disappear, and new ones would take their place. So, the first thing we'd need to figure out is what principalities were active in the last thirty years. I'm Hans, by the way."

Elisa smiled and shook his hand. "A pleasure to meet you, Hans."

For the next two months, Elisa's life revolved around the archive. She and Hans poured over the records, looking for any marriage between a prince and Clever Gretel. Elisa couldn't resist looking into a few moments of her own personal history, however. She couldn't find anything about Prince Joseph and Princess Henriette, but a notification of a large briar being cleared to reveal an entire palace behind it in the year 1764, followed by a marriage between a Prince Henry and a Lady Briar Rose brought a smile to her face. *I guess the right person came along sooner rather than later after all.*

It was a cold February morning when Hans announced, "We've got five Gretels total. Now we just need to figure out which one you're looking for."

Elisa sighed. "I guess I'd better start travelling again."

Hans frowned at her. "Why? There's no reason we don't have enough information to figure this out here. Besides, my wife wants to meet the mysterious woman who has me looking through marriage records."

Elisa chuckled. "I'm not staying long."

"Surely, one of these days, you can stay for dinner."

Elisa gave him a smile. "I'll think about it."

It only took them a couple of days to rule out their first Gretel – an old widow who had scandalized her family by marrying a soldier on a pension, and died a few years later.

The second took a full week, but it was ruled out as soon as they found the princess' age. This one was an arranged marriage between a ten year old princess and a prince in his late teens. Elisa had smiled wryly as Hans showed her the records. *Even now, I still don't understand how the nobility can tolerate doing marriage this way.*

The third, fourth, and fifth took longer to sort out.

All three of them were young women, and none of the three had come from a pre-existing princely family. Any one of them could be Clever Gretel.

"It's a pity we can't just go looking to see if they died," Hans lamented. "That would make this a lot easier."

Elisa's eyes widened. "But we *can* do that. The Gretel I'm looking for wouldn't have died."

Hans stared at her. "Are you sure? A lot can happen in thirty years."

Elisa nodded. "I'm positive. If she's anything, she's a survivor."

The snow was beginning to melt by the time they discovered that the third Gretel had indeed died just before the Holy Roman Empire was dissolved. That left two, both with raven black hair.

Elisa stared over the records, lost in thought, birds chirping just outside the window. On paper, the two were indistinguishable – and both had married their princes between the years 1788 and 1792. But in reality one was a young woman who had been lucky enough to marry above her station, while the other was a centuries old wish granter who delighted in playing sadistic games with the lives of the people around her.

Elisa blinked. Games. Clever Gretel liked to play *games*...and to do that, she needed one thing above all else.

Privacy. She needed to be left alone in her chosen playground.

Elisa began to smile. "Hans, do we have maps for the general area of both of these principalities that we can compare?"

Hans nodded. "Give me a moment." He headed off into the depths of the archives, returning a few minutes later with his arms full of rolled up maps.

They covered the table with them. As Elisa looked over them her smile widened. One of the principalities disappeared from the maps within a couple of years of the marriage.

Her smile turned into a wide grin. "I found her."

It took her a day to copy the last map showing Gretel's principality. During it, Hans begged her to come and have dinner with his wife before she left to find Clever Gretel.

"You'll love our children," he declared. "They're wonderful, and happy, and—"

"I'm sorry," Elisa said. "After my husband died, I...I'm just not ready for something like that yet."

The next day, she left Regensburg heading north-west, to find Clever Gretel.

As she walked, stopping every night to stay at a decent inn, her mind churned. *It's been over thirty years – what if Gretel has changed? What if she's repented her sins?*

She made her principality disappear from the map, she reminded herself. *Gretel hasn't changed.*

But that was almost thirty years ago too, her mind objected. *What if she's changed since then?*

Elisa sighed. She's just have to confront Gretel first, and find out.

It only took her a couple of weeks to reach Clever Gretel's principality. It was small, but at first glance, the village at its border looked normal. Nobody appeared to be living in fear.

Perhaps Gretel has changed, Elisa thought, leaving the village and heading through a forest towards the palace. She found it at the edge of a small town, a couple of church steeples rising above the buildings from the distance.

She rented a room at the only inn left open. "You're lucky," the innkeeper declared. "We're closing next week. You can't run an inn when nobody comes here anymore. We can't even support ourselves with the tavern any longer either. Princess Gretel claims everything will change soon, but she's been claiming that for years."

"What about the prince?" Elisa asked.

"Nobody's seen him in years," the innkeeper replied. "There are rumours, but...well, there are always rumours."

"I'm sure things will improve soon," Elisa said, heading upstairs to leave Karl's rifle and her pack in her room, and then heading back down into the street.

As she left the inn, what little crowd there was made way for a small procession on horseback. At its centre was Clever Gretel.

Elisa took a deep breath. Gretel was just as she remembered. As soon as she saw Elisa, Clever Gretel held up her hand, stopping the procession.

"Elisa the Penitent!" she declared. "It's been so long."

"I'm just Elisa Mueller now," Elisa said.

Gretel glanced at Elisa's jacket. "You married a soldier? How pedestrian of you. Please tell me he at least died bravely."

"He died," Elisa stated. "He was a good man."

Gretel laughed. "But not a prince, like I married. Soldiers die so easily, and you get much less from them once they're gone. Next time, marry a prince."

Elisa forced herself not to scowl. "I'll keep that in mind."

"If you're here to resume our game, I'm happy to

oblige," Gretel said. "I think I'm running out of things to amuse myself with here. But, the hunting is good, and it makes for a fun daily activity. So, you wait here, and I'll fetch you when I'm ready." She turned to one of her guards. "Toss her an alm, will you? She's a war widow."

With a neutral expression that had to be forced, the guard tossed her a coin. It landed at her feet. Gretel laughed and trotted away. Elisa picked up the coin and passed it to the man standing next to her. "I think you'll need this more than me."

"You know Princess Gretel?" the man said.

Elisa nodded. "We're not friends, if that's what you're wondering."

Elisa took a deep breath. There could be no mistake – Clever Gretel was still the evil wish granter Elisa remembered her being. And that meant she had to be stopped. It was time to go to work.

She spent the next couple of days in the forest watching Gretel hunt, using everything Karl had taught her to remain unseen and move silently through the cover. Gretel didn't use dogs. Instead she would send her guards away before heading to a single particular clearing, wishing the game to appear before her so that she could eviscerate it, delighting in its screams of pain and terror.

After four days of observation, Elisa decided it was time to act. She unrolled Karl's rifle from its blanket and gave it a proper cleaning. Then she checked her powder and her ammunition. Both were good. The last thing she did was check the flint. It was nice and sharp.

The next morning, she left with Karl's rifle covered in a blanket, slung over her shoulder, her powder and ammunition on her belt. She moved silently into cover and picked her spot, a bit of brush that would provide her with perfect camouflage and cover. She loaded the rifle, measuring her powder charge with care. Then she want into a prone position, steading the muzzle of the rifle on a tree branch, and settled down to wait.

Birds twittered above her, and she heard the rustling of small animals, but she didn't move. She stayed prone and still, concentrating on her breathing and the clearing before her. Clever Gretel had come here like clockwork every day after dismissing her guards. She would be here again. All Elisa had to do was wait.

"Leave me," she heard Gretel say in the distance. Elisa concentrated on her breathing, remaining still. Invisible as only a skirmisher sharpshooter could be.

Gretel entered the clearing and stopped. Elisa placed her finger on the trigger.

"I know you're here, Elisa," Gretel declared. "If you wanted to spend time with me, you didn't have to follow me all the way out here. You could have just come to the palace and asked for an audience. I would have seen you."

Elisa forced herself not to react. Gretel was standing still. Elisa lined up her shot and began to exhale.

"Want to know how I know you're here?" Gretel asked. "I imagine you're curious. My guards had no idea I was being followed. I can sense you – I can always sense other wish granters." Gretel's eyes locked on hers. "There you are. Now what shall I wish?"

Elisa held her breath and pulled the trigger. Gretel dropped to the ground. As soon as Gretel fell, Elisa was up on one knee and reloading. The moment she was done, she rose to her feet, leveled her gun at Gretel's still form, and began a cautious approach.

"It's okay," the Devil said, emerging from the far side of the clearing. "You got her."

Elisa realized she was holding her breath and exhaled. "You shouldn't be here," she said. "Her guards will have heard the shot. They'll be here soon. I'll shoot at them, and when they return fire I'll join my husband."

The Devil shook his head. "No they won't. I clouded their minds – the least I can do for an old friend. They didn't hear a thing, they won't hear a thing, and they won't suspect anything is wrong for hours."

Elisa stared at Gretel's body. *Should I feel this numb?* she wondered. Then she sighed and fired the rifle into the air. "You have any idea of how hard it is to unload one of these?"

"I can't say I've ever had to learn."

She slung the rifle over her shoulder. "It's less trouble to just fire the shot." She paused. "My husband, is he...?"

The Devil gave her a kind smile. "He's not in my care."

Elisa breathed a sigh of relief. "Good."

The Devil stepped over to Clever Gretel's body and leaned over it. "Game over," he said to her. "I win."

A chill went down Elisa's spine. "This was all one of your long games, wasn't it? Right from the very beginning at the festival."

The Devil rose and nodded. "The longest I've ever played. I gave Gretel those powers. Her deal with me was that I would give her the ability to grant her own wishes, and when she died in her old age, her soul would be mine. The first thing she did was wish herself eternal youth."

"And you didn't see that coming?"

The Devil laughed. "Of course I saw that coming. I just wanted to see if she would do it. But, she never understood that age is measured in years, not wrinkles. She could have died at any time in the last few centuries – somebody just needed to kill her."

"So why didn't you do it yourself?" Elisa asked. "Why bring me into this?"

"Those were the rules I set," the Devil replied. "I wouldn't take her life, but arrange for somebody else to want to do it instead – and no hiring mercenaries to do it for me."

Elisa sighed. "And I was the perfect pawn."

"You came into your abilities with a show of power that would have put an exploding volcano to shame," the Devil said. "Every single one of us across Europe felt it. Most of us came to see what had happened, Yitzak, Gretel, and myself included. And once I saw what you were, and, far more important, how good a person you were, the strategy was obvious."

"Little nudges to keep Gretel and I in each other's paths."

The Devil smiled and nodded. "Precisely."

She closed her eyes. "Were you the one who told that insane princess that Snowy was alive?"

"I made sure she knew. You were in a rut, after all – you needed something to pull yourself out of it. And, I knew you'd be able to keep little Snow White alive."

Elisa opened her eyes. "Did you get my husband killed?"

The Devil shook his head. "Once I saw how happy you were together, I left you alone. Your husband was killed by a shot from a volley of muskets, just as so many others have been."

"So what you told me about being my friend after you saved my life, was any of that true?"

The Devil blinked. "All of it was true."

"But you still used me as a pawn in your game," Elisa stated.

A confused look crossed the Devil's face. "What difference does that make to whether you're my friend?"

Elisa chuckled despite herself. "Of course you wouldn't understand. You're the *Devil*."

"You Christians can be very odd sometimes, you know," the Devil said.

"So, what happens now?" Elisa asked.

The Devil looked thoughtful for a moment. "This was

my last bit of business in the German lands. They've amused me for a very long time, but I think it's time to see some new places. America sounds like it has plenty of promise, or maybe I'll check out what's happening in the far east. So, I'm leaving. As for you, that's a much more interesting question."

"Oh?"

"Look around you," the Devil declared. "Humanity has finally figured out that it doesn't need wish granters to reshape the world as they would have it. They'll always have a need for a devil, I think, but the days of fairy godmothers are ending, if not already over. Your powers won't last much longer." He looked thoughtful. "If you go to a city named Kassel, and visit the taverns there, you may find two brothers collecting stories. Talk to them, and you'll understand what I mean."

Elisa frowned. "So what happens when these powers are gone? Do I keep going on living forever, or will I become just another mortal?"

The Devil shrugged. "I haven't a clue. This has never happened before." He gave her a kind smile. "If you happen to make to the end of all things, I'll make sure there's a place for you among the rest of the immortals. And if you don't...well, thank you so much for the friendship and the wonderful conversations. They meant the world to me. Goodbye, my friend." He grinned. "Who knows...if we both make it to the end, perhaps Yitzak will finally talk to me!"

Elisa glanced down at Gretel's body, thinking of all the suffering she had gone through on account of the Devil's game. When she glanced back up, he was gone, and she stood alone in the clearing.

"Two brothers collecting stories in Kessel," Elisa muttered, and then shrugged. "I guess it can't hurt to check them out."

Chapter XI – Journey's End

The first place Elisa's trip brought her was a familiar house on the outskirts of a village. It was a Sunday afternoon, so somebody should be in.

She took a deep breath and knocked on the door.

There was the sound of approaching footsteps and the door opened, revealing a dwarf in his forties.

The dwarf broke into a wide grin. "Elisa. I'm so glad you're safe!"

"Hi Fritz," Elisa said. "I was on my way to Kassel, and I thought I'd stop by and see how everybody is doing."

"Please, come in!" Fritz declared. "It's so good to see you!"

Elisa smiled and stepped inside. Fritz led her to the large table that she had come to know so well. She sat down opposite him. The table seemed massive with only the two of them sitting at it.

Fritz pointed to her jacket. "So, you got mixed up in the wars."

Elisa nodded. "My husband was a sharpshooter in the Seventh Bavarian Infantry." She sighed. "He died on campaign last year."

"I'm so sorry to hear that," Fritz said. "If there's anything you need, please, just let me or Freidrich know, and it's done."

Elisa gave him a fragile smile. "Thank you – I really appreciate it." She looked around. "You could start by telling me where everybody is. How is it just the two of us here on a Sunday afternoon? Where's Gunther, or Albert, or Christof?"

Fritz gave her a sad smile. "A lot has changed since you left. Gunther passed away about six years ago. He's buried in the cemetery, if you'd like to pay your respects. Albert's there too – that cough of his finally caught up to him. We tried to get him to stop working, but...well, you know how he could be."

"What about Christof, Harald, and Eric?" Elisa asked.

Fritz sighed. "They went to war. They decided they wanted to try their hands at being sappers, just like Gunther had been. I just wish Gunther had still been alive to talk them out of it. I haven't heard from any of them since they left. I pray for them every night, though."

"They didn't send any letters?"

He shook his head. "They can't read or write. Besides, you didn't send us any letters either."

Elisa stared at the table. "I'm sorry about that. I should have done better."

Fritz smiled. "Well, you're here now. That means a lot."

"And where's Freidrich?"

"In the village, with his fiancee." Fritz chuckled. "He actually managed to find a woman who was into dwarfs, the lucky bastard."

"I'll need to congratulate him," Elisa declared. "Have they set a date yet?"

"Not yet," Fritz replied. "*She's* into dwarfs. Her father is considerably less enthusiastic about the prospect. He can't stop them from getting married, but they both want his blessings before they set a date."

"And what about Snowy and Max?" Elisa asked.

Fritz grinned. "They were smart. They gave careful consideration to making a claim on the principality, and all the politics they would face when they took it to the College of Princes...and then they went to America instead. They've got a farm in some place called 'Virginia' and four children so far. They write pretty often – I'll show you some of their letters. Snowy wants Freidrich and I to come join them. And, if you ever came back, they wanted me to extend that invitation to you too."

Elisa stared at the table. "A fresh start...now *that* would be a nice thought."

"Going to take them up on it?"

Elisa shrugged. "I'm still figuring out what I'm going to do."

"That's fair." Fritz got up and fetched them both steins of beer. When he returned to the table and put one before her, he asked, "So, are you still doing the fairy godmother thing?"

Elisa shook her head. "That's long behind me."

"Well, we kept your room, just in case you ever came back," Fritz said. "If you need a place to stay for the night, or a place to live while you figure out what you're doing next, you're always welcome here."

Elisa smiled. "I think I can afford to stay the night."

Freidrich returned that evening, and the three of them talked long into the night. Elisa told them all about what had happened to her – her husband, the end of Clever Gretel, and the Devil's long game. Finally, she told them about her trip to Kassel.

"Collecting stories?" Freidrich mused. "I wonder if they're telling stories about us."

"Why would they tell stories about us?" Fritz asked.

Freidrich raised his eyebrow. "A mad princess tried to poison Snowy because she thought Snowy would be more beautiful than her, and then danced herself off a cliff. You think that's not worth telling?"

"I don't know what's worth telling," Fritz declared. "What makes Snowy's story any more worthy of being remembered than the butcher's courtship of his wife?"

"You mean besides the mad princess, the poisoned apple and the dancing off a cliff?"

"Okay, that's out of the ordinary, but the world is full of out of the ordinary things," Fritz pointed out. "I mean, think about those giant bones we found in the mine seven years ago. Is anybody going to tell stories around their kitchen table about us coming across *those*?"

"Maybe it's not about that," Elisa said. "Maybe all its about how many people find it memorable and pass it on. People are still telling stories about Ella's courtship, and that was just her uncle, aunt, and I trying to get her out of that house."

"Well, regardless, it's not up to us," Freidrich stated. "But, it would be nice to be remembered that way, wouldn't it?"

Elisa shook her head. "Not for me. I was a penitent. And, I don't think I want anybody remembering my great sin."

Elisa checked five taverns in the city of Kassel before she found them. She knew she had the right place the moment she stepped through the door.

"And *then* the prince jostled Snow White, and the piece of the apple fell out of her mouth," the patron nearest to her said to his companion.

"After she was placed in a glass coffin for years," his companion said.

"That's how I heard the story," the patron said.

Elisa allowed herself an inner smile. *There was no glass coffin, and there was no prince*, she thought. *It was a cobbler's apprentice, and she married him and they moved to America.*

She glanced around the tavern. Two men sat in a corner, their table covered with paper. One of the looked at the other and said, "We've got all of these, Wilhelm."

Wilhelm shrugged. "It was worth a try. We'll go back to our usual sources next week."

Elisa took a deep breath and walked over to their table. "Excuse me," she said. "I understand you're collecting stories?"

The brothers looked up at her. "We are indeed," said Jacob. "Please sit down."

Elisa nodded and pulled up a chair.

"I'm Jacob Grimm, and this is my brother Wilhelm," Jacob said. "We are trying to collect the stories of the German people. I take it you have one to tell?"

Elisa shrugged. "I guess. My father told me this story a long time ago, about this lazy wife named Trina. Her husband got so tired of her laziness that one day when he found her sleeping, he decided to play a prank on her and cut her dress short to the knee. Then, when she woke up, she was afraid that she might be somebody other than herself, and when she came to the house and asked if Trina was there, he said that she was. So, Trina became convinced that she was somebody else, and ran away, never to be seen again."

Wilhelm gave her a kind smile. "And the husband's name was Hans, right?"

Elisa blinked. "I believe so."

"It's a good and fun story, but I'm afraid we've heard it before," Wilhelm said.

Elisa frowned. "I see."

"Don't feel bad," Jacob added. "There are a lot of versions of the same story out there. Just take Cinderella, for example."

"Her name was Eleonore," Elisa muttered.

Jacob raised an eyebrow. "That's new. We hadn't heard 'Eleonore' as a name before."

"What names had you heard?" Elisa asked.

"Quite a few," Jacob replied. "This is a tale that's told across Europe. There's Aschenputtel, Asken Pel, Cendrillion, and Finette Cendron, just to name a few. And there is quite a lot of variation in the story as well. The French story in which she's named Cendrillion has a fairy godmother who–"

"There was no fairy godmother," Elisa stated. "She was helped by the spirit of her mother."

The brothers exchanged glances. "You seem rather certain about that," Wilhelm said.

"I am. There was no fairy godmother in the German lands."

"How are you so certain?" Wilhelm asked. "You see, there are a lot of stories with wish granters, but they're almost always animals. It seems odd that there isn't a human wish granter of some sort as well."

Elisa shrugged. "There just wasn't. If I may ask, why are you doing this?"

Jacob leaned forward. "This world is changing so quickly. Napoleon is rewriting the map, the Holy Roman Empire is no more, and factories just like England's are starting to appear on our shores as well. These stories are the record of who we are – the soul of the German people. If there truly is a greater Germany, these stories are what defines it. It doesn't matter if they're true or not, or how many variants there are, they need to be remembered. To forget them is to forget ourselves as the world changes around us."

Elisa smiled. "I think I understand." Then she thought, *What's the harm of granting one last wish?*

She focused on their wishes. She could barely read them, they seemed so faint, but they were also the same – that their work would flourish and grant them enough money to take care of their family. She went to pull on the thread attached.

Nothing happened. The thread, and the brothers' wishes, faded away. *So the Devil was right after all*, she thought. *This really is the end for wish granters like me.*

"Thank you for your time," Elisa said, rising from the table.

Jacob glanced at Wilhelm and said, "We'd like to discuss this with you further, if we might, Ms..."

"Elisabeth Mueller," Elisa said. "But, I'm afraid I can't. I'm just passing through, and I've got a long trip ahead."

"If I might inquire, where are you going?" Wilhelm asked.

Elisa gave him a smile. "Honestly, it's time that I finally went home."

The waters of the Baltic sea were calm as Elisa rowed towards the island on which she had been born. The air was a bit chill, but her husband's jacket protected her from the worst of it.

She rowed to what had once been the docks, but now were little more than a rocky beach. Another rowboat was already pulled up onto it. She stared at it for a moment, and then rowed towards it, hopping out and pulling hers up beside it.

She placed some rocks on the seat to mark her boat, and then looked around.

The docks were gone, but then again, so was everything else. Elisa sighed. There was no point in being surprised. Most of the buildings on the island had been made of wood – those that survived the fire wouldn't have survived elements in the years to come.

She made her way inland, trying to find the streets she had once walked on with her best friend. She frowned. What had her best friend's name been? Caroline? Charlotte? Christina?

"I've been away too long," she muttered.

She looked at the horizon. A figure stood on it, standing in front of or behind some sort of board on legs. Elisa shrugged. She might as well introduce herself.

Elisa walked closer to find that the figure was an artist, painting on an easel.

"Hello!" Elisa called.

The artist turned and waved. "Hello there! I guess I'm not the only one who comes out here. What brings you here this fine day?"

"Just visiting to take a look around," Elisa replied. "You?"

"I'm painting the ruins," the artist said, pointing at the crumbling remains of the royal castle. "Capturing their essence, or at least, as much as these imperfect hands and eyes can manage."

"Have you been here often?" Elisa asked.

The artist nodded. "I love this place. The ruins are so...melancholy. Nobody knows how old they are, or who lived here. If this place had a name, it's long forgotten. The locals just call it 'the island'."

Elisa tried to bring the name back to mind. Nothing. She tried to remember the name of the king she had watched lose his head on a block in the town square. Nothing.

She resisted the urge to cry.

"I'm pretty sure they were Christians," the artist declared. "I've found the ruins of two churches." He pointed. "I think that one was the larger of the two."

"I'll have to go check them out," Elisa said. "Enjoy your painting."

The artist smiled at her. "I will!"

As she began to walk away, she stopped, turned, and said, "Just in case, I put some rocks on my boat, so that you know which is which."

The artist nodded. "Thank you! I appreciate that."

She made her way towards the smaller church. The grass was soft under her feet. She imagined that if she scratched away at it, she might still find the cobblestones that had once lined the streets.

She smiled, and then as she walked she imagined her husband walking beside her.

"I've missed you," she said. "I've missed you so much."

"*You know I'm not really here*," Karl replied. "*I'm just your mind giving a voice to your memory of me.*"

"I know," Elisa stated. "I'm indulging myself, just for today. I always wanted to bring you here one day, when the wars were all over and we could travel in safety."

"*So this is where you grew up*," Karl stated.

Elisa nodded. "We never had enough to eat, but in every other way, it was a good life. We were safe, and happy. I didn't appreciate it back then." She smiled wistfully. "I don't think I learned how to appreciate what I had until I married you."

She came to the churchyard. The roof was gone, and the walls were crumbling, but it was still recognizably a church. She made her way into the space that had once been a cemetery. Most of the headstones were gone, the few that remained so worn away by the elements that only their shape gave any hint as to their purpose.

"My brothers are buried somewhere here," Elisa said. "Their names were...were...Joseph, Franz, and Anton." She wiped a tear away. "I can't remember what they looked like, or sounded like. I can't remember what anybody looked like. The priest who baptized them, the baker who gave me bread whenever she had an extra scrap, they're gone now. I can't remember any of their names."

She sat down on the ground and wept. She imagined Karl giving her shoulder a comforting squeeze. *"You've lived longer than just about anybody else,"* he said.

Elisa chuckled. "No, I didn't. I didn't live *at all*. I *existed*. I lost myself in my penance, I forgot who I was, or that I could ever be something else. I became my penance so much that I ceased to exist before my penance began, and barely noticed the world becoming something completely new and different. I may as well have been a wish granting frog, or bird, for all that my life has been. And, then, when I finally did start to live and found a man to love, you were taken from me."

She wiped the tears from her eyes and stood. "I've got a lot of catching up to do, don't I? In living, I mean."

She imagined Karl smiling. *"I think so."*

Elisa couldn't remember where in the field her brothers had been buried, and her parents probably hadn't been buried at all. She knelt and said a prayer for all of their souls. Then she rose and began making her way back to the boat. She imagined Karl walking beside her.

"You will always be in my heart," she promised as she reached the boat. The artist's boat was still there.

"And I will always be watching you from Heaven," Karl's imagined voice replied.

She took the rocks out of her rowboat and tossed them back onto the beach. Then she pushed it out to sea and hopped in.

Elisa began rowing.

"*Where are you going?*" Karl's imagined voice asked.

Elisa shrugged as best she could while rowing a boat. "I don't know."

Karl's imagined voice became quiet, almost inaudible. "*What are you going to do?*"

Elisa smiled. "I'll figure that out when I get there."

As she rowed towards the shore and the island receded behind her, Elisa cast her mind back, remembering Ella, her aunt Anna and uncle Jakob, her Prince Karl, along with Prince Joseph and the young wish granter Princess Henriette, and all the other people she had met once upon a time.

A Note on Sources and Fairy Tales

Some truly amazing things happen when you match up Grimm's Fairy Tales to early modern German history.

This story began shaping itself in my head when I was watching a Youtube review of Disney's movie *Wish*. As the concept was explained, I remember thinking, "This would make a great origin story for a fairy godmother, if you just let her be the accidental villain of the first act."

That was the first seed. The second was finding a discounted copy of a leather bound edition of *Grimm's Complete Fairy Tales*, with 201 fairy tales and a selection of children's stories. It was after I had read it cover to cover that I realized that *The Fairy Godmother's Tale* would be the next novel I wrote, regardless of the complication that there isn't a single fairy godmother appearing in any of Grimm's Fairy Tales.

Grimm's Fairy Tales are not what you expect them to be. Many of them aren't really what we'd think of fairy tales at all – some of them are little more than funny stories. It was within the first ten stories that I found myself putting down the book and wondering, "What did I just read?"

But once you pair these tales up with actual German history, incredible synergies start to appear, and parts of the tales resonate in a way that they wouldn't otherwise. The entire festival and hunt for a bride in Cinderella (along with the sheer number of princes running about looking for the same) suddenly makes far more sense once you learn how the Holy Roman Empire worked, and that failure to produce a male heir meant the principality would cease to exist. Maid Maleen escaping her tower to discover her kingdom has been destroyed preserves actual events that occurred over and over again throughout German history. I set my adaptation during the Nine Years War, but it could have just as easily happened in the Thirty Years War, or the Seven Years War. The twelve hunters who Elisa meets during the Seven Years War (and treat her quite badly) stand in a very real phenomenon in the early modern period of women dressing up as men and joining armies as soldiers.

What was left was to flesh out these stories and bring them to life.

The fairy tales I adapted or referenced were, in order of appearance:

- The Good Bargain
- Cinderella
- The Robber Bridegroom
- Little Red Cap
- Maid Maleen
- The Two King's Children

- Clever Gretel
- The Sleeping Beauty (Briar Rose)
- The Twelve Hunters
- The Three Apprentices
- The Devil and his Grandmother
- The Shepherd Boy
- Godfather Death
- Hansel and Gretel
- The Gnome
- Little Snow White
- Hans's Trina

On the historical side, I tried to get as much correct as possible. For my depiction of German peasant life (including the practice of using getting pregnant to check fertility before marriage), I relied on *The Story of Everyday German Peasant Life: 100 BCE-1850*, by David Kohler. For the sweep of Germany history, my main source was *Germany and the Holy Roman Empire, Volume II: The Peace of Westphalia to the Dissolution of the Reich 1648-1806*, by Joachim Whaley, with some additional material from *Prussia and the Seven Years' War 1756-1763*, by Johann Wilhelm von Archenholz (Leonaur Press edition).

The first two parts were mainly on the periphery of history – the third dove right into it. Information on what it was like to be under French occupation during the French revolutionary wars before Napoleon came from *Civilians and War in Europe 1618-1815*, edited by Erica Charters, Eve Rosenhaft, and Hannah Smith. Elisa's encounter with a dying soldier shortly before Austerlitz is based on *1805: Austerlitz – Napoleon and the Destruction of the Third Coalition*, by Robert Goetz and *The Ulm Campaign: 1805 – Napoleon and the Defeat of the Austrian Army during the War of the Third Coalition*, by

F.N. Maude (Leonaur edition). My main source for Elisa's life in the Bavarian army was *Women, Armies, and Warfare in Early Modern Europe*, by John A. Lynn II, and *A Solider for Napoleon: The Campaigns of Lieutenant Franz Joseph Hausmann, 7th Bavarian Infantry*, edited by John H. Gill and translated by Cynthia Joy Hausmann (from Frontline's Napoleonic Library). My overview of the Napoleonic Era overall was *Napoleon's Wars: An International History*, by Charles Esdaile.

For a depiction of what Elisa sees as she follows her sharpshooter husband around the Napoleonic Wars (in particular, the sieges), I relied upon *The Art of Warfare in the Age of Napoleon*, by Gunther E. Rothenberg, and *Tactics and the Experience of Battle in the Age of Napoleon*, by Rory Muir.

Frontline's Napoleonic Library was invaluable in this project. Not only did *A Soldier for Napoleon* give me a full rundown of where the Bavarian 7th Infantry was during the campaigns I was depicting, but quite a lot of the details were fleshed out using this series. One of my additional sources for Elisa's first campaign was *The Jena Campaign 1806: The Classic Study of Napoleon's Total Defeat of the Prussian Army*, by F.N. Maude. The remarkable story of the "Pionniers Noirs" (in English, "Black Pioneers") chasing cannonballs comes from page 53 of *With Napoleon's Guns: The Military Memoirs of An Officer of the First Empire*, by Colonel Jean-Nicholas-Auguste Noël, edited and translated by Rosemary Brindle. And, to figure out Napoleon's wish, I relied upon *In the Words of Napoleon: The Emperor Day by Day*, edited by R.M. Johnston.

These sources, I hope, have enabled me to do justice to the period of German history that I have depicted. Any errors are my own.

I would also like to thank my wife Johanna for

ensuring that I didn't make too many embarrassing errors while writing a devout Catholic protagonist, my neighbour Peter Scott for giving me a rundown of how aiming and firing a rifle works, and my beta reader, Clarissa Pattern.

Robert B. Marks
September 24, 2024

About the Author

Robert B. Marks is an author, editor, researcher, and publisher. He is the author of *Diablo: Demonsbane*, the e-book that launched the entire Blizzard fiction line back in 2000, as well as *The EverQuest Companion*, the *Garwulf's Corner* pop culture columns, he is the author of the fantasy novels *Magus Draconum* and *War of Succession*, and he is the co-author of *The Eternity Quartet* with Ed Greenwood.

As a non-fiction author and historian he is the co-author of *A Funny Thing Happened on the Way to the Agora: Ancient Greek and Roman Humour*, with R. Drew Griffith, as well as the translator of Grandmaison's *Training of the Infantry for Offensive Combat*, the French doctrine of 1913, the first volume of Joffre's Memoirs, and Moltke the Younger's *Memories, Letters and Documents*.

Put another way, he wears many hats. One is a Stetson, and the other a Tilly. He lives in the area of Kingston, Ontario, with his wife and children.